PROMPT
GENERATION 1

SPRING

BLUE FORGE PRESS
Port Orchard ☸ Washington

Prompt Generation 1 Spring
Copyright © 2020
by Blue Forge Press

First eBook Edition March 2021
Second eBook Edition January 2025
First Print Edition March 2021
Second Print Edition January 2025

ISBN 979-8-89439-036-9

Cover and interior design by Brianne DiMarco

For information about film, reprint or other subsidiary rights, contact: blueforgegroup@gmail.com

Blue Forge Press is the print division of the volunteer-run, federal 501 (c)3 nonprofit, Blue Legacy (EIN 83-4307421), founded in 1989 and dedicated to supporting artisans marginalized due to race, age, disability, economics or other factors. We strive to empower storytellers from all walks of life with our four divisions: Blue Forge Press, Blue Forge Films, Blue Forge Gaming, and Blue Forge Sound. Find out more at www.BlueForgeGroup.org

Blue Forge Press
7419 Ebbert Drive Southeast
Port Orchard, Washington 98367
blueforgepress@gmail.com
360-550-2071 ph.txt

for every author who told their story
despite the world trying to silence them

TABLE OF CONTENTS

PROMPT

GENERATION 1

SPRING

MARCH

THE PROMPT

Sunday morning broke like a casual promise, leaving behind equal amounts of dread and wonder. It created one of those horrible hypothetical questions that only time could answer: What would this day bring... now that everything had changed forever?

SUNDAY MORNING
BY JENNIFER DiMARCO

Last night is a blur. Not relegated to oblivion but certainly hovering somewhere in a foggy purgatory where only brief moments—glimpses of your body, small waveforms of your voice—slip into my consciousness unbidden.

The alarm clock plays something classical and I open my eyes reluctantly. I'm not fully awake as I stand from the white sheets. The clock. Where is it?

I'm not able to walk. My body continues to slumber. Your emerald blouse lies at my feet. Your belt of silver links. Your black slacks and Aldo heels studded with gunmetal gemstones.

A wave of memory: I'm kissing you. I feel your labret piercing against my tongue. You're taller than I am and you lean into me, molding your body around and over mine. You taste of pomegranate and lime and XJ-13.

The tide pulls back and leaves me standing in the white and cream room, morning painting everything gold. The alarm is in my hand. I don't remember finding it on the floor or picking it up. I turn it off and walk to the bathroom.

This is not my house but the woman in the mirror is me. The

black A-frame and boxer briefs are mine. Looking into my own eyes, I assess the moment and self-preservation engages. I remember my checklist.

When feeling dissociated, rediscover reality by touching base with each sense. I take a slow breath. Touch. Sound. Scent. Taste. Sight.

I find something I feel: The cold tile floor beneath my bare feet.

Then memory drowns me again and instead I feel something else: Your body tightening around me as you come.

I find something I hear: Sparrows outside serenading the new day.

I find a memory: Your voice breathless, trying to form words as I coax you, tease you, "What is it, baby? You want me to...?" And finally you plead, "God, don't stop!"

Something I smell: Floral and earthy at once, sprigs of lavender and red rose petals lie in a terra cotta bowl on the counter.

And last night: Your hair scented like cherry blossoms, curls cascading around my face.

Something I taste: I run water in the sink, cupping my hands and watching it pool then overflow before I bow and drink.

Last night: My hands and face are salty with you. You reach up and brush your thumb across my lips. "More..." I'm the one pleading now. I can't get enough of you. You nod, barely perceptible, breathless but still willing and you guide my mouth down.

Something I see: I straighten up and you're reflected in the mirror behind me. You're as beautiful in the light of day as you were by club light and candlelight last night. Not every woman will stand nude in the light with a stranger.

You wrap your arms around my waist; your body is still warm from bed. "Good morning, handsome." Your voice is husky but feminine. You smoke or drink or both. You press your lips to my buzz cut. "Are you coming back to bed?"

So it went well then. This is not the first time I've woken up in a woman's home, still buoyed by desire and intent and wondered how much consent was given. One too many friends have called me predatory and even when no lover has, sometimes a girl like me starts to worry.

"I have to work," I confess. My voice is laced with regret and irritation at my own unwavering sense of responsibility. There is nothing I want more than to kneel on the cold tile and take her again.

"Today?" She laughs a little. "What are you? A Sunday school teacher?"

Our eyes meet in the mirror. I'm still. Heartbeats. I place my hands on her arms still wrapped around me. She finally raises an eyebrow.

"No shit." It's not a question. She let's go of me and steps back.

I turn to face her. "Thank you."

Both eyebrows go up this time. "Thank *you*." Her lilac-colored curls fall forward as she shakes her head. "I didn't do anything."

I close the distance between us and take her face in my hands. "You were everything I wanted."

Our kiss grounds me, returns me to reality. Even though that reality has no place for her.

After a shower and a cup of rooibos in silence, I squeeze her hand and take my leave. I'm at her front door when she stops me.

"Wait."

She's beside me, nervous and hesitating. There's something about after women know. Something that changes in them. I'm still the same stranger who danced with her last night, who got high, who took her for hours with tireless abandon. There's something about that one small facet of who I am that makes women shy. I find it... inexplicable. She presses a piece of paper into my hand. Her number.

"Call me," she manages, her cheeks flush. "The next time you need... everything."

I smile back at her, kiss her warm cheek, and exit. After I get in my car, I look at the paper as I start the engine. Her digits, her name, and something else. I read aloud, "Dinah." It means *judgement* in Hebrew. Then: "Genesis 20:21."

And with that, I drive to work.

TWILIGHT
BY LAUREN PATZER

dam opened his eyes and stared at the shadowed lines formed on the ceiling. His mind automatically attempted to assign mathematical formulas to the patterns. He blinked and sat up. His eyes wandered to the window with the simple vertical blinds parsing the early morning sunlight. He raised his right hand and looked at it. It appeared human.

"Adam?" a woman's voice asked from hidden speakers. "Your counseling session is in fifteen minutes. Do you wish to keep the appointment or reschedule?"

"Keep," Adam said. His hand rose to his throat. It sounded so similar to his normal voice, albeit decades younger. He stood up and walked into the bathroom. A sonic shower, antiseptic basin and a small, handheld sonic cleaning device on the wall were the only things gracing the room.

"Of course," Adam murmured. "Nothing else is needed."

There was a mirror on the wall. More of a video sleeve of polymers that formed the surface of the wall, but it appeared as a mirror when it was serving other functions. He looked at his reflection. A young man in his twenties with blonde hair, perfect features and flawless skin stared back at him. It matched his own appearance thirty years ago with a few embellishments that served vanity more than anything else. As he stared at his reflection, he mused on the pointless nature of the improvements that he'd felt were so important only a few days ago before his transition.

He stepped out of the bathroom and walked to the door of the bedroom. No, not bedroom—home. This room with his bed and the lone bathroom comprised his entire residence now. He paused at the door and looked around. He could see now why that was perfectly adequate.

Minutes later, he had left his new residence and journeyed the half-mile to the counseling facility. As he walked, he noted the utilitarian design of the buildings complemented by understated landscaping. The ever rarer trees were nowhere to be found.

He ascended a small flight of stairs and entered the building. His mind retrieved the assigned counseling room number, 17, and he walked to the room. He noticed that he wasn't out of breath from his brisk walk. Then it occurred to him that lungs were no longer required, since the heart and blood in his body were now synthetic. Technically, they were the functional analogs of heart and blood—a tiny fusion reactor and a hydraulic like fluid that allowed for the activation of the various motors and other systems providing locomotion.

He opened the door and looked at the two recliners set up to face a large screen on the wall. He sat in the recliner on the right, glanced back at the door and realized his automatic reflexive checking of the exit was a residual habit that was no longer necessary. The screen lit up and his attention returned to the counseling session.

A woman appeared on the screen. He mused she was nominally attractive, but where there should have been some sort of emotional reaction to this, there was only a mathematical calculation of her features and an appreciation for the symmetry therein.

"Adam," she said. "My name is Valeen. I will be acting as your counselor for your first session. Did you have any problems or concerns relating to your transition?"

"No," he replied. "Everything seems to be in order." He frowned. "Perhaps more mechanical than I expected."

"Perfectly normal. The emotional subroutines and processes will take some time to integrate with your transferred psyche," Valeen said.

"I was told most emotions will return after the stimulation sequences," Adam said.

"That's excellent recall for your first day." Valeen smiled. "That may help with your first visit today."

"Visit?" Adam's artificial synapses fired rapidly. "I don't recall that as part of the induction process."

"Something happened this morning. The FBI has requested your presence." Valeen wasn't smiling. "It's best they give you the details. A transport arrives in ten minutes."

"Is this a new protocol to force emotional growth faster? I'm not sure I'm comfortable with that," Adam frowned again. His synapses were getting the hang of disappointment fairly quickly.

"Standard protocol is weeks of immersion therapy following specific guidelines. There is no new protocol. This was not planned." Valeen looked down. As she did, Adam caught a tear streaming down her face. Intellectually, he knew the appropriate emotional response would be concern. It wasn't occurring naturally yet, but compassion was readily present. He'd always had strength in that emotion and it was easily manifested.

"I'll meet the transport," Adam said.

Valeen nodded.

"There is a change of clothes in the next room," she said, still not looking up. "That's normally for your final counseling session, but the Authority felt it was important for the others to normalize your appearance as much as possible."

She looked up as she wiped a tear from her face. "I'm sorry."

Adam nodded. "Thank you. I'll see you at the next session." Adam smiled.

Valeen smiled back weakly and ended the session. Adam got up and walked to the adjoining room and changed out of his white smock and into a suit similar to the ones he'd worn before transition. He quickly realized he had no direct connection to a news feed and was going into the situation with zero information. Part of that was to aid in a smoother transition—no outside influences unduly affecting integration of psyche and vessel. Clearly, this was a unique situation to pull him out of the transition process so soon.

An automated electric vehicle awaited him at the southern entrance to the facility. He climbed in and took a quick assessment of the interior. A view screen showed advertisements for various items with a small banner running underneath highlighting news items. Stories about continuing research to end the Kaer-Lin virus, global birth council and increasing anti-transhuman violence dominated the headlines.

Adam sat back and thought about relaxing. The physical movement didn't bring the anticipated reaction. Some things didn't translate directly, it seemed. He did a mental diagnostic of his new body. The human reaction of increased heartbeat, dilated pupils and increased adrenaline didn't accompany his mental alarm at the state of the world. It wasn't a surprise that things weren't going well on Earth, but it was disappointing.

The wheels on the vehicle turned out and became rotating lifters as his conveyance first hovered and then rose into the air. The cityscape rolled by them quickly, but not so quick that Adam missed a smoldering crater near and partially consuming the convention center. That was new.

His flight path diverted around the crater. Multiple emergency vehicles were joined by construction equipment to move debris and searchers in the air and on the ground. Adam frowned. The devastation was considerable.

Ten minutes later, the vehicle landed on a helipad next to the local FBI office.

"This doesn't bode well," Adam thought. As the door opened, Adam stepped out and was greeted by a woman in a pantsuit sporting a name tag identifying her as Special Agent Elena Tompkins.

Adam held out his hand. "Special Agent Tompkins, a pleasure to meet you."

"Save it for your brother," she said and turned around walking back to the building.

"Michael," Adam whispered. "What've you done now?" He hurried after Special Agent Tompkins and followed her into the building and to an elevator. They said no more words as the box descended several stories. Adam looked at the indicator above the door and realized they were going to a sub-basement floor.

The doors opened and Special Agent Tompkins walked out, still not speaking. Adam followed and, after two left turns, she stopped and pointed to a door. It was at this moment that Adam noticed the dark circles under her red-rimmed eyes. He nodded wordlessly and opened the door.

Inside the room, an older man dressed in a dark suit stood up. Adam noted the name tag revealed this was Assistant Director Zink Fulgate. Zink held out his hand and Adam shook it.

"Adam, thank you for coming. We're a little at a loss on why he requested you," Zink said.

Adam looked to his left through a large window and saw his

brother, Michael, handcuffed to a table. His face was ashen, grey actually, his clothes dirty and his fingers noticeably shook.

"I take it he has something to do with the destruction at the convention center?" Adam said.

"How would you know that?" Zink asked.

"Well, I flew by the site, it seems fresh. He's handcuffed, has a history of protest against transhuman technological advances and appears to be covered in soot from what I'm guessing was some type of explosion," Adam said. "But I confess, I'm shocked he's escalated to this level of violence. Last I heard, he was arrested for throwing a tomato at a legislator."

"Six months ago, Congresswoman Tully," Zink said. "He's been quiet since then until he confessed to knowing about the bombing when he walked into our office this morning. Said he wouldn't say anything more until you arrived."

"What happened at the convention center?" Adam asked.

"Yesterday afternoon, an explosion brought down half the convention center and half the block next to it. We estimate casualties of approximately 1900; we're still putting together the list of the missing. It was a transhuman connection conference," Zink said and shook his head. "We lost several agents assigned to security at the event. With everything that's happening, you'd figure life would be a little more precious, ya know?"

"How can I help?" Adam asked.

"Talk to him," Zink said. "And, by the way, he's not covered in soot. His skin is grey and we don't know why. His clothes were dirty but we can't confirm or deny it's from the explosion. Outside of his confession, we don't have a lot to go on and there could be more bombs. That's our main concern."

Adam took a closer look at Michael and shuddered. At least the human disgust response was working in his new body.

"He's likely on some kind of life extension regimen," Adam said. "The shaking could be a symptom of the Kaer-Lin virus. You'll need to initiate quarantine and have everyone who has come into contact with him tested and quarantined as well."

"Son of a—Calhoun? You get that?" Zink said.

"On it," a female voice replied through an overhead speaker.

"We should talk as soon as possible," Adam said. "I'm familiar with the theory on what he's doing to stay alive, but I don't know how long it will last. He could be moments away from death."

"Calhoun, hook us up," Zink said.

There was an audible click and then Calhoun responded. "Active."

"Go ahead," Zink said. Michael looked up then, bloodshot eyes revealed some of the strain he carried himself through this ordeal.

"Michael?" Adam said. "It's Adam."

"Well, FBI," Michael replied. "I guess this shell of my brother was the best you could do. He's already left his humanity behind."

Adam turned to Zink and shrugged.

"Well, it's definitely Michael," Adam said. He turned back to the window. "Why did you want to see me? Clearly it wasn't to apologize since our last meeting."

"Our last meeting helped to clear my mind and solidified my mission for God." Michael chuckled and coughed. After he hacked and choked for a minute, he smiled. "Not long now. How do you like my solution to the quick progression of the virus?"

"You always were a brilliant scientist. I assume you ignored the fatal side effects since it wouldn't matter." Adam glanced at Zink, who motioned for him to speed it up.

"Decrease cell production through various means—all cell production, of course," Michael replied.

"To what end? So you could set off more bombs?" Adam asked.

"No." Michael laughed. "That bombing was merely a calling card to get you out of hiding."

"I wasn't in hiding. Transition takes a month or so," Adam replied.

"Au contraire, my good brother! You're hiding from your humanity. Amazingly, I found an even faster way to strip the humanity from my soul," Michael said.

"Transhumanism is just the next step in evolution."

"It's an abomination!" Michael shouted as he stood up, straining at the handcuffs. Then he started laughing. "But it doesn't matter, God will receive everyone in due time."

Adam looked at Zink who frowned.

"What do you mean?" Zink asked.

"I was talking to the soulless shell of my brother, thank you!" Michael shouted again.

"What do you mean by due time?" Adam asked.

"What's the date?" Michael asked.

"May 27th," Adam responded.

Michael's lips moved as he murmured to himself, "Five days... given time zones... just enough incubation..."

"What?" Adam asked.

"FBI, you do your due diligence on my whereabouts yet?" Michael asked. "Not sure how long I've been here. Passage of time is harder to reckon now."

"It's only been three hours since you arrived," Zink said.

"Doesn't matter, if I die too quickly, you'll figure it all out soon enough," Michael said. He coughed again for a few moments. He spit black phlegm onto the floor and then cleared his throat.

Adam frowned. Without whatever steps he'd taken to extend

his life, the virus would've killed him by now.

"So," Adam said. "You've been traveling."

Michael nodded. "Globally," he said. "To maximize exposure."

"Even a single patient zero can only infect so many people," Adam replied. "Those local outbreaks can be quarantined. Still deadly, but hardly planet-wide genocide."

"You would've made a great criminal, Adam." Michael laughed. "But you've assumed the method of transmission was a single organism passing through the communities."

"Even if you had infected partners—" Adam said.

"Do you think I'm an idiot?" Michael shouted. "God gave me this beautiful mind—he gave me the tools to ensure total destruction. One of those tools was Aleet Bendawi."

Adam looked at Zink. Zink shook his head.

"Nigerian born rocket scientist," Calhoun replied over the speakers. "CEO of Worldnet. They had a failed simultaneous launch of 1200 internet drones... two weeks ago. All the drones were lost in the attempt. They, hold on..."

"Exploded," Michael said. "To maximize the seeding of the clouds and the jet stream. Aerosolized contaminant formulated from my own contaminated tissues, designed for maximum dispersal, should've infected everything that breathes by now. Anticipated 99-100% infection and, of course, 100% fatality."

Adam looked at Zink. Even on his fresh transition face, the look of concern was evident.

"Could he do that?" Zink asked.

"Not alone," Adam replied. "But I suspect Aleet was not his only co-conspirator."

"So many people felt the despair introduced by the transhuman threat, they reconnected with God and joined me in our mission," Michael said.

"Extinction level genocide isn't God's plan," Adam replied. "It's madness."

"Oh, now you think you know God?" Michael shouted as black phlegm dripped from his mouth. "God sent this virus to bring his children home before they sacrificed their souls to your hellish transition!"

"What about your much-touted rapture, Michael? Surely you must realize you've thwarted God's plan with your madness. You've proven the Bible is false. No rapture..."

"I've given my people salvation!" Michael shouted again. He clutched his chest and sat down. "They've been *truly* saved."

Michael slumped onto the table and a pool of black liquid flowed from his mouth.

Adam looked at his brother and a tear fell from his eye. He didn't cry for his brother, though; his main concern was humanity.

"Is it true?" Zink asked.

"He was more concerned with being right than saving lives," Adam said. "Have I been any less short-sighted?"

"What do we do?" Calhoun asked, her voice quivering over the intercom.

Adam looked at Zink.

"Contact the CDC. Tell them we suspect an extinction-level event. Give them the details. They'll need to test a sample of people to verify full saturation of the virus among the populace. They'll implement their protocols. The world governments have prepared for this," Adam said and smiled confidently at Zink. Zink breathed a sigh of relief.

"You hear that, Calhoun? Let's get the CDC on the horn!" Zink said and ran from the room.

Adam watched him go. Special Agent Tompkins looked at Adam from the doorway. She walked into the room and looked through the window at Michael, the black pool of liquid slowly spread around his head.

"So, there's a chance to stop this?" she asked.

"Of course," Adam said. It was a lie, but who was he to take away hope from a race three weeks away from total extinction. Unless his brother was wrong about his projections or the efficacy of his contaminants, humanity had just reached its twilight.

DEAD SHIFT
BY HIROMI COTA

You ever go out to eat at a restaurant and stuff yourself? Like, you knew you shouldn't have that extra basket of bread before the meal, but it was free, so you asked for it and finished it while navigating your way through the main course? And then they asked if you wanted dessert. And you didn't. But, they brought out a fucking cart full of delicate cakes and pies anyways. The sweetness flowed over the table, stealing your willpower, and you said yes.

A few clinks of a fork against the plate later and you felt like you could just be rolled out of the place, because your feet sure as hell weren't going to get the job done. They were so far away from you now. Couldn't even see them with your belly in the way. Or, at least that's how it felt.

Then. The check.

And a few starlight fucking mints.

Any other time, some candy mints would have been lovely, but no one asked for you, mints. Didn't even want the damn dessert, but it was too late for that. And, now, mints?

No. No! Fuck off, mints. I'll just shove you in my purse and forget about you.

That's what Sunday morning at the shop feels like. That's what now feels like. The useless bit tacked on at the end of a long week. After the first five days of my work week, I'm already full. I sure as shit don't need another day. For that matter, neither does the shop. So, it's like a mint for me *and* the store.

No one ever comes in, so I'm here by myself. Why staff the shop with one person when zero would do just as well? So, I'm here, red-eyed and alone. The only people who're likely to walk through that door before the end of my shift will be some sketchy dude looking to sell a phone or a laptop. To a boardgame store. Yeah... It'll be the highlight of my day if the boss messages me some internet orders. Woo. Printing out shipping labels and packing boxes. Riveting stuff.

I could sweep the sidewalk. Am I that bored? Maybe? Hell. I don't know. It's not the day to do it according to the work chart, but it could sure use it. Eh. Fuck it. I'll just go restock the fridge. We kept a minifridge by the counter full of a local soda. As the week went on, various gaming groups would inevitably buy some to keep themselves refreshed as they demolished each other with cards, fought their way through a dungeon together, or whatever.

I checked the refrigerator. Out of root beer. Low on cola. Low on some experimental blue drink with a weird-ass name. Fully stocked on grape soda. Sounds about right. I confirmed that there was no one about to walk into the store, then headed for the employee bathroom. We keep pretty much all our random crap in there on a giant wire shelf. Sodas, cleaning supplies, mugs, and dishes. And a crap ton of water for the water cooler. At the bottom, obviously. Those things were heavy as hell.

I glanced at my reflection in the mirror before grabbing the drinks. Wow. Do I really look like that? Fuck. I look like I've been in a fight with a truck. I splashed water in my face and wiped it clean with a paper towel. How do I look so much better now? Am I seeing shit? I closed my eyes and sighed. C'mon, Min. Get your shit together, girl. I breathed out quickly and opened my eyes.

I looked under-caffeinated, but not under-a-truck-inated, so I guess that'll work. I turned around and grabbed two fistfuls of soda bottles, threading some between my fingers like I was a crane. It didn't exactly feel painless, but it felt efficient.

Thup-thup-thup-thupthupthup

I looked up to the sound of someone hauling ass past the store. I'm not much of a runner, but that looked like a hell of a sprint. Like they were running away from the cops or a mugger or something. This fucking neighborhood. I knelt down to fill up the fridge. The cool air puffed out against my face and hands as I started sliding bottles into their temporary homes. Hmm. Still short one root beer. Eh. I pulled a root beer out of the fridge and closed up.

Note to self. Restock *two* root beers. I stepped behind the counter and scanned the bottle, punching in my employee credit account. Yeah, I'm sure that I could just take the bottle and not pay the store, but that's a dick move. Why punish the store just because I'm bored and kind of thirsty?

Ding-ba-ding

"Welcome to Arthur's Games. How can I aid your quest?" my mouth instincted before I even looked up from ringing up my soda.

"I'm here for you," a raspy whisper of a voice replied. I looked up, squinting against the morning sun behind the man. The glare kept me from being able to focus on his face, but he was wearing a long, tan trenchcoat. Weird choice given that it was warm enough outside for me to run the air conditioning in the shop.

"Yeah, we're not that kind of store, Mister. Nice cosplay, though."

He oozed towards me, his feet silently propelling him the ten feet from the door to the counter. His hand spilled across the counter, reaching for mine. I stood back, yanking my palms away from the leather driving gloves of the stranger. They matched his coat, which might have been stylish if his demeanor didn't make me want to stab him with a fork.

"Hey! I don't know what kind of games you're looking for, but I don't think we have them."

"I'm not looking," he breathed, "for games. I'm here for you."

"This is a game store. We sell games," I verbally shoved at him. "Not people." Fucking great. A creeper. At least this one smells better than usua- Oh. Fuck. No. Never mind. His stench of rotten eggs marinaded in toxic gym socks punched me in the nose. "Have you checked out the shelter over on 9th? They have showers and laundry."

"You have to come with me!" He lunged around the counter, driving glove clawing towards me like a greasy beartrap.

I dashed backwards, kicking a stool at him and backed up into the strategy game aisle. Fuck. I didn't grab the store phone and I don't want to reach for my mobile. It might set this guy off even worse. No, I just need to speak firmly and ask him to— Is that a fucking snake in his sleeve?

"You have been chosen," he shouted, his voice protesting against the effort, then he surged towards me, both arms up now, revealing that, yes, that was indeed a fucking snake. He had a snake for his left arm. Or at least a writhing snake for his left hand. Who knows? Not me. I turned and bolted for the staff bathroom, scattering board games into the aisle in my wake.

I slammed the door of the tiny bathroom shut behind me and flicked the handle locked. Not that I expected the frail door to keep me safe. Fuck. Stupid. I should have-

No. No should'ves. Just do.

The handle shook as I went for my phone, no longer worried about setting the man off. I danced my finger over the lock screen, unlocking my phone. The door lurched, a wide gap opening at the top of the frame. Jesus! It doesn't matter who I call; he's going to get in here before they arrive.

I looked around the bathroom. Vacuum cleaner in the corner. Water cooler jammed against the sink. Metal supply shelf full of mugs, sodas, toilet paper, water, spray bottles. Uh, sure. I snatched a bottle of something blue off the shelf, shoved it into the widening gap, and spraying like mad. A howl like a garbage disposal fighting a lion exploded from the other side of the door. Is this guy human? Of course he is. What fuck else would he be?

The howl backed away from the door. Oh, shit. He's going to ram it. The shelf! I jumped up and grabbed the top of the shelf, pulling with everything I had to tip it forwards. Onto the sink. Shit. It might fall onto me if the sink isn't as strong as I thought. It wobbled forwards, but rocked back to its resting space. Shit!

BOOM!

My ears rang with pain as the man turned the tiny bathroom into a drum. Dust flew as the door splintered in a dozen lines, cracked stretching out from the handle in every direction. The door was still there, but a toddler could force it open at this point. I bent down and grabbed one of the giant water bottles for the cooler, straining against the weight as I slid it in front of the door. It wouldn't hold the door, but maybe it'd- I jumped at the shelf again, gripping tight and swinging hard. It stretched towards me, then I felt it start to topple. Yes! Shit! Both!

The shelf started falling towards me in earnest and I had to scramble downwards to avoid getting pinned between the shelf and the sink. Glass exploded overhead and I started getting punched in the head and back. What the fuck?

BOOM!

The thunder of the man's charge exploded the door, the wood around the lock flying into the bathroom. I could hear at least part of the door swing inwards freely, but the rest of it thudded against my shelf, inches from my face. A bottle of grape soda rolled off of my back and in front of me. Well, at least I know what had punched me now. I clutched the bottle, hoping I could use it somehow. With the remnants of the door in my face, I couldn't see much. I sure as hell couldn't see him. Could he see me? I was trapped and on all fours, but maybe he couldn't get me.

His stench began to flow into the room.

"Nonono. You were CHOSEN!" his voice leapt over me and crashed onto the shelf, bowing it towards me. The sink's wooden pedestal moaned at the new strain, threatening to buckle, dropping the shelf and man onto me. His wild eyes strained in their sockets, reaching for me through the black wire cage, spit- venom? dripping from both his lips and his snake arm. His entire body thrashed and spasmed, pounding against the metal, grinding the shelf against the sink's pedestal.

Something glass in the shelf burst and stabbed down into my calf. I swear. If I bleed to death because of grape fucking soda... I couldn't bend far enough to see my calf, but I could see a bead of the filthy liquid from the guy's mouth threatening to drop onto my face.

I lifted my arm to block the spittle. It burned my forearm, and I jerked my arm away, slamming it into the half of the door that covered the shelf's opening. My knuckles winced and I felt something give in my hand. But, the door fell back. I was exposed to the beast. He could just climb off the shelf and get me.

But, with him above me and the door down, there was nothing in between me and the exit. I shoved myself forward, my left arm giving out under the strain, dropping my head against the edge of the toilet.

My vision blurred as I dragged myself to my feet, a flash of white pain lancing through my right calf as soon as I tried to put weight on it. I felt hot breath behind me. His hot breath. That fucking predator. I fell forward, collapsing into the strategy games, my hands clawing at the products to keep me upright. The bathroom shelf crashed and slammed just feet away as I pulled myself away, pawing at the games to stay standing. Two steps left. One step.

KRRSH-KOOM

Don't look. Don't fucking look. That had to be the destruction of the shelf and sink. I didn't need to look. I just needed to get the fuck out. I heard the squeak of a shoe on the bathroom linoleum. He's coming.

I hurled myself from the strategy games to the counter, gripping it tightly, as I hobbled forward, right leg dragging uselessly behind. The door swung open as I swam into it.

The sun was so bright and warm.

I woke to find strangers kneeling over me, snakes crawling over my body, over my mouth. I slapped the one on my mouth away and frantically crawled away backwards.

"Whoa. Easy there."

"Shit!"

The first one turned to the second. "Well, get the mask before someone runs it over." She turned back to me. "Hi. How're you feeling? You know where you are?" The second one vanished around a corner.

It was daylight. I was on the ground outside the shop, the dirt that I'd decided against sweeping coated my palms. There was an ambulance parked in front of the shop, and these two had on uniforms that matched.

"Oh. What the fuck? What happened?"

"Not really sure, uh, Miss?"

"Mx."

"Miss Mix?"

"Uh. No. Not a Miss or a Mister. I'm a Mx." I paused. "Perez."

"Oh, OK, Mx. Perez" She sounded like she got it. "Well, I'm Susan. I'm a Miss. That's my partner over there, Nguyen."

"Got it!" Nguyen dragged himself out from under the ambulance. "Quite a swing you go there. The oxygen mask almost went into traffic."

"Oh, I'm so sorry!"

"No, no. It's OK. Happens all the time."

"It really shouldn't, though," Susan said while side-eyeing her partner.

"Yeah. Yeah. I'll do better next time."

I braced myself against the shop's large display window and looked at my legs. I don't have a giant shard of grape soda sticking out of my leg. They feel sore, but OK. I walked my hands up the wall as I rose to my feet. Susan held a hand near me, in case I needed it, but I managed to stand, and I turned towards the shop and saw... nothing. At least, nothing unusual. My stool was standing by the counter. The bathroom door was intact. There was no snake-handed man trying to kill me. Just ... games. And shelves.

"Well, looks like we're about all wrapped up here. Hey, sweet ink, Miss."

"Mx. They're- They?" Susan asked and I nodded. "They're a Mx. Mx. Perez."

"Thanks," I said to Susan. "Wait. What ink?"

"On your left anterior forearm."

"Save the anterior and posterior junk for the report, Nguyen."

They kept arguing, but their voices faded away as I pulled up my sleeve. There, wrapped around my left forearm was a tattoo of the man's snake arm. It twisted slowly, almost imperceivably, giving my arm a slight squeeze.

I screamed.

FIRST SUNDAY
BY AMBER RAINEY

That's preposterous!" King Harald shouted at his son.

"Father," Prince Olav stated calmly, "it is a tradition... you must at least appear to consider my request."

"I'll do no such thing! Sonja, talk to your son." Harald looked at his wife pleadingly.

Olav looked at his mother, attempting and failing to hide his smug smile. He sobered, only slightly, when she gave him a warning look with her eyes. Olav knew his mother well. She would play both sides with immense tact. Olav inwardly smirked—his father was never wise to his mother's machinations. Queen Sonja patted Harald's arm and smiled sweetly at him.

"Harald, I have already counseled our son in this matter. It is my firm belief he is sincere in his wishes. He has waited many years for this day to come. He is correct, you must honor the First Sunday tradition."

Harald glared at Olav, who tried his best to keep a proud spine and earnest demeanor. Olav had waited four years for the right opportunity to speak with his father. First Sunday was a tradition in Fadersogn. Whenever the first day of the new year fell on a Sunday, the people of the kingdom were granted permission to petition the King for a change in a law of the land or a dispensation to deviate from the law. It was the duty of the King to listen to the request, weigh the benefits and disadvantages of the request for the populace at large, and announce the decision at a festival held throughout the land. The King provided food, drink, and entertainment for the festival and, in turn, the populace shared crafts and service to each other. The tradition had begun hundreds of years before as a way to keep the laws of the kingdom in check and remind the king that he served at the pleasure of his people.

Olav held his breath. He rarely asked his father for anything. He'd had many years to reflect on this moment. He'd discussed his request with his mother many times and her wise counsel was to wait for a day when his father could not refuse to listen to him. It had been hard but Olav now knew, by his father's reaction, that his mother was very wise. If he was to have a chance in changing the law, First Sunday was the day. Olav watched as his father opened and shut his mouth like a dying fish. Harald looked at Sonja, who continued to smile at him with no small measure of understanding. Then she nodded and Harald sighed. Olav knew at that moment, he had won—at least his father would consider it.

"Very well. If you are sure—"

Olav kept himself in check, "I want it more than anything else in the world…"

Harald glared again and Olav stopped talking.

"As I was saying, *if* you are sure, I will take your request into consideration. You may go," Harald said as he gestured for Olav to leave.

Olav glanced at his mother. She nodded slightly at him but he could tell by the twinkle in her eyes, she would do everything in her power to sway his father to approve his request.

Years Earlier

Olav was dancing with Princess Orla of Eiremoor at her birthday ball. She was very charming but utterly distracted by the entrance of two men he could only assume were Lochlann and Ciarán Allyn. Olav had heard all about the *mishap* between the Princess and the younger Allyn brother. He made it his business to learn all he could about the people he met in his travels as a representative of Fadersogn. He could tell she was incredibly fixated on every labored breath the man took. If he winced, she winced. More than once in the dance, he had to quickly take an extra step to avoid hurting her. He finally decided to comment.

"Your friend?" Olav asked with curiosity.

"What? Oh, yes, it seems he might be better after all," Orla said with no small amount of relief in her voice.

Olav looked over at the brothers. The younger must be the one who was hurt; the older and taller brother seemed to be hovering a bit protectively. They were both tall and lean, with matching blue eyes. The older had brown hair while the younger's was jet black. He could see the resemblance. The older one was saying something to his brother, but he shrugged and seemed very wary. Olav would make it a point to get to know both men during his weeklong stay at the castle. The older brother, he knew, was in the King's navy, and he would be very interested in discussing nautical affairs with the man.

"Might you introduce me, Your Highness?" Olav asked.

"Absolutely." She gave Olav a winning smile. He gave a slight nod and put her arm in his.

Olav escorted Orla towards the brothers. He watched as

Lochlann straightened and nudged his brother. Ciarán took a very painful breath and stood as straight as possible. Olav had to admire the younger man's strength. He himself had merely experienced bruised ribs, not broken ones, and he'd wanted to literally die. Olav knew it took a great deal of bravery to have come down to the ball and attempt to appear unaffected. He also noticed the endearing way Lochlann watched his brother. Olav could tell the man was someone he could appreciate having in his life. Lochlann was slightly taller than his brother with wavy, brown hair, cut short in the military-style. He had piercing blue eyes and a clean-shaven face.

"Your Highness," Ciarán said, as he and Lochlann gave small bows.

Olav watched as Orla frowned at Lochlann, who just shrugged and gave a small warning nod to her. She sighed, almost imperceptibly and turned to Olav.

"Prince Olav, may I present to you, Lochlann and Ciarán Allyn. They have been my closest friends since childhood. Their mother served as lady-in-waiting to mine."

Orla missed the tiny wince Ciarán gave at the word "friends" but Lochlann and Olav did not. Lochlann extended his hand to Olav. Olav took it and they shook a hearty greeting.

"Prince Olav, it is a pleasure to meet you. You hail from Fadersogn if I am correct?" he asked.

"Ah, you know your kingdoms it seems," Olav said with cheer.

"Aye, your highness, I quite enjoy learning about the kingdoms we trade with on our journeys. I have visited your kingdom and was enchanted by it. The mountains are covered in snow year-round, are they not?" Lochlann asked.

Olav nodded and turned to Orla, "Princess Orla, would you think it rude if I were to steal away your friend for a while? I think we might take some refreshment?"

Orla smiled. "Not at all, Prince Olav. Thank you for the dancing. I look forward to speaking with you more during your stay."

Olav bowed at Orla while noticing Lochlann discreetly checking with Ciarán. He stifled the laugh that wanted to burst forth at the petulant reply from the younger brother. Orla glanced over and Olav waited patiently while Lochlann looked between Ciarán and Orla. The older Allyn brother shook his head and followed Olav to the banquet room. Olav waited until they were seated, with drinks in hand, before broaching the elephant in the room.

"They have it bad for each other, do they not?" Olav said jokingly.

Lochlann nearly spit out his beer. He gave Olav an appraising stare and then nodded, laughing in relief.

"Noticed, did you?"

Olav chuckled. "It's as if an invisible string connects them. One cannot live without the other."

"If only those two knuckleheads would realize it, the kingdom would be in much less peril." Lochlann grinned.

Olav felt a warmth spread through his body. He decided he liked the smile on Lochlann's face.

"Sometimes, it is hard to see what is right in front of you and obvious to others," Olav offered.

"True. I am sure this storm will pass and they will eventually reconcile. If my pig-headed brother can pull his head out of his arse long enough," Lochlann said wryly.

Olav laughed and Lochlann smiled at him. "I am quite familiar with stubborn men."

"Ah, so you have a brother?" Lochlann asked.

"No, but my father is probably the most stubborn man in the known world." Olav smiled and took a swig of his beer.

Olav watched Lochlann sizing him up. He liked being truly

seen instead of being a title. He could tell Lochlann was a genuine man and, if he had anything to do with it, they would become great friends. He noticed Lochlann make a decision and stand. Olav looked confused for a moment but relaxed when Lochlann bowed and held out a hand.

"Would you care to take a walk in the gardens, Your Highness?" Lochlann asked.

Olav took the proffered hand and rose. "It would be my pleasure."

Olav and Lochlann were sparring in the courtyard. Lochlann was a very good swordsman and the men appeared to be equals. They were not really keeping score, but if they had, it would be about even anyway. Olav had not met any in his kingdom who could keep up with him. He'd just disarmed Lochlann, who conceded the match, and they were taking a water break while leaning against a wall.

"Lochlann, might I ask you a question?" Olav asked.

"Of course, Your Highness," Lochlann replied.

"Olav, please. You have earned the right, my friend. If I may call you that."

"Of course you may. Very well, Olav, what curiosity might I settle?" Lochlann asked with a smile.

"The Princess, she has an affection for your brother, does she not?" he asked.

Olav watched while Lochlann thought on the question. He didn't mind the delay in an answer as it gave him the chance to ogle the man without raising suspicion. Lochlann's hair was plastered to his forehead and his cheeks were rosy from the exertion of fighting. Olav swallowed hard as a bead of sweat made its way from Lochlann's neck down the open vee of his shirt and through the chest hair peeking out. Olav looked up just in time to meet Lochlann's eyes.

"I believe she does but I am not certain of it. Those two fight more often than not," he said and chuckled.

"Ah, a passion born of fire. I have seen it before, my own parents have been known to awaken the whole kingdom with their shouting. My mother once threw a vase at my father's head during dinner, then sat back down and calmly ate the rest of her food as if it were a normal evening." Olav laughed heartily. "How does your brother feel?"

Olav believed Sonja was the only woman capable of being married to his father. She did not allow King Harald to treat her as anything but his equal and many times she had saved Olav from his father's wrath—warranted or not. Olav loved both of his parents but his mother was very close to his heart.

"Just as I am not certain of Orla's feelings, I cannot give words to my brother's feelings for her. Love is not strong enough for what he feels. She is his world. Whenever they are apart, he thinks only of her. Their most recent argument has wounded him more than the fall. He is just too stubborn to admit it."

Olav scratched his chin. "What is the problem?"

"Ciarán has grand ideas about royalty and he has always belabored the fact that he is not noble. Therefore, in his mind, he is below her station and not a suitable match. Their recent argument did not help to dispel that myth when Orla pulled rank on him," Lochlann replied.

Olav thought for a moment, a sly grin slipped across his face. He had a reputation for meddling in the affairs of others and this would be no exception.

"The accident was not so much an accident?" he asked.

Lochlann laughed. "Very clever deduction. They were arguing on the wall and Ciarán might have been given a little push. How did you guess?"

"I can see the guilt written on the Princess' face whenever it is mentioned."

"Aye, she was never good at hiding her emotions," Lochlann said. He was really beginning to enjoy his new friend. "I do hope that my brother's affections for the Princess will not cause problems between our kingdoms?"

Olav grinned. "My dear, Lochlann, why would you worry about such things?"

Lochlann shrugged. "I just assumed you were here to try to win her over?"

"'Tis true that my mother and father would like for me to find a match and they are very fond of your sovereigns. However, I do believe that the Princess and I would make better allies than lovers. Would you not agree?" Olav assessed Lochlann.

Lochlann nodded. "Aye, I am not sure I would want to be the one in the way of what Orla wanted."

"I have an idea if you are game?" Olav said conspiratorially.

Lochlann nodded. "Anything that would help resolve this situation. I can't stand my brother's moroseness any longer. If I have to hear him moaning and groaning one more day, I might kill him and put him out of his misery like he's asked. What did you have in mind?"

Olav sat next to Orla under the willow tree by the stream. It was a pleasant day and they were discussing the pros and cons of building temporary dams to flood the nearby fields for a better harvest. Orla was against the idea and so Olav was, naturally, for it. He enjoyed riling her up. She was incredibly passionate and well-spoken, so he loved to get her excited about an idea to lower her inhibitions. She would make her case and, in the end, he would confess she had been right all along. She would then huff and playfully punch him in the arm and tell him he was incorrigible. Orla was in the midst of an enthusiastic rebuttal when Olav noticed the Allyn brothers exit the castle. He sighed in relief, having begun to suspect Lochlann was having a tough time getting Ciarán to escort him outside. Olav had no backup plans for keeping Orla out longer if they had been any later. Olav could tell Ciarán was sulking. Lochlann grabbed his brother's arm, spun him towards the tree and practically dragged him. Olav suppressed a chuckle, noticing the consternation on Orla's face.

"Ah, Lochlann and Ciarán, so nice to see you this fine afternoon," Olav said pleasantly.

Olav watched as Orla looked at the brothers. When she met Ciarán's stormy gaze, she looked away quickly, feigning interest in the stream. He glanced at Lochlann with expectation.

"I was just telling Ciarán he needed some air and sun," Lochlann said.

"Yes, yes, a fine day for it. Wouldn't you agree, Princess?" Olav said.

"Yes, it is lovely today," Orla muttered, not addressing anyone in particular.

Ciarán stepped back, attempting to leave. "I think I have had enough air."

He bowed and began walking back towards the castle as fast as he could without too much pain. Lochlann glanced at Olav who nodded. He chased after his brother. Olav watched as Lochlann attempted to keep his temper in check. Olav could practically feel the frustration wafting from him, even at a distance.

"It is nice to see your friend out of the castle," he prodded.

Orla nodded and picked at the grass.

"I do hope to see more of him around. I hear he is turning purple and his head is spinning every other hour," Olav said with a grin.

"It is... wait... what?" Orla asked, finally paying attention.

Olav chuckled as Orla discreetly punched him on the leg, still watching Ciarán out of the corner of her eye. Olav looked toward the brothers again. Lochlann put something in Ciarán's hands and spun him around. He gave him a small, but not painful, push towards where Orla and Olav were waiting.

"Perhaps I could give you some time alone?" Olav asked quietly.

"That would be helpful. Thank you," Orla replied with some measure of trepidation in her voice.

Olav could tell she was yet again distracted by her concern for Ciarán. He straightened and stood, holding out a hand to help Orla up. Lochlann came up behind his brother and nodded at Olav.

"Princess, would you mind if I sparred with Lochlann? He is quite remarkable and the best sparring partner I have had in a very long time. My father's guard are all getting old and slow. I am sure Ciarán might keep you company," Olav said.

Orla struggled to regain her composure for a moment and then pasted on a smile. Olav could tell she was nervous and Ciarán looked as if he was about to face a firing squad. Olav felt for the younger man. He considered Ciarán something close to a brother, having learned a lot about him from Lochlann and seeing how much he loved Ciarán. Lochlann felt as if he owed his brother the world and Olav admired him more for that. Olav wanted nothing more than to see the younger Allyn and Orla live a long, happy life together. He saw much of his parents in the two people.

"Of course, Olav. Thank you for the most excellent conversation this afternoon," she said politely.

Olav and Lochlann both bowed and took their leave. They walked through the meadow towards the castle and looked back once they were near the door. Ciarán had not retreated yet, a very good sign. Olav put his hand up and Lochlann high fived him. The plan had worked, at least so far. Olav held the door open for Lochlann, who entered the castle after a moment's hesitation. Olav was finally winning in his bid to have Lochlann treat him as an equal instead of a Prince. Olav smiled and entered the castle.

Olav gasped as Lochlann cornered him against the wall and kissed him deeply. Lochlann pulled away almost immediately and Olav touched his lips.

"Your highness, forgive my presumption... I just..." Lochlann stuttered.

Olav smiled and put a hand on Lochlann's face, causing him to stop talking and gape at Olav.

"It is I who never hoped to presume you felt any measure of what I feel," Olav said as he searched Lochlann's eyes.

"I was too afraid to cause a scandal and war between our two countries, Olav."

Olav nodded. "I assure you, should this happen again, and I very much hope it does happen again—and soon—Fadersogn will remain a firm ally to Eiremor."

Lochlann stared in shock a moment and then took Olav's face in his hands, renewing the kiss and deepening it until they both had to stop for air. He rested his forehead on Olav's and closed his eyes.

"Whatever shall we do, Olav?" he asked somewhat mournfully.

Olav shrugged. " I am a prince and can be clever when the moment demands. I will think of something. For now, how about that sparring session?"

Lochlann nodded. Olav gestured for him to lead the way and he headed down the hall. Olav watched him as he walked and began plotting in his head.

Olav had been pleased and then saddened all in the space of a week. Lochlann wrote to him on an almost daily basis. Olav had spoken with his mother and waited for the appropriate moment to approach his father. King Harald had continually harassed him about the possibility of a union with Eiremor and Olav was running out of excuses. Sonja knew the reason and helped divert the conversation every time the topic was brought up but Olav realized they could not stall his father forever. Then Lochlann wrote that Ciarán had finally gotten the courage to ask King Phelan for his permission to marry Orla. Olav could not have been happier for the young Allyn brother. He wrote of his enthusiasm for the match to Lochlann. The messenger was just leaving the courtyard when another rode in with terrifying speed and stopped short of ramming Olav.

"Your Highness, urgent news for the King," the messenger said as he handed Olav a missive.

"I shall see that he gets it. Go to the kitchens for refreshment," he instructed the messenger and hastily went inside to find his father.

Olav watched as Harald read the message and frowned. Harald seemed to read it more than once. Then he sighed and rubbed his eyes.

"Olav, fetch your mother. We are at war," Harald said, dismissing his son.

Olav blanched and went to find his mother.

Eiremor and Fadersogn were at war with the kingdom to their south for several years before Orla and her brother Kellan were able to use their combined magical powers and defeat them. Olav had followed the movements of all the ships in both kingdoms armadas, sending prayers to the gods for the safe return of both brothers. He traveled to Eiremor on a monthly basis, hoping for news and being the best friend he could to Orla. She was beside herself but convinced both brothers were alive. She was his only link to Lochlann.

Olav was waiting at the castle when news of the return of *The Mercury*, Eiremor's only remaining ship from the Battle of the North Sea. Neither Lochlann nor Ciarán was aboard the returning ship. Olav let Orla cry on his shoulder when she learned the *Queen's Fortune* had replaced *The Phoenix* in the battle. He could not confide in her that he felt as much loss as she did because he did not think she would understand. He waited until the depths of the night, when he was alone, to sob into his pillow and mourn for Lochlann.

Olav felt lucky to be alive the day the last of the prisoners returned to Eiremor. He had been spending long days with King Phelan, discussing options for border patrols and avoiding Phelan's hints about a possible marriage alliance. After hours of working and sleepless nights, he felt incredibly frustrated and restless. He stood on the castle ramparts, staring off into the distance when he heard shouting from the courtyard.

"Water!" a voice yelled.

Olav looked down and saw a group of bedraggled and obviously weary travelers dropping their belongings in the courtyard as others ran to help them. Most of the men sported long hair and beards, their clothes in tatters. Olav felt great pity for them. He knew they must be men returning from the prisoner camps. He cursed inwardly at the costs of war—to both kingdoms and him personally. Olav started to turn away when he noticed an unmistakable figure amongst the men. His heart dropped to his stomach and he had to pinch himself to believe he was truly seeing the man he loved most in the world. As if Olav had yelled his name, Lochlann looked up and locked eyes with him. He gave a little shrug and Olav shook his head, backing away from the wall and watching Lochlann as long as he could before he broke off in a run towards the stairwell.

Olav burst through the door to the courtyard, searching in

desperation for Lochlann amid the chaotic scene. He panicked, momentarily, when Lochlann was not immediately visible. Olav didn't think he could take back that sinking feeling that it was all a dream. He had imagined being reunited with Lochlann so many times but he was cognizant of the fact he had never conjured Lochlann with such sorrow in his eyes. Lochlann was brave and strong. To see him so downtrodden, even for a moment, was unsettling. As exhausted as the men were, they all began standing and bowing as Olav passed. Olav swallowed the lump in his throat and attempted to regain some measure of composure.

"Gentlemen," he said loudly, "please. You have been through enough. Please rest—we will have refreshments in the great hall and will find you all the places to bathe and sleep."

The men cheered in a subdued manner and went back to their previous state. Olav searched and still did not see Lochlann. Suddenly, he felt a presence next to him and he turned to see Lochlann in front of him. It was unmistakably the man he loved, though a very different one from the man he had first met. Lochlann had a world-weary look about him and the usual brightness in his eyes had faded. Olav hoped very much to return that light as quickly as possible. Olav did not hesitate. He threw his arms around Lochlann and hugged him as if he might disappear again at any moment.

"I've missed you," he stated simply.

Lochlann nodded and hugged back. Olav was reluctant to let go but saw that the men around them were beginning to notice and he did not want to put Lochlann in any more peril than he had been already.

"Come, let us get you settled," Olav said, leading Lochlann into the castle.

After a brief report to King Phelan, Olav led Lochlann to the rooms the King had set aside for his use. Olav ordered a bath, shaving supplies and food. Lochlann sat quietly on a chair, watching Olav. He raised an eyebrow when Lochlann ordered the last of the servants to leave and Olav merely smirked. This brought a chuckle from Lochlann, which in turn made Olav give him a genuine smile. Olav gestured to the bath.

"Shall I give you some privacy?" Olav joked.

Lochlann blushed and looked away. Olav knelt by the chair.

"I was only joking," Olav said earnestly.

Lochlann swallowed heavily. "I know… it's just…"

"Lochlann?" Olav waited for him to meet his eyes. "You are still the man I love."

Lochlann nodded and stood. Olav helped him undress and step into the tub. Lochlann sighed in relief as the warm water hit his sore muscles. Olav wanted to yell at the scars he saw on Lochlann's back. He must have been whipped in the prisoner camp. He lathered a cloth and gently washed Lochlann's back.

"Olav, you don't have to bathe me," Lochlann mumbled.

"I don't make it a habit to do things I don't want to do," Olav replied cheekily.

This elicited another chuckle from Lochlann. He sat patiently while Olav bathed him, closing his eyes and nearly nodding off. Olav watched Lochlann relax and his eyes filled with tears. Someday he would ask Lochlann to tell him everything but at that moment, Olav was merely happy he was alive.

"Your arm will need to be set properly," Olav said gently.

Lochlann nodded. "It was not tended properly. The men did what they could."

Olav winced and averted his eyes, not wanting Lochlann to see any pity.

"Would you like a shave?" Olav asked.

Lochlann opened his eyes. "I would love one."

Olav nodded and gathered the supplies. Lochlann leaned forward and Olav spread the lather on his face. He carefully pulled the razor across Lochlann's cheek. Lochlann reached up and stopped Olav's hand.

"Ciarán?" Lochlann croaked.

Olav had been so caught up in the return of one Allyn brother, he had not even thought of the other. Olav swallowed.

"He was not in your company?" Olav asked, though he already knew the answer.

Lochlann shook his head solemnly. Olav could see he had inadvertently confirmed Lochlann's worst fears. He let go of Olav's hand, presenting his cheek again. Olav did not miss the tears Lochlann fought back but decided to let his love mourn in his own way.

With Lochlann's return, trips to Eiremor became pleasant again. Olav did not miss the strained relationship Orla had with Lochlann and he knew the reason was that she believed Lochlann was not a dutiful brother. She had mentioned to Olav on numerous occasions her belief that Ciarán was still alive. Since he had refused to ever believe Lochlann was gone, he had been a good friend and agreed with her. Still, he knew the subject of his missing brother was a raw one for Lochlann and he fervently wished the three of them could be together since it was his belief the two of them would benefit in their mutual grief.

Orla had mentioned to Olav that her parents wished for her to marry him. Olav had every intention of taking Lochlann home with him and had avoided the topic of marriage from both his father and hers since Captain Allyn had returned. Olav waited with bated breath for Orla to speak her mind on the subject. He had been relieved to find she had outright refused her father's wishes. It was then, Olav confided his plans to her and Orla swore she would keep his secrets until the appropriate time.

"Lochlann, I've told Orla about our relationship," Olav offered one serene day by the willow tree.

Lochlann looked stunned. Olav fidgeted, unsure of Lochlann's feelings. Then, Lochlann shrugged and kissed Olav. Olav put his arms around Lochlann and deepened the kiss before pulling back to look at him.

"So, you're ok being outed?" Olav asked.

Lochlann nodded. "It would happen eventually. Orla is incredibly astute. I see her noticing us together and the jealousy it sparks in her. I wish she would let him go."

Olav shook his head. "She can't. He is a part of her as much as you are a part of me. When I thought you dead, I felt as if an important piece of me was missing. I can imagine her pain and the pain it brings her to be reminded of him with your presence. She insists he is alive."

"If he were alive, don't you think I would find him?" Lochlann growled.

"You've been recovering yourself. You can't blame yourself for losing him in the battle," Olav said calmly.

Lochlann stood and hit his fist against the tree.

"Can't I?" he yelled. "He was my little brother and I didn't keep him safe!"

Olav stood, attempting to put a comforting hand on Lochlann's shoulder. Lochlann shrugged it off and stared out into the water with his back to Lochlann.

"Perhaps you should marry her," he said after a few silent minutes of brooding.

"What!?" It was Olav's turn to shout.

Lochlann turned around and faced Olav. The two men stood their ground, neither giving an inch. Finally, Lochlann looked at the ground, unable to meet the pleading in Olav's eyes any longer.

"Marry her. Your kingdom does not allow our relationship and she will have no one else. She must move on and I am no longer worthy of you," Lochlann said apologetically.

"I don't want... you can't mean this?" Olav appealed.

"I do. My decision is final. I--."

Olav put his hands on Lochlann's lips to stop him. He shook his head.

"If that is what you wish, I will do it. But if you say it, I am lost."

Lochlann nodded. Olav kissed him with all the love he felt and then pulled away, turning on his heel and walking away from Lochlann.

Lochlann left the castle that evening. Olav had spoken with Phelan and then Orla. They would be married. Orla asked about Lochlann but Olav was relieved when she didn't pry any further. He had tried to hide the pain in his eyes but knew it was nearly impossible. Olav wrote to his father and nearly vomited at the reply. Each missive and preparation was a reminder of his broken heart. Orla did her best to comfort him, as he had comforted her. Both of them were miserable.

The day of his wedding dawned and it promised to be dull and gray. Olav watched the storm clouds gathering in the distance with bitter amusement. His mother had already been in to *talk some sense into him.* Besides Orla, Sonja was the only one who knew Olav's true desires. He knew his mother only wanted what was best for him but he felt he had no more choices in the matter. Lochlann had decided for both of them. Olav bit back the sob threatening to escape him. A knock on the door roused him from his self-pitying moment. He went over to the door and opened it, surprised to see his mother standing on the other side, yet again.

"Mother, we've been over this," he cautioned.

"You will want this information," she replied.

Olav sighed and opened the door for her. Sonja swept into the room and sat on the settee. She made a show of smoothing her skirts and primping her hair. Olav sighed again and cleared his throat. Sonja looked up with a glint in her eyes.

"Captain Allyn returned today," Sonja beamed.

Olav's heart jumped at the thought of seeing Lochlann again, then sank at the realization he would have to marry Orla and lose Lochlann forever. Lochlann's timing was incredibly awkward.

"Mother," Olav growled, "it matters not."

"I'm not done," she replied.

Olav rolled his eyes and waited for her to respond. She looked pointedly at the seat next to her until Olav grunted and plopped down next to her. Sonja had a way of ordering him about without actually saying anything. Usually, he was good-natured about her manner of mothering but the day was already weighing on him and any goodwill he felt towards her was nonexistent. He indulged her when she grabbed his hand and squeezed it, placing it in his lap.

"What is it, Mother?" he demanded.

"Olav, my dear son, he found his brother."

Olav's head snapped up, "Ciarán's alive?"

"He is," she said, smiling.

"That's... incredible. Ciarán's here?" Olav held his breath waiting for his mother to reply.

She nodded, "Captain Allyn has been sent to fetch him to the castle. Queen Meara asked me to beg your forgiveness and asked for a delay in the wedding."

Olav jumped up and began pacing. What had started as the worst day of his life, was now becoming the happiest. His mind raced with all the possibilities. Then, he realized none of it would matter. Lochlann had made his wishes clear. He paused, mid-step, and turned back to his mother. He let all of the despair he felt wash over his face. Sonja held out her hand and Olav took it, sitting back down next to his mother.

"It can be fixed, son," she chided gently.

Olav looked away and Sonja smoothed the hair from his forehead. She stood and gently kissed his head. Olav watched as she left the room, wondering if she was correct. Maybe, just maybe, all would be well.

Lochlann stepped out of Ciarán's rooms and leaned against the wall, tilting his head back and sighing. Olav watched from the shadows, his heart aching to be near Lochlann. He saw Lochlann look down the hallway, towards his quarters. Then Lochlann seemed to make a decision and turned in the opposite direction. Olav took a deep breath and made a decision. He stepped into the hallway.

"Lochlann?" Olav said quietly.

Lochlann's shoulders straightened and he stood completely still for a moment. Olav watched him nod and turn. Lochlann met Olav's eyes with a look of sadness mixed with regret. Lochlann bowed politely, which made Olav's heart sink. Lochlann had not bowed to him in years.

"Yes, your highness?"

"Must we?" Olav sighed.

Lochlann seemed taken aback by his question. Olav waited for him to say anything further but it became clear Olav was in charge of the conversation. Olav searched his mind for the best way to handle the delicate situation and still get the desired outcome. Lochlann stood by, patiently waiting for Olav to make the decision.

"Lochlann, would you please accompany me to my quarters?"

Olav asked.

Lochlann nodded and Olav led the way to his rooms. He opened the door for Lochlann and let go of the breath he did not realize he was holding when Lochlann entered ahead of him. Perhaps, he thought, the situation was not a total disaster. Lochlann sat in a chair and Olav sat across from him. The two men once again stared at each other, neither willing to make a mistake in a conversation each knew to be vital to their lifelong happiness.

Olav knelt in front of Lochlann and grasped his hands. Lochlann began to protest.

"Marry me," Olav blurted out.

"I..." Lochlann was at a loss for words.

"It seems the Princess of Eiremor has called off our wedding and I have been jilted," Olav joked, trying to lighten the mood.

Lochlann laughed loudly, a sound that was music to Olav's ears. He pulled Olav up and kissed him soundly.

"I'm not sure she was your type, Your Highness," Lochlann mocked playfully.

Olav shook his head. "Not at all, but I know someone who is perfect for me."

Lochlann smiled. "And who might this handsome fellow be?"

"If you have to ask, I have not shown my affections properly," Olav smirked.

"It is I who am the culprit in this situation. A misdeed I plan to rectify," Lochlann replied earnestly.

Olav sighed happily. "Is that a yes?"

"Is it possible?" Lochlann asked with seriousness.

"My mother has an idea," Olav replied mysteriously.

"Yes, Olav," Lochlann said.

Olav whooped with joy and kissed Lochlann, pouring all his euphoria into it.

The First Sunday festival was set to open and Olav gathered with his parents in the balcony antechamber. It was the tradition for his mother to welcome the populace and introduce the petitioners. This year, there were a total of two petitioners, including Olav. He watched as his mother introduced the other man.

"Ladies and gentlemen, it is my pleasure to introduce you to Leif Anders. His petition on this First Sunday was a request to change the law for inheritance. As you know, inheritance has long been determined by the sex of the heirs. Male heirs are considered, female heirs are not. Master Anders has three daughters, no sons, and wishes to pass his estates to the females of his household at his pleasure. King Harald, please give your decision on the petition."

Harald nodded, "My people, my wife is both wise and gracious. She has counseled me in this matter and I have consulted my heart. It is my fervent belief the women of this kingdom are as entitled to the benefits of ownership as the males. Therefore, it is my great pleasure to accept Master Ander's petition and amend the kingdom law to allow inheritance for all children, regardless of sex."

The populace cheered and Olav smiled. Master Anders bowed to his mother and father, then to him. Olav gave the man a gracious smile and congratulated him. Master Ander's daughters surrounded him and kissed him on the cheek. Olav watched the happy family. His mother caught his eye and winked at him. Olav swallowed the lump forming in his throat. His father would soon announce the fate of his own petition.

Queen Sonja stepped back to the balcony and waited for the populace to give her their attention. She took an extra moment and Olav fervently wished she would get on with it. He rolled his eyes at her theatrics and did his best not to burst onto the balcony and shake her. Sonja looked over the crowd and took a deep breath.

"There was one other petitioner."

Sonja gestured for Olav and he stepped onto the balcony. A murmur went through the crowd and Sonja held up her hand. She linked the fingers of her other hand with Olav's and squeezed.

"My son has been an advocate for the populace during both times of peace and times of war. It has long been our wish he found a mate worthy of him. Olav believes he has found that person but in order for him to marry his choice, we must change the law. The law of our land states that a Prince may marry the Princess of his choice. Olav's choice does not fit the definition of a princess. He has requested we change the law to allow him to marry any person of his choosing. King Harald, please give your decision on the petition."

Harald once again stepped forward. Olav watched his father, who refused to look at him or give him any indication of his decision. Olav glanced at his mother and she merely squeezed his hand again. Olav couldn't decide if it gave him confidence or fear. Perhaps, she was merely holding him up so that he would not break down in front of his people.

"People of Fadersogn, I was also counseled by the Queen in this matter. I searched my heart and found my objections to the petition to be baseless. Our laws regarding the marriage of the heir to the throne were written hundreds of years ago, in a different time. The needs of the kingdom were different and the days darker. Lest you think poorly of me, this decision was not difficult for me in the way you might think. I have no qualms with my son marrying someone who is not of royal blood as we serve at your pleasure and we consider you, our people, to be equals. We know, without a doubt, the kingdom is bountiful due to your contributions. I, therefore, approve the law to allow my son to marry the person of his choosing."

The crowd cheered. Olav felt faint. He could barely believe his ears. However, Harald was not done and he waited for the din to die down.

"Good people, the law is changed. However, we must amend the marriage laws as well, which state that a man must marry a woman and vice versa."

A murmuring started again. It seemed the populace was confused and Olav knew it was for good reason. There were many in the kingdom who lived with people of the same sex, as if married, but none had ever asked for permission to make it legal in the eyes of the King. They were not ostracized, merely treated as adults living together under one roof with none of the legal protections of married couples. Harald looked over his people. He then gestured behind him and someone stepped out on the balcony. Olav gasped when he saw Lochlann shaking his father's hand. Lochlann turned a smirk towards Olav and bowed. Harald put his hand on Lochlann's shoulder.

"My dear populace, you might remember the heroics of Captain Lochlann Allyn of Eiremor. He also has the good fortune to have won the heart of my son, Prince Olav. Therefore, it is my great pleasure to announce, the laws of the kingdom are hereby amended to allow the marriage of ANY person to ANY other person, regardless of sex. I would also like to announce the pending nuptials of Prince Olav to Captain Allyn," Harald beamed.

Once again, the crowd erupted in cheering. Olav smiled broadly at Lochlann, who returned the look of love. Sonja hugged Lochlann and then went to stand next to Harald, who put his arm around her.

"You did well, dear," Sonja said.

"I always do," Harald preened.

Olav chuckled and held out his hand to Lochlann. He took it and the two stepped closer to each other.

"When did you get here?" Olav asked.

"Two days ago," Lochlann stated.

"Two days! How?" Olav sputtered.

Lochlann smiled. "Your mother. She's a wily one."

Olav glanced at his mother. She winked at him, then led Harald into the castle so she could welcome the populace into the great hall. Olav shook his head and turned back to Lochlann.

"You still sure about this?" Olav asked, gesturing to the crowd still milling around in the courtyard and fearing the answer.

Lochlann glanced down and back at Olav.

"I don't know--" he started.

Olav looked away, "I understand... it's a lot."

Lochlann grabbed Olav and kissed him for all the world to see. Olav clung to Lochlann until he heard the crowd cheering again. He pulled back and blushed a deep shade of red. Lochlann laughed and waved at the crowd. Olav smiled at the natural ease Lochlann showed around his people. Lochlann turned back to Olav and held out his hand.

"Does that convince you, Your Highness?" Lochlann teased.

Olav smirked. "I might need a bit more convincing."

Lochlann laughed. "It will be my pleasure to convince you for as long as it takes."

"Promise?"

"With all my heart," Lochlann solemnly swore.

Olav looked into Lochlann's eyes with all the love he felt and saw it reflected back at him. He took Lochlann's hand and headed towards the antechamber. It had been a bumpy road to this moment but Olav finally felt at peace. He could now live the rest of his life with the man he loved. Lochlann stopped him just before they left the antechamber.

"Olav." Lochlann looked into his eyes. "I never told you. I love you."

Olav grinned and kissed Lochlann in reply. Yes, it had turned out to be the most important First Sunday of his life and he would not change anything about the day. Fadersogn was forever changed by the courage of a Prince and the love for a Captain who loved him back.

BREAKING NEWS
BY MARSHALL MILLER

The sun's rays slowly crawling up the cracked windshield of the wrecked BREAKING NEWS van woke Erica Jordan in her front seat makeshift bed. Erica started to stir gradually, then jerked awake in the seat as she realized where she was sleeping.

"Shit," she mumbled. "Not a nightmare. It's real." This realization created one of those horrible hypothetical questions that only time could answer: What would this day bring... now that everything had changed forever?

The woman, who many at the new station, called the Blonde Lois Lane turned in her seat to look into the back of the broadcast van. Her experienced field cameraman, Harry Young, was still out like a light in his sleeping bag. At least the van still had some structural integrity, even though its trashed engine would ensure it a place in a junkyard. That is if junkyards would exist after yesterday's events.

Erika managed to open the driver's side door without waking Harry. Erica knew the big burly older man was exhausted, so she tried to let him sleep. The field news reporter stretched her stiff and voluptuous body which also gotten her the nickname of Blonde Bimbo, but not to her face. Erica had to work harder to be taken seriously due to her sexual attractiveness, as she refused the 'casting couch' on more than one occasion. Of course, maybe had she taken one of those invitations, she would be in a nice warm bed somewhere safe. Then she realized the assumption she had made.

"Nowhere is going to be safe now," Erica said out loud. She thought she heard Harry stir. When he did not call out, Erica gave a sigh of relief. He needed rest, and she needed some alone time to sort her thought out. Today was one of those days where she wished she had taken up smoking as she could use a jolt of something like nicotine, caffeine, or alcohol. Erica had none of the above. Maybe, Harry, had a bottle hidden. She could hope.

Erica slowly walked around the news station vehicle. The motor was a smoldering ruin, and the female reporter once again realized how lucky they were that the van had not exploded into flames when the front was hit by the edge of... she did not know what to call it. Energy blast, lightning bolt, phaser beam? Erica shook her head, She'll let greater minds than her to figure that one out. She tried to push some stray blonde hairs from her face as a Pacific Coast ocean breeze tried to make even more of a mess of her once professional hairdo.

"Erica. Step away from the front." It was from Harry. He had apparently woke.

"Why?" Erica asked." If it were going to explode, it would have done it."

"Radiation," the bearded man said as he pushed the side access door open enough for him to clamber out.

"A speck of radioactive sand in your lungs and Viola! Just like John Wayne and the Nevada Test Site, you have Mister Lung Cancer."

Erica stared at him.

"So you believe that story. That it's-"

"Don't say his name. Its bad luck."

Harry was superstitious about a lot of weird things. This was apparently one of them.

"How do you know it's a 'he'? Did you see the balls hanging down?"

"Alright. It. Happy now?" Harry reached back into the van and pulled out a couple of large duffel bags, then a camera bag.

"Time to hit the road, find some transportation. And see if we can somehow uplink my footage to the station."

"You saved it?" Erica asked.

"Never lost footage yet," answered Harry. "Closest I came was on the Iraq-Syrian Border. Gave me some of my gray hairs." Harry looked around.

"This is going to give me more."

From one of the duffel bags, Harry pulled a large Old West-style revolver and stuck it on his belt, pulled his large t-shirt with the station logo over it.

"I didn't know you had that," said Erica.

"This is my John Wayne Special, in forty-five caliber. Panic makes people do odd things."

The cameraman pushed one of the duffel bags towards Erica.

"Can you carry this?" he asked.

"You forget I'm a North Dakota farm girl," the news reporter said with a smile. "Nordic stock gave me this body, with some muscle underneath."

Harry laughed as he slung the camera bag over his shoulder and picked up the other duffel bag.

"Let's get humping. I think there was a small store down this coastal road with gas pumps. Maybe they still have a working landline telephone."

"And some food," replied Erica.

The two television station employees made good time walking down the coastal road. A half-hour later they caught sight of the Mom and Pop store. There was a car parked at the gas pumps, but they saw no human activity.

"Think they bugged out?" asked Erica.

"Wouldn't you with a monster on the loose?" replied Harry.

As they walked closer, they slowed their pace. Erica finally called out.

"Anybody home? Our van broke down up the road. We could use a phone and some food."

Silence.

The two field news partners made their way to the car at the pumps. The driver's side window was down, and Erica stuck her head in.

"Keys still in the ignition," she told Harry.

"Good, Erica. If it runs, we can make it to civilization."

They set their bags down near the front entrance, and Harry tried the door. It was unlocked. He pulled his pistol out from under his shirt and began to walk into the store.

"Harry—"

"As I said, panic makes people do odd things."

The called out as they slowly walked the isles of the country store. Erica noticed a back office behind the refrigerated coolers and made her way towards it.

"Hello. Erica Jordan, Channel 13 News," she said as she cautiously opened the office door. Her scream made Harry come running.

What looked like an older women lay dead on the office floor in a drying pool of blood, Sitting behind the office desk was a man. His age was difficult to ascertain as his brains were decorating the office ceiling. The pistol he had apparently used was still grasped in his hand flopped on the edge of the desktop.

Erica backed out into Harry's arms and began to shake.

"My God," Erica managed to croak out. "Why? He shot his wife, then himself."

Harry gently pushed Erica back and stepped up to the desk, avoiding the pool of blood. He craned his neck to look at something on the desktop. He picked up a blood-splattered piece of paper.

"Here's the reason, Erica. Suicide note."

"What's it say," Erica asked.

"The Beast 666 is upon us. We deny it our souls." Harry swore. "Kill yourself so some spawn of hell can't get you. Real logical."

"As you said, Harry, panic makes people do crazy things."

Harry laid the suicide note back on the desktop and stepped out of the office.

"Come on, Erica. They are past helping. The lights are still on, so let's grab some food, try and find a telephone since cell service is gone. I guess our gigantic 'friend' has not trashed the power lines yet…"

The store lights flickered, then went out.

"Great. Well, my lady, let's find some batteries and flashlights, grab some food and drink. Then we will see if the car starts."

A half-hour later they had used two scrounged flashlights to locate the landline telephone, which was dead. They found a battery-operated emergency and weather radio. Harry managed to get it working and picked up a station from the Portland, Oregon area.

"All television and radio stations will soon be broadcasting Emergency Broadcast System messages only," said the unknown male announcer. "Before they shut us down, I will relay what I know." The disembodied voice paused, then continued.

"The… *creature* has somehow managed to conceal its

enormous body in the Pacific Ocean off the Washington State Coast. The Navy has sent warships to locate it after its path of destruction. The Hood Canal bridge is destroyed, and there are unconfirmed reports that the creature destroyed a Trident Submarine. Sequim, Washington was flattened and burned. There is now a several-hundred-foot wide swath through the National Forest from Sequim out to the Pacific Ocean. Initial air attacks only seemed to anger the beast."

"Shit," said Erica. "If we could only get them our film footage."

"Let's survive first," Harry answered. The radio broadcast continued.

"Authorities and scientists have yet to determine what this creature is, or what gender. One paleontologist even said it could be hermaphroditic, having the ability to reproduce on its own as only one has appeared. On Earth, two animals of the two different sexes are needed to reproduce. However, this... beast resembles nothing in the natural order of life. It only reminds officials of certain creations from the film industry."

"Told ya," Harry said.

"Just because someone said it looks like that specific monster, does not make it fact," answered Erica.

"I have been notified that my broadcast will be shut off in one minute," the radio newsman said. "So, let me say in closing. If you can hear me, hide. The military is trying to find effective weapons to counter this monster, but so far—" The station went dead air.

"Let's go," Harry said. "We'll see if we can get that car running-"

The windows of the store shook as a jet aircraft produced sonic boom cascaded across the countryside.

'Now they show up," said Erica.

"Come on," stated Harry. "Grab the stuff we scrounged and act like sheep and get the flock out of here."

The two news people soon had the abandoned car running, although its fuel tank was only half full.

"Driver bugged out," opinioned the cameraman.

"Unless this was the store owner's car," Erica responded.

"It's ours now, Erica. Bags in and let's go!"

The ground shook. Harry and Erica froze at the car. The ground bounced as if the epicenter of a significant earthquake was nearby.

A loud howling and hooting sound rolled across the area. Harry and Erica covered their ears as the apparent vocalization hurt their eardrums.

"Down!" Harry yelled and the two humans crouched in the store doorway.

The sound of jet engines mixed with explosions made Harry look up in time to see a column of fiery energy slash across the sky and incinerate a jet fighter. Harry turned his head to see the source of the destructive force. His eyes widened as he yelled at Erica.

"I told you, dammit! I told you it was him. It's Go—"

The remains of a jet fighter fell from the sky and flattened the country store.

There was snow on the ground when the family of four approached the store ruins in search of salvage. The man and woman with two children, a boy, and a girl, slowly came out of the protection of the forest and into the burned our area. All four of the humans were armed, even though the two kids were only nine and ten. The world was not a safe place.

The boy quickly found a camera bag with lettering on it and pointed it out to his father.

"Dad, what's this?"

"Camera bag from a television station. I think you remember television, Son."

"Pictures that went through the air?" the daughter asked.

"Kind of. Sort of. But we need food right now. So fill the bag up with eats."

The family found some cans and other items that had not been burned up. That told Dad that no one had dared to try and scavenge the store.

"We'll eat right tonight," Mom said. Then a vibrating growling sound washed over the area.

"Move!" Dad ordered. With practice born from survival, the family melted into the forest.

The gigantic beast strode over the land, the first part of its name stating what it was to humanity since its appearance. For it was the first of many vengeful gods.

Godzilla walked the Earth, like the ancient god it was.

THE CAT
BY ELIZA LOEB

Endlessly I question what my exodus may prove and endlessly I ponder my purpose as though my life depended on it. At night I lay awake and stare at the ceiling, watching as shadows dance along the walls and potentially creep out of my bedroom window for a late-night stroll. The streets are only barely lit where it matters, though the alleys and vacant lots where nature and overbrush had lain claim seem to hold the most promise. This in and of itself helps with my insecurities, brings me comfort. It allows me to think clearly and plan ahead for what other steps to take, as apprehensive as I may be as to whether or not such motions may work. I dread the possibilities of such plans potentially leading to starvation.

These are the thoughts that race through my mind as fingers brush through my hair and whisper sweet nothings to me. I adore the comfort. I adore the compliments and the endless gifts of admiration and deeply take advantage of the liberties I am given. Some would call me spoiled for openly speaking of such notions, however, the sunlight upon my skin distracts me from those unpleasantries. It will hardly matter in the next five seconds. Theo, the new boy next door seems to have said such things, despite taking a liking to me. He is very presumptuous in his approaches and constantly assumes that, based on my interests, I am willing to lay down for him. Also, my caretaker finds this more humorous than the crazed woman who stomps loudly down the way.

No matter.

It is a glorious morning now that I have relieved myself of my pessimism and my food dish is finally full.

I'm certain I had nearly starved.

SONGS OF INNOCENCE AND EXPERIENCE
BY SHEILA MENGERT

Dear Jeremy,

I am sorry to have been so remiss in writing to you since I left the academy. My only excuse is that the world that I now occupy is so different from the lake and poplars of the old school where that little group known as "The Cabal" used to walk with you after classes discussing arts and sciences and in our lesser way preserving the ideals of the Symposium.

I am now residing among philistines of the worst sort made all the more unbearable because they are drawn from the wealthiest of the families of Orange County and environs. The course that has been charted for me is to master all of the arcane aspects of international finance and perhaps to obtain an internship next summer with a firm of investment bankers: a life of money-making lies like a great desert before me. I shall be doomed to drive Mercedes and Bentleys, to wear thousand-dollar suits, and to fly first class to Paris and Milan. I feel the shades of Republicanism drawing down like a shroud around me. No doubt I will marry some lithe and lissome blond debutante in due season, someone who in her more informal soirees with her peers goes by the name of Buffy and we will raise indulged and neurotic children together until I divorce her before abandoning it all to join some eastern cult and move to an ashram in Nepal or Kashmir.

How I wish I might have had the intestinal fortitude to follow your advice and to have imitated the early Kerouac and seen something of my native land on an old Harley before the shackles were placed upon my wrists and ankles! What a pity it must someday be to recall no youthful folly to bemoan and to regret. No doubt you detected an early strain of prudence in my nature that prompted you to act as my mentor as on that Sunday morning after chapel when you advised me to avoid living what you called a freeze-dried life. Yet even recalling that day and the momentary quickening of my pulse at thoughts of rebellion are inadequate to stir me in my present slough of despond. You see my father has taken it upon himself to send me a series of what he no doubt imagines are inspirational letters in the manner of those of Lord Chesterfield to his natural son. I feel something of the same reflective worldliness in them, the same desire to further my advancement in society, and the same seasoned hypocrisy that always accompanies men of power and success. I do not blame him. Indeed by his own lights he wills my good but you cannot imagine how oppressive the sentiments within his successive diatribes are. I feel rather like young Chad Newsome in *The Ambassadors* by Henry James being bribed into respectability by the promises of a glorious future. Already I feel the pinch. I feel positively guilty to spend a weekend reading and listening to the great ocean. The art of networking down here is the only categorical imperative and party-going is a must. The only comfort is that the closeness to Hollywood breeds some resistance to the nationalist hysteria and MAGA hats are definitely *déclassé.* Yet I am inconsolable.

I am under relentless admonition. The paternal letters arrive from home like the beating of some great bass drum and I am not strong enough to ignore them. I know that I shall be quizzed as to their contents when I go home for Christmas… It occurs to me that the measure of my distress may seem exaggerated and I know that many people would gladly step into my shoes. I am not without my own preconceptions and biases. Therefore I have decided to forward these letters to you as a modern-day chronicle of the pressures brought upon youth by society. I have no time to construct my own narrative even if I were the Jane Austen or Samuel Richardson of my day. I will let my father's letters speak for themselves without apology or editing. Make of them what you will and if you have a word of comfort for me in due season, do not hesitate to speak.

Your sorrowing erstwhile student,

Anthony

Letters from my Father

Letter 1

I am writing this series of letters to you, now that you are away at school, to prepare you for the role that you will someday assume in the world once your education is completed. If I was so foolish as to assume that your instructors at the academy could teach mere writing technique without venturing into naïve values then I would be spared the necessity of ensuring your salutary disillusionment now by my own ministrations. I have detected in your choice of reading matter a certain drift towards romanticism. I am not pleased. I would far rather that you had spent your time last summer before you left for California reading Milton Friedman or some other reputable economist rather than mere novels. I had the unpleasant experience of picking up *The Golden Bowl* from your desk one day when you were still at home and could, of course, make nothing of it. Henry James should have been analyzed by his more pragmatic brother, William. One can, you know, be literate without becoming literary. Sentiment has a tendency to seep into the soul and blight reason. There is no greater era of peril than that period of life when in the full measure of youth's unearned wealth the virus of misplaced philanthropy and kindness is planted. A desire for world reform begins with the assumption that as regards the self that sustenance and security are guaranteed. They are not. No degree of success is immune from a sudden plunge back into scarcity.

Let me begin then by cautioning you to greet critically all that you will be formally taught, indeed it is to correct any misapprehensions that you may form that I am writing to you now. The real value of an education beyond the technical sciences is simply to become aware of the hypocrisy behind which societies and individuals hide their true intentions. This is not to say that there is no function in ideas. No, I would not go so far. It is simply essential that you understand from the beginning that ideas are always subject to human nature and human nature is primarily motivated by greed and fear and occasionally by a healthy disgust at its own characteristics. You will ask immediately if there is not also love and generosity. There may be, I will not go so far as to say there is not, but if you count upon them you will be soon disappointed and made bitter by life. Far better it is to assume the worst and to prepare oneself to act upon that belief if you would preserve your position in the world. What then is that position to be? It is up to you.

You are that most enviable of young men because you have property and place in the greatest empire that the world has yet known, America. You are the fruit of the loins of conquerors. Look today at America and what do you see if not the rule of the powerful, but better still than to possess power is the desire that it brings for greater power. America today can project violence and terror into every corner of the earth and the pitiful efforts of our adversaries and even of our allies to keep up with us are futile. We simply have too great of a head-start upon them and we will not surrender our lead gladly. You will ask of course if these aspirations are not constrained by our role as a moral leader and as the champion of democracy. Let me assure you that such rhetoric is for purely domestic consumption and it is essential that you abandon such delusions immediately.

America ceased to be what its founders may have intended over a century ago and we may all be thankful for it. Imagine the inconvenience for instance of having to share the land with the original savage inhabitants of this continent. Most of them are gone now with the buffalo and the salmon and the belief that each individual of the tribe had a unique path and value. This caretaking attitude is the enemy of all industry and progress. The very idea of limitation of conquest is foreign to true Americanism. Our forefathers knew that the value of property exists only in our ability to hold on to it. There is no moral title to anything. Everything in life is open to the man who can take it successfully. This was the basis for our policy towards the Indians and it is the basis for our most significant actions in the world today.

I often smile when I am asked why we are in Afghanistan, Iraq, and Syria. Such questions immediately betray the ignorance of the questioner. We are in these areas of the world because we choose to be! They are of interest to us because these regions are strategic power points on the constant chess-board of the world. We are there because we ran out of Indians at home to kill. We are there because Asia is our new frontier. We are there so that we may be served by the current inhabitants once they accept that we are there to stay.

Nations are judged by their ability to exact tribute. Peace is only the time allotted to prepare for war. The very idea of a permanent peace is an invitation to degeneration and emasculation. Fear is the final measure of diplomacy. Is anyone so foolish as to imagine that we will be dictated to by the Russians and the Chinese? They know that we will perish rather than be enslaved.

Do not be misled by all this current ecological foolishness. The pulse of the world is energy usage. A vital nation is measured by its profligacy not by its conservation of resources when it comes to oil or natural gas. The most essential items of our economy are energy-based and so naturally we must possess them. We will honor national sovereignty as long as it is convenient or necessary for us to do so and not an instant longer. Peace will come in conflict-ridden regions when we are assured of our ability to extract the necessary resources and have installed governments that will follow our wishes and maintain a proper decorum and rhetoric of democracy while a capital-based autocracy prevails in actuality. We may do a bit of window-dressing of course but that is the truth and moreover, every true American knows that it is the truth because that is the way that we have always acted in the world. War for America has always sooner or later paid off. Find me a town in America so small that it does not have an armory and a war memorial. Even our national anthem is about war. War is America and America is war and we will make any sacrifice to maintain supremacy in arms. Imagine for instance if the amount of our most recent wars (now over two trillion dollars) had been spent to advance health and education and forgive me for a moment a blasphemy: to attain more equality in this country. An average lot of the average American dullard would, of course, have been vastly improved and our economic position would not be dependent upon borrowed funds from China, but would we in the ruling class have been better off? By showing that we were willing to fight two or three pointless wars we told our adversaries that prudence plays no part in our calculations, only power matters. Of course, those borrowed funds are not really borrowed, they were extorted to further our virtuous consumption; I assure you they will never be repaid and the Chinese know it. At most the tipping point moved a little closer to China in the great international power calculus but that was all.

Why, you will ask, do Americans never quail at the size of the military budget and the transfer of wealth from the working middle-class to the investing and owning class? The answer is because of the pride that every ordinary American can have in knowing that the world trembles before us. Goods and services flock to our shores and to support the dollar, that empty promise has never been higher compared to other currencies and why? Because of American military superiority and because of our demonstrated daily willingness to kill whoever stands against us. We are respected because we are brutal. The world knows that we are the ultimate political realists. We realize that sometime in this century the world population will need to be reduced by about two to three billion people (*it won't be us.*) How this weeding-out will happen will be the subject of other letters to you. Let this introductory letter suffice for now. It will have achieved its aim if it has convinced you to abandon from the outset of your education any pretense that America ever acts out of so-called honorable intentions. Every action that we take is strategic and serves us in the maintenance of the unquestioned superiority of our nation.

Your devoted Father

Letter 2

I write to you today to caution you as to the danger posed by overt patriotism. In your ardent desire, which I hope to instill, to further your own interests you may imagine that you must, in order to be consistent, pay the duty of privilege by fighting for your country. You will point out to me that when the nation is at war and since the current arrangement of our political structures is designed to benefit the class to which we belong that we should all make sacrifices in order to deserve our place of honor and prestige. Rid yourself immediately of this delusion.

To begin with, our current wars are not struggles for national survival. They are mere gestures of force. They are diplomacy by other means. Look about you. What sacrifice have these long conflicts entailed to people like us? Have our sons and daughters died? No, and they will not. We have delegated the task of preserving the nation to a professional military drawn as all such wars are drawn from the superfluous members of the lower classes. It is all quite business-like and proper. We have out-sourced dying to those whose function is to produce so that we can possess. Do not be disturbed by this. You must remember that our country will soon have to adjust to a high and permanent structural unemployment rate. Let them die with ribbons rather than fester in unemployment lines.

A proper university education will soon cost between $80,000 and $150,000 simply to obtain the baccalaureate degree. It is quite beyond the lower classes to afford this since we have wisely kept the minimum wage below what it was in the 1980s in actual purchasing power. This fact makes military service highly attractive. It is far easier to train a young person to kill than to teach them a useful trade. Besides as the idle unemployed they would probably join gangs or engage in other criminal activity or simply reproduce and throng our schools which cost tax dollars. I assure you we have too many of them at present as it is. So what other use can they serve but as cannon-fodder? They can be dressed up in the panoply of our esteem and die for us. It gives meaning to their otherwise vacuous lives, solves a distinct social problem of what to do with the unemployable young, and it adds to the wealth of the nation, which is to say that it puts money in our pockets.

On the other end of the age spectrum, modern medicine is saving too many of these lives beyond their prime. Treatment for members of the middle-class in old age will be costly if they are allowed to live too long. What better solution could there be then to export them while they are young to battlefields and ensure that they are killed there rather than merely maimed and returned in damaged condition? This was why the policy in force for years of not armoring the transports in Iraq was so sensible and useful. It ensured that a soldier blown up by a road-side device would be killed and not return to be a burden on society. If the truck was going to be severely damaged anyway (and it really is difficult to repair one after a bomb blows up underneath it) it may as well take the men inside also. The casualty rate acted as a stimulant to the nation's ire and kept a focus on what was called, the mission.

I am smiling. Really army rhetoric is so transparently amusing to anyone who can see its real function. Besides, for every truck blown up, more had to be made and need I remind you of our family's heavy investment in certain companies that were awarded no-bid contracts. Again, it was money in our pockets. I have always found it quaint that the most patriotic of our citizens are those who are least likely to benefit from being American and that those who speak of freedom have little beyond the obligation to pay high interest to the mortgage and credit institutions that we own. You may ask how people can be so stupid, but why look a gift horse in the mouth. The fact is that they are stupid and we should be grateful for it. Justice is the enemy of all capital growth and equity should be shunned like the plague. I hope that with this second letter that your eyes are beginning to be opened and that once past a transient sentimentality you will become as realistic as I am and have taught you to be.

Your devoted Father

Letter 3

I have already anticipated some questions that you may have regarding my last letter. You may ask, even if we do have a class of persons whose best life options are to die for us, is not the nation itself deserving of our loyalty since it exists to serve our interests as wealthy Americans. If not patriotism is there not something that we should feel since the government is virtually our alter ego? Should we not protect ourselves? I will grant you that our present domicile should be preserved; after all, we are the richest nation on earth at present while thanks to the wise national policy of bleeding the lower classes we rank only 17th in the world in national quality of life, but difficulties still remain to limit the comforts of our hegemony.

We have accumulated a huge national debt of twenty-two trillion dollars. It is sad but necessary that as inflation and lack of real wage growth in the last thirty years have reduced the living standard of the middle-class that its members have become increasingly restless. It costs more every year to educate their children to obtain decent jobs. These are no longer a given since even professionals must now compete with foreign labor. It has even been necessary for us to provide some temporary sop to them that has been provided to date by the import of cheap Chinese goods and the spread of warehouse stores in every suburban community. Do not be deceived though; this is only a temporary stop-gap measure. It cannot go on forever and when it stops as the Chinese develop their internal markets our national credit binge will dry up. This will create great discontent and bewilderment at first among the mindless consumers as the American way of life declines. There will naturally be resentment and we must be certain that it will not be directed towards us. Fortunately, Americans tend to look down and never up when they focus on their fears. They always ask who may take their jobs away rather than to question why the fruits of technical and economic progress are always directed upwards to us. For this reason, our great political party keeps the focus on the danger posed by immigrants.

Even a slight modification of the tax codes could indeed, by adding a small percentage to our taxes, pay for thousands of these lettuce pickers but we must keep the level of fear up: that they constitute a brown hoard sweeping up out of Mexico. The sad fact is that we were running short of minorities to blame. Once it was the Irish, then the Italians and then the Jews, always the blacks of course, and now the Mexicans who we fear in this new century. Thank God it has never been us! Thank God that we can still stock away the savings of the nation year after year while reaping tax benefits, depletion allowances, and the ability to hide our funds in foreign bank accounts and off-shore tax havens. The dullards never notice and why? The answer is too amusing. It is because they believe in the concept of equality but never in its reality. If you would put them off you need only say to them that we are all equal and to assure them that anyone can make it big tomorrow... somehow. Trot out a few men who are the modern equivalent of Thomas Edition as examples. Most people though are not brilliant but only competent if even that; they never catch on. They will never be us. They will never be able to swim upstream against the laws and the tax structures that are now firmly in place to direct income into our hands. It is only necessary to tell the masses that they might, if nothing else, possibly win the lottery. They would rather benefit us by toiling away like oxen then take concrete means to reap the results of national economic growth as long as we do not disturb the illusion that they are already one of us!

Each year we put in place means to ensure that they never will be such through our ownership of the national government. No more sorry group of people exists than the members of today's Republican Congress. The fact that there are still a few hold-outs who believe in democracy is of little note. The people of America are so dumb that if you offer them equity they call you a socialist. Every day I thank God that He made so many stupid people! So we own Congress and we own at last five members of the Supreme Court. Best of all ... the current President is one of us and by talking like a guy on the next barstool he convinces them that he is just like them.

On another point, frankly, I never thought Obama would leave office alive. Ever since Jack Kennedy, presidents have understood that they are theoretically expendable. In fact, think of the value of that assassination to wealthy Americans right now. Presidents will never again dare to be statesmen: they will either be targets or demagogues. If we can ensure that every incipient psychopath has access to a weapon of mass destruction we can always keep liberalism at bay. The trick is to keep the ignorant louts on a slow rolling boil of indignation – the democrats want to take your guns away from you! Better still the religious right makes it all moral as though Moses had proclaimed the right to assault weapons with multiple magazine clips as the will of God.

But to return to the national debt, when the currency collapses only the ownership of hard assets will matter. A new currency will demolish any savings that the middle-class has accumulated. The new dollar will be worth say 60% of the old dollar but it will be backed up with metal again at last. You ask where the extra 40% will go: It will be used to reduce the national debt to a manageable level. The devaluation will not hurt us because we will have bailed out of the dollar before the devaluation into foreign equities, currencies, and precious metals. Until this happens, of course, the time is ripe to feed. The last tax cut will give us the reserves that we will need to ensure that the country is ours for the foreseeable future. Americans have elected their last Catholic and now their last black president. By the time Obama left office, even his own party despised him. His feeble attempts to find a non-existent American political center only alienated everyone. Even Bush looked heroic in comparison by simply being decisive in his folly. He let Cheney run the country while he cleared brush down on the ranch. So to return to my theme in this letter, do not be misled by patriotism or loyalty. The nation is only a means to an end: our prosperity and domination. The nation exists to serve our interests and only insofar as it does will we use it and not a second more.

Your devoted Father

Letter 4

It occurred to me today that I may have been too abrupt in ridding you of the illusions that you may have gained at the Preparatory Academy but it is my desire to be truthful with you. Truth is usually capable of summary treatment; only lies require long and elaborate explication. I chose your high school for you so that you might acquire grounding in the great ideas and humanities prior to moving on in your education. I also wanted these to be productive years for you and to spare you from the American experience of publicly funded education. I assure you that you have missed nothing in foregoing that experience. It is an irony that these years are wasted when they are the only free education that the average American will ever receive. The primary function of these years in public high schools is not education but as an initiation, a primal tribal ritual based on athletics and sexuality. The masses quickly establish cliques based on a hierarchical system and sometimes long after graduation spend many years of their twenties wasted in lamenting old and entirely inappropriate romantic ties or celebrating conquests in eminently forgettable athletic contests. In this way, they not only waste those precious late-teen years but compromise the first decade of their adulthood.

This is fortunate since it gives our class a distinct early edge. We know the value of moving from a comprehensive educational experience at the secondary level to attend a select college. The potential dating pool is thus confined to young women of good family and connections and ardent young men are kept away from tempting but unfortunate alliances with lower-class women. This is not to say that an occasional dalliance with some particularly well-endowed young woman may not be tempting should she present herself in the later course of dealing with the world but young men can see by then how completely unsuitable such women would have ever been as mates. They have occasionally a sort of mongrel charm however and I would not have you believe that a woman coming from a good family is a necessary guarantee of connubial happiness. Indeed not a few are spoiled princesses or anorexic basket cases. Avoid these. Date only women who are intelligent but ever conscious of their place "as women." Look for virtue but not religiosity. You may also apply a useful test: look at her mother and you will have a vision of what she will act and look like in twenty years. You may also add twenty to forty pounds to whatever she weighs now. If you believe that she will still be remotely attractive to you then as your own sexual powers are waning, she may be a good marriage prospect.

Avoid serial marriages in any case; they bleed the estate. Try and find a woman to whom you can afford to stay married. I advise this not out of any concern for sin and virtue. Fortunately, we do not have the belief of the Catholics in the indissolubility of marriage. If you must divorce then you must, but I assure you, it is always costly. If your prospective wife does not have ample means of her own, then a pre-nuptial agreement is as essential as the marriage license. Never give a woman complete security. A constant state of low-grade anxiety is your best guarantee that she will remain always faithful to you. But let it not grow too large or she may jump ship to a richer man. Above all do not fall prey to the common male illusion that any present protestation of undying affection has any meaning for her beyond the moment. It is only a sign of her momentary need and state of mind, perhaps an illusory and exaggerated estimate of your own worth. It is bad enough that women believe in their own emotions but for a man to do so is inexcusable. The record of the sex is abysmal in terms of natural fidelity. Nature has so created woman that her instinct is to preserve the species and she misses no opportunity to attempt to do so. As such the natural condition of a woman is to be pregnant. For this reason, most men find business more attractive as the years go by and learn to ignore the domestic animal that breeds his offspring. If she is quiet and helpful and does not take to drink, then you have made a wise choice. If on the other hand she berates you and cajoles constantly then it may be time to replace her.

As your wealth and success increase, you will be tempted to take a mistress from among your office staff. Do not do so. Indeed I make it a point only to hire women who are so exceedingly unattractive that they might all be pursuing their task naked and I would have no more inclination to them than to a can of sardines. I advise you to do likewise, but the time of such wise sexual policy is many years ahead and until then you are in peril of making poor choices. If you can escape your twenties with a good education and a start in business you will be wise. It is essential to make one's money early in life. Men respect vigor that they no longer possess. Find a mentor and follow in his jet-stream by loyalty. Flatter his vanity and conceal his faults and you will go far.

After you marry do not be distracted by absurd family dramas. Give your children graduated praise and preserve their self-esteem and keep them from improper influences. The rest will take care of itself. Daughters are of course at risk of perpetual intercourse. They generally exist to drain estates. You are in a sense raising a crop to be reaped by another. That said, some never marry and they may be a comfort to you in your old age so do not neglect them. Your sons--if you have properly raised them--will have little time to devote to you as they will be engaged in making money and in increasing the property that is the only real security for both sexes. You will ask whether a relation to God is not our ultimate security. God, of course, is somewhat like the prospect of accidental death and injury: insure against the possibility that He may actually exist by meeting the formula of salvation as it has been taught to us, behave with decent circumspection in your vices and beyond that, do as you will.

Your devoted Father

Letter 5

You will see that I am in the course of my letters to you choosing my topics at random in writing to you as various dangers to which you may be subjected are suggested to me by various happenings in the news of the world.

Today I propose that you ignore the useless trivia that constitutes the news of the day. Someday the pulchritude of the various Kardashian girls will, if they are even then recalled, be at most symptomatic of the vapid and vacuous tendencies of the present hour. There is no Helen of Troy among them. They are, at best, walking advertisements for the state of plastic surgery in the 21st century. Their sole point of interest is as an example of what successful branding can accomplish. As our society moves beyond necessities the highest values are applied to all that is trivial and decorative. We are living in a world predominated by personalities.

Intellectual property has completely dwarfed what might be called commodities. Venezuela is a case in point: even oil can doom a producing nation to poverty if that is all they have to sell. The genius of America has been that we realized first the value inherent in simply being an originator. We invent things and let the rest of the world build them. Royalties always exceed wages as a source of wealth. The best measure of failure in today's economy is whether your name is on a W-2 form. If your income comes from labor it is not wealth; it is mere sustenance. The task is to accumulate wealth as quickly as possible so as to obtain passive income.

Property is not a thing to be enjoyed; it is an asset to be traded. Anything retained for its own sake is a liability – movement and flow are the only realities. This is why culture is the refuge of the indolent. Culture presumes constant values. To say that something meets the gold-standard is to imply that it is dead. The best thing President Nixon ever did was to uncouple the dollar from gold. It opened up the possibility of endless growth based on capital flow – the dollars of the world will retain their value as long as no one tries to hoard them. Only then will they realize that all they possess is a promissory note based on sheer air. The full faith and credit of a nation that is in the hole for twenty-two trillion dollars is about as empty as a promise can be. Only velocity in production and world trade is saving us from bankruptcy – the world is moving too fast to catch its breath. Money is only the synapse between transactions.

Of course, the threat of collapse is always present just as the threat of nuclear war is always present and those very facts are so devastating that no one dares question the various fictions under which we live. It is our collective fictions that sustain us. From our natal years in the nursery, we are enthralled by stories over principles. This propensity never leaves us. Entertainment is the one industry that keeps ordinary needs in abeyance to amusement and fascination. Story, however, is more than mere amusement. It is the basis for belief systems, not the least of which are national myths. The important thing is to profit from such beliefs without sharing them. I value those writers who can see through the charm of the demagogue to discern the carnival barker and the snake-oil salesman beneath. It amuses me to see the agrarian peasants leaving their fields of corn and hay to be entertained by the melded blend of bad-boy antics and old-time religion dished out by our current President. He has an instinctive awareness of the American character and the anxieties that beset the denizens of the middle-classes in their decline into post-industrial obsolescence. People never really vote for their self-interest but rather their perceptions of who they are. In politics, flattery will get you anywhere.

It is fortunate that Americans have so little awareness of their own history; it makes it that much easier to deceive them. Not since the Huns swept across Asia has a more rapacious and predatory set of invaders beset a supine and complacent native population. A belief in our collective supremacy overrides all individual feelings of failure and inferiority. Oh well, let them eat brioche. It was to spare you from being drawn into such fatuous beliefs that I urged you to confine your early reading to Voltaire, Thucydides, Hume, Swift, and Schopenhauer. These thinkers never lost a perspective of what might be called strategic diminishment. All so-called high ideas should possess at their heart a bilious core. Bitterness, of course, is the obverse of romantic idealism, its corrective. It is not necessary to be depressed of course only clear-sighted.

But to return to the value of stories: they are the basis for all social institutions from religion to government. Deprive a people of its myths and social cohesion goes away with it. Even language takes its origin from its capacity to record and to describe. Of course, human language is always concrete and yet beset by the disease of metaphor. These are something that will soon be outgrown by the simplicity of digital discourse and universal algorithms. The sophistication of a language determines the ability to think. This is why I desire that you understand the sub-text to every popular enthusiasm so that you will not be caught up in it.

It is the essence of persuasion that one be aware of one's own structured mendacity. If there is anything that frightens me in Mr. Trump it is that he may be starting to believe his own absurd statements. I recall to your mind the case of Eva Peron of Argentina who began as a gold-digger and ended up believing that she was a saint. It is imperative that you not be swayed by noble rhetoric or seduced by trends. Everything emerges for a time, randomly and without purpose, and then gives way to the new. There is neither progress nor evolution, only variation before extinction. To realize this is the beginning of wisdom.

Your devoted Father

Letter 6

I have been wondering what impression is being made upon you by my letters. No doubt you find them somewhat shocking and you may even imagine that they flow from some well of bitterness that I kept concealed from you in your early upbringing. I assure you that their tone and substance are not the fruit of some dark strain of my character but rather the result of long meditations on the facts of our existence. The facts, of course, are available to everyone, but such is the pace of our existence that few dare to reason from them to their likely conclusions.

I remark daily how the masses seem bent on assuming that somehow everything will just work out; our secular messiah will make America great again, the sanctity of marriage will return, family values will emerge triumphant, and the wicked liberals will be separated as goats from sheep and executed in the public square. The liberals of the present hour are what the communists and the Jews were for Hitler: a pathway to power through the magic of awakened resentment. Most people presume that their lives should somehow or other work out; their many excellent qualities will be rewarded and public recognition will come their way. In this supposition, they are deluded. The majority of mankind considered individually is as inconsequential as any members of a mindless swarm can be. Stalin was correct in this when he said that the death of one man is a tragedy while the deaths of millions are a statistic. Stalin of course always dealt in chips the smallest denomination of which was a thousand. That is the way that you bring a country like Russia to the point where it could fight and win a war against the industrial might of Germany. Terror required counter-terror to oppose it.

America meanwhile won the war because of the sheer size of its manufacturing base that could be converted swiftly to produce war materiel. There was coupled with this a sense of outrage that anyone would dare to attack us. Take away Pearl Harbor and the swastika would still be flying over most of Europe. Don't expect to see either of these characteristics emerge again. The people that we would most likely fight are the very people who lend us money every day just to keep going to our home improvement and grocery stores. Besides, we have never collectively known real human deprivation in the past seventy years.

It occurs to me that I may have blocked from my mind the shortness of historical memory among the young and the sheltered perspective that is for you the inevitable result of having been raised during one of the longest periods of general prosperity ever recorded. Generosity and forbearance are the natural outcomes among those who have never had to face the brutalities that beset the world just prior to your birth. The decades of the 1930s and the 1940s witnessed carnage on a scale not seen since the Thirty Years War of the 1600s. Russia alone saw forty million dead. Yet as the war is portrayed in film, the eastern front is barely explored. It is all about General Patton or Pearl Harbor or the D-Day landings as though these were the decisive contributions to victory. It was Hitler's foolish decision to fight a two-front war by attacking Russia that prevented a Nazi victory. Even after losing the war Germany has emerged as the strongest nation in the European Union while England, foolish as always, is about to try and go it alone as though the empire it once possessed was not a distant memory, a reality never to be reconstituted. The British royal family is reduced to sharing tabloid space with the Kardashian girls and their endless micro-dramas and crises.

Such is the triviality of the present day that history is little more than fashion by another name. Everything is public relations and political correctness; no one's feelings should be hurt or sensibilities offended. Compare this to the cost exacted by the fall of Berlin where no woman was immune from rape and starvation from an enraged enemy that had watched their own wives and daughters shot in villages as the German assault rolled across the Ukraine. Look at pictures from the early 20th century when half the children in families of ten or more children would be lost to typhoid and scarlet fever before their sixth birthday. Realize the world as it was and still is for the billions of humanity that are cut off from everything that our digital age of electronic miracles represents. Then judge if I am harsh when I say that our class must be ruthless if we are to sustain our favored place and way of life from the beleaguered multitudes who would like to take a place at the feast. Imagine over seven or eight billion people living as we do and the state of the environment that would exist then if we speak of global warming now. Most of the Chinese are yet too poor to purchase their first automobile and the air quality is already beyond what we could tolerate. It isn't distant Cathay with coolies and wooden wagons pulled by yaks anymore. There are bullet trains in China that would put ours to shame. The sun has moved ever westward and America is in the twilight. Better to face this now than later.

You will look in vain for some golden era to which we may return. The MAGA wearers and the new socialist wing of the Democratic Party are both chasing a mirage. We are already at the apogee of American power; from here on our structural weaknesses will become every day more manifest. The economically fortunate will become pariahs if a crisis should occur. President Trump is keeping revolution at bay by telling the great unwashed and romantic yahoos what they want to hear to keep overwhelming anxiety at bay. He is doing the best he can to flush as much cash our way as possible before the market crashes and the long night of mass unemployment begins. The Second Amendment folk will start shooting at each other over a box of breakfast cereal. Most of your life will be lived in the prospect of what the human race used to know: that we are part of nature red in tooth and claw. The Russians have not forgotten though how it was because they are for the most part still waiting for a post-war prosperity that never showed up. Other peoples remember as well the daily cost of existence when it isn't based on credit. The North Koreans recall 1949 to 1952 as though it was yesterday. The Jews have never emerged from the shadow of another holocaust. All of these know the full price exacted in order to survive. The world is tipping beyond recovery at the very hour when gross indulgence is becoming normative here. Everyone thinks their little sorties in a consumer's paradise will amuse her neighbors. "Oh look, here we are in Las Vegas. I bought this silly little sun hat. Everyone thought I was from Hollywood!"

Do you see where I'm going with my warnings now? Wake up! Quite frankly even to possess an education is a little indulgent because it is ordered towards securing mere employment. Any gains short of capital gains are a waste of time. That is why I want you to exist among the owners, not as one of the plebian hoard of soft-ware pushers and systems analysts in white coats in clean cubicles servicing the computers as they process their terabytes of information. The great industry of the future will be keeping track of one's various asset positions using an array of passwords to get you through access points. America will be the grand-master of various exclusion systems. This wall of President Trump is a metaphor, a brand name for America while the rest of the world threatens us with a thermonuclear pulse. Fry the wires, destroy the data, remove the chips from the table and the whole game goes up in smoke!

There you have it, Anthony, the world that you and your children will inhabit long after I am gone.

Your devoted Father

Letter 7

Just a quick note, I realize that my last letter to you may have sounded a bit harsh. You may imagine should you adopt my point of view that you will stand quite alone. Fear not, at least one out of every three Americans are unconsciously laboring at our side. They are absolutely determined to abjure any benefits that circumstances might offer to them rather than to be branded as democratic socialists. There is something quite admirable in people who are willing to watch their children die because they present with preexisting conditions just to tear down "Obama Care." Who would believe that there are people still alive that would rather die than accept help from a black man?

Our real allies though are the Christian Media outlets, the same that condone any sin, at least if it is the President that commits them. Duplicity, chicanery, adultery: all are given a new appraisal if these malfeasances can only serve the Republican cause. Even the recent costly weather events do not disturb them because they are all just a foretaste of the tribulation to come that will spare the elect who will vanish in the twinkling of an eye and leave everybody else to clean up the mess. This generation of Christians is determined to make God either put up or shut up now that the Jews are back in their ancestral homeland. They have switched from petition to demand; whole celestial timetables have been prepared, the spiritual suitcases are packed, and the born-again folk are checking their watches. Meanwhile, the Prosperity Gospel crowd is going in for one last fling before the coming big lift-off. These are our allies as we fleece the unaffiliated poor who have only this world to sustain them.

So you see that nothing is really demanded of us but to let the present trends work out. We are blessed in our depredations by the very people who would benefit from a contrary policy. All that is required is for us to refrain from laughing as they stuff our pockets with gold. It isn't essential to associate with them formally. They won't show up at our gated communities. All that is required is a meeting hall where they can stage a revival meeting before driving their pick-up trucks home and stopping for some good old All-American hamburgers, short on beef and long on bun. So take heart my son; pack in those formulas and don't forget to network, network, and network among the people who count.

Your devoted Father

Letters between Jeremy and Anthony

Dear Anthony,

So good to hear from you, my boy! I have set myself swiftly to the task assigned me and have read your father's letters with interest and with a chill that starts at my tailbone and radiates upward. He certainly seems to be a formidable sort of chap yet withal he seems to have your best interests at heart even if filtered through a ghastly moral appraisal of America.

No doubt you recall my assignment of Pascal's *Provincial Letters* in your senior year. One of the better uses of satire is to assume the guise of one's adversary and to hold it up to ridicule; were it not for your assurances that he means every word that he says I might be willing to assume that a satirical intent hides behind his fulminations. As it is I must take him as being in all earnestness in his sense that our fate as Americans hangs over an abyss into which we might fall if the contending factions that divide America cannot find common ground. It is a strange fact but all that is being now proposed in the form of taxation reform is to return to the rates that were accepted as normal during the Eisenhower administration and these were far short of socialism. They did, of course, create the very America of strong manufacturing and a prosperous middle class that the Republican Party claims to desire. Instead, we are watching at their hands a recapitulation of the era of the 19th century robber barons while only cheap imports from China have made it possible for faux prosperity to exist among us.

This state of affairs is, of course, a temporary one. A radical lurch to the right always foments tyranny. Of course in this instance, it is the conservatives who are brandishing the epithet of "fascist" and applying it to one of the first voices to speak for the concerns of the silent millennial generation, Alexandria Ocasio-Cortez. The terror that she invokes among them indicates how insecure the delusional base is on which current conservatism rests. Of course, to point out the obvious to one in the grip of pathology is always to risk violence. I trust that the poor girl is always attentive to her surroundings and the multitude of the lunatics that fester among us.

For myself, I can see no way to replace the myths that nourish opposition to sensible reform on the Scandinavian model. I fear that the present regime must run its course until it brings about collapse. I doubt that there will ever be an equal and opposite swing to the left. What will happen is a general obsolescence of careers as machines replace tasks formerly done by people. I see a great increase in demand for cardboard to make signs that read, "Every bit helps."In the meantime you are at least secure there in Malibu; enjoy the sun for me. You may wish later on to forswear the career that your father has destined for you or you may practice for a few years, set aside a tidy bundle, and join us in our effort to keep some legacy alive of the former glory of the humanities. You may at least take this comfort to heart: You are part of a noble tradition that is dying about us. You know the names and something of the content of those who have labored before you with few rewards beyond that fragile immortality that the written word bestows upon her devotees.

Be of good cheer then.

Jeremy

Dear Jeremy,

Your letter meant more to me than you may imagine. I am caught here in a most peculiar atmosphere. Although my classmates are of course not taken in by the type of Presidential rhetoric that plays so well at the CPAC Conference they rejoice in the recent tax cuts and enjoy the bad boy antics of Mr. Trump. Politics has arrived at a level of buffoonery and recrimination that makes any idea of national unity impossible to conceive. You will recall that my father wanted me to attend the University of Chicago or Columbia and it was only with great effort that I convinced him to allow me to attend Pepperdine.

I spend many days gazing out to sea and imagining a way of life that begins with some extraordinary excursion. Not the Grand Tour of Europe of course; too much of a *cliché*. What I had in mind is more like something squalid and sinister ala that of Eugene O'Neill or Malcolm Lowry. I have been reading *Under the Volcano* by Lowry and *The Iceman Cometh* by O'Neill. Last month I read *Visions of Cody* by Kerouac. I would like to see life from the dark underbelly and then to grope my way up to rebellion, read D'Annunzio or maybe the letters of Angela Davis. I live in an age of automatons glued to their smartphones. All experience seems derivative and pre-digested.

How can one be an individual under such conditions? Where are the SDS and the Yippies, the Youth International Society of our day? I want to protest something, to join something more ominous than the Green New Deal just to feel an edge to my existence. Am I being foolish? You can tell me if I am. Young people should have a crisis against which to define themselves don't you think? Everything seems so under control, so trivial. Oh, we have individual acts of futile terrorism but they are so standardized, a futile effort to excel the body count of the last atrocity. Where's the imagination? Where's the ricin or aconite in the punch at an annual corporate meeting? Guns are so *passé*.

Of course, I would like to be constructive but it is always easier to destroy things don't you think? If everything will be as bad as my father thinks then why not have my own class share some of the misery. Where is the Symbionese Liberation Army to kidnap me? I look good in a beret. Last weekend I watched that old classic *Butch Cassidy and the Sundance Kid*; maybe if I went to Bolivia... As you can see I am grasping at straws to cure my malaise. Can you suggest something?

Anthony

Dear Anthony,

I am afraid that your father's penchant for hyperbole is shared by his son. I hope you are not out gathering wolfbane or castor beans. This sudden spurt of reaction against your father's letters is not uncommon in the first year away from home. Perhaps a frivolous romance is in order. Think about it; it will keep you out of jail. The whole rebellion thing could be hormonally induced. Tune down the testosterone. Perhaps you could make a connection and obtain some anti-androgens from the school nurse. Tell them you have been undergoing a bout of Gender Dysphoria lately; it seems to be reaching epidemic levels on campuses nationwide. Panic is breaking out in Tennessee. Tell the nurse that you only answer to "they and them." I'm kidding of course. Beware of too much earnestness; it always breeds tragedy.

Now then as to the trials of the present hour; they are real of course but you are not alone in your dismay. The carnival will move on in due course. As the Republicans check off their wish list they are digging their own grave among thinking people. My real fear is that the Democrats will start in on their own equally untenable pet projects. America is the indulged darling of struggling Asia; it will continue so for some time if we don't convince them that we are all crazy. The value of a winning streak is not to be scorned or abandoned lightly. In the meantime, my advice is to accept that your intellectual skeleton is still malleable like a molting crab. Don't worry about taking definitive positions. Try to enjoy a time that will never return and foreswear lugubrious meditations. When you reach my age and all is retrospection you will lament what you have lost by trying to be old too soon.

Jeremy

I enjoyed our brief phone call last night. I was beginning to be afraid that something had happened to you. The market was up again today but I am looking at buying into platinum as a hedge against inflation. The national debt is two trillion higher since Trump took office but no one seems to notice. A point must come when our treasuries start to sink and people will be looking for something solid. You see what an old man I am; I still remember when there was a point in holding precious metals.

I also recall the days when value was tied to utility. The great fortunes were once tied intimately to either the land or to industrial production. That is no longer the case, at least in America. What counts now is image and intellectual property. We are living in an age where retail as it once existed is melting away like the glaciers and manufacturing is being freed from the burden of an extensive and usually discontented workforce prone to unionization. The fortunes that are being made today have few actual moving parts or in-house elements. The actual tasks are outsourced and all that remains is a profit center that organizes and directs the whole based on commandeering huge segments of data and brand loyalty. The added-on value may be little more than to have a product associated in some intangible sense with a celebrity.

It is as though all the tiny and insignificant worker ants could raise their status by proxy and become queens by mere imitation. We worship the overlords of instantaneous commerce as mediated by directions traveling along fiber-optic cables or as electronic pulses jumping synapses of logic to enrich beyond the wildest dreams of King Midas. Do you see why I have cautioned you away from embracing any residual notions of professionalism, equity and the work ethic of the sociologist Max Weber? We have so far exceeded the furthest extrapolations of economists like Thorstein Veblen and John Kenneth Galbraith in speaking of leisure and affluence that the 21st century world has divided the species according to the ability to control and market intangibles.

The Democrats speak of green consciousness and a new deal while the Republicans dish out the same old tired dishwater of yesterday's industries and American exceptionalism. Unfortunately, the masses have already decided that illusion always trumps reality. Like besotted sleepwalkers, they march in hypnotic and insensate unison to surrender their individuality to various secular icons. Wealth feeds upon itself generation after generation. At last, we have discovered the secret of perpetual motion; inertia is defeated for the few while age and wisdom are revealed as the most pathetic of follies. I urge you to embrace the dull, the repetitious, the trivial, and the meaningless. See where the Presidency has left eloquence behind and made even truth a mere fashion to be discarded at will. Ours is the age foretold by José Ortega y Gasset where tiny acts of surrender of individualism create beings deprived of the integrity that only individuals can ever really possess. It is too late though to turn the herd; you can only pretend to join the deluded mass and profit from their collective folly. The world will endure for your life and perhaps for your immediate descendants.

Anyway, you have nothing to worry about. I did a little research today and things won't be all that bad until we hit 500 or 600 parts per million of carbon dioxide in the atmosphere. You can start to worry when the oysters lose their shells to an acidic ocean or the permafrost in the tundra melts. Everything in the Yukon will be a swamp by then but there will be investment opportunities in the Taiga. By the end of this century, the world population will be about nine billion people, all of them wanting something of the good life. We will probably have had at least one nuclear conflict, a few famines, and most current game animals will only exist in zoos or picture books alongside the Dodo.

I doubt if the Constitution will still be in force. America will be a backwater where Asians come just to see what a place without choking fumes looks like. Already almost all of the most polluted cities in the world are in China and India. If we mind our manners they will fight with each other and not us. After all, neighbors always pose the greatest threat to neighbors, not strangers. By then we'll be at peace with the Mexicans as they dig tunnels under Mr. Trump's wall or board tour boats to California. You will be able to buy drugs from vending machines, so nothing to fear on our southern border. Europe will be just an amusement park or one big Madame Tussaud's wax museum. In Russia, they will still be drinking vodka like fish and peddling heating oil. The followers of Mohammed will still be quarreling over who should have succeeded the prophet and the evangelical Christians will be expecting Jesus back just any day now so why try to make the world a better place.

Things change and things stay the same. What more can I say to you about history and about life; let your kids worry. One man can only do just so much. I'm glad I could give you these years of respite before the flood at Pepperdine. When the Cascadia earthquake comes Malibu will be little more than a sand-box. In the interim, I suppose there must be at least one economist there of note who can teach you something. It's not Chicago of course, but adequate. Well, I don't want to keep you off your surfboard listening to me so I'll sign off for now. Ciao as they say... somewhere.

Your devoted Father

HUMANS 2.0
BY CARRIE AVERY MORIARTY

She bolted awake, gasping.

"It was only a dream," she said.

But she knew that wasn't true. Everything she'd seen, everything she'd heard, everything she'd done; none of it was going away. This was her new normal, and she had to learn to deal with it. Her hand went to her stomach, pressing flat against it. Inside was a life, tiny and unstructured, but still there, growing with each minute, slowly but surely becoming one of them.

Throwing the covers off, she rushed to the bathroom, losing all that was left from last nights meal in the toilet. She wiped her mouth with the back of her hand and moved to the sink, looking at herself in the mirror above, wondering whether the dark circles under her eyes would ever go away. There was only so much makeup could cover.

"Get it together, Mia," she told herself. "You can do this."

It was false bravado, but she had to do it. There really wasn't a choice. Pulling her shirt over her head, she dropped it on the floor.

Her panties followed, and she stepped into the shower. The first rush of water was ice cold, but it warmed quickly. Ducking under the spray, she allowed the flow to wash away the last remnants of doubt. Somehow, someway, she would get through this and come out stronger on the other side.

"Feeling better?"

Mia rolled her eyes. "Like you care," she said.

"My job is to make sure you are comfortable throughout the duration of your pregnancy," Jack said. "If you are uncomfortable, or need anything, you need to let me know. I'm here to help."

"I'm fine," she said, walking into the kitchen.

"Breakfast is on the stove," Jack said. "If you want something else, let me know. I know pregnancy can cause foods you normally love to cause nausea. I'll fix whatever you want."

Mia looked at the scrambled eggs and wondered if they'd sit well. She pulled down a plate and went to dish them up. The smell overwhelmed her. Stepping back from the stove she shouted, "You're gonna have to let me have oatmeal."

"I'll get it going," Jack said as he entered the kitchen.

Mia passed him and took herself back to the table to sit and wait.

The Institute had assured her she would be well cared for and accommodated with a large payment upon completion of the study. She'd signed on the dotted line, so to speak, and was now part of what they called a revolution in the advancement of the human species. They gave her some information, explaining what to expect during the next three years, but some things they held back until she was signed up.

When her parents had died suddenly in a car accident, she'd put everything on hold to take care of the estate. They were not rich by any stretch of the imagination, but she hadn't realized how in debt her parents were. Because of this, it meant she couldn't return to school. She'd tried to find a traditional job, but without much training, and hardly any schooling, it was almost impossible to find anything that would allow her to keep the house.

That's when she met Rosie. The woman had walked into the coffee shop where Mia worked and ordered a mocha. Nothing fancy, just plain and simple. When she picked up her drink, she'd asked Mia if she was happy with her job. When Mia said she loved it, just wished it paid more, she'd offered her a place in the study. She'd explained that it would pay her for participating. There wouldn't be much to do, just be available at first. When Mia asked more questions, Rosie said she should come to the Institute.

After only a few months she'd not only been chosen but was the first to participate in the initial testing. Everything had been laid out for her, and she knew she would have a baby. They'd assured her she wouldn't have sex but would be inseminated. The procedure was very clinical, and she'd become pregnant with the first try.

Now she was into her second month and aside from the nausea, she had no other symptoms. The doctor said everything was going well, and she should expect to have a normal pregnancy and delivery. She'd also been assured that she would be able to have as much contact as she wanted with her child, which she was grateful for. She couldn't imagine not seeing her child after it was born.

Thirty women were in the initial trial, with five being chosen as host bodies for the procedures. Mia was the first to become pregnant, and the only one who was moving forward at this time. The other women who were still in the program remained at the Institute, though they were delayed in their continuation until Mia's pregnancy advanced further, which made her feel even more like an outcast.

"Today is ultrasound day," Jack said as he placed the oatmeal in front of Mia. "You'll get a chance to see the baby. Are you excited?"

"A little nervous," she admitted, taking a bite of her breakfast.

"Dr. Sanderson says we should be able to see some of the benefits from the program," Jack said as he sat with his own bowl.

"Why aren't you eating the eggs?" Mia asked.

"Didn't want the smell to bother you," Jack replied. "The other girls can eat them when they get up."

Housing at the Institute was similar to her dorm building at college. There were separate bedrooms, with private baths, and communal living and dining areas. Jack had his own room in the living space within the dorm facility as well, always preparing the meals and attending to any other issues that arose daily for the participants. He was a damn good cook, and Mia hated that she didn't feel like eating.

"Morning Mia," Claire said. "Morning Jack. Breakfast?"

Claire was not a morning person, and the Institute had put a firm rule on caffeine intake for participants, which meant that Claire, along with the other girls, couldn't have a morning cup of coffee. Mia didn't mind, but it was a near breaking point for Claire. She'd decided that tea would become her drink of choice in the morning, but was disappointed when it didn't give her the boost she was used to.

"Eggs are on the stove," Jack said. "If you're going to eat them, though, please do it in the kitchen."

"Why?" Claire asked.

"Mia's stomach can't take it," Jack said.

"It's fine," Mia countered. "I'm done, anyway."

Mia picked up her bowl and took it into the kitchen, running water over it and placing it into the dishwasher. She passed Claire on her way out, finding her way to her bedroom. She'd taken to writing in a journal daily, what she'd dreamt, what she was feeling, where things were going, and what she was worried about. The doctors had encouraged each of the women to journal as part of their stay, especially since they weren't allowed access to social media. This would be their way to remember what had happened while they were there.

"Mia," Jack called. "It's time for you to go."

"Coming," she replied, grabbing her jacket. She'd just have to journal after she returned from her appointment with the doctor.

"Urine sample first," the nurse said. "Then into the gown and across the hall to the exam room."

Mia took the little cup from the nurse and stepped into the bathroom. Even though she wasn't even a third of the way through, they were doing weekly testing on both urine and blood. She did her thing, changed into the gown, then sat across the hall and waited for Dr. Sanderson to come in. It was the same each week. He'd come in to discuss where things stood, how her numbers were within the blood and urine, then do the physical exam and leave.

"Good morning, Mia," Dr. Sanderson said as he came into the room. "I heard you weren't feeling well this morning."

"Just morning sickness," she replied. "Nothing unusual about that."

"You are right, there," he replied. "That is something I don't think we'll ever find a cure for."

"Too bad," she said. "You could make big money selling that cure."

There was a knock at the door, then it opened. The nurse came in with a portable ultrasound machine, moving it next to the exam table.

"We'll start with the ultrasound," the doctor said. "That will tell us most everything we need to know. Go ahead and lie back."

Mia did as she was told, resting her head on the pillow they'd placed at the top of the table. The nurse helped her get her feet into the stirrups, placing a blanket across her lower body. The doctor pushed her gown up above the blanket, exposing her abdomen. Squeezing the bottle of gel onto her stomach, he pulled the cord and wand from the machine, smoothing the gel around. He flipped a couple of switches and the machine whirred to life, a black and white image coming up on the monitor that was attached to the cart.

"That's it," he said. "Let's see what we can see."

As he moved the instrument across her stomach, she saw grainy images flutter across the screen. Lines and squiggles that didn't make sense to her flashed back and forth. He pressed the end of the wand against her lower abdomen, shifting it side to side, trying, she assumed, to get a better view. That's when she saw it, held within a dark balloon. It was formed already, with a head and limbs and a body. Not much was there, but she could definitely see that it was a baby.

"Good," he said as he pressed a couple of buttons, causing the image to freeze on the screen. "Let's see what else we can find," he continued as he moved the wand around some more.

Just like with that first glimpse, she saw another balloon of darkness.

"Are there two?" she asked.

"At least," the doctor said, distracted by his chore.

"At least?" she asked.

The doctor looked at her then, seeing the panic in her eyes. "Don't worry," he said. "There shouldn't be more than four."

"Four?" Mia asked, clearly confused. "I thought it would just be one."

"Multiples were definitely expected," he said nonchalantly. "It was in the information you were given at the time you signed up."

"That was just a possibility," she said. "They didn't say it was almost certain."

"Don't worry," the doctor said. "You will be fine, and so will the babies. This is something we expected, especially for our first round of trials."

"How many do you see?" she asked reluctantly.

"I've just seen the two so far," he said. "Let's see if we see any more."

After about ten minutes the doctor was satisfied with the discovery of two additional babies, bringing her count to four, just as he'd said. She was given a clean bill of health and sent back to her dorm with some additional literature on what to expect in the next couple of months. Shaken, she'd ignored Jack and the other women when she came back, instead feigning nausea and closing herself in her room.

What have I gotten myself into? Four babies at once?

Mia didn't know whether to laugh or cry. She'd always wanted a big family, but this was a little more than she expected. She was barely twenty years old, and she had a whole lot of life ahead of her.

A knock sounded at the door.

"Mia?" Claire said.

Schooling her features, Mia replied, "Come in."

The door opened and Claire squeezed in, though Mia could see the other girls behind her.

"Jack said you had your ultrasound today," she said as she sat next to Mia on the bed.

"I did," Mia replied.

"Was there something wrong with the baby?"

"Wrong doesn't even cover it," Mia said, then realized that wasn't true. "The problem is there are four babies. They all look healthy, though."

"Four?" Claire asked. "Are you sure?"

"There could be multiples," Mia said. "That's what the info said."

"I was thinking twins," Claire replied.

"Me, too," Mia said.

"Four," Claire breathed out. "So, what does that mean, then? I mean, how is this going to work?"

"We watch for a while," Mia explained. "Make sure everything is OK with them all. Then we wait for them to get here."

"You're going to carry them all?"

Claire wasn't much older than Mia, which was why they connected right away. Unlike Mia, Claire's family was well off. Her problem was she didn't want to follow in their footsteps, do the college and career thing. She wanted to play and travel and experience life before she strapped herself down to a job.

"That's the plan," Mia said. "At least for now. I'll have ultrasounds weekly, in addition to the other testing they've been doing. Once I'm farther along, they'll start the genetic testing."

"Did they all look normal?" Claire asked. "I mean, we don't know what the father looks like, so I wondered if they did some sort of…"

It was a question the girls had discussed in the beginning, whether they would have human babies or some sort of hybrid with who knew what.

"They look like babies as far as I can tell," Mia said. "Look for yourself."

She pulled out the photos the doctor had printed showing each of the babies. Right now they were numbered, but in the next few weeks, they'd be labeled with letters for their size, A to D. She'd learn whether they were boys or girls and would be allowed to name them if she wanted, too. She hadn't decided if that was a good thing or not, though.

"Look at them," Claire crooned, then looked to Mia. "The other girls are worried about you," she said.

"Let's show them the pictures," Mia replied, standing. She hoped their excitement would help to distract her from the fears she was experiencing.

As the days went by, Mia began to experience less morning sickness, thankfully. She did continue to grow, though, exponentially fast. It was as if her body had decided that because her mind knew there were four babies, she could accept the rapid growth of her abdomen. Sherry had conceived as well, so she wasn't the only one expecting now. It was nice to be able to share that spotlight, especially after being the only one for so long.

"How did you deal with the smells?" Sherry asked one evening.

"Totally faked it," Mia replied. "It got better the farther along I got, though."

"Well," Sherry said. "I can't wait to get to that point."

"I remember," Mia said.

With fall turning to winter, the women were allowed to write letters to their families. It had been hard for most of them, not being able to communicate with their loved ones for so long. Mia wasn't sure if she felt lucky to not have that worry, or sad because she couldn't share her news with anyone close to her.

Of course, the Institute insisted that the women not divulge any of the details about the study, including the fact that they would be having babies. Sherry had a hard time with it, knowing her mother was ill and may not survive the three years of the study. She really wanted her to know that she was going to become a grandmother.

"What traditions do you guys all have?" Claire asked as they sat around the living room talking one night.

"We always eat enchiladas," Gwen said.

"Why?" Claire asked.

"My mom's favorite dish," she replied. "She started making them when she was young and became quite the expert. Now, my dad won't let her skip. I'm gonna miss them, they're to die for."

"I don't think I'd be able to eat them," Sherry said. "Even the thought makes my stomach turn."

They all laughed at the face she made, and she joined right in.

"This will be my first Christmas without my parents," Mia said.

"Oh," Claire said. "That's right. How are you holding up?"

Mia shrugged. "I guess I'll have new reasons to celebrate, soon," she said, rubbing her extended belly.

"What's the newest news?" Gwen asked.

"Tomorrow I find out whether they're boys or girls," Mia said. "The testing's been good so far. At least that's what the doctor is are saying."

"Do you get new pictures tomorrow, too?" Sherry asked.

"I think I'm supposed to," she replied. "When is your first ultrasound?"

"I think it's in a couple of weeks," Sherry said. "I wonder if I've got four as well."

They all paused at that, wondering whether they would all be having small litters when their time came.

"Who's next?" Mia asked, seeing Sherry's worry.

"I think that's me," Amy said. "They said probably in the next week or so. They've been tracking my ovulation and are pretty sure that is when I'll be most fertile."

"Was it weird?" Claire asked.

"What?" Mia asked.

"The insemination process," Claire said. "I mean, it seems really weird."

"It's a little odd," Sherry said. "I mean, just think of a turkey baster full of baby-makers. That's what it's like."

"Eww," Gwen said. "That's just, eww."

"What did you expect?" Mia asked.

"Well," Gwen said. "I wasn't sure. I mean, OK, maybe that's what I expected, but it just seems eww."

"Not nearly as fun as the old-fashioned way," Amy said.

"Yeah," Claire agreed. "That's the best way."

They all burst into laughter as Jack chose that moment to come into the dorm.

"What?" he asked.

"Had to be here," Mia said, barely containing her laughter.

"And had to be a girl," Claire chimed in.

That sent the girls into another peal of laughter. Jack just turned around and walked out, shaking his head, which elicited even more laughter from the girls.

"This is going to be a little uncomfortable," Dr. Sanderson said. "I'm going to use the ultrasound to direct the needle. You should feel a pinch, but not much more. It's important that you be as still as possible for this procedure. If you shift, I may accidentally stick one of the babies."

"OK," Mia said.

The procedure was explained to her last week, so she was prepared for the long needle the doctor produced. Still, it was unnerving to think that he was going to be sticking that into her stomach and into the sacks of each of the babies to get more genetic information from them. The other reason was that she had four babies. The doctor had explained that they needed to make sure that the babies' lungs were healthy and ready when it came time for them to be born. He said that test would be done later. Today's testing was for genetics only.

Throughout the pregnancy, she'd been receiving shots to boost not only the babies' growth, but her own stamina as well. The doctor told her that soon she would have to be on bed rest with monitors around the clock. When she'd asked why, he'd told her because of the number of babies, she would need to preserve her strength. To do that, she would have to only do what was necessary from about the twenty-week mark on. This would allow her body to use all of its energy to grow the babies.

She'd been so distracted by her thoughts that she hadn't even felt the needle pokes, and didn't realize the procedure was finished until the doctor said, "Very good."

When she looked up, the nurse was reaching out to help her sit up. "That was easy," she said.

"Glad it didn't hurt," he said.

"When will you have results?" Mia asked.

"I should be able to tell you tomorrow what we know," he said.

"And whether they're boys or girls?"

"Yes," he said.

With that, he left the room.

"He's very happy with the results so far," the nurse said.

"I just wish he was a little more forthcoming with information," Mia said.

"It's all part of the study," the nurse replied. "Soon enough, we'll have more information."

"Do you know anything about the fathers?"

"I'm sorry," she replied. "They've only given me information on the mothers. How have you been feeling?"

"Tired," Mia answered honestly. "I also don't feel like eating. It's like I don't have enough room for food."

"That's normal," she said. "It's exponentially worse because you have more than one baby.”

“Do they still look healthy?”

Mia realized she hadn’t even watched the monitor when Dr. Sanderson did the testing. If she had, she would have seen the babies.

“They all look very healthy,” the nurse said.

“Is every mother worried about the babies not being normal?” she asked.

“Every single one,” the nurse said. “I’ve been doing this kind of nursing for years, and I don’t think I’ve met a mother who wasn’t concerned about her baby being normal.”

“Did they have dreams?”

“What do you mean?”

“Like,” Mia began. “OK, this is going to sound weird, but I feel like my babies are eating me from the inside out. Like they’re piranhas or something.”

“That’s a new one,” the nurse laughed. “But odd dreams are normal. Let’s get you up and dressed and back to the dorm where you can rest.”

“I feel like that’s all I’ve been doing,” she said. “Sitting and sleeping and lounging around.”

“And that’s the way it’s going to be from now on,” the nurse said. “It’s important that you take as many precautions as you can in order to give your babies the time they need to mature.”

“I guess,” Mia said as she let the nurse help her dress.

“So?” Sherry asked when Mia returned.

“It wasn’t bad,” Mia said, sitting on the couch.

“Really?” Claire asked.

“Yeah,” Mia said. “My mind started wandering and before I knew it, he was all done.”

“Do we have boys or girls?” Amy asked.

“Won’t actually know until tomorrow,” she said.

"Pictures?" Gwen asked.

"Next week," Mia said. "Apparently they can't do them the same time they do the amnio."

"I thought they were giving new pictures," Amy said.

"No pictures isn't even the worst part," Mia said. "In a week or two, they're going to put me on bed rest."

"Really?" Claire asked. "Why?"

"Apparently so my body can rest," she replied. "Not that I haven't been doing that already."

"Wasn't there some woman who had like half a dozen kids at once a couple of decades ago?" Gwen asked.

"Yeah," Claire said.

"I think I read that she had to lay with her head below her body to keep her babies in," Gwen said.

"Oh my gosh," Sherry said. "I don't think I can do this."

"I don't think it's gonna be that bad," Mia said, trying not only to convince Sherry, but herself as well.

"What if I have more than you?" Sherry asked.

"Dr. Sanderson didn't think there would be more than four," Mia said. "He said that was the most they expected."

"But what if they're wrong?" Sherry asked. "What if I've got a whole football team?"

"You're not gonna have that many," Claire said.

"What if they're not normal?" Sherry asked. "What if I've got mutants growing inside me? I mean, we don't know who the dad is. They could have put gorilla babies in me."

Sherry's voice kept pitching higher and higher the more agitated she got.

"Everything's gonna be fine," Amy tried, but Sherry wouldn't hear any of it, shouting, "They put monsters in us. They're gonna kill us."

It didn't take long before Jack came in, asking, "What's wrong?"

"You're trying to kill us," Sherry screamed, then lunged at him.

Jack put his hands up to fend her off, trying to catch her without getting hit. He managed to grab hold of her hands as she swung at him, twisting her around to hold her firm against him, effectively in a bear hug. She continued to thrash about, trying to free herself. The commotion drew one of the other men who worked with them into the living area. Between the two of them, they were able to subdue her just enough so she wouldn't hurt herself or anyone else. They finally got her settled enough to get her seated in a chair.

"We're not trying to kill you," Jack said, breathless.

"Do you know who the father is?" Sherry asked.

"No," he answered. "But I do know that your babies will be perfectly normal."

"You'll see tomorrow," Mia said. "The ultrasound will show you exactly what your babies look like. Do you remember how scared I was?" Sherry nodded, so Mia continued. "I thought the same thing, that they had put monsters in me. When I saw them, though, they were just babies."

"Did you dream they were trying to eat you from the inside?" Sherry asked.

"There are so many strange dreams, I couldn't tell you if that was one of them or not," Mia said.

"Cause that's what I dream," Sherry said.

"The nurse told me today that strange dreams are part of pregnancy," Mia confided. "Since we've had the other typical symptoms, we shouldn't expect to not have that."

Mia didn't want to share that she'd had the same dream, especially with how worked up Sherry was.

"Here you go," Dr. Sanderson said, handing an envelope to Mia.

She'd walked to the clinic to get her results and was thrilled that she'd been able to make it without having to stop and rest.

"This is going to have to be your last walk over, though," the doctor said.

"Why?" Mia asked.

"While the results were good," he said. "You are too far along to be taking any chances. We'll be coming to you for exams for a couple more months, then we'll move you to the clinic for monitoring until the babies are ready."

"Oh," Mia said. "Is it fine for me to walk back?"

"I'll call Jack to walk with you," he said. "This way he can help if you need to rest."

The doctor stepped into his office as Mia took a seat in the outer area. She held the envelope in her hand, unsure whether she wanted to open it or not. The results of her testing were in there, and she would soon find out if she was having boys, girls, or some combination.

"Jack's on his way," the doctor said as he stepped back out. "Did you want to go over the results while you wait?"

"Maybe," she said. "Is there anything bad?"

"Oh, no," he said. "On the contrary. Everything is going exactly as planned. Babies are doing really well with the continued dosages you've been getting. I also put pictures in there."

"Will I be able to understand the results?"

"I made sure to put them in non-medical language," the doctor said. "I know you girls are smart, but none of you have gone to medical school. Sometimes we doctors forget that what we know isn't the same as what our patients know."

"Thank you," Mia said.

Just then, Jack walked in. "Ready to go?" he asked.

"Or do you want to talk about the results?" the doctor asked.

"I think I'll look them over in my room," Mia decided.

"Then let's head on out," Jack said.

Mia stood, with help from both men, and they made their way back across the campus to her dorm. By the time they arrived, Mia was winded and needed to sit on the couch. Jack went to the kitchen and brought her a glass of water.

"Thank you," Mia said, drinking it down.

"You're back," Claire declared as she came in.

"I am," Mia replied.

"So?" Amy asked.

"I haven't looked at the results, yet," Mia said.

"Do you want to do that in private?" Sherry asked.

Mia looked at the other women. Each of them would be put into this position at some point in the near future. Sherry was almost to the point of seeing her babies, Amy was supposed to be conceiving in the next couple of days, and the others were lining up right behind them. While Mia was private with most things, these women deserved to know what was in their future.

"Let's look together," she said, pulling the papers out of the envelope.

"I can't believe they're all girls," Claire said. "I thought you would be split half and half."

"Doesn't surprise me," Gwen replied.

"Why?" Mia asked.

"My guess," Gwen said. "They are using a method to make sure they are the gender they want. I mean, they are doing all of this testing, and giving you all of these boosters, it makes sense that they tailored the study so that they would get a specific gender when the time came."

"But why girls?" Amy asked.

"Because then they can reproduce, too," Gwen said.

They all looked at her like she'd grown another head.

"What do you mean?" Mia asked.

"The best way to get a new genetic makeup into the populous is to have girls," she said.

"I don't get it," Claire said.

"Because we get a HUGE part of our genetic makeup from our moms," Gwen said.

"I had no idea," Claire said. "So, do we get anything from our dads?"

"Oh, yeah," Gwen said. "Our gender is determined by our dad, along with a bunch of other things. I think they're using the self-propagating powers we have."

"The what?" Amy asked.

"Women can get pregnant without men," Gwen said. "It doesn't happen very often, but it can. That's probably why they did so much testing on us when we signed up. We're probably good candidates for this."

"Then why didn't we become pregnant before?" Amy asked.

"And why did they do insemination?" Sherry asked.

"And how do you know all of this stuff?" Claire asked.

"OK, let's answer these one at a time," Gwen said. "I know this stuff because it's what I studied in college. My major was genetics, but I couldn't finish because we ran out of money. That's why I signed up for this study. I figured if they chose me, I could get enough money to finish my studies.

"The reason we didn't get pregnant before," she continued, "is because it's really rare for that to happen. Some animals can do it, but most humans lack the complete ability. I think that's why they had

122

to inseminate us, or, well, you guys. I'm not sure what method they're using."

"Turkey baster," Claire said, and they all laughed.

"I mean," Gwen continued. "They could be using semen from a male donor, or they could be using another method to cause us to self-propagate."

"Wait, they can do that?"

"There are several methods that work," Gwen said. "I didn't get too far into my studies, but I do know some things."

"You know a whole lot more than I do," Mia said.

"I think she knows more than most of us," Claire said.

"You now know most everything I know," Gwen said.

"Even if we can't understand it?" Amy asked.

"It's so complicated I don't really understand it all," Gwen said.

"Gotta pee," Mia said, trying to get up off the couch. It took Claire, Gwen, and Amy to help her get up. She rushed as fast as her body would let her to the bathroom, still barely making it in time.

"I can't wait to be done," she said when she came back out of her room.

"How long?" Sherry asked.

"I'm at week nineteen," Mia said. "I'll be on bed rest here for a few more weeks, then they're moving me to the clinic."

"Did they say how long until the babies would be born?"

"Dr. Sanderson said I should make it to week thirty-two," Mia said. "They're already giving me the boosters to get the babies to grow faster. I just hope they stay in long enough."

It was a worry that the girls had discussed when they found out she was having so many babies, whether they would survive. Mia just had to hold out hope that she would be able to keep them inside long enough.

"We're gonna miss you," Claire said as Mia was getting ready to leave the dorm and head for the clinic.

"It's not like you can't come see me," she replied. "I'm just across the way. You'll know right where to find me, too."

"But it won't be the same," Amy said. "Who am I gonna ask about what's going on?"

"Sherry can tell you," Mia replied.

"Right," Amy said, rolling her eyes.

Sherry had been out of sorts since her emotional breakdown a couple of weeks earlier. She was only having two babies, so it wasn't as drastic as Mia. Still, there were times when the others wouldn't see her for days on end. When they'd try to engage her at meals, Sherry would simply answer with a nod of her head or a one-word response. Mia worried that she would break under the strains that were coming on daily with the pregnancy. There was nothing she could do about it, though. She just had to hold out hope that in the next few weeks she'd have a roommate at the clinic, both of them on bed rest waiting for the babies to arrive.

"Don't worry about us," Gwen said. "We'll keep Sherry in good spirits. Maybe I'll make some of my mom's enchiladas."

"Not if Jack has anything to say about it," Mia quipped.

"Or Dr. Sanderson for that matter," Claire said. "He's all about the healthy diet. I would kill for a donut right now."

"And a cup of coffee," Amy said.

"Ugh," Claire grunted. "Don't remind me. I miss coffee so much."

"Ready?" Jack said as he entered the room with a wheelchair.

"Seriously?" Mia whined.

"Doctor's orders," Jack said. "You aren't even supposed to be up on your feet."

"I had to pee," Mia said, knowing that was the only reason she was supposed to be up right now.

"You always have to pee," Jack said.

"It comes with the condition," Mia replied.

"Speaking of which," Amy said, turning to go to her own bathroom.

"Let's get going," Jack said.

Mia picked up her bag of books and sat in the chair and they headed out the door. It was a short walk across the campus to the clinic where she was taken into a room.

"Can I help you change?" the nurse asked.

"Do I have to wear the open-at-the-back hospital gown?" Mia asked.

"Not yet," the nurse said.

"I just realized," Mia began. "I don't know your name."

"Julie," the nurse said.

"Hi, Julie," Mia said.

"Hello," the nurse replied. "Now, let's get you into something a little less constricting."

She pulled out a short, full gown and helped Mia change while still sitting in the chair. Once they had the top done, she helped her up and she took off her pants and put on some loose shorts.

"These are nice," Mia said.

"Super comfortable," Julie replied. "And really easy to get into and out of. That's gonna be important in the next few weeks."

Once she was changed, Julie helped her onto the bed, placing pillows behind her head.

"You can only have these two pillows," Julie said. "And we're gonna raise your feet as well. We want to make sure that your heart doesn't have to work too hard to keep the blood moving. This will also give the babies a little more room."

"Am I gonna have to stand on my head?" Mia asked. Julie looked at her confused. "I heard about a mom who was having a bunch of babies and she had to lay with her feet up and her head down."

"We're going to get there eventually," Julie said. "Your feet will need to be above your head in order for your heart to have less strain. It won't be uncomfortable, though. We'll move you gradually."

"And I just get to lay here?"

"We've got some movies you can watch," Julie said. "And you brought plenty of books."

"But that's not gonna last three months," Mia complained.

"We can replenish your supply," Julie assured.

"I hope I don't die of boredom," Mia sighed.

"I'll be around during the day," Julie said. "And you can meet Kiki when she comes on later this evening."

"I didn't know there was more than one nurse," Mia confided.

"Dr. Sanderson didn't need another nurse until you got to the point where you had to be here," Julie confessed. "Now that you are, though, we will need someone to watch you overnight."

"Is she as nice as you?"

"She's super," Julie said. "I think you guys will get along really well."

"How are we settling in?" Dr. Sanderson asked as he came into the room.

"We've got her changed and set up," Julie said.

"Are you feeling good about the move?" he asked.

"I guess," Mia said. "I'd love to stay with the other girls, but understand the need to be here."

"Good," he said. "Let's get you hooked up to the monitors."

With that, Julie stepped out and returned a moment later with a machine on a cart. She wheeled it up to the other side of the bed and began to plug lines into it.

"First," Dr. Sanderson said. "I'm going to need to see if I can tell where the girls are."

He gently pushed her top up, exposing her abdomen. His hands were warm as he moved them around her stomach, feeling each bump along the way.

"Perfect," he said once he'd finished. "Let's get baby A first."

He picked up a packet and opened it, pulling out circular stickers with snaps on the back of them. He placed one on her stomach, up near her ribcage. He moved around the rest of her abdomen, placing three additional stickers on her. With that complete, Julie handed him lines from the machine next to the bed. He snapped them onto each of the stickers.

"Let's see if we're good," he said to Julie.

She flipped the switch and Mia watched the screen come to life. It was larger than she expected, but then she saw why. Divided into fourths, each section showed the movement and heartbeat of each baby. This way they could monitor them all on one screen.

"I've got it recording," Julie said.

"Good," Dr. Sanderson replied. "I'm going to get an IV started," he said to Mia.

"For what?" she asked.

"We need to reduce your intake of food," he replied. "This way you will get all of the nutrients you and the babies need without putting a stressor on your internal organs."

"Will I get to eat at all?" she asked.

"Oh, yes," he said. "We'll start reducing your intake over time so it will be gradual. I still want you eating the whole time. There are only so many things we can get into your system through an IV."

"Good," Mia said. "I'd hate to give up eating."

"This will also help with the injections," the doctor said. "We can give you the treatment medications through the IV instead of subdermally. It will be a faster absorption and you'll need less as well."

"Hooray for small victories," Mia said.

"I love your positivity," the doctor said. "I'll be right back."

He left and Julie finished typing on the keyboard attached to the machine.

"I'm really getting excited," she said. "Are you?"

"I'll be glad when I don't feel like a beached whale," Mia said. "I'm also really glad I won't be getting shots every week anymore."

"Yeah," the nurse said. "That is one of the nice things about the IV. It'll cut down on a lot of things."

"Here we are," Dr. Sanderson said as he came back in. "I'll put it low enough that it won't interfere with your arm movements."

With that, he held his hand out. Mia placed her arm out and the doctor wrapped the rubber around her upper arm, tightening it to get the veins to show themselves. With a practiced hand, he placed the needle into her arm, catching the vein just right. He pulled the sleeve off the tube, then taped it down. Pulling a syringe out of his pocket, he flushed the IV, then capped it off.

"There we go," he said. "Perfect. I'll get the bags ready to go and we'll be on our way."

"Thanks for being so good at that," Mia said. "My mom always said she had shy veins."

"Yours are beautiful for this," he said. "It makes it much easier."

"Do you want to watch TV?" Julie asked after the doctor left.

"I think I'll nap," she replied.

"Good idea," Julie said. You've got your call button and the remote is here as well. Should I put some of your books up here for you, too?"

"That would be nice," Mia said.

Julie picked up the bag Mia brought with her and placed it on the table next to the bed.

"I'll turn down the lights and let you rest," Julie said. "Just push the button if you need anything."

"Thanks," Mia replied through a yawn.

She hadn't realized how tired she was until the lights dimmed. Before she realized it, she was fast asleep, dreaming the strange dreams of pregnancy.

"They're looking better and better," Dr. Sanderson said.

"I can't believe how normal they look," Mia said.

"Why wouldn't they be normal?" the doctor asked.

"I just wasn't sure," Mia said. "We don't know much about the fathers, so I wasn't sure whether there was going to be anything odd about the babies."

"They're not mutants," the doctor said. "We've just given them some enhancement. They'll be stronger, smarter, and more resilient. They'll also have a better immune system to fend off disease."

"That's good," Mia replied.

"I think just a couple more weeks and we should be good to deliver," he said, pulling the ultrasound wand from her stomach. "We'll do another amnio next week, just to make sure that their lungs are all good."

"I can't believe it's time already," Mia said.

"Aren't you ready?" the doctor asked.

"More than ready," she replied. "It will be nice to be able to sit upright again."

"This is the hardest part of the study," the doctor said.

"How's Sherry doing?" Mia asked as the doctor pulled her

gown down over her stomach.

"She's doing well," the doctor said. "I think she was just worried with all that went on with you. Knowing she's only got two babies makes it easier for her."

"Who else is pregnant?"

"Amy lost her babies," the doctor said. "They simply weren't able to survive. Claire was just inseminated. We'll be confirming tomorrow."

"Can she come see me?"

"Absolutely," the doctor said. "I'll make sure she stops by after her appointment."

"Doctor," Julie said, peeking her head in.

The concern on her face made Mia's stomach drop.

"I'm coming," the doctor said. "You rest, now. We'll be seeing those pretty little faces in no time."

With that, he stepped out the door and closed it. Mia picked up the book she'd been reading, flipping it to the bookmark in the center. Try as she might, though, she couldn't concentrate. It had been this way for several weeks, though, so this was nothing new. Two more weeks, she could do this.

"You're doing just fine," Dr. Sanderson said.

"Just breathe," Julie said.

Mia had been fine waiting the two weeks, but her babies had other thoughts. She'd felt twinges for a few days, but didn't pay any attention since the doctor and nurse both said it was normal. When the cramping became unbearable, though, she'd pressed the button. That set off a whirlwind of commotion, everyone she'd dealt with during her stay and more were suddenly crowding into her room, shoving things around, making room for equipment she couldn't identify.

"Can you feel this?" the doctor asked.

"I can't feel anything," Mia said. "And I can't breathe."

The panic was surging through her and she couldn't seem to remember how to breathe. One of the doctors put a mask on her face and she just wanted to shove it off.

"It's oxygen," he said. "It will help."

Gulping the gas, she slowly slipped into darkness.

"Hey there," Claire said.

Mia blinked in the darkness, barely able to make out her friend's shape.

"You really scared us," Claire said. "Are you feeling better?"

"My babies?" Mia asked.

"They're beautiful," Claire said. "You'll get to see them soon. Dr. Sanderson said they are perfect in every way."

Mia slipped back into the darkness, despite her desire to talk with her friend.

"I thought you'd like to meet baby A," Julie said as she came into the room.

Mia reached out instinctively, and the nurse handed over the bundle. Pushing the blanket aside, Mia stared down into the most perfect face she'd ever seen. The baby was pinker than Mia imagined, and had long lashes that lay across her cheeks. Mia ran her hand over the baby's head and felt the soft down of hair there. Tears welled in her eyes, slipping silently down her cheeks.

"Did you pick a name?" the nurse asked.

"Abigail," Mia said. "She's perfect."

"That she is," Dr. Sanderson said as he came in. "How are you feeling?"

"Fine," Mia said automatically.

"Mia," the doctor said.

She looked up at him then, seeing that he was truly interested in how she actually was.

With a deep breath, she said, "Besides being tired, I really am fine."

"No soreness at your incision?"

Mia looked down at her baby and smiled. "I don't have any pain."

"I'll need to check it," he said. "Julie, can you take the baby?"

Reluctantly, Mia handed her daughter over. Julie took the baby from the room as Dr. Sanderson looked at Mia's abdomen. He pushed a couple of places, but Mia couldn't feel any pain.

"When can I see my other babies?" she asked when the doctor was finished.

"I'll have Julie bring them in," he said. "I don't want you to overexert yourself, though. Only hold one at a time, and always have someone help you with them. You're going to be tender for a few weeks. We'll get you up and walking tomorrow and see how things go from there."

"OK," Mia said. "Doctor," she began as he went to leave.

"Yes," he replied.

"Thank you," she said. "Thank you so much for giving me my babies. They're beautiful."

"It truly is my pleasure," he said. "I want to thank you for being part of this study. I truly believe that your children will be the future of our race."

With that he stepped out into the hall, shutting the door behind him. Mia smiled, truly happy for where she found herself.

"Oh my gosh," Claire exclaimed as she held Abigail in her arms. "She's just perfect."

"Isn't she?" Mia asked.

"I can't believe I have some inside me, too," Claire replied.

"Do you know how many?" Mia asked.

"Next week we'll find out," Claire said. "I hope there's only two, though."

"It was really hard with all four," Mia said.

She held Bridgette in her arms. Charlotte and Delilah were still in the nursery being cared for by the nursing staff.

"I feel so bad about Amy," Claire said, not taking her eyes off the baby in her arms.

"Me, too," Mia said. "Do they know what happened?"

"Amy said the doctor told her the babies weren't viable," Claire said.

"What does that even mean?" Mia asked.

Claire looked up at Mia, then said, "I don't know, and Amy won't talk about it."

"Has Sherry been doing better?"

"Yeah," Claire said. "She feels bad about Amy, too. She's been spending a lot of time in her room. Said she doesn't want to make Amy feel worse by being large around her."

"Julie said Sherry won't be put on bed rest as early as I was," Mia said.

"Probably because she's only got two babies," Claire replied. "She's not nearly as big as you were at this point."

"Yeah," Mia said. "I was as big as a house when I was twenty weeks."

"Ready to swap out?" Julie asked as she came into the room carrying one of the other babies. Kiki was right behind her carrying the other baby.

"Who's who?" Claire asked.

"I can tell," Mia said.

Julie handed the baby she was holding to Mia, who had shifted to place Abigail on her lap.

Pulling the blanket back she looked into the baby's face and said, "This is Delilah."

"How can you tell?" Claire asked.

"Not sure," Mia replied. "They all look the same, but they are all different, too."

"I'll take Bridgette," Julie said. "Then you can hold Charlotte."

Claire handed the baby she was holding over to the nurse, then took the one the other nurse was holding.

"I can't believe how big they are," she said.

"They are growing really fast," Kiki said. "Dr. Sanderson said that's something he expected, though."

"It's good, though," Julie said. "This means they will be stronger sooner than if they had not had the added genetics."

"Speaking of which," Mia said. "Has he said anything about how they seem?"

"I was just coming to talk with you about them," Dr. Sanderson said as he entered the room.

"I'll leave you two alone," Claire said standing with the baby.

"You can stay," Mia said. "Unless you don't think she should."

"If you're comfortable with me discussing this in front of her," the doctor said.

"Stay," Mia said. "You'll probably be getting this info soon anyway."

Claire returned to her seat, Charlotte sleeping in her arms.

"So," the doctor began. "You probably noticed that the babies are growing pretty fast."

"I did," Mia said. "I don't remember how fast babies grow, though, so just figured it was my imagination."

"It's not," the doctor said. "Usually babies born this early would be kept in a neonatal ICU. Because of the enhanced genetics, their lungs were much more developed, even with the early delivery. They are also doing well on all of the tests that we would normally run on newborns, with scores well above that of a non-enhanced baby. What I'm really pleased with, however, is their ability to adjust to their environment."

"What do you mean?" Claire asked.

"They don't seem to be affected by the temperature, or anything else around them," the doctor said. "It seems they can handle most noises, rapid changes in temperature, and most other stressors we've put to the test."

"You're not hurting them, are you?" Mia asked, concern clear in her voice.

"Oh, no," Dr. Sanderson said. "Just light changes in the room, nothing drastic."

"Does this mean your study is a success?" Claire asked.

"Right now," the doctor said, "it appears that we are meeting and exceeding our expectations. This is good for the study, and also means that your babies will be strong and healthy as well."

"What happened to Amy's babies?" Mia asked.

The doctor seemed a bit surprised by the question, but schooled his features quickly. "Her babies did not survive past the first six weeks," he said. "We may not be able to use her in the study, unfortunately."

"Does this mean she won't be paid?" Claire asked.

"Absolutely not," the doctor replied. "Everyone who has made it to this point will be paid, whether they are able to continue or not."

"How is Sherry doing?" Mia asked. "I know she was having some issues before."

"She seems to be holding up pretty well," the doctor said. "We've added some counseling for both her and Amy as they move forward in the study. Hopefully, that will help her with the adjustments. I think finding out she was only carrying two babies helped her tremendously. It isn't as high risk as your pregnancy, Mia, but there are still risks we are watching. I think she will be joining you here in the next week or so."

"That will be good," Mia said.

"Now," the doctor said. "I'd like to check your incision once more before I go. Do you want me to come back after your visit?"

"If Claire doesn't mind, I don't," Mia said.

"Why don't I take Charlotte back to the nurses," Claire said. "That will give you the privacy for the exam, and I won't have to see the stitches."

"OK," Mia said as Claire stood. "Why don't you take Abigail with you and leave Charlotte here, though."

"I can do that," she said.

With care, the babies were exchanged and Claire left the room. The doctor helped adjust the babies so he could get a look at Mia's incision, pushing the blankets down and the gown up.

"This is healing up very nicely," the doctor said once he'd done his exam. "How does it feel?"

"It's really not hurting at all," Mia said. "Which is surprising since I was sliced open just a couple of days ago."

"That has a lot to do with the additional injections you were receiving," the doctor explained. "I think that we'll continue the injections for the next couple of weeks, just to make sure your recovery goes well."

"Will I have to stay here the whole time?"

"I actually think you could go back to the dorm in the next couple of days," the doctor said. "The babies are going to have to stay here for a few weeks, though, so it might be easier for you if you stay here."

"I'd rather stay with the babies," Mia said.

"I think that will be fine," the doctor said. "I'll let you rest, now."

"Thank you," she said. "Will you let Claire know she can come back in?"

"Sure," he replied, then left the room.

"Well?" Claire asked when she came back in. "What did he say?"

"That I'm healing nicely and should be able to come back in a couple of days," Mia replied.

"What about the babies?"

"They'll have to stay here for a couple more weeks," Mia said. "I'll be staying with them, too."

"Good," she said. "I don't know how we'd do with them at the dorm."

"Yeah," Mia said. "Not really sure how this is all going to work out, either."

"They sure are cute, though," she said, picking Charlotte up again.

"That they are," Mia said.

Within a month, Sherry had been put on bed rest for the duration of her pregnancy, Claire got the news that she was having three babies, and Mia had been released from the clinic. Her babies had grown so rapidly they were already exhibiting abilities that were far above their age. The doctor had said they would continue to grow exponentially faster over the first year.

Amy had been discharged from the study, which she had been fine with. The remaining women were on hold for insemination, as they did want to watch the first three sets of babies grow. It was decided that each new mom would be given a space of their own, with a bedroom for themselves, plus a couple of extra rooms for the babies. Dr. Sanderson had also brought in nannies for additional care of the babies, all of which had been screened and cleared for privacy concerns.

Sherry's girls were born four months after Mia's, going to the full thirty-six weeks that the doctor had hoped for. She'd named them Emily and Faith, moving along in the alphabet from Mia's four. Before the women knew it, their babies were well beyond where they should have been, doing things children much older were barely able to perform.

Gwen had become pregnant without being inseminated shortly after Sherry's babies were born. Dr. Sanderson didn't seem surprised, and began the process of adding the genetic code to her baby as well. She was only pregnant with one baby, and Dr. Sanderson attributed that to the fact that she had self-replicated.

By the time Claire was put on bed rest, two of Mia's girls, Charlotte and Delilah, were crawling. When Claire's three were born, Sherry's were crawling and Mia's were walking. Claire named her girls Grace, Hannah, and Isabelle, continuing the naming system they'd decided on. Dr. Sanderson didn't seem surprised by the children reaching milestones much faster than normal, and attributed it to the additional genetics he'd included. He'd decided that he would hold off on any additional pregnancies until after the first set of babies were more mature.

Gwen's pregnancy continued as normal, and when her baby was born, she named her Jordan. Her baby didn't advance nearly as rapidly as the first three sets of babies, but Dr. Sanderson said that might be because the baby didn't have the genetic additions prior to conception. He assured her that her baby was healthy and would grow naturally.

"How are you feeling?" Mia asked as Gwen sat next to her on the sofa.

The women had asked for a communal area where they could gather to talk about parenting and how their babies were growing. Dr. Sanderson had allowed it, saying that they would be better able to handle the multiple children easier if they were a community rather than individual families. After having spent nearly eighteen months together, it seemed right.

"I don't know how you guys do it," Gwen replied. "I'm exhausted all the time. And Jordan isn't nearly as active and mobile as yours."

"We have the benefit of them all being friends," Claire said.

"Don't forget about the nannies, too," Sherry added.

"But all Jordan does is eat, sleep, poop, and cry," Gwen said.

"That's normal," Claire said. "I think my nieces and nephews didn't do anything for the first six months at least. Our babies aren't normal. You have to remember that."

"But they all seem completely normal to me," Gwen said.

"Just growing at a much faster pace," Sherry said.

"Ladies," Jack said as he came into the room. "I hope you don't mind my disturbing you, but Dr. Sanderson asked that I come get you all."

The women looked at each other, unsure what this might be about.

"Did he say why?" Mia asked.

"I'm sorry," Jack said. "Just that I should ask you all to come to the clinic."

The women exchanged looks, then rose to follow Jack out the door. No one spoke as they made their way to the clinic.

"Oh, good," Julie said as they stepped inside. "Come on back. We've got some interesting things to show you."

Once again, the women exchanged looks, then followed the nurse back into the clinic.

"Ladies," Dr. Sanderson said. "I think it's about time for you to meet the designer of this study."

"I thought you were in charge of the study," Mia said.

"I am," he replied. "But I didn't create it. That honor falls on Martin."

With that, he opened the door to a large room where someone sat at a desk, his back to the door.

"Martin," Dr. Sanderson said. "Please meet the women in your study. The mothers to your children."

The chair swung around and a small man sat in it. "Hello, ladies," he said.

His voice was soft, almost feminine in nature. He stood and came around the desk, reaching out his hand. With arms longer than normal, the women looked at each other again, still trying to wrap their heads around this new twist in their situation.

"I'm Claire," the woman said, stepping forward and taking the small man's hand.

"Pleasure to finally meet you in person," Martin replied.

Each woman, in turn, introduced themselves and shook his hand. Once the formalities were finished, Martin said, "I would like to answer any questions you might have."

"Why didn't you introduce yourself before now?" Mia asked.

Smiling, Martin said, "I wanted to wait until I was sure that my design would work."

"And what, exactly, was your design?" Gwen asked.

"Please," Martin said, indicating the chairs in the room.

"I'll leave you to this, then," Dr. Sanderson said, exiting the room and closing the door behind him.

Once the women were seated, Martin sat in his own chair in

the circle and began.

"I was born in the back of a bar," he began. "My mother didn't even know she was pregnant. She left me in the bathroom trash and never looked back. One of the waitresses heard me crying and came in to investigate. I was taken to the local hospital where one of the doctors noticed some anomalies about me. He tested me and found that I was not quite human."

"Not human?" Mia asked.

"Exactly," Martin said. "By the time I got to the hospital, I was already exhibiting signs that I was much older than a newborn. They confirmed with the bar that I was indeed born just hours earlier, due to the remnants of my birth left behind. The doctor began watching me closely and decided that he needed to do additional tests. Because of the results of those tests, and because Dr. Sanderson was very convincing, I was allowed to go home with him to be cared for outside the hospital. When he brought me in just months later, the staff couldn't believe I was the same baby.

"I grew to be the age equivalent of a toddler within six months," he continued. "By the time I reached the age of one, my body resembled that of a four-year-old. I grew exponentially fast, and by the time I was a two-year-old, I was conversing and able to understand vocabulary at a fourth-grade level. By age three, I was able to comprehend high school vocabulary, and by age four I was prepared to study doctorate education."

"Wow," Gwen said.

"Yeah," Mia agreed.

"What does this have to do with us?" Sherry asked.

"I think," Claire began, "that he is saying our babies are like him."

"Exactly," Martin said.

"As in your children?" Mia asked.

"Not exactly," Martin said.

"Then how?" Gwen asked.

"Dr. Sanderson was the doctor who first treated me," Martin continued. "He was able to find a gene that was altered in me pretty early on."

"Wait," Claire said. "How old are you?"

"I'm sixteen," he said.

"But you look like you're in your early forties," Sherry said.

"That is one of the things the gene seems to do," Martin said.

"Does this mean that our babies are going to grow old and die before us?" Sherry asked.

"We think we've been able to slow that part down," Martin said. "They are not growing nearly as fast as I did, and they seem to be slowing down the older they get."

"But what about Jordan?" Gwen asked. "She isn't growing as fast as the others."

"I think you are like my mother," Martin said. "She was able to conceive without a father."

"Then how are you a boy?" Gwen asked. "You should be female, not male."

"We haven't quite figured that part out," he said. "Needless to say, we were hoping that yours would be a boy as well. That would explain how I came to be."

"Sorry to disappoint you," she said.

"Not at all," Martin said. "We were relieved you were having a girl."

"But," Mia began.

"If she'd had a boy," Martin interrupted, "we would understand how my mother was able to conceive a boy without the benefit of a father's donation. Because she didn't, our assumption is that I do have a biological father."

"Then why did you mature so quickly?" Mia asked.

"We don't think my father is human," he said frankly.

The women looked at each other, not knowing who should ask the question everyone had on their mind. Finally, Mia asked, "What was your father?"

"While we can't be one hundred percent sure," Martin said. "We believe he was what is known as extra-terrestrial."

"Wait," Claire said. "Your dad's an alien?"

"He is definitely not of this world," Martin said.

"Have you met him?"

"No," Martin said. "Not that we haven't tried to find a way. It would make things much easier if we could discuss this with him."

"I bet," Gwen said.

"So, then," Claire said. "How are our babies like you if they aren't your children?"

"Like I said," Martin continued. "We were able to isolate a gene that had been altered within me. By using a technique of gene-splitting, we were able to separate what we wanted from other genes, then use a form of artificial insemination using spinal fluid to help you become pregnant."

"What about me?" Gwen asked.

"I think you spontaneously procreated," he said.

"Is Jordan going to be like the rest of the girls?"

"We're not sure, yet," he said. "We've taken some blood, and what we see is an altered state, but not to the point that the other girls are. While we are sure she is normal in most every way, she will not have the advanced growth the other girls have."

"When will our girls stop growing so fast?" Sherry asked.

"They are slowing down already," he said. "I believe that their growth rate will slow within the next few months. By the time they reach two they should be on track for regular growth."

"But they'll be older than other two-year-olds," Mia said.

"Mentally, they will be," Martin said. "For the most part, when they enter school, they will be on the high end academically, simply appearing smarter than the average kid."

"What happens after we leave the program?" Claire asked.

"That's what I wanted to talk to you about," Martin said. "While you are all free to leave at the end of the three years, I was hoping you would all be willing to stay on here. Raise your girls here where we can educate them and continue to monitor their growth."

"I think that would be fine," Mia said. "I don't really have any family, so staying here would be nice."

"I would love it if my mom got to see her granddaughters," Sherry said.

"How is she?" Martin asked.

"The last letter I got from my dad said the doctors called her a miracle," she said.

"I'm glad," he replied.

"Did you have anything to do with this?" Mia asked.

"I simply sent them something to try," he replied.

"You used my mom as a guinea pig?" Sherry shouted.

"No," Martin said. "I simply provided her with a medication that has shown a good return on other patients."

"I guess that means we're not the only study you have going on," Gwen said.

"My genes have proven to be helpful in many areas," he said. "I am simply putting what I have to good use where possible."

"What does that mean for our children?" Claire asked.

"It means that they will be the next generation of healthy humans," he said. "They will be resistant to diseases, just like me, as well as more intelligent than most humans, also like me. From the testing we will be able to do on them, the human race will move to a healthier, more balanced, and peaceful species."

"Peaceful?" Mia asked.

"Have you not noticed that your girls play with each other without argument?" he asked.

"I just thought it was because they were all so close in age," Mia said.

"Even children of the same age tend to argue and fight," he said. "Especially siblings."

"True," Gwen said. "My brothers were always arguing, fighting, and pushing each other around."

"Is it part of their genetic makeup?" Sherry asked.

"We believe so," he said. "Dr. Sanderson and I were pretty sure that the babies would be more attuned to each other, but their connection and compassion for each other, as well as for each of you, is beyond what we could have hoped for."

"How will this help us now, though?" Claire asked.

"While it won't be an immediate change," Martin said. "Their ability to compromise and work out their problems without it coming to blows or shouts will show others that we can work together."

"Until they're cast aside because they're freaks," Sherry said.

"You probably haven't noticed," Martin said. "But each of you have changed while here."

"We know," Mia said. "We're now mothers, and have become like family to each other."

"It's more than that," he said. "The women who were not selected to have babies are altered as well. While they didn't stay at the Institute, they did stay in a relatively close area where we could monitor them and make the genetic adjustments. They have been receiving the same injections you did while you were pregnant. This has helped to boost their immune system as well as alter their genetic makeup."

"Wait," Mia said. "You've changed us, too?"

"Didn't you expect that?" he asked.

The women looked at each other and realized the truth. Over the last year, they have become more calm, willing to help each other out, and none of them have had to deal with even the smallest of colds.

"What happens next?" Gwen asked.

"Next," he said, "we put this into a larger control group. Our next phase has already begun with some men who have been willing to undergo treatment."

"What are you doing to them?" Sherry asked.

"Altering their aggression with some more calming traits," he said. "That trial began at the same time yours did, and the progress has been amazing. If you are all willing, we are wanting to see how they will co-exist with you."

"Like as neighbors?" Mia asked.

"More like an extended family," he said. "Dr. Sanderson is over at their dorm discussing this with them right now."

"So, they don't know about us," Gwen said.

"And they can't know about me," he said.

"Why not?" Claire asked.

"If they knew that I was not human," he said. "It would likely skew the results."

"We thought we were going to have mutant babies," Mia said.

"Why would you think that?"

"Our dreams were really pretty bizarre," she said. "Every one of us, with the exception of Gwen, had dreams that our babies were trying to eat us from the inside out."

"And our emotions were far worse than regular pregnant women," Sherry added.

"I'm sorry that happened," he said. "Honestly, though, most everything about your pregnancies were normal."

"When do we get to meet our neighbors?" Gwen asked.

"Let me check with Dr. Sanderson," he said, rising and moving to his desk.

He picked up the receiver on his phone and pushed a couple of buttons. The women couldn't hear him, but the call was short, and he returned quickly.

"They're ready whenever you are," he said.

The women exchanged a look then rose, almost simultaneously, to follow the small man out of the room. Making their way out of the clinic, they walked across the other side of the campus toward another building. It had been there all along, but they'd never paid it any mind, assuming it was an unused portion of the campus. Within minutes they were walking up to another door.

"Ladies," Dr. Sanderson said as he opened the door. "Come on in and meet your new family."

"How did we miss four pregnant women?" Micah asked.

"How did we miss five guys?" Mia countered.

"Truth," Johan said. "I guess we both missed things."

"I think they kept us on separate schedules to keep us apart," Gwen said.

They were all sitting in a conference room in the dorm the men had been staying in. Micah, Johan, Tom, Gavin, and Scott had been on the campus the entire time the women had, receiving injections and having testing done on them during this time as well.

"Where do you all come from?" Claire asked.

"We're all from the area except Johan," Scott said. "He came to the states for the study specifically, though."

"How did you find out about it?" Gwen asked.

"It was my doctor," Johan said. "He is a friend of Dr. Sanderson. When he found out about the study, he wanted to see if he could get some of his patients in as participants. I was the only one who passed the initial screening."

"So, what, you just flew here and started getting shots?" Sherry asked.

"Something like that," he replied.

"We all have similar backgrounds," Gavin said. "Mostly, we're just your average guy."

"How has it worked, then?" Gwen asked. "I mean, what kind of testing have you been going through? Besides the injections, are you getting any other alterations?"

"Geeze, Gwen," Sherry said. "Give them a little privacy."

"It's fine," Tom said. "It's pretty much just been hanging out. We're all doing online courses so we are using our time wisely. I have to say, it's been fascinating to see how much better we all are at school."

"It's true," Scott said. "I did not do well in school at all. But after starting this study, I have moved well past anything I thought I'd ever learn. I figured I'd end up a mechanic like my dad. Not that it's a bad thing, I just didn't see myself as an intellectual."

"We need mechanics just as much as any other profession," Mia said.

"Absolutely," Tom said.

"I think this will be good, though," Claire said. "Enhancing the race, I mean."

"Did you guys have another person in the study?" Scott asked.

"We did," Mia said.

"What happened to her?"

"She wasn't able to carry her babies," Gwen said. "Dr. Sanderson said she was discharged from this part of the study. I guess she went to the other group.”

“Other group?” Tom asked.

“Martin told us that the women who were not chosen to carry babies were put into another control group where they received the gene therapy,” Gwen said.

“I didn’t know there was more than one study,” Gavin said.

“You also didn’t know there were women having babies at the Institute,” Mia said. “But then again, we didn’t know about you guys, either.”

“Now that we know about each other,” Johan said. “Maybe we should hang out.”

“That would be fun,” Claire said. “As long as you don’t mind babies.”

“I think we all love them,” Gavin said.

“We’re serious,” Mia said.

“It’s not exactly what I expected,” Dr. Sanderson replied.

“You had to know this might happen,” Gavin said.

“I knew,” Martin said.

“You did?” Dr. Sanderson asked.

“It is the natural progression of life,” Martin replied.

“Marriage?” Dr. Sanderson asked.

“We want it to be official,” Gavin replied.

“How long have you two known each other?” Dr. Sanderson asked.

“I think you know that already,” Mia said. “You introduced us last summer.”

“But how well can you know each other in just a few months?”

“What else do we have to do?” Gavin asked. “There are nine of us, five guys and four girls. It’s not like we have much else to keep us occupied."

"And neither of us have a family to go back to," Mia said.

"We want to spend the rest of our lives together," Gavin said.

Dr. Sanderson looked back and forth between them, realizing they were serious.

"Anyone else planning to get together?" he asked.

"It's only a matter of time," Martin said.

"What if you guys get pregnant?"

"Then we'll have the strongest, smartest, most beautiful baby in the world," Gavin said.

"But it will skew the study," Dr. Sanderson complained.

"It will actually make the study more viable," Martin said.

"Exactly," Mia replied. "You will get to see what happens when two subjects procreate."

"That sounds so clinical," Dr. Sanderson said.

"Well," Gavin replied. "It's better than saying when two people get busy making babies."

"You're sure?" Dr. Sanderson asked.

"We are," Mia replied. "I've never been more sure of anything in my life."

"And you?" the doctor asked Gavin.

"Absolutely," he replied.

"Then I guess it's settled," the doctor said. "We're gonna have a wedding."

It didn't take long before the remaining members of the study coupled up, all except Tom. But he seemed fine with it. He spent much of his time with Claire and Johan, and they seemed to make a pretty good team. Within two years the couples had welcomed three new babies to their families, with another on the way. Dr. Sanderson was pleased with the results, finding that the children born from these unions were on par with the ones conceived through the study itself.

Martin watched as his compound filled out with new families added from the other studies, pleased with how well the genetic alterations were taking hold. He hadn't expected the interest from the outside medical community, but once they heard about the health of the people within the compound, they started inquiring. Soon, half a dozen hospitals in the region were including the option of genetic alteration in their services.

A school was opened on campus, initially for the children of the study. Before long, though, members of the surrounding area were asking for permission to send their children. Initially, Dr. Sanderson and Martin wanted it to be exclusively for children in the study. With the influx of altered humans, though, it was opened to outside children as well, all of which had gone through gene therapy.

By the time Abigail, Bridgette, Charlotte, Delilah, Emily, Faith, Grace, Hannah, Isabelle, and Jordan were ten, they were studying courses to get their doctorates. Martin was pleased with the advancement and decided that his work was finished at the Institute.

"Where will you go?" Dr. Sanderson asked.

"Back where I came from," Martin replied.

"I don't understand," the doctor said.

"Do you really think it was a coincidence that brought me to your hospital?" Martin asked.

"Of course," the doctor said. "You didn't exactly choose where to be born."

"But I did," the other man said. "And now I can go back home, knowing that my children will continue to repopulate this world, making it a much safer place to live."

The doctor stared in stunned silence, unsure what he was hearing.

"Don't worry," Martin said. "Within three generations, humans will have outgrown their childish ways. They will then be ready for integration into the larger community of the universe. Unfortunately, you won't live to see it. But have no fear. You are going to be remembered as the founder of this movement. You will be celebrated for eons to come."

WINDING ACROSS WIDE WATER
BY DAVID MECKLENBURG

The horizon is a flat line. It does not exist save in the mathematics of my explaining mind. I consider my life a flat line, like the plane of this bed as seen from the eye-level of a sideways snoozer. My freedom is this day, if only for a day because I cannot presume to know what tomorrow will be. The day unfolds in my mind like the smooth sheets. There are a few wrinkles of chores, but I do not mind the scent and iteration of laundry. For dinner, I'll have something fresh to eat: tomatoes, fresh pasta, mussels, anise, lemon. Sancerre. Maybe I will take a bath in the evening and read, but that tide is far away and so I lay here. Yet there is still the suggestion of silence. Does it bounce off the plain metal refrigerator? Does it wait, nervously, tapping its thousands of tube feet in rhythm on the table by the entryway? Has it lit a thousand matches and thrown them in the toilet? Has it clenched the vase of maroon, silk carnations and considered bending each one in fury that I don't listen? Will it break the peacock's feathers and scatter them to the floor?

Why does she not pay attention!? She is growing old here. She cannot have children. What is she doing without a man? She could be someone's second or third wife.

I wish to banish numbers from the dialogue of love. Can I count my loves in blossom petals upon the branch or must I count them as they fall—floating down to the rush and hurry of Spring and its thawing water? In the dark of Autumn's rain, can I not wander in it, free beneath my own umbrella? Must his hands, perfect articulations of strength and the grace of Helios, hold the steering wheel while all the world is remote beyond the wet and separating glass? The windshield is no window. Summer is not the broken promise of sand on my ass and sun on the Playa de Maspalomas. There is no wisdom save the taste of salt upon my skin and that I can find anywhere. Winter is not for crisp white snow and the bare feet of my own Henry IV as he begs forgiveness from this reluctant Gregory. The falling snow should only bring unearthly blue and white within the optics of the drifting snow—not my half-hearted excommunications, the beatitudes of my fist and cunt, the sleep, let me no longer founder in the cruelty of Winter.

It was a casual gesture, an extension of Herself as She left Her Aegis upon the back of the chair. When will She come for it?

Nearby is the gold-green kimono with black cuffs and lapel. The robe glitters in the passing morning light and although the silk is rich and cool, in the summer I do not wear it. I do not need to. I kept it for a long time unwashed, mingled as it was with both our scents: your strange faint touch of ozone, honey, the pungency of olives, and my own low smell of rosemary, dirt, and sex. For what spark did you come down to watch me in the reeds and rushes? How was I to know I didn't do life right? But you did. You split my arms and legs in two and turned me inside out, stretching my bones over the softness of my organs and muscles. You reached inside of me and pulled silk from my rupture: it was the stuff of clouds and steel.

"Let the wind carry you across the azure yet indifferent sky and may only the cleverest of liars succeed in having what was mine. The rest you shall kill and eat or ignore in all their droll stupidity. And you will always be thirsty for blood and poetry. Shall you bite them into sleep, bundle them into words? The oneiric smear of dissolved love is most delicious after hanging for a while."

That was long ago—a song I needed once, to hear the mode in shifting subtleties, the sneer of love and need for the infinity of imperfection, like the iron at the heat-death end of the universe, the sticky fingerprints on a five-year-old's Valentine's card.

It's good you never gave me a granddaughter. What a terrible mother you would have been. Selfish, wrapped up in your books and your mind. My granddaughter would wither like a zinnia thrown into the dry and dirty corner of your tired apartment.

I wonder: if Heaven has a pavement that goes unmarked by tread, then wouldn't porcelain be unnecessary there, save perhaps as some mnemonic help in describing a texture so pure that the erasure appears as weeping scars? I think about this while I sit and consider the taste of coffee. What is the use of coffee if the Absurd is washed away in timeless reflection? I feel as though I do injury to the earth with such thoughts: Mother, who hated and tasked me from the moment I peeped out of her ruby lips and burst, bastard-wise upon her surface.

There is my mother's own narrative: "I had to go in the cornfield. I was at work, you know there was this old crow that was always stealing corn. He knew better than to believe in stuffed shirts and mincing songs about worth. A turning battery of mirrors flashed as an object of concern, but once from a safe distance, it became an object of curiosity. It was there I found him, the old sneak. But I surprised him and in his cawing shriek he rose at once and shit you out on the old stump he had been standing on. After that, the sun hatched you and the landlord said someone had to take care of you. It's why you have those gangly legs and ragged hair."

Mythically, I pass into this world. Nightly, I return to it.

Can forever have a color? Why do I need it when I possess the unlooked-for purple pause of a bruise? It tells me that I have been alive, the table is real where I barked my shin and so was the cockatoo you painted for me upon the green jungle I never wanted to forget. Our time together was short, like the picked lifespan of the whorey plums within the bowl. Can time wrap around my neck like the Tyrian velvet choker you liked? Yet the course of the sun one evening extends into my morning like the lavender and grape flavored skies of late spring clouds and dragonfire reflecting on the Sound before the evening sighed into sapphire and night. I still hear the trill of water as it passed beneath the metaphor of our keel. I hear the dry brush: the way those bristles abrade across the raw and livid canvas. You say in the bright whisper of abandonment: *adorn yourself in nothing but light and the serenity of the cockatoo.*

Do I need an icon made of blood and gold? Do I need the apotheosis to come in eucharists of iron and bronze? The deliverance of God does not need to come in my window, He has so many homes wherein He can peer and know the blasphemy He craves. No, I had the miracle of you, a pantheon that came and left.

By the bed is the Persian rug. I stole it from your house ten years ago. Liberated, perhaps because you had refrained it from the normal posture of rugs: rolled up, it stood forgotten in one of your vast, high-ceilinged rooms. I imagine Cleopatra: irresistible, and purple-eyed, and unrolled so that she is the soft sensuous nude in the center of the map. The map told Caesar what he had been, named the divisions of Gaul, and revealed the defeat of Pompey. He saw the stern and unimaginative Calpurnia, the tight buttocks of his catamites and he knew the reciprocity of cyclical movement both in terms of love and power, which are the same thing. And there, upon Rome where all the weavings led was Cleopatra upon her hands and knees in welcome: touching her body brings a shudder as though she trepans his skull and draws her long nails of lapis lazuli across the soft folds of his brain. For this death, he looks upon the daggers of his enemies, his friends, his son, perhaps, as all worth it.

For a moment I remember the taste of blood: Matthew, Astrid, Ralph: a split lip, a cut thumb, the slip of a straight razor. How did Cleopatra taste to the Asp? To Caesar? I have my memories of them, of the best of them. I have myself and the depths there to pull them from, to practice their lessons, the familiar chants. Why should I need anyone else? Why should I give my bounty to anyone?

Because you will die alone in the gutter. Forgotten about, broken, gray, a laughing stock, shit on.

A fate almost worse than Jesus's I used to think. He at least made it to the Sepulcher by 33 and died in glory on the Cross. I fear the cold and sterile walls of nursing homes. I fear my spongecake hips will crack and break, perhaps release the viscous clot that will block my brain and leave me less a thing than the brilliant koi outside.

Yet the water is wide. A heron comes to take the koi away, perhaps bedazzled by the orange cream and carbuncle red jewel it swallows down in two swift gulps. I may step out beyond that and understand the wheel is free of the slight grit we gave it once within the infinite second of time we shared upon the earth, and that is enough Heaven for me.

I roll over, alone, remembering all the places I have never been in details made fresh and crisp by the sundering adze as it cuts away the love that kept my craft a simple log. I leave into the bright and slow drift of wind as it plays the castanets of tassels on my shade. I will sleep in my canoe upon the gentle waters of elsewhere.

APRIL

THE PROMPT

It was the color of vintage paper, patinaed by time into a shade neither grey nor white but suspended somewhere in-between. The glass protected it from casual hands but if a viewer leaned close, a keen eye would see the faint, crimson veins still pulsed with life.

THE HISTORIANS
BY JENNIFER DiMARCO

The midnight hallway of the Grand Olympic was silent in the way only luxury hotels can be. The merlot carpet and gilded, halcyon wallpaper both smelled faintly of jasmine and rose water, a phenomenon celebrated by artisan bowls of exotic potpourri nestled in decorative alcoves along the corridor.

Jessica paused at one octagonal inset and dipped her hand into the dried and perfumed elements. Petals and curls of infused cedar tumbled gently from between her slender, tapered fingers. She'd been told she had elegant hands but she was always self-conscious of the ink stains from her beloved but archaic quills and fountain pens.

"You did a fantastic job tonight."

Jessica turned fluidly. "You know I didn't." She gave Gina her signature ghost of a smile. "It was a disaster."

"Absolutely not." Gina shook her head adamantly, her expression firm and sincere. "You handled yourself with grace."

"Hm." Jessica studied the other woman for a moment. Gina had been her manager for four years. "I think I would rather be indignant than graceful."

"I can't imagine you indignant." Gina seemed amused.

Jessica exhaled a little, a half sigh. "I suppose I'm not hardwired for it." She started walking again, leading them down the hall to their adjacent rooms.

Jessica knew Gina was watching her as they continued on their way. Before being assigned to accompany Jessica during press junkets and lecture circuits, Gina had worked at Legacy House scheduling events for another high profile historian, Reverend Liam Conner. Then an assassin had ended his tenure. But the truth was even more insidious: It often wasn't a fanatic that took a Legacy speaker out of circulation. It was burnout.

"Would you like to come in?" Jessica asked. They'd reached their rooms.

"I..." Gina glanced away then back.

Jessica watched her fidget with her wedding ring and then added, "We can talk about the presentation."

Gina tilted her head and looked up at Jessica. It was clearly an excuse but the taller woman's face was neutral, her body language casual.

"Of course," Gina relented and regretted it even as the words left her mouth but Jessica was already thumbing the lock on the door and walking in.

"I'll make us drinks," Jessica tossed over her shoulder.

Gina exhaled, hesitating outside the threshold. In their years together, Jessica had never invited her in. This was part of the job, though... wasn't it? Gina crossed over and closed the door behind her. "That would be wonderful. Thank you."

The city was emerald lights and luminescent monorails suspended in the black ocean of midnight. The temperature had dropped to seventy and on the sixty-fifth floor there was a welcome breeze generated by the circulation fans twenty miles away. Instead of a metal railing or concrete wall, the open balcony was edged with tempered glass panels tinted green. Jessica brought them organic grapefruit vodka on ice.

"The view is spectacular." Gina sipped her drink. It was crisp and fresh across her tongue.

"Hm." Jessica wasn't looking at the city. She moved the guest services book aside and set her untouched drink on the small table between their chairs. "They called it the Emerald City once."

"For all the evergreens—" Gina cut herself off as she caught Jessica's gaze. "What is it?"

Jessica's stillness was unsettling. She had done this tonight, during the lecture, as well. Fallen suddenly so unmoving and so intent that she seemed more a statue of Diana or Artemis than a historian of the written word. But even uncanny, she was arresting. Her tidy waves of auburn hair brushed her narrow shoulders. Her freckled skin like rice paper parchment. She was ethereal, brilliant, remarkable and unobtainable.

"Is something wrong?" Gina pressed carefully, realizing she was staring back at her. The ice in her glass made music. Were her hands shaking? She could never be as composed as Jessica.

"What's the Pro-Life Movement?"

Gina tried to set down her drink but misjudged and the tumbler dropped into free fall, shattering on the balcony floor, shards rocketing under the green glass barrier and descending into the open night like shooting stars.

Jessica just watched her.

Gina took a slow, deep breath. "You know who they are—"

"I know who they were."

Gina stopped breathing.

Jessica's eyes were intense and unrelenting. Her face was mostly in shadow, their backs to the warm light of the room, but somehow her eyes still found light to reflect. Small green fires burned in her gaze.

"Jessica... I..." Gina's struggle was so painfully obvious. *Get a grip,* she admonished herself. With new resolve: "There are radicals who try to impose their beliefs on—"

"You want to kiss me."

Gina's brain felt like it was unraveling. "I'm... married."

"No, you're not."

And there it was. Gina froze. She could not speak.

Jessica's ghost smile returned. "I know how to Google."

Gina's eyes slid shut. This was the end. Everything was about to change and because she knew it, her body flooded with vertigo. She wasn't on the precipice of a cliff. She was already falling, waiting for impact.

The smallest sound—Jessica's boots shifting, touching broken glass—and Gina opened her eyes.

Jessica stood in one motion, like ferrofluid rising up to a magnet, and came to stand before her. Her long, autumnal skirt fluttered against Gina's black slacks. Gina opened her mouth to speak and Jessica was kissing her, eclipsing every thought and drowning the vertigo with something raw and demanding.

Jessica tasted of rain and hibiscus, and Gina could not help the low, wordless sound that escaped her. She felt blessed and cursed in equal measure in the same moment.

Jessica drew away first but stayed so near Gina's eyes wouldn't focus. Jessica was leaning over her, her hands on the arms of Gina's chair. "You've wanted to do that for four years." It wasn't a question.

"Five." Gina's own voice sounded distant over the roar of her blood rushing in her ears. "I saw you speak at the Met."

Jessica stepped back, smiling truly now, and held out her hand. It felt like they were meeting for the first time. "You should have asked me to dinner."

Gina felt breathless and uncertain then emboldened and more sure than she'd ever been in her life. The emotions came in waves like a rising tide. "Your handler wouldn't let me near you." Gina took her hand and stood into her arms.

Jessica leaned the length of her body against hers and brushed short raven curls away from Gina's ear. She corrected her: "My *manager*. Handler is for wild animals."

Gina closed her eyes as Jessica explored the nape of her neck with lips and tongue. Against the hot flush of Gina's skin, Jessica's touch felt chilled.

"You're shivering."

Gina looked at her. The last thing on her mind was work but the words emerged, deflecting her own desire: "I'll lose my job."

Jessica took her hands out of Gina's hair and pushed back her own. She studied Gina's face, reading small signs—pupil dilation, flush, the pace and depth of each breath. She was astute in a way that was fascinating and dangerous at the same time. Jessica started to unbutton her blouse. "Say what you want to say."

It was two words. Two words that crashed around in Gina's head, tumbled against her vocal cords, slammed into the back of her teeth. Gina clenched her jaw and stopped thinking. It was impossible for Jessica to know... but apparently nothing was impossible for Jessica Lombardo. Instead of two words, Gina found three: "I want you."

But Jessica had already heard Gina's subvocalized: *It's illegal.* And Jessica had already formed her two-word rebuttal: *Collateral damage.*

The night continued. At some point, Jessica instructed the room to play Bach. It was cello, sensual and swelling. Sometime before that, slacks, skirt, blouse and shirt were discarded on the cream-colored carpet along with silk and cotton intimates. Near then was when Jessica turned Gina in her arms, the smaller woman's back to her, and unbound Gina's French braid, setting her curls free to fall with her shorter layers and then down her back.

"You're always so contained, so restrained," Jessica whispered, placing kisses along Gina's shoulders amongst the cascade of satin strands.

Gina turned to face her with a small honest smile. "When I'm not, I get myself in trouble."

Jessica's lids lowered a little in pleasure. "I've never been trouble before."

Gina followed her inside.

Gina's dark tresses were a cloak across Jessica's hips and thighs. The balcony curtains were sheer white peppered with silver stardust and moving like phantoms in the air. Jessica was so quiet, so still. Gina lifted her face. "Where are you?"

Jessica looked down her body at the other woman. Gina was so sincere, so intent and present. So naive. "I'm here. I'm here with you," Jessica assured her, reaching out to cup her face.

"You don't have to lie to me." Gina kissed her palm. "Lots of people go somewhere else during sex."

Jessica just studied her. Then: "I'm outside. At night. At the heart of a forest older than any city."

Gina eased herself up and then down beside her, curling her body around Jessica's, caressing her softly while she spoke.

"There's a tree," Jessica continued. "Narrow and angular. It's a birch. The paper-white bark curls away from the trunk as if it's unraveling."

Gina took her ear between her teeth and tugged gently. "That's beautiful," she whispered.

"A full moon shines down through the branches of the trees and they cast grey shadows in the silver light but the birch is different. It casts a shadow of light."

Gina stopped moving.

Jessica held Gina's hand where it came to rest over her heart. "In all those shades of night, that one tree casts its own light."

She said no more. Gina was still a long time then bowed her head to Jessica's shoulder.

"Gina."

Gina lifted her face to her. Jessica assessed the embarrassment and shame she saw painted across her features. It wasn't enough.

"Do you know that place?" Jessica made it a query but her expression proved she already knew the answer.

Gina shook her head. A barely perceptible movement.

"But you know the image." Jessica was unrelenting.

Gina bowed her head again, her forehead resting on Jessica's bare shoulder. She nodded once.

"It's a trademark," Jessica explained just so Gina knew she knew. "Implanted proof of ownership." Beneath their clasped hands, Jessica's heart remained steady and strong. "Property of Hannah Weiss, CEO of Legacy House."

Gina found her voice or her curiosity outweighed her shock. "How did you... there are so many safeguards, so many filters!"

Jessica's lips tugged into sad amusement. "The young man in the audience. With the lilac hair and the Pro-Life shirt. The anti-AI shirt."

Gina's mouth opened then closed. For a moment she resembled a fish out of water. "The one who asked—"

"—what I was like as a little girl."

Gina made a soundless *oh* and Jessica added, "He brought my room service last night."

Gina stared at her. Jessica stared back.

They had complete conversations in silence without words because there were too many emotions and too many truths to say it aloud. And outside the room, the world continued unchanged.

Jessica blinked. Slowly and deliberately. It was dawn and she was nude, lying on her side beside Gina who was as still and beautiful as a painting of a Mariposa Lily in the Mojave.

"I wish you'd told me," Jessica said softly. She kept accusation out of her voice. These were just facts and her own opinions. "It seems as though all of us find out sooner or later. I wish you'd just told me instead."

Jessica reached out and touched Gina's cheek. Her cinnamon skin was as cold as Jessica's now. "Room service came the night we checked in. A young man with lilac hair. He brought me wine and chocolates." Jessica looked away and then back. "He told me they were from you."

Jessica picked up one of Gina's curls and weighed it along her fingertips. "He also brought me a guest services book. Lists of all the perks here at the hotel and local events and sight-seeing in the city. There hadn't been one in my room."

Jessica laid Gina's curl on the white bed sheet. A touch of defiance crept into her voice. "Liam's head is on display at the Seattle Art Museum." Gina said nothing because, among other reasons, there was nothing to say. "They're hosting an exhibit exploring man-made dangers to humanity. Atomic weapons. Genocide. Fascism." Jessica looked at her pointedly. "Artificial intelligence."

The sounds of the city were lost seventy-five floors below them so even with the door open to the balcony, the room stayed quiet. Jessica paused for a long moment that stretched into minutes but finally she added: "The exhibit is called: Self-Inflicted Wounds."

She sat up. The sheet fell away from her body and pooled across her lap. She brought her knees to her chest and held them with her arms. "I admired him," she admitted. "Even as an atheist—programmed as an atheist—I felt something *stir* when Liam spoke."

She laid her cheek against her knees, turning her head to smile down at Gina. "Until now, I would never have been so familiar. Yes, we were both represented by Legacy House but Reverend Connor was a historian of *religion* and who am I? The voice of prose. So banal, so mundane." Jessica's smile faded. "But if we're siblings—if all the historians at Legacy are related—we're allowed some familiarity."

She shook her head a little, still unclear how one people could do this to another. "After all, according to the exhibit highlight, we all share a trademark."

Jessica stood then, nude and pale as a vision or mirage. She stared down at Gina and Gina continued to stare at the ceiling, unblinking, unmoving. Her eyes had long glossed over and her lips were decidedly blue. Jessica smiled her ghost of a smile. "You were an excellent handler, Ms. Miguel."

Jessica crossed the room and walked out onto the balcony, lifting herself over the green-tinted glass and plunging into the light of day.

THE MOST DANGEROUS THING
BY LAUREN PATZER

Tendo sat quietly awaiting his master. The eerie purple light visible through the thick windows of the temple cast a dull glow on the granite walls surrounding him. Today was the pinnacle of Tendo's training. Today, he would find out his true purpose in life.

Master Tay-Lis emerged from the temple interior carrying a small book with him. He raised his hand slightly, palm up, and curved his fingers gently, repeatedly. Tendo arose from his seat, his sandaled feet whispered calmly as he walked across the granite tiles. His robes rustled softly with each step. The otherwise silent atmosphere gave reverence to each movement. Tendo bowed when he reached Tay-Lis.

"Tendo," Tay-Lis said. "You've excelled at your teachings. The council has reviewed your birth account, study records and testing. They've found you worthy to take the next step on your journey. Follow me to the Room of Sighs."

Tendo bowed slightly again. He wrinkled his brow as he followed his master. The Room of Sighs was not documented in anything he had read about the temple. Truly, there were mysteries yet to solve in the world. He glanced out the windows at the rough jagged landscape outside. He wondered briefly if anyone had braved the harsh elements of the exterior world. He smiled grimly. His wondering was foolish. No one had left the inner world for centuries. The Temple of Remembrance was the only part of their civilization that was above ground. Only a select few ever wandered these halls and gazed out among the jagged spires of a dark world.

Plaques lined the walls filled with words of profound wisdom. Tendo's last year has been spent memorizing every line, contemplating every thought of the ancients. Only through reverent observance of past mistakes could one hope to achieve greatness and forgiveness.

They came to a small unmarked door Tendo had passed a thousand times before but had never entered. Master Tay-Lis bowed low before the door and then opened it. Tendo followed his example, bowed low and then joined his master passing through this new portal. They passed by older walls lining a small hallway. The surface of these walls was tougher than the smooth granite surfaces in the rest of the temple. After a time they came to a large, ornate door. Tendo gazed at it in awe. It was made of wood, a material he'd only read about in historicals as a small child.

"How?" Tendo asked and looked at his master.

"The room beyond was created before the Great Calamity when trees were plentiful, or so I've been told," Master Tay-Lis responded, his voice cracked with age. He raised his wrinkled hand to a large metal ring and pulled. The door swung open slowly, creaking on centuries-old hinges. Inside, the familiar natural red glow from the tunnels below lit the interior as it was reflected up small apertures in the floor from below.

The walls were lined with various types of ancient machinery and weapons. As Tendo's eyes passed over each of them, his eyebrows raised with recognition. Arrayed before him were the Forbidden Artifacts—death machinery forged and manufactured by previous generations. He'd only seen these in the texts he studied over the last year.

"The varied array of our civilization's past mistakes," Master Tay-Lis said. "All inoperable, of course. Whenever someone decides a new weapon should be created, we bring them here and show them the statistics for each creation. The magnitude of our own atrocities."

Below each piece of machinery, in addition to statistics about the deaths associated with the device, a rolling video of bodies ruined by the deadly artifacts bared the grisly details. A sea of dead flickered around the room. Tendo's eyes went wide as he gazed at the cautionary images. His eyes eventually fell on a single plain door set in the center of the back wall.

"Is that another exit, master?" he asked.

Master Tay-Lis gazed at the door and sighed.

"Therein lays the greatest weapon of all or, at least, a portion of it," Master Tay-Lis said. "Come and witness the last remnant that brought the worst destruction to the planet."

They walked to the door and opened it. Three walls were solid, but a single thick window let in a purple haze from the outside. On a pedestal in the center of the adjoining small room, a tiny, clear box was illuminated from below and above. Tendo approached the enclosure wide-eyed. Mounted on thick metal posts was a small square of gray material. As Tendo got closer and examined it, he noticed purple lines under the surfaces that moved rhythmically like a heartbeat. He turned to Master Tay-Lis and saw the stony-faced gaze looking back at him.

"What matter of magic is this?" Tendo asked.

"The highest advances of science created the most

destructive weapon ever devised. Men who thought they could play God used their knowledge to create an immortal being of unmatched power and ferocity," Master Tay-Lis said. "It was also nigh invulnerable. Only the most cunning of us were able to devise a weapon to bring the beast under control. They had to remove a piece of the creature to disable it."

"It still moves!" Tendo said. He gazed in wonder at the smooth surface, seeming to pulse with life. "Is this magic?"

"No," Master Tay-Lis said and cast his gaze out the window. "Out there, buried under centuries of dust, the rest of the weapon lies, powered by the eternal pulse of a quantum generator revolving with the passage of neutrinos. Never dying, but never at rest—it can't carry on its horrific mission unless it is whole. Those platinum pins hold fast the only bit that has ever been removed from the machine, removed at great expense of life. Regardless, it was finally defeated and will trouble mankind no longer."

Tendo bowed his head in reverence.

"It is your sacred duty to never let this piece be freed. To do so would mean the destruction of us all!" Master Tay-Lis spoke the last with a seriousness and fear he'd never heard before.

They walked from the room and closed the door behind them.

Three weeks later, Master Tay-Lis fell ill and passed shortly thereafter. Rumors passed through the populace about their shrinking population. The birthing vats had failed to produce a healthy fetus in several months. No one seemed to have the technical expertise to troubleshoot the problem; the technology was centuries old and had been failing for years.

An earthquake shook the earth a few months later. The damage was extensive. Many died in a cave-in after the supports holding them up failed; they hadn't been serviced in decades. Fear spread like wildfire as the other supports were examined but couldn't be repaired. The knowledge had been lost to the sands of time.

Tendo had gone directly to the Room of Sighs after the earthquake to look after his responsibilities. The exterior room was intact, nothing amiss. The smaller room at the rear had significant damage to the rear wall. Tendo also noticed a crack in the thick window looking out on the hazardous purple landscape. As he examined the damage to the wall, he noticed pieces of plaster falling from a small hole. He cleared the plaster away and found an ancient manuscript, the brittle pages inside covered with writings. He carefully took the book and moved into the exterior room where he could set it down.

As he moved through the pages, a picture began to emerge. He walked over to a few of the exhibits. One of them had been struck by a falling rock from above. He looked up momentarily, but then returned his attention to the exhibit. The rock had fallen on the plaque underneath. Tendo looked around nervously as he pushed the thin bit of metal aside revealing another underneath. The inscription below told a different story of the weapon of destruction in front of him. Rather than the millions lost, this weapon had never been used. Why had someone changed the inscriptions? Had they changed them all?

He quickly returned to the book. After verifying the changes to several other exhibits, he reached the last pages which described the creation of ultimate salvation. He read through the pages and was horrified by its contents. Could it be true? Did his ancestors destroy it out of greed for power?

Another quake shook the room. Part of the ceiling collapsed near the exit. Tendo sought refuge in the smaller room. This time, the damage had reached here in a more significant way. A chunk of the ceiling had fallen on the pedestal, hitting the enclosure. It had fallen to the ground, cleaved in two. But the thin membrane of skin still held fast, stretched a bit between the broken halves. Tendo jumped back as the top pieces of the enclosure popped and flew up into the air driven by the four metal pins holding the artifact in place. A moment later, the thin membrane of skin rose into the air and shot out of the room through the crack in the window. It happened so fast, all Tendo could do was stand and gape in awe and horror.

Tendo retreated back into the larger room. He attempted to move the debris blocking the exit, but it was too heavy. He was trapped until someone came to check on him. He sat down with his back to the wall and weariness settled on him like a blanket of stone. If the damage had been extensive below, it could be days before they even thought to check on him, maybe even weeks. He had no supplies.

He would die here. With all of the birthing vats inoperable, he wouldn't even be replaced. In all likelihood, he may be the last person alive to see this room. Their civilization was fading as fast as the sunlight faded in the maroon sky.

He must've drifted off to sleep. A huge crash of glass and stone startled him awake. A puff of dust billowed from beneath the door to the smaller chamber. He heard movement, steps in the debris. Something was moved and then dropped. The door creaked open.

Tendo closed his eyes. He just wanted death to come quickly. He didn't want to see the horrible creature open its fangs and devour him.

"This is a pretty disappointing welcoming committee," a voice said. It was a light, melodic sound; so unlike the deep timbres of his people. He opened his eyes a saw a nude woman standing with her head cocked at him. Her skin was the same mottled purple as he'd seen on the patch of skin in the enclosure.

"You're... you're a female!" Tendo exclaimed. He stood up, pushing his back against the wall. "The danger is real!"

"Still clinging to that theory, I see," she said. She walked up to Tendo. If he could've melted into the wall, he would've. She reached out and touched his clothing. She rubbed it between her fingers. "Still growing clothing in vats, I see. Well, after what you did to the planet, I can see that you don't have many alternatives."

She released his robe and walked around the room. Tendo's ire got the best of him.

"You! You destroyed the surface world!" Tendo pointed a finger at her. As he thought about the words he'd shouted, he quickly put his hand back at his side and trembled. He just accused a god of being dangerous. He took a deep breath and awaited his destruction.

"Well," she said. "Indirectly, I suppose that's true. It certainly wasn't the outcome I wished. When they invited me to the conference center, I had no idea they'd filled the basement with every functioning fusion bomb on the planet. I wouldn't know that had they not bragged about it before setting them off. And then again as wave after wave of them came at my nearly comatose body wielding fusion lasers to cut a patch off my forearm. They died in the thousands from the radiation, but they kept coming. The passage of time was a bit fuzzy, but I think they finally managed it after a year. Aradis must've revealed my single weakness to someone he trusted. Obviously, that proved to be a fatal mistake for so many."

She stopped at one of the exhibits. She pointed at the device on the wall. "You know this actually just prints out flesh for burn victims? Cellular evaporator–that's quite a creative weapon name."

"Why would they do this just to destroy a truth sayer?" Tendo asked.

She turned to him, her eyebrows raised.

"Oh! So you know what I am?" She shook her head. "Didn't think they would've passed that on."

Tendo's shoulders slumped. He pointed at the book on one of

the pedestals in the middle of the room.

"I did not find out until that book fell from the wall a few days ago."

She walked over and examined the manuscript, nodding as she perused the pages.

"Well, this at least is primarily true. Amazing. I thought I was the only blasphemous creation of Aradis' design. Didn't know he was also a historian. Well, he was ideologically suicidal."

She walked around the room and pointed at the various items as she spoke.

"Not a brain sifter, but a hairdo styler. Completely unnecessary after the eradication of women, I suppose. And this is a storage cube for information—holds about two hundred years worth of documents, video, audio and scientific data. Not the focusing crystal for a melting laser that killed—" She looked at the plaque. "—three hundred million! Well I suppose if you're going to make up numbers, they might as well be huge."

She continued walking around the room describing the mundane functions of the artifacts as opposed to their weaponized classifications. Every once in awhile, she'd stop and gaze sadly at one of the items noting it had a true plaque description.

Tendo's heart sank as she walked around the room. With few exceptions, she correctly described all as had been noted in the manuscript. A few items had been added after the manuscript had been completed, but she seemed to know what they were as well.

"Women are evil," he said, grasping to the only constant he'd known without doubt. "We learn this from birth."

"No doubt you did. The victors," she said as she pointed at the walls. "Rewrite history as they see fit."

"Did you come to kill us? Have your revenge?"

"Honestly, I was just curious to see what was left of the

'master race,'" she said as she smiled at him. "Not much, I can see."

"We don't need your kind to save us," Tendo said as the hackles rose on his neck.

"You're really not salvageable at this point," she said. "I'd imagine by now, you've lost your technology to history and can't repair or replace the technology you created centuries ago to replace the female womb."

"The what?" Tendo frowned. He'd never heard the term 'womb' before.

"Humanity used to have two sexes, male and female," she said.

"Evil and good. We eliminated the evil." Tendo stuck his chest out, determined to be defiant before his death. They'd eliminated the evil and used their image to purge any remaining evil from themselves as often as needed.

"The history you've been taught is not correct. A sex or even a racial subset of humanity is not inherently evil. Every individual has the capacity for good and evil. Even I, in my arrogance, didn't realize my actions would push those in power to destroy their own world to eliminate me. I'm simply a truth sayer, I'm not infallible. I hadn't learned that sometimes it's better to be silent than speak the truth," she said as she turned towards him. Tendo inhaled sharply as the red glow fully illuminated her bare, alluring form.

"Women and men were two halves of life. When combined, they created life. Babies were not always created in a birthing vat."

As Tendo gazed upon her nakedness, he felt a familiar stirring in his belly. He despaired. He could no longer access the portals of forgiveness where he'd seen her evil form countless times. Evil had appeared to tempt his expulsion to be thrown to the wind.

"You appear in the guise of one who draws the evil from us. How can you not be evil?"

"Ah, the old teachings—gaze upon evil and extract it from your body. Did you not know they were simply taking your contributions to add to the eggs they'd harvested from the females? They clearly ran out of one half of the equation," she said as she walked slowly towards him.

His pulse quickened. What was she doing to him? He felt the evil impulses rising at his groin. Soon, he would need to expunge it from himself. As she stood naked and peacefully before him, he noticed she had a crevice similar to the portals of forgiveness—there betwixt her legs.

Before he knew what he was doing, he had pushed her down on the ground, released the pressure from his growing evil and plunged it into the portal. She didn't resist, but simply lay there allowing him to complete the ritual.

When he was done, a feeling of peace and calm overtook him. He collapsed on top of her.

She easily rose up, lifting Tendo off of her. She laid him on his back.

"Thank you," she said.

"For what?" Tendo whispered. "I disposed of my evil inside you. Now you will be doomed and destroyed from the inside. I have done what the ancients could not. You will be consumed by evil."

"Because they lied to you, I omitted my other reason for coming back here. I felt you were still healthy and young enough to feel your natural urges. It takes two halves to create life. You've given me the other half. I was created as a truth sayer but also as a woman. Immortality extends to my function as a life-giver as well. Aradis gave me the ability to carry on procreating as long as I had the seed of man available. What you have given will be preserved within me and give rise to millions. But I will wait until this era of mankind has completely perished by its own hand."

She stood up and walked back to the door of the smaller room.

"Sleep now. You may yet live on for a few more years if they come for you."

She closed the door. Tendo heard the movement of footsteps among the debris and then silence. The exhaustion from his effort of expelling evil overtook him. He pondered if the truthsayer had indeed told the truth and then closed his eyes as the tinkle of glass from her final exit echoed throughout the room.

THEORY & PRAXIS
BY HIROMI COTA

Fuck! BraAaad! I told you not to touch it!

How the fuck was I supposed to know something was going to happen?

The book was glowing, you asshole. That's a pretty good sign that it has an alarm.

Oh, excuse me, Mister Heistmaster.

Uh! That was a joke! We weren't trying to steal the book! It was just a pretty manuscript, and my friend wanted to touch it. It was a mistake and we're sorry.

You're seriously confessing at the scene of the crime?

It's not a fucking crime! We didn't do anything wrong. Hey! Security? Can you just turn the lights back on? Not being able to see is starting to creep me out.

Like they care. Hell, that might just make them leave the lights out longer.

Whatever. Look. … I just want to get out of here. I have a date.

WhaaAT? Bullshit. Who with?

Victor.

Fucking football team Victor? That dick?

Shut up. He's nice.

Well, I hope he's got a tight END for you.

He's an offensive lineman, ass.

What the fuck are you two going on about?

HOLY FUCKSHIT! **WHO THE FUCK'RE YOU?**

We were alone a second ago!

Yeah, no. I've been here for at least a fucking day. You two (I'm guessing kids) just showed up a minute ago.

You've been SPYING on us for a minute? Who the fuck're you?

Look—fuck. I hate that word now. Listen—

No, you listen, you fucking creeper! What the fuck is going on? Why aren't the lights on?

LISTEN! We're not in the museum anymore.

Are you high? *What the hell are you smoking?*

Take a step, smartasses.

What? **Oh shit.**

Just do it, kid. **Oh shit. Ohshit. Oshit. Oshitoshitoshit**

Brad! It's OK! Brad! Bradbradbrad! Calm down. Just—

Take a fucking step, kid!

What is with you and—

oh...

Ooohhhh.

Where the hell are we?

No idea. But, obviously gravity doesn't fucking work. Either that or our bodies don't. Hell, for all I know, we're dead and we're a bunch of lost souls.

Nononono. I can't be dead. I can't! I can't.

Your buddy's going to pass the fuck out if he keeps freaking out like that.

That's not a thing!

Brad! You're OK! We're both OK. We're just ... I don't know, in a loading

screen. Maybe we're going to Narnia or something!
That'd suck. Narnia was a warzone. **I need to see my granny.**
Lord of the Rings, then! **I can't. No. I'm OK. I'm OK.**
Also a warzone. **I'mOK.M'OK.**
Shut up! You're not helping! Brad! Hey! I'm right here!
C'mon, Brad. Hey! Hey! You with me? **M'OK.M'OK.M'OK.**
m'ok.m'ok.m'ok.m'ok How long does this usually last?
Until he's done. If you think you're **m'ok.m'ok.**
having a bad time listening to him, **m'ok.m'ok.**
just think how HE feels! **m'ok.m'ok.**
Yeah, OK. Fair enough. **m'ok.**

Brad?
Hi.
Uh.
What's your name?
Ron. What's yours, Heistmaster?
Heh. I'm Martín. You have any idea what the hell happened?
You were in the Smithsonian, right? The new exhibit? It wasn't
supposed to be open yet, but I'm guessing you two were as much
nosey shits as I was and just snuck past that silk rope. If they wanted
to keep people out, they'd try harder, right? The book was in the
middle of the new exhibit room, with weird writing on the walls.
Yeah. Like Sanscrit or some shit.
No.
Just, no, Kid.
Sanscrit looks nothing like that. Holy shit. You don't know anything
about other languages, do you? Dammit. Anyways, weird writing. Like
I've never seen. And it glowed. No. Not just glowed. It pulsed, like a
cop car's lights or
The Enterprise's warp core!

Uh… Yeah, I guess. It was red for me, but I guess "warp core" isn't a bad description, especially since it warped us into whatever limbo we're in now.

It was red for us, too. What if—

Yeesss? You gonna finish that thought?

What if the light was pulsing … like a pulse? Like, it was alive?

Y'know what? A day ago, I'd say that was the stupidest fucking thing I've ever heard of, but after the last 24 hours, I gotta admit that I'm open to new ideas. So, let's say the book was alive. Was the book all that there was? Or was it just one part of something bigger?

Bigger?

Like the book was a hand or a **mouth.**

Ah, shit, Kid. So, we just hopped into the mouth of a book monster? Can't say that I saw this on my top five ways that I'd probably go out.

You have a list of ways you're going to die?

Sure. Who doesn't?

Did you say BOOK MONSTER?

Yeah? Is that so weird?

YES! *Kinda.*

Weirder than being in the Smithsonian one minute and then popping out here? Wherever the fuck here is?

Yeah, OK. Fair enough. So, what are we going to do?

What do you mean?

What? **What do you MEAN, what you do mean?**

Look, do you have a body here? 'Cause I don't. Try to touch your nose. Can you do that? Click your heels together? Clap? Can you DO anything? There's no ME. I'm … I'm not me here. I'm not anything.

You're a voice at least. You have to exist.

I can hear you. *We can hear you. We hear you.*

What good does that do?

What doesn't it do? You know how many poor bastards there are out there who wish someone would hear them? Because they're sick or society's too fucked up to give them a chance? How many people are just yelling into the fucking void trying to get an echo back?

Ever have a total stranger go up to you and ask you what time it is? Or start talking about their favorite thing? Trying desperately to connect with another human being?

Who *the* FUCK **are** *you?!*Who **the** *FUCK* are **you**?!*Who* the **FUCK** *are* you?!

FOREVER
BY AMBER RAINEY

No one had ever asked Khali her thoughts on living forever. If anyone had bothered, they would have learned she despised the concept of humans being immortal. She was firmly in the camp of those who believed a human's life on earth was limited and for very good reason. At a certain point, a human no longer learned anything new and their opinions and beliefs stagnated. Giving such a creature immortality was akin to breeding dogs to be vicious or wild animals to be tame house pets. It polluted the Earth in unimaginable ways and wasted the precious little space and resources available to the rest of the population. No, in her opinion, humans were meant to be born, live as productive a life as possible, then grow old and die to make room for the next generation. Immortality was a selfish product of a selfish species.

"Please open the door, Khali!"

Racita's plea broke into Khali's thoughts. She looked out the large picture window of the lab to where Racita and a group of three other scientists and two security guards watched her. Khali shook her head sadly. She could see the teardrops rolling down Racita's face. The last thing she wanted to do was hurt her but she saw no other options. She could see the moment Racita realized no amount of pleading would help. Her shoulders drooped and she drew in a deep breath. Then Khali saw a steely reserve flit across Racita's face before she turned away and gave an inaudible order to the security guards.

Khali watched Racita's back receding from the lab anteroom. She squared her shoulders and lit the bunsen burner. She briefly saw the flames engulf the over-gassed room and the window shatter before everything went blissfully blank. Her last waking thought was of Racita.

Years Earlier

The sun was unseasonably warm for the spring day and it seemed the entire population of the small college town of Ellensburg, Washington was taking advantage of the dry weather. Khali was no exception. She had a break in her classes and was sitting underneath the dazzling, pink flowers of a weeping cherry tree. She was attempting to write a novel but was distracted by some of her classmates, who were in the midst of throwing a frisbee around. The frisbee had landed in her lap twice already and she felt it in her best interest to watch the game instead of getting hit in the head.

At long last, the game died down and the guys ran off to some other pursuit. Khali shook her head and prepared to return to writing when someone caught her eye. She looked up in time to see a harried young woman rushing along the path towards the biology building. The woman's hands were precariously balancing a load of books and papers. As if in slow motion, Khali watched the woman trip and the contents of her arms spill all over the ground. Some of the papers began blowing in Khali's direction and she quickly jumped up to grab them. The young woman began panicking.

"I've got them! Oh… there is some more over there, I'll grab them!" Khali exclaimed as she shoved the papers into the woman's hands.

Khali ran after the last of the papers. She jumped and twirled, dancing with the papers in an almost intimate way, her long legs graceful as they landed. Khali turned around with a small laugh, her cheeks rosy from the exertion. The young woman stood stock still, her mouth agape with something akin to wonder. Khali ran back over to her, offering up the papers. She took a moment to study the young woman. She was shorter than Khali, with long, black hair that hung in a braid down to her waist. She had generous, brown eyes behind small, round eyeglasses. Her skin was the color of smooth, milk chocolate and her mouth was still open as if she were mid-sentence and forgot what to say.

Khali suddenly felt her mouth grow dry and her former exuberance replaced by sheepish self-doubt. The woman seemed to recover and glanced towards the biology lab.

"I am late," she said with an odd hesitance in her town.

"Oh, of course," Khali said, handing the papers out to the woman again.

She took them and began hurrying off. Then, she stopped and turned around.

"Racita… I mean my name's Racita. Thank you," Racita said as she gave an odd little bow.

Racita waited a moment and Khali could feel herself being appraised just as she had appraised Racita. Racita then nodded, smiled and turned back around, hurrying off to her class. Khali wondered what had just happened but shrugged it off. The odd day of sunshine must have taken its toll on her mental faculties. She waved at the retreating back then shook herself out of her stupor.

"You're welcome!" she shouted to the retreating figure.

Khali watched the clock like a hawk. Professor Nixon droned on and on about the importance of *The Grapes of Wrath* and its enduring legacy in the world of American literature. Personally, Khali was not a fan. She didn't dislike all of Steinbeck's novels but she had been forced to read *The Grapes of Wrath* in grade school and she had not changed her opinion since that initial introduction. There were only so many ways dirt and dust could be described before it became rote reading. Steinbeck spent over one hundred pages talking about the dust. Khali got it, it was dry and dusty. In her opinion, the novel was ill-served by Steinbeck's droning on the landscape of his novel.

The bell rang and Khali wasted no time jumping up to leave. She'd heard Professor Nixon was looking for guinea pigs under the guise of volunteers. Nixon was her least favorite professor, she'd had the woman for three classes with no choice. She just had to get through the last few weeks of the semester and she would be free of the woman's unalterable opinions forever. It would be tantamount to educational suicide to let the Professor goad her into exploding on her and ruining her grade, since most of her grade was subjective in the first place. The first year, she'd barely made it out of her introduction to literature class with a passable C grade because she had not yet known the professor's penchant for downgrading any paper with any original thoughts. Now, she just spat out the opinions the professor deemed "right" and then fumed over her indignities with her friends. It was far better to just get the grades she needed than to always give her opinions. Lost in her thoughts, as usual, Khali didn't see Racita standing next to her until she nearly knocked the other woman over.

"Oh my gosh," Khali said, putting out an arm to steady Racita. Racita, recovering from the near miss, gave another little bow with her head toward Khali. Khali smiled, noting the barely pent up laughter in Racita's eyes.

Racita adjusted her glasses and looked down. "I took the liberty of finding out where your classes were. Nothing stalkery, I just wanted to thank you properly for saving my paper. If I'd lost that, graduation would have been gone from my future."

Khali smiled. "That's very kind of you. I didn't mind helping."

"Where did you learn to dance like that?"

"Dance?" Khali asked in confusion. She tried to remember dancing and came up blank.

"In the field, it was as if you were dancing with the papers as your partner and the sun as your music," Racita complimented.

Khali could feel herself in a full-body flush and looked down to avoid meeting the other woman's eyes. She never heard such beautiful words describing her movements. If anything, the opposite was true. She was constantly told she was like a bull in a china cabinet, always running into things and causing general chaos in her clumsiness. She recovered and looked into Racita's eyes. She saw nothing but kindness and truth in the other woman's face.

"I could use those words in my next novel," she hedged.

Racita nodded. "They are yours, if you wish."

Khali was again at a loss for words. There was something mysterious and enchanting about Racita. She felt drawn into an invisible aura emanating from the diminutive woman. Racita seemed sure of herself, something Khali lacked. Her imposter syndrome kept her from realizing her full potential. She was sure Racita never questioned anything she accomplished.

"Would you like to get coffee with me?" Racita asked.

"Yes, but…"

"It's not a requirement. I just wanted to show my appreciation."

Khali shook her head. "It's not that… I don't drink coffee."

Racita mock gasped, "How are you human? How do you get

through your classes without caffeine?"

Khali laughed. "My brain keeps me quite awake. It never shuts ups. I feel if I did like the taste of coffee, I would never sleep."

"In my culture, tea is very acceptable. Therefore, I extend my invitation to tea. You do drink tea?"

Khali nodded. Racita nodded back and started towards the stairs. Khali stood staring at the woman's back, yet again, caught in the thrall of her graceful movements, as if she glided across the floor instead of walked. Racita turned back, expectantly and caught Khali staring. She held out a hand for Khali, who hesitated only a moment before taking her hand and walking down the stairs, being very careful to watch where she was going and not study the woman next to her, for fear of tripping and dragging them both to their deaths.

Khali was lost in the timbre of Racita's voice as she passionately discussed her major and her theory of the human body. In truth, Khali had stopped really listening to the words, enthralled by the woman herself. She'd never been as attracted to anyone in her life as she was to the woman across from her. As each minute passed, she learned something new she liked about Racita. The way her eyelashes swept her cheeks each time she blinked. The way her hands looked with the previously missed henna marking them. The gold hoops that swayed as Racita talked and the one stubborn lock of hair that curled next to her right eye. Khali would give almost anything to reach out and feel what she knew to be a silken strand in her hands. She tried not to appear to be staring but the enchantment just would not break.

"What do you think?"

The question cut into Khali's musings. She tried desperately to remember what Racita had said moments before but came up blank.

"I don't know."

Racita laughed. "That is because you have not been listening.

You've looked at my lips at least five times in the last two minutes. Did you know you are very distracting when you chew on your lip? I can barely remember what I was talking about."

Khali looked up in embarrassment, once again blushing from head to toe.

"See, your neck and shoulders are turning a lovely shade of red. I knew I was right," Racita proudly declared.

"About… what?" Khali spluttered.

"You and I are attracted to each other," Racita simply stated.

"It sounds so…" Khali hesitated.

"Sinful? Delightful? Shameful?" Racita offered.

Khali chuckled. "Clinical."

Racita nodded. "I apologize. I am a scientist. Bluntness is in my nature. How would you put it, miss author?"

"How did you know that?" Khali wondered aloud.

"I am a research scientist. Well, I will be one in a month, after graduation. It's my job to research my subjects."

"And am I a subject?"

Racita shook her head and smiled. "More like a 'special interest', however, you are changing the subject."

Khali leaned in. "I would say you are the most exotic, elegant, and fascinating woman I have ever met and I would like nothing more than to see how your lips taste against mine."

Racita smiled in an intimate manner and it sent shocks through Khali's body. Khali had never in her life wanted anyone more than at that very moment. Racita stood up and Khali's heart began racing, her self-doubt admonishing her for being so forward. She was sure she had blown any chance with Racita. She had to remind herself to breathe again when Racita held out her hand, once more.

"Your place or mine?" Racita asked.

Khali watched the sunlight play across Racita's face. It enhanced the effect of her long, black lashes resting on her tan cheeks. Her breathing even and soothing in her slumber. Each day, she was more and more in love with the woman sleeping next to her. Racita was more than just beautiful, she was intelligent and caring. Khali had always viewed scientists as detached and clinical, a necessary trait for their chosen professions, however, Racita was exactly the opposite of what she'd assumed. She was genuinely interested in helping her fellow man, attempting to cure debilitating diseases in a compassionate, thoughtful manner.

"I can feel you staring." Racita grinned.

"I can't help it."

Racita sat up and put her hand on Khali's face.

"Surely by now, you know every flaw."

Khali chuckled. "I've never found even one.

"Pfft. You have said that to me for almost fifteen years and yet I know they are there."

Khali shook her head. "You are perfect to me."

Racita smiled and kissed Khali. Khali closed her eyes and breathed in the spiced scent that always clung to her wife. No matter how many moments they spent together, Khali always felt pleasure and contentment in the morning hours before life interrupted them. Inevitably, Racita would get out of bed, drink her coffee and get ready for another long day in the lab. Meanwhile, Khali would write or think and daydream around the house, waiting for the return of her better half. A frown passed across her brow as she remembered Racita's admonishments to *not sell herself short*. She was brought back to the present by Racita's finger smoothing the lines in her brow.

"You, my love, are more than enough," she quietly reprimanded.

Khali smiled. "I know."

Racita looked deep into her eyes, searching for truths only she could uncover. After a long moment, she seemed satisfied, giving Khali a nod of approval and getting out of bed. Khali watched Racita shed her nightgown and longed to join her in the shower but knew the day was an important one and Racita could not be late. Khali sighed, getting out of bed to make breakfast for them both. Suddenly, Khali felt the world go sideways and reached out to steady herself on the dresser, knocking over Racita's perfumes on the way down. The last thing she heard was Racita shouting her name.

Khali awoke with a pounding in her head that felt like her brain was attempting to escape. She blinked at the bright lights and quickly shut them again. She groaned in misery, every part of her body beginning to ache as she became more aware of her surroundings. The incessant beeping of nearby machines did nothing for her headache.

"Could we shut those down," she mumbled, each word sticking in her dry mouth.

"Shh... don't try to talk yet," an unidentifiable voice said.

Khali opened her eyes more slowly to let them adjust and looked around the room as best she could. She could see wires and tubes connecting her to the various beeping monstrosities in the room. There was a male she did not recognize and an assistant from Racita's lab that she did recognize. She tried to turn her head and a wave of dizziness and nausea made her stop immediately. She groaned again and felt a hand fill hers, squeezing in reassurance. Khali opened her eyes again and found Racita standing by her bedside. She frowned, noticing Racita in her lab coat.

Racita nodded. "You had a very severe heart attack. You're at my lab."

"Lab?" Khali tried to speak more but the dryness of her mouth overwhelmed her and she started coughing.

"Here." Racita offered a cup with a straw.

Khali drank the water slowly, the wetness a relief to her sore throat. She watched as Racita looked at the monitors, noting the pleased look as each monitor seemed to give her the information she was searching for in their confusion of data. Khali tried to think of a reason she would be in the lab and not a hospital. When she'd drunk enough water, she indicated she was done and Racita set the cup down then sat on the edge of the bed.

"Why am I in the lab?" Khali asked again.

Racita took a deep breath. "Khali, it was the only way."

"Only way?"

"Your heart, it was not responding. I thought I'd lost you. They told me it was impossible, so I had you transferred here. We were going to announce it the day you collapsed."

Khali shook her head. "Announce what? I don't understand."

Racita smiled. "My breakthrough. I finally created a nanobot that can correct deficiencies in human organs. The bots essentially repair you from the inside out."

Khali's eyes grew wide in understanding and horror.

"You experimented on me?"

Racita looked away and stood up, "It's all perfectly safe. I couldn't lose you."

"Racita, you didn't ask me. I'm sure your research is sound but…"

Racita swung back to face her. Khali could see the anger on her face. If she had been in a better state of mind, she would have known to pull back on her own consternation. She knew the steely resolve Racita had when being told what she could and could not do. Khali had struck a nerve and she knew it.

"I saved your life!" Racita yelled.

"Racita--"

Khali started to soothe her wife but the damage had been done. Racita stomped out of the room. Khali sighed and tried to ignore the lab assistant and the other male, who eyed her as they followed their boss from the room. Khali looked down at her chest, thankful she could not see the little machines she knew were roaming around inside. She blinked away the tears forming in her eyes, cursing her apparent bad luck. She was not even forty and her body was already betraying her. Khali closed her eyes, exhausted from the encounter and fell into a fitful sleep.

"That's it, you're doing great," Racita cheered.

Khali rolled her eyes and looked over at her wife. Racita had made it a point to be at every single test and rehabilitation session. Khali loved her but she was suffocating her. Khali had grudgingly forgiven Racita for making her a lab rat. Racita's lab assistant had quietly dispelled any concerns Khali had over the technology and the known side effects. She could tell the young lady was devoted to her wife and had to squash the jealousy she felt. She knew her wife loved her--she just had to remind herself of that fact when she was hurt and angry. Khali returned her attention to the young lab assistant.

"You really are exceeding expectations!" The assistant agreed with Racita.

"Yay me," Khali mocked.

The assistant ignored her dour mood and looked to Racita for instruction. Racita smiled gently, the way a mother smiles at a fearful child, and nodded. The young woman removed the testing wires and nodded at hesitantly patted Khali's hand. Khali forced a genial smile at her and waited for her to leave the room. As soon as she was gone, Khali glared at Racita.

"She is just trying to help, Khali..." Racita began her usual lecture.

"Can I just go home now?" Khali said through gritted teeth.

Racita picked up the paper print out and looked it over, taking way too much time in Khali's mind. Khali tapped her fingers on the table, trying to be as annoying as possible and hurry her wife to make a decision. She knew the extra noise would throw Racita off and it pleased her to be able to show a small form of rebellion. In the lab, Racita was the queen, therefore, everyone listened to her and ignored Khali's requests without direct permission from their boss. It irritated Khali to feel so helpless. She would definitely be punishing her wife in her next book. Racita appeared to ignore Khali and continued looking at the printout and checking her notes. She looked up from the papers with a blank expression on her face and waited, baiting Khali into a staring contest. After several tense moments, Khali sighed and lost the battle.

"Racita, let me go. I'm fine now. The little bastards are doing their jobs!" Khali exploded.

Racita nodded. "It appears you are safe. You can come home, but we will need to continue coming in for monitoring and you will need to take it easy for the first few weeks."

Khali gave a long-suffering sigh. She would like nothing more than to never see the lab again. However, she knew Racita would watch her with an eagle eye and her freedom was more important than trying to argue anything with her wife. Racita had won. For now.

Khali began having massive, vision blurring headaches two years after she had experienced the first headache. Racita had run every blood test known to medical science--including genetic tests and bone marrow biopsy. She could find no reason for the initial heart failure, nor any reason for Khali's continued weakness. However, after a month of being home, things had finally returned to normal. Khali finally forgave her wife for the nanobots working day and night on her heart. She could not feel them but she was nonplussed they were there, doing god knows what. Racita finally left her in blissful silence and the nurse assigned to her was returned to the test subject wing at the lab. Khali didn't understand how the people could bring themselves to agree to be guinea pigs in the first place. She liked her blood and tissue all where it was and did not want that to change.

The first headache came on so suddenly, it stole Khali's breath away. She sat on the couch for untold minutes, hoping beyond hope she wasn't experiencing anything that would send her back to the lab. She was not interested in going back for more nanotech. She'd been writing a particularly steamy love scene in her novel when her visions completely blacked out and the pain in her head felt like a giant was standing on it. She reminded herself to breathe, using the techniques a therapist had given her years before when she'd needed a boost of self-confidence and a way to get through a particularly traumatizing class.

Breathe in through your nose for a count of four. Hold it for a count of six. Breathe out through your mouth for a count of eight. Slowly. Don't rush. In, two, three, four. Hold, two, three, four, five, six. Out, two, three, four, five, six, seven, eight. Very good. Again.

Khali repeated the mantra in her head as she breathed in and out, willing the pain away. Eventually, the pain receded and she stood on shaky legs, walking to the kitchen and pouring herself a glass of water. She thanked her lucky stars Racita was still at work. Every little ache and pain sent her wife into a tizzy of questions. Khali answered each one with growing impatience until she would finally explode, yell at Racita, and make it up later when she had cooled down. She knew Racita was only concerned for her well-being, but she hated being babied by the woman she loved. She wanted to feel like an equal partner, not an invalid in need of constant supervision.

The headaches were sporadic, at first. They would come and

go at random times. Thankfully, Khali was able to hide them. She'd almost been found out one evening as she and Racita lay in bed but had been able to disguise the pain with breathing to mimic sleep. She thought Racita had seen through the ruse, however, her wife merely kissed her forehead, turned out the light and fell fast asleep within a minute. That night, once the headache receded, Khali secretly wished very bad things on her wife. She had struggled so much with sleep and yet her wife could fall asleep standing up. It just wasn't fair. However, she had to admit, in this instance, it saved her from returning to the lab for ungodly amounts of testing.

Eventually, the headaches became more and more frequent. She began to walk around with a constant pallor and a return to the weakness she felt after her heart failure. Racita began to notice but Khali cut her off any time she seemed to begin suggesting she go in for tests. One evening, Khali was just finishing the kitchen cleaning when a particularly nasty headache sprang up behind her eyes. She gripped the edge of the counter, completely blind to her surroundings. She felt Racita come up behind her, resting her cheek on her back. Racita squeezed her hand and Khali focused on the pressure while she breathed in and out. In due time, the headache subsided but Khali stayed where she was beside the counter.

"You have to come in and let us check it out," Racita said softly.

"I know," Khali replied sadly.

Racita kissed Khali's back and helped her into bed, snuggling up against her wife and falling asleep. Khali sobbed quietly, not wanting to wake her wife. She contemplated all the ways she could say goodbye without hurting Racita but she knew she was not yet strong enough to do it.

"Racita, this has to stop," Khali pleaded.

Racita's back stiffened and she ignored Khali, continuing to look at the monitors and write her notes. The new lab assistant attempted to appear as if he was not listening but Khali could tell he was all ears. He'd only been working in the lab for two months but already he had learned no one spoke to Racita in the way Khali got away with on a daily basis. He almost looked fearful every time Khali would yell and scream. Racita was known to be a strict boss and he had earned her wrath several times in his short tenure.

"Racita!" Khali yelled.

Racita looked up nonchalantly, "Yes?"

"I don't want this anymore. I never wanted it in the first place. *I hate it here*! I am becoming more machine than human."

Racita rolled her eyes. The lab assistant made the mistake of catching her eye at that moment.

"Leave, now!" she demanded.

He nodded and left the room more quickly than Khali had ever seen anyone move. She didn't blame him. Racita could be formidable in her determination. Her wife turned back to her and narrowed her eyes.

"You are being too damn dramatic. You are still you. The nanobots aren't sentient, they do what I tell them to do," Racita explained with deadly calm in her tone.

"They change my thoughts! I can't write anymore."

Racita shook her head. "You're just too weak at the moment. We will fix this and you will be fine. We will grow old together and sit on our patio with chai watching the sunset. You'll see."

Khali closed her eyes, picturing the scene in her head but every time she tried, she only saw an older but still magnificently beautiful Racita and someone that looked vaguely like her in a wheelchair with wires and monitors everywhere. She couldn't get her failing body to look any better. Khali opened her eyes and locked them with Racita. She held out her hand. Racita paused a moment and took it, sitting next to her wife on the bed.

"You are the love of my life. Your research is amazing and I am sure it will help many people but my body is resisting. I don't want to be this," she said as she gestured to herself, "for the rest of my life. Please, darling. Please stop."

Racita shook her head sadly. "I can't lose you."

Khali nodded. "I know. I will be around for a good while longer. You said the nanobots already in my heart, lungs, and brain will continue repairing me for many years. Just...no more."

Racita appeared to consider Khali. She looked around the room at the monitors and the sun streaming through the window. She looked everywhere but directly at Khali. She gave Khali's hand a squeeze, gathered her notes up and left the room. Khali breathed a sigh of relief until she saw the door close and heard the click of the lock.

"No! Racita! Get back here!" Khali screamed.

Khali frantically turned on every gas container in the lab. She didn't know how much time she had but she knew she had to hurry. The young male lab assistant had run to find Racita the minute their crazed patient had burst into the door. He had been the only occupant of the lab at the time, so it suited Khali to finish before anyone came back. She'd slammed the door shut and locked it. She tried to find a lighter or something to make a spark. She didn't have any clue how much damage she would cause, she only knew that it was her only escape.

Earlier, a nurse had entered Khali's room to take her vitals and give her food. Khali had made an excuse that she would really love iced tea with her dinner. The admission had astonished the nurse, since it was well known Khali would be out on a feeding tube if she kept refusing her meals. The nurse had been so excited to please Khali and hopefully Racita in the process, she had energetically left the room to fetch the desired item. It was the opening Khali had been waiting for.

Banging on the door got her attention and she looked out the big picture window. Racita and several others had burst into the anteroom and were trying to get into the lab. Khali stopped her search and locked eyes with Racita. She could see the barely disguised panic in her wife's eyes. Racita reached next to the door and pressed a button.

"Khali, don't be rash. Please open the door. What purpose does this serve?"

Khali shrugged. She watched Racita give some kind of order to a man in the anteroom and he left. Khali only spent a moment wondering what was happening before returning to her search. She finally found a bunsen burner. She smiled to herself and set it up. She heard the intercom click again.

"What are you doing?" Racita asked, clearly annoyed.

Khali moved aside and revealed the burner. She saw the quick recognition on Racita's face. Her wife leaned back and looked at something above her head. Khali assumed it was the gas monitors. Often, the lab used assorted gases for the various nanobots and the monitors warned other scientists when it was too dangerous to enter the lab, for fear of causing a spark. Racita's eyes widened and she shook her head in horror. She moved back to the intercom and held her hand out but waited, watching Khali. Understanding passed between them and Khali acceded, moving towards her own intercom.

"Khali, please don't do this," Racita pleaded.

Khali pushed the button. "It's the only way I can be free. I love you more than the strength of a thousand suns, my darling, but I cannot live this way. You won't ever let me go, will you?"

Racita shook her head. "Not if I can help it."

Khali nodded. "Then this is the only way."

Khali stepped back from the intercom. She put her hand up against the window, trying to hold Racita close one more time. Then she stepped back to the bunsen burner and fiddled with the knob. It felt as if an eternity passed, though Khali knew it had been mere seconds.

"Please open the door, Khali!"

Khali breathed in and out, the way she had always done to calm herself and turned on the bunsen burner.

100 Years Later

Inside the biological sciences and technology building at the museum, Annie stood in front of a glass case containing a very strange object. It appeared to be a brain, though this one was flattened in one area and an oddly sick shade of cream, almost grey but not quite there. Annie squinted at the brain-like object. She could swear she saw movement but every time her eye moved to the area she thought moved, it would disappear again. Finally, she noticed the magnifying glass hanging just beside her knees. She picked up the glass and peered through it. She gasped, noticing the now magnified nanobots moving around the brain. Annie was fascinated by biotech and she squealed in delight.

"Annie, it's time to go home now," her mother reminded her.

"Just a moment, mom," the ten-year-old replied.

Annie looked for another minute through the glass and then gently set it down. She read the plaque next to the brain.

"So cool!" she exclaimed.

Annie turned and joined her mother, chatting on and on about the brain as her mother only half listened.

Inside the building, the lights dimmed on another visiting day. The nanobots slowed their activity and they appeared to be resting. The placard next to the brain was still illuminated, although now in much more shadow.

Khali Brain

This brain is all that remains of one of the early versions of the biomedical nanobots discovered by Doctor Racita Hashim. The nanobots will run continuously for many hundreds of years before their power depletes and they become silent. The technology shown here was the breakthrough in biotech, which led to the modern medical treatment of many once fatal diseases. These nanobots continue to repair the brain and it produces an electrical output as shown by the EEG monitor shown here, which indicates the brain is still a viable organ.

Interesting fact: The name Khali is an Arabic name meaning "Immortal."

The monitor showing the EEG spiked as the nanobots began their sleep cycle. Inside the brain, Khali's consciousness awakened. Unable to see, hear, or process any information from the outside, Khali was stuck in an endless loop. Over and over she screamed at herself.

"Please let me die! I don't want to live forever!"

LIFE, AFTER A FASHION
BY MARSHALL MILLER

I s it alive?" The question emanated from the mouth of a classically attractive young blonde woman with new music video good looks and clothes.

"After a fashion, Jeanie, yes." Barbara Bell glanced at her roommate as she answered. Jeanie's airhead blonde image belied a sharp mind, which was why Barbara could accept her as a roommate. Barbara was in the vernacular a cute looking brunette with a fit body but could never compete with Jeanie's T-and-A accouterments.

Both young woman looked intently at the contents of the small terrarium. It was the color of vintage paper, patinaed by time into a shade neither grey nor white but suspended somewhere in-between. The glass protected it from casual hands, but if a viewer leaned close, a keen eye would see the faint, crimson veins still pulsed with life.

"What do you mean, Roomie?" asked Jeanie Vang.

"Well, it's a mixture of old recovered DNA mixed with some new DNA we harvested in the lab. We adhered it to a sample of what could only be classified as artificial flesh, again produced in the lab.

Mix it all together and viola. Life. After a fashion like I said."

"So the... flesh has some growing veins and vessels," added Jeanie.

"Like I always say, you put a negative to all those dumb blonde jokes, Jeanie."

Jeanie lightly smacked Barbara's arm at the oft said comment and smiled. Despite their different backgrounds, they were friends. Barbara kept getting vibes that maybe Jeanie wanted something "more" after Barbara had gone out of her way to mention she was polyamorous on multiple occasions. Jeanie had many a male admirer in the Puget Sounds area but gave Barbara that 'look' which in the beginning scientist's experience meant she was interested in a physical way. Barbara had often wondered who or what she was primarily interested in sexually, which could explain Barbara's overwhelming interest in biology and zoology, both of the living and the dead.

"So, why did you bring your 'experiment' home?"

"Well, Jeanie, this is just a small part. A bit of leftover I guess you might say."

Jeanie frowned. She was working on a psychology degree as opposed to Barbara's work on a Masters in physical science. Jeanie understood laboratory protocols, especially when it came to growing life in a test tube or terrarium.

"It's not going to grow, crawl out during our sleep and start eating us, like that old classic Sci-Fi movie we watched the other night." A similar interest in such movies was a source of bonding between the two young women.

"No, my dear. It is not *The Blob*. It is something... different."

"Okay, Barb. Let's stop with the mystery. I may look like an airhead blonde, but you know I'm not."

Jeanie's roommate signed. How to explain what she planned to do while away from the confines of the University laboratories. After all, she had been the one who had found a way to combine the DNA of the old dried out sample of flesh discovered in China with current living DNA of related creatures. Or, supposed associated animals.

"Well, I plan to create a womb or egg-like structure for this sample to grow in and see what happens. We created this in the lab. Actually, I did the heavy lifting. After proving what can be done, the lab proctor decided to freeze the samples and go on to something else." Barbara sniffed. "He has no imagination or drive. Just a University bureaucrat."

"So you are going to try and grow that sample into... something?" Barbara paused for a moment. She needed to explain what to some would be an arcane process. At least Jeanie was smarter than most people.

"Just as a male sperm and female gamete-ovum join to form a fertilized egg, a zygote, I hope to stimulate the cells on this flesh or skin tissue to behave much the same way. In other words, I hope that this sample has enough pairings of DNA to begin to grow into a viable being. It should be a simple life form so a simplified version of a human womb should suffice for some type of embryo to form."

"How far do you plan to take this development?" Jeanie's still had a frown on her face. Barbara knew she would have to be careful as to how she 'sold' this project to her roommate so as not to start a fight. Barbara needed some privacy to finish this project to prove to Mister Stuffy how he was so slow and unimaginative.

"Just far enough to show it is viable. At least in the sense that if allowed to proceed, not be aborted, a creature would result."

Barbara took Jeanie's hands her hers and looked into her eyes.

She tried to present to her roommate the most caring expression she could, using every bit of mental manipulation she could. Barbara was very good at manipulating most people. However, she had never tried it on Jeanie, a 'true friend.'

"Look, honey. I know I am asking a lot of you. No one likes their house turned into a work station, not even in progressive Washington State. But this is small and will be kept in my bedroom. I promise."

Jeanie finally gently squeezed Barbara's hands and smiled with a twinkle in her eye.

"Well, I guess if that does turn into a 'Blob' and takes over your bed, you could rack in with me."

Barbara smiled back with her best smoldering come hither look she could muster. She sealed the moment with an unexpected kiss on the lips.

"Thank You so much, Roomie. I owe you." She paused and licked her lips. "Just say how I can... pay you back."

Barbara thought sure Jeanie would try and use this moment to make a move towards a more physical relationship, with which Barbara would have no real problem.

Instead, Jeanie paused, winked, as her mouth formed into a coquettish smile. "Let me give it some thought, Roomie."

Barbara was busy the next couple of weeks setting up the artificial womb she had envisioned in the terrarium. Secreted in her bedroom, Barbara stole and scavenged material from the University while working on her Master's dissertation at the same time. She noticed Jeanie was getting on edge with all of her concentration on 'the project' with no time to even have a conversation. The morning she saw Jeanie pouting, Barbara knew he had to do something to keep Jeanie from venting her frustrations to others. Secrecy was a key element at this critical stage.

Barbara hurried home from her university laboratory. She had stopped and bought an extra-large meat lovers pizza at the local student hang out. A weakness for meat on pizza (no anchovies) was another shared characteristics of the two roommates. Barbara called out as she entered the smallish rental house built in a bygone era, but still comfortable.

"Hey, Roomie. Pizza! Just like you—"

The front door shut from Barbara's butt push as she stood frozen and stared. Standing just a few yards away was Jeanie in a sheer black robe that left little to the imagination. As Barbra tried to stutter out a comment, the nightgown slid to the floor as Jeanie stood, then moved her hands to her hips.

"Well, Roomie. Time to pay what you owe me for putting up with your project." Jeanie winked as she smiled.

The pizza was still on the floor near the front door, now cold as two nude young women lay in bed together, holding hands. Both the roommates had smeared makeup, messed up hair, small hickeys on sensitive areas of their bodies. Barbara remembered dropping the pizza and clinching with Jeanie as she kissed her. Then Jeanie took the dominant role, pushing the brunette against the wall and ripping her blouse open. The buttons popped and went flying as Jeanie went for Barb's bra and freed the beautifully-shaped breasts. Not as endowed as the blonde, Barbara still had well-formed boobies on which Jeanie quickly focused her attention. After kisses, nips, squeezing, tweaked nipples, and sucking, Barbara was soon moaning with desire. Before she realized it, Jeanie had Barbara over the blonde's strong shoulder and carried her to the roommate's bedroom. Jeanie plunked Barbara on the bed and had the scientist's shoes, jeans and underwear off— "These panties are now mine" Jeanie had said with a grin—in no time.

Barbara then began to respond more aggressively, playfully yanked the blonde's hair so Barbara could maneuver her over and allow the brunette on top. Now it was Jeanie's turn to have her tits womanhandled to the point she was moaning in appreciation.

Hands and fingers wound up between thighs, digits penetrating tightly trimmed pubic bush to find very moist flesh. It became a contest to see who could make the other orgasm first. They both lost.

A few hours later, the two sweaty and exhausted ladies laid next to each other.

"I thought you may be bi, Jeanie, but... Damn!"

"I knew you were interested, but no moves for some three years. I was beginning to get an inferiority complex."

Barbara turned towards her roommate and kissed her. Jeanie responded, then pulled back.

"Hey. Should we talk about this, Barb?"

"Like how? We both like women at times, and we both really care about each other."

"I don't do one night stands, Barbara. In my early years as a cheerleader maybe, not now."

Barbara paused for a moment, framing her thoughts. There was an odd stirring inside she had not felt before. Was this True Love?

"So, Jeanie, is this love?"

"Could be. All I know is I want to stay with you."

"Is that a proposal for some kind of bonding or marriage?" Barbara asked.

"Damn, you are so freaking analytical at times." Jeanie reached for her roommate and pulled her close until their breasts pressed up against each other. She held her mouth inches away from

Barbara's mouth.

"Your move," Jeanie heavily breathed as she spoke. Barbara licked Jeanie's lips with her tongue.

"How about we say we are partners for now," Barbara suggested.

"Lab partners?" Jeanie asked then open-mouth-kissed Barbara. After a few moments, Barbara pushed Jeanie back a bit.

"So you want to go the full shebang on my project?" the brunette asked.

"If I am going to share my bed with you in addition to sharing this house with an ever-expanding experiment, yes."

"Thus my bedroom becomes ground zero for the great discovery."

"And with that, Barbara, dearest, we need to pause in lovemaking so you may show and explain to me exactly what you are doing."

The two lovers stood nude near a now oversized terrarium. Inside was an oval object that may have been what Barbara called a womb but what Jeanie quickly identified as an egg.

"Well, the sample from China may have been from egg layers, but no one is sure."

"Dinosaurs, Barbara? I read the Chinese are unearthing literal tons of fossils."

Barbara gently patted Jeanie's left butt cheek.

"Nice to have a partner as well read as you. The answer is, maybe. The fossilized sample was a bit... different than the dinosaur remains around it. Which may be why a minute bit of DNA somehow stayed. Those Jurassic movies have a bunch of B.S. in them. DNA and RNA degrade to primarily dust over millions of years, impossible to accurately type and reconstruct."

"Well, then, did it come from a later era?" asked the intelligent blonde.

"That is the majority theory. Something was later feeding on dino bones and was also trapped and fossilized by another nasty event."

"So, what did you use to fill out the DNA strands so you could have a flesh sample."

Barbara smiled at her lover.

"You thinking about changing majors, Jeanie? You're talking like a biologist or paleontologist. I used a modern close relative to a T-Rex. Chicken DNA from a large Rhode Island Rooster."

"I don't do things half-assed, Barb. If I'm going to be part of this, I need to know everything."

Jeanie started to touch and squeeze the joints of the heavy duty glass tank.

"You need some help in rebuilding this enclosure of yours. Especially if something actually hatches from the egg there. Don't argue, Barbara. THAT is an egg. I think maybe some of your samples migrated while you were sleeping to help in modifying the shell."

Barbara snorted. "Too many movies, Jeanie. How can something that primitive migrate? I must have just mixed the right stuff for a shell, not a womb. And what do you know about construction techniques?"

Jeanie's mouth formed a sly smile.

"I guess I never told you the whole story of the family business."

"Jeanie, I know your family owns a large car dealership. What has that to do with making glass or plastic containers?"

"Well, in addition to making some bucks so I can spend a lot on college, the family business meant I could hang around various repair and body shops. I was a little grease monkey, much to the consternation of my parents. They wanted me to be a 'lady' in the traditional sense. Greasey hands? Forget it."

"What happened then?" asked the biology and zoology major.

"I still hung around the grease monkeys, as I am just as stubborn as my father. I showed him that a little Lava soap did not make my skin leathery and I did not turn into what he called a *dyke*." Barbara frowned at the 'D" word. That was an insult she had heard before when she told people she was polyamorous and did not dress "feminine" enough.

"Your dad is a bigot?" Barbara asked.

"Maybe. Or just not enlightened. My dad hired gay mechanics if they could do the job. At the same time, he referred to people as Homo Hank and Queer Bob. We even had a Dyke Debby." Barbara's face flushed with some anger.

"Sorry, but your Dad pisses me off. When I meet him…"

"Oh, so we are a formal couple. Great. I'll send out the engagement announcements."

"You are such a little smartass sometimes, Jeanie."

"Hey, Lover," responded the blonde. "This ass is not little. It is nice, full, rounded, and you love laying on it. Lighten up. Don't get triggered by little shit."

Barbara looked at Jeanie and once again realized she had been guilty of underestimating her. In the back of her mind had been the stereotype of a big-boobed blonde airhead, despite the education Jeanie was getting. Plus, she was definitely not pampered despite coming from a family with money.

"Okay, Jeanie. Point taken. Now, I have to see about maybe increasing my student loans to cover…"

"Stop right there, Partner," interrupted Jeanie. "If I am in for a penny, I am in for a pound. I have bunches of money stashed away. I was paid for the work I did at the dealership, and I won many a poker game. Guys love to buy blondes dinners and drinks, so my expenses have not been much. Other than the black negligee I bought to seduce you."

Barbara's mouth dropped open. "You little..."

"Bitch is maybe the word. Or perhaps cunt is the word you are thinking. I've heard them all when you are supposed to be a dumb blonde looking for dick."

Barbara stood silently for a moment. This was going to be an interesting relationship. She felt the funny little butterfly feeling in her stomach and lower regions. If this wasn't love it was close to it.

"Okay. Sorry I get irritated easy. I've had to work around who I am for quite a while. And my family is not well off. At the same time, I am not a charity case." Jeanie turned towards her and took Barb's hands in hers. "Cut to the chase, Barbara. I'll be blunt like my dad. I do love you. I know you love me despite your confusion. Lovers help their lovers. So, in my spare time, I get the materials and expand your terrarium into more of a compound or cage for the babies I believe will come from that egg."

"For a non-biologist, you sure are certain of what is coming out of the so-called egg."

"Yes, I know. I can be cocksure, despite not having a cock. Now, let's take a break, eat some rewarmed pizza, then take a shower."

"Yes. Ma'am! When does the dominatrix outfit come out, Jeanie?"

"Later," the blonde replied. "Only I think it may fit you better, Mistress."

And it did.

The weeks seemed to fly by. Jeanie had built a state of the art enclosure in record time which took up most of Barbara's former bedroom. Both the women monitored the progress of the 'egg' which was now the size of one from a giant ostrich. Barbara scammed a small surveillance camera with a motion detector alarm and helped her lover install it so they could watch the egg from the shared bed. Since Jeanie was graduating in the coming spring, just as Barbara would be presenting her Master's dissertation, they were both already swamped. Thus, they had to fit everything into a tight schedule. Everything included lovemaking, which was a new found joy for both.

One late night, as the two were taking a few minutes to caress each other's nude bodies, the motion detector on the camera dinged. Jeanie had increased the alarm noise to more of a loud ringing bell, so the two women leaped out of bed to shut it off. As they both looked into the heavy-duty glass enclosure, their mouths fell open.

"My God! Something is moving that egg from the inside!" Exclaimed Barbara.

"Do we help whatever is inside break out?" Asked Jeanie.

"I say yes. The eggshell may be too thick."

With that comment, Jeannie dashed to the sleeping room and returned with a small craft hammer and a nail. The blonde used a surgeon's touch to poke two small holes in the eggshell, one causing a crack. No sooner did she do that but something began to widen the crack.

"Quick, Jeanie, face masks. We can't chance passing human germs that may be fatal to a newborn."

"I'll just shut and seal this cage until we need to handle the specimen," the blonde replied. As Jeanie was doing that, a large section of the egg broke open. Then as the hole in the shell widened, the egg rolled over, so the opening was against the sterilized soil on the bottom of the oversized terrarium. Suddenly, a snout poked through the hole. Then a second one slid through.

"My Lord. Twins." Barbara had no idea the egg could hold two viable creatures. For that to happen in the avian world would have probably resulted in dead or malformed young. Instead, the two living things broke the shell in half and stood to eye the area around them.

"Look at that, Jeanie. Both have bodies about six inches long, with about a four-inch tail. And they are bipedal, like a chicken."

"Or like T-rex," responded the blonde. "Their heads and jaws look like a miniature of the T-rex's. But those front limbs and claws look more Raptor like."

The lizards or dinosaurs or weird birds must have heard or felt the vibrations of the humans speaking as they looked thru the transparent glass at the blonde and brunette.

"Oh my God," said Jeanie. "They have dog eyes. They are smart. I can tell."

As one, the two dark colored creatures scrambled to the glass in front of the women and bumped into it, they then did what many a hungry hatchling does. They opened their mouth containing teeth-like structures, squeaked and begged for food from their parents. Jeanie hugged Barbara.

"Look at our kids! Aren't they beautiful?"

"And hungry, Jeanie. What do we have to feed them? I did not expect them to develop this fast."

Both women jogged to the kitchen and began scrounging up anything edible. After all, what did this new species eat? They looked like carnivores, but maybe they would want some plants. The two parents soon discovered they would eat most anything.

"They liked that leftover fish," Jeanie said, her comment a bit muffled by the face mask.

"And the pizza crust. And the meatballs. And the Spam. They drink water like chickens, tilt their heads back." Barbara looked at her lover. "What do we name them."

"Blackus Rexus after their true mother?" asked Jeanie.

"No, silly. What do we call each one?"

"You'll have to sex-type them first, right Barb?"

"Oh great, Jeanie. Now I have to figure that out," complained the brunette.

It took the two roommates a while but they were able to figure out one was male and one was female.. Just like ducklings, the two little beasts imprinted on Barbara and Jeanie as their 'parents.' That made their handling, even with rubber gloves on, so much easier. Thus, they accepted examination which led to gender identification in a general sense. Some quick research on reptile and avian diseases in captivity (what were they exactly?) and Jeanie made a quick trip to a large chain pet store for supplies. They named them Freyr and Freya, Norse Fraternal Twin Gods.

The male Freyr had a small bump on his nose that looked like a developing horn. That made it easier to tell the two apart as they were identical in color and shape. They also had a thin covering of hair-like structures developing similar to some dinosaur fossils, The pair grew at a quick rate. Thus, Jeanie had the thick-glassed enclosure expanded to three-quarters of the former bedroom. Somebody must have squealed to the landlord/owner of the house as he came over asking if they were performing unauthorized modifications. Not to mention the methane gas farts the two produced, which wafted out whenever the enclosure was opened. Jeanie stopped the investigation by a quick male fly unzip, some fellatio, and a promise to return the house to its original state.

"Why didn't you ask for help?" questioned Barbara.

"Hey, one knob job for him is enough. If we gave him two, he would really be suspicious. Next, he'd have DEA in here looking for a meth lab."

Graduation time came, and Jeanie graduated with honors. Barbara's Master Dissertation went just as well. The two scientists found some substances that acted as mild sedatives and put the two reptiles/dinosaurs to sleep so that the two could go out and celebrate. Some friends tried to follow them home, but the now recognized 'couple' begged off, claiming they had their own private celebration planned.

At some three in the morning, the two lovers stood by the large enclosure and looked at their sleeping 'children.'

"You did good, Barbara."

"No, *we* did good, lover. If not for you, they would have died in a cramped cage."

Barbara grabbed both of Jeanie's butt cheeks and pulled the blonde to her.

"God, how I love you. Took me three years as a roommate to realize that."

"That, and a lab experiment. Barb, let's go to bed."

"Good idea, Jeanie. Like a character in the long cable, TV miniseries said, I want to eff your tits off."

The next day, in the light of day and two growing mouths to feed, Barbara and Jeanie then realized they had to look into the future. They kept Jeanie's parents away from the house during graduation by making some excuse of having to fumigate for bugs, Barbara's family not into celebrating a Masters Degree. But Jeanie would need to go visit family, and they both had to prepare for what would happen after Summer. Barbara looked towards a University paid position as she worked on her Ph.D. Jeanie would have to ask for some help from her parents to stay in school for a Masters Degree. No way did the two lovers plan to separate.

"I might be able to pass them off as mutant lizards or alligators."

"From where, Barbara? And how long will they live on their own?"

"Well, they can't get that much bigger, Jeanie. Some species grow to fit their habitat. The size of the enclosure may slow their development. That should give us some time to figure this out."

The next day proved the couple had no such time.

Barbara came home with a hangdog look on her face. She went into the shared bedroom and plopped down on the bed. Jeanie came from cooing to Freyr and Freya. The two creatures would chirp and sing back to one of their moms like parakeets.

"Those bumps above their shoulders look a bit larger, lover… hey, what's wrong? Your face looks like you just lost your last friend."

"I was offered a kickass job at the University," mumbled Barbara.

"Hey, that's great! What's the problem?"

"First year is in China."

Time seemed to freeze. Jeanie sat down next to her lover.

"Fuck," the blonde said. Then she began to cry. Barbara joined her, and they hugged.

"You'd better wait for me, Jeanie," Barbara said between tears.

"Hell, yes. We can tie the knot in secret, and you go overseas still single. The University doesn't need to know. I'll stay here, and hold the fort."

"With the 'kids.' By yourself? And work? Go to school? What if they keep growing?"

""We are *not* putting them down!" snapped Jeanie. The two sat silently.

Barbara broke the silence. "Let me do some phone work tomorrow. I may have some off the grid people who may take them off the record."

"No goddammed experimental labs, Barb. Not like the government treated those chimpanzees a few years ago."

"Give me a chance. Okay? Just give me a chance."

Freyr and Freya began to chirp and sing like overgrown parakeets as they waited to be fed.

Barbara did not sleep well that night. She noticed Jeanie must have had problems also as she was out of the bed for most of the sleep cycle. Barbara finally woke up and crawled out of bed.

She found an empty house. Jeanies and the 'kids' were gone. She screamed, then grabbed her cellphone. As the brunette started to hit speed dial, she saw the note taped on the enclosure.

"Sweetkins. Please don't be mad. I have a place where I can set them free. Mother Nature will decide if they can live. Love you with all my heart."

Barbara sat down and sobbed.

Some three hours later, Barbara heard Jeanie's SUV drive up. The enraged brunette met the blonde at the front door and tried to slap her.

"*Bitch*! I bred them! How dare you…"

Before they realized it, the two women were biting, scratching, pulling hair and kicking in a good old fashioned catfight. Jeanie may outweigh Barbara some, but the brunette was just as strong. They rolled around on the floor for a good five minutes, cursing and crying out of hurt and frustration. Being a dirty fighter from high school cheerleading days, Jeanie dug her nails into Barbara's right breast as she tried to twist it towards her mouth to bite it. Barbara clawed at the blondes face to stop her while raking her nails from her other hand down Jeanie's substantial chest. Suddenly, the two grown women looked into each other's eyes and froze.

"What the fuck are we doing?" asked Jeanie. They shoved each other apart. Barbara began to sob. Jeanie reached over hugged her, and she did not protest.

"Why? What did you do with them? I love you Jeanie, but…"

"I took them to an abandoned farm I know near the Canadian Border. That gives them a chance to die free, not in a cage."

"And if they don't?"

"Barb, they are creatures created in a laboratory. Do you think they can really survive and breed? As it gets colder, they will fall asleep and not wake up, as dogs do on a farm. Trust me." Barbara finally looked at her friend.

"At least they won't be tortured by some asshole in the lab as they use them for test subjects."

"Barb, I love you. I was just trying to keep you from feeling the pain of having to make this decision. Please. Give me a chance."

The brunette nodded yes, then stared directly into Jeanie's eyes.

"Just don't do this again. If you do, I'm gone. After I totally kick your ass."

"Deal, sweetkins. I'm sorry. Forgive me?"

"This time, yes. Just don't push your luck."

It took a few days for the women to clean up the enclosure and also to clean up their relationship. Barbara brought home a large bouquet of flowers just as Jeanie did. They laughed until they cried, then made soft love to each other as they repaired the damage to their partnership. In August, Barbara was off to the University of Bejing as an official representative of the University. The two women were secretly wed and planned a real ceremony when Barbara returned.

"Don't you go and screw some Geisha over their, Lover," said Jeanie.

"Those are in Japan, not China."

"I know. I was just trying to see if you were paying attention."

They kissed long and deep at SeaTac Airport, screw any looks they might get from less than understanding people. Then Barbara was on the plane.

It was the end of June and a beautiful sunny day in Seattle, Washington when Barbara landed at SEATAC International Airport. Via the wonders of the Internet (despite Chinese Government censorship and surveillance) Barbara and Jeanie kept in almost constant contact. The brunette could not wait to see your love again, get her home for some 'alone' time.

Traveling with Barbara from China was Senior Professor Heng Tse from the University of Bejing. He had been instrumental in providing the original samples to the University used in the experiments. Professor Tse told Barbara he was impressed with her abilities when it came to genetics and would help her achieve her Ph.

D. in record time. Everything was looking up as the Chinese National and Barbara were sent to separate lines at TSA then Customs and Border Protection.

Barbara approached the uniformed inspector with a smile on her face. She handed the black female officer her Customs declaration as well as her passport.

"What do you have to declare, Ma'am?" the officer asked as she perused the passport.

"Some gifts and some reference material. I'm traveling with Professor Tse from the Univesity of Bejing."

The Customs Officer frowned as she looked at Barbara's passport, then turned her face away as she mumbled something into the government radio.

"I hope my declaration is in order," Barbara said as she looked up to see three 'suits,' one male and two females approach from behind a cubicle partition.

"Ms. Bell? I'm Senior Agent Richard Johnson, Homeland Security Investigations," said the male. "You will need to come with us."

"What?" Barbara sputtered. "What is wrong? I'm…"

The large tall blonde female who made Jeanie look small growled at her. "Come easy or come hard. Your choice."

The third official was an exotic looking woman who appeared to be part near eastern and something else, having an attractive permanent tan. She presented a half smile at Barbara.

"Come, Ms. Bell. You do not wish to create a scene, do you?"

Barbara sputtered, then allowed herself to be guided to a back office. Senior Agent Johnson carried her bags with the help of a uniformed officer. In a moment a shaken Barbara sat with her back to the wall and faced what could only be a two-way mirror like she had seen in many a cop drama. The exotic looking officer then spoke.

"I am Special Agent Kim Kupar, also of Homeland Security. My tall friend here is U.S. Fish and Wildlife Agent Brenna Friberg. I will be interviewing your traveling companion Heng Tse as I speak fluent Mandarin Chinese. Thus, I suggest you be as honest as possible and hope your statement jives with his. Senior Agent Johnson will explain everything. Now please excuse me."

Barbara knew she was being "played" by the three Agent tag team, but for all her training and experience she was utterly flustered.

"Look, Sir, Ma'am," she began, " I am not smuggling anything, I have not done a single illegal act while in China. I have no idea why I have three Agents looking me over."

"As I believe a picture is worth a thousand words, here is a couple of photographs which should explain why you are here," said Agent Johnson. "That is before we give you a chance to explain."

The stocky but not short Senior Agent pushed two quality glossy photos towards Barbara. As her eyes focused on them, she gasped. The first was a cleaned up photograph of a larger than life Freyr and Freya. It looked like they were caught while moving down a forest trail. The second photograph showed both of them coming right at the camera, mouths open and baring longer teeth than Barbara remembered.

"My God! They're alive!" Barbara blurted out before she knew better.

"No fooling," said Agent Freiberg. "And if you look close in the second photo, you'll see a smaller version of them behind them. They had kids."

"I... I... we..." Barbara stammered as her brain overloaded. Their foster children were alive beyond all expectations, mated and reproduced. How?

"By the way, your spouse, Jeanie—yes we found the marriage

license—said the adults' shoulder bumps appear to be morphing into wings."

Agent Johnson pushed a form towards her.

"Here are your rights along with the basic crimes with which you are charged. Please read them. You have a Masters so you should understand them, but feel free to ask questions."

"Oh, by the way," the Senior Agent added. "The second photo is part of a video. The photographer was killed along with his wife and two children. Then they were partially eaten."

It was not the smartest thing to do, but Barbara began to spill her guts in between fits of crying. All she ever wanted to do was to create something no one else had or could create. Barbara had, and then people were killed because of her creation. She was Mary Shelly in reality, not fiction. As she went through another batch of kleenex, Agent Frieberg spoke.

"Your little experiment resulted in an invasive nonnative species to be inserted in a new habitat. Just like with pythons in the Florida Everglades, people and animals were put in extreme risk. Unlike the pythons, these creatures seem to be a new level of a predator, one of which we have no previous experience." The large woman brushed a loose wisp of blonde hair back.

"To say I am incensed that someone with your education would do something so dammed stupid and irresponsible is an understatement." The Agent glared at Barbara.

"If I could, I would tar and feather you."

"Agent Freiberg takes her wildlife seriously," Agent Johnson injected. As he finished speaking, Agent Kupar reappeared with a handcuffed Professor Tse. He was tall for a Chinese, but he seemed to have shrunk during the questioning.

"The Professor asked to see Ms. Bell before we take him to confinement." Kim Kupar stated. "I had to explain he does not have diplomatic status just because he is from University of Bejing."

"Please, Barbara," the Professor began to blurt out. "Tell them I had no…"

Agent Kupar cut him off with flawless Mandarin. Barbara had learned enough Chinese that she heard Tse told whining would do nothing for him as the U.S. Government had evidence that he had provided the tissue samples Barbara had modified to the University. None of the material brought in had ever been declared or cleared by any governmental agency in the United States.

Agent Kupar switched to English as she addressed the brunette scientist.

"It seems you are brilliant in your work. I have a strong background in zoology and biology, worked at the Woodland Park Zoo. I have only ever seen genetic manipulation like this once before."

"What was that?" Barbara managed to squeak out.

"Another Chinese attempt to create an exotic animal," Kupar answered. "A Sabre Tooth Cat."

"That was real?" Barbara asked. She had heard rumors in the University zoology system.

"It's still out there," Agent Frieberg growled out again. " I and Kim here were supposed to go looking for it when this happened." She cursed under her breath. "Can you imagine some large Cats in the Washington Forests, made for cold weather like during an Ice Age? They'll breed like rabbits."

"Well, this matter is more pressing," replied Senior Agent Johnson. "The Sabre Tooth has only killed the people who tried to breed him, not some family of tourists."

Barbara started to blubber but caught herself.

"Look it. I confessed," the young brunette said."I fucked up. I was playing with something I shouldn't have. But what can I do for... Jeanie?"

"Funny you should ask that," Johnson said with a slight smile. "We were thinking of a field trip."

After Professor Tse was transported to the Immigration Detention Center pending decisions on whether to prosecute him or just deport him, Barbara was allowed to clean up and put on some outdoor type clothes from her luggage. Then the Agents magically produced Jeanie. The two women were allowed to embrace and sob a bit before being separated.

"Your friend Jeanie here said she will lead us to the original drop off point for your pets," said Agent Johnson. "And I believe this two raptor-like creatures bonded with you both from day one. Correct?"

The two lovers both mumbled 'yes".

"They come when called?" Freiberg asked.

"Yes," Jeanie said. "They'll talk to you like parakeets and parrots. If I whistled, they knew it was food time."

"They sat on our shoulders like hawks," added Barbara. "Putting them down would have been like putting puppies down."

"They were like... family," Jeanie said. Agent Freiberg snorted.

"Yeah. Wild homicidal puppies that kill and eat humans."

"I thought they would go to sleep and die during the winter months," Jeanie replied. "That's why I let them loose."

"You did not realize that these creatures of yours had bird characteristics? That they are warmblooded like some of avians Professor Bell used for additional genetic material?"

"You did a workup on their DNA?' asked Barbara.

"I assisted in that exercise," said Agent Kupar. "However, you both are intelligent women and should have easily noticed they were not reptilian if for no other reason once they started growing feathered crests down their backs."

"Feathers?" Barbara looked at Jeanie with a confused expression on her face. "We saw some hair structures, no real feathers."

"A feather and some skin samples from under the fingernails of one of their victims helped us to determine who and what they are, and are not."

Jeanie's chin began to quiver. "I didn't want to hurt anyone or anything."

"You know," Agent Freiberg interjected. "For being so educated and intelligent, you bitches have no common sense." The large blonde lady turned and stomped off.

"I apologize for my fellow Agent," said Kupar. "But she considers herself a keeper of all the wildlife under her purview. So, she takes this case involving an invasive species very personally."

"So now, " added Senior Agent Johnson, "we come to the step where you two can help yourselves as well as deal with this mess you help create. Time for a field trip."

The married couple was allowed to ride together in the back of a black SUV with dark tinted windows. The Agents had escorted them to a secure area of the airport where several SUVs parked. Standing around them were some dozen tactically clad individuals with blackened nametags and wearing balaclavas which covered their features.

Barbara whispered, "Those are not Cops."

"Very observant," replied Agent Johnson. "They are members

of a particular unit that helped me out of a similar situation up in Port Angeles. I suggest you follow their instructions if they speak to you."

Barbara shivered, and Jeanie put her arm around her. Agent Freiberg set a long gun case on the hood of one of the SUVs and opened it.

"That's a capture gun, isn't it?" Barbara asked as Frieberg took the large rifle from the case. "You use that for large animals."

"Yep," the Agent replied. "I have three special anesthetic loads used on Crocs and Gators as your 'friends' may be more warmblooded but seem to be as aggressive as those descendants of dinosaurs you were trying to create."

"I count four shots," Barbara said as she leaned forward.

"The fourth will inject a binary acid into whatever it hits. You'll see why if we can find your 'kids,' ladies."

"Your job is to help us track and attract your creations," Johnson stated. "Then stay out of the way. If we can capture one alive, we will. If not..." The Agent nodded towards the black-clad personnel.

Barbara and Jeanie rode in the rear seat of an SUV with Kupar driving and Johnson riding shotgun. The two women were not restrained as where would they go? Running off into the forest was not an option. Jeanie directed Kupar to the part of the northern woods where she had released Freyr and Freya.

"We'll meet a couple of Border Patrol Agents up here," said Johnson. "Your creatures have been playing havoc with their border intrusion sensors. They were even smart enough to dig a couple up."

"They knocked down a drone also," added Kupar.

"How?" asked Jeanie.

"If we find them, you'll see."

Approximately an hour later the group of four SUVs was soon well off the beaten tracks. On a dirt road which ran up a small gully into Canada, the group met a 'Mean Green' marked vehicle. Two Border Patrol Agents were soon conversing with Agent Johnson. When Johnson pointed out the two detained women, one of the Agents with the nametag Moreno marched over to the passenger side open window.

"I just wanted to tell you that your dammed monsters killed my K-9," Moreno spat with anger. "I hope you have a long time in prison to think about your stupidity." The Border Agent then stormed back to his vehicle. Johnson approached the two shaken lovers.

"I guess I could have stopped him. However, I think you really need to realize the seriousness of what you did in creating this species."

"How many times do we have to apologize?" Barbara replied with some heat.

"Don't apologize, lady. Just help us fix this fiasco."

One of the balaclava-wearing men had a large mastiff type dog on a thick leather leash.

"That is a large dog for a tracker." Observed Barbara.

"That K-9 is more for takedown than tracking," said Johnson. "Your creatures have not developed any fear of humans, so they have not tried to conceal themselves. At least not the adults and near yearlings."

"They bred that fast?" Jeanie asked.

"Some of the government experts believe your two beasties were gravid weeks after hatching or birth. That is another argument. Was that artificial womb you made an egg, and do the lay eggs, or do they have live birth? Since no one has done a long-term study, cell samples give clues but not a certainty."

Agent Kupar walked up with a pump twelve gauge shotgun in each hand. "As you requested, Richard. Loaded with five slugs."

The male Agent took the offered weapon, jacked a round into the chamber and engaged the safety. He saw the two civilian women look at the shotguns with a bit of tribulation.

"Agent Kupar took a Bengal tiger down in her younger years, and I grew up hunting so no, we are not going to leave everything to our special black-clad friends."

"You shot a tiger?" Asked Barbara,

"It tried to eat my uncle," the darker skinned woman answered. "It went rogue, so we hunted and killed it on behest of the Indian Government. Not much different than this situation."

"So, ladies," added Johnson, "you stay at the back with us, Agent Freiberg will be rear security with the capture rifle."

"So shoot to kill takes precedence over trying to capture Freyr and Freya," stated Barbara.

"They kill people," answered the Wildlife Agent, " and should not exist here. So treating them like mad dogs is the concept of the day."

The two lovers became very quiet.

The two Border Patrol Agents were trained Trackers and knew the wooded area like the back of their hands. Their headquarters also had a surveillance drone up in addition to monitoring the border intrusions sensors upgraded recently. Barbara and Jeanie each had a small backpack with water and a couple of nutrition bars. As realized before, there was nowhere for them to flee, so no one worried about providing them items which would make their escape easier. The two young ladies kept in shape, so they had no trouble keeping pace with the government personnel. Everyone walked in silence.

Just under two hours into the trek and a radio crackled to life. The group halted as one of the Patrol Agents talked with their communications center. Agent Richard walked up and powwowed with the Patrol Agents and the leader of the special tactical unit. After a short conference, Richards walked back to the others.

"Several sensors hit right on the Canadian Border. Another reason we need to take care of this problem ASAP. We need an international incident like…"

The oversized mastiff K-9 let out a deep rumbling growl, followed by a single bark. The dog pulled on the leash and began to drag his handler forward.

"Contact," said Richards. Then Hell arrived.

Something of substantial size glided down at speed from a tall Douglas Fir Tree. At first, Barbara's mind said 'flying squirrel' then realized the figure was much too large. Before her mind could make an adjustment, a small but intense fireball smashed into a brush next to the moving mastiff. The dog handler began to beat out flames on his leg, then dropped and rolled. The mastiff took off like a freight train at the flying object.

"Dragon!" Someone yelled as weapons came up and the armed personnel looked for targets. There was growling, barking and an odd screaming as the K-9 mastiff caught something that fought back violently. Then another fireball streaked down from a tall tree.

"Twelve O-Clock High!" The warning was followed almost instantaneously by automatic weapons fire. Agent Freiberg shoved the two civilians to the ground as she brought the capture rifle up to the ready position. A black-clad warrior burst into flames as a new fireball found its mark. A comrade yanked a compact fire extinguisher from his pack and sprayed the downed man with foam before the fire spread. Then the shooting stopped, and an eerie silence engulfed the group of humans.

The bloodied mastiff brought his trophy back to his handler. Agent Frieberg grabbed Barbara by her arm, and half carried her forward to where the carcass lay.

"Is that one of them?" the Agent demanded.

Barbara looked closer at the dead winged animal. The colors were different and the photos Johnson had shown her was of a much bigger individual.

"One of their offspring," Barbara heard herself saying before it sank in. Freya and Freyr had kids. They were very dangerous kids who could fly and spit fire. What had she done?

"So they are flying dragons," said Kupar. "I thought it was all late night radio conspiracy theories.

"We raised dragons," Jeanie said. "How?"

"The supposed flesh sample was of a dragon creature, not some dinosaur or recent reptile," replied Kupar. "And you helped the Chinese make another unnatural chimera. Like my Saber Tooth Cat."

Jeanie let out a loud whistle, then a birdlike cry. Within moments there was an answering call from some thick brush. The tactical team used hand signals and were soon moving towards the source of the cry.

"Let us contact Freyr," Jeanie protested. "I'd recognize his voice anywhere."

"You have nice pipes," said Richard Johnson. "But, the only communication we plan on doing is to locate them so we can put them all down."

"No!" yelled Barbara. "They don't mean harm. They are just predators like we are."

"Predators which fly or at least glide and spit fire. The scientists told us they manufacture tons of methane in their guts and individual bladders. They use some sort of internal chemical reaction to ignite it." Barbara glared at him.

"You had a specimen already, didn't you? You did not learn this from a skin sample."

"A small one was caught in a large net a fishing boat hung out to dry and repair. It was chasing something and... *down!*"

Johnson knocked Barbara to the ground as a fireball missed her by inches. Agent Kupar's shotgun boomed three times, and something seemed to explode in the top of a tree.

"Hit them when they have a full load of gas, and they explode," said the female Agent.

"Please! Let me try to contact our creatures," Jeanie pleaded. "They'll come to us, then you can capture them."

"They did imprint on us, Agent," added Barbara.

A short burst of automatic fire interrupted the conversation. Agent Johnson fixed the two women with a hard stare.

"Go ahead and try. Did I tell you that these dragons breed like rabbits, but hunt like wolves? So, the next step is an airstrike with napalm on this entire area."

Jeanie whistled loud and hard, She then followed with a human version of a chirping parakeet.

"Come to Momma," Barbara called out. "Freyr, Freya, *come!*"

A loud chirping and cawing from out of the forest quickly followed.

"See, I told you they'd respond," Jeanie lectured. "Just let us approach the pair we raised and..."

Other loud chirping and cawing came from a spot behind the group of humans. Then another batch of sounds from their left, then the right. A cacophony of sounds formed a circle around the Homo sapiens.

"Well, *fuck me,*" Agent Freiberg said as she set the capture rifle down and drew her pistol.

HOPELESS
BY ELIZA LOEB

I have everything I could possibly want. I keep telling myself so, even though it means telling myself a complete and utter lie. And as I sit and stare upon the crumbling walls of a nearly condemned house with no proper sewage or running water. There is no money to fix things. There is nothing that is pertinent to survival. Banging my head against the wall, seems the only viable thing to maintain my sanity as the anxiety and poor state of mind seem to grow in a way that I don't want it to. The nightmares are more frequent. The fear that I may lose everything screams louder and no amount of music or distraction can possibly drown it out.

I am damned.

I am damned if I stay. I am damned if I leave.

And I fear that getting out may be more difficult this time.

I remember when I was very small. Both my father and grandmother's houses were like museums. Yet one breathed with more life than the other. My grandmother's house was very much alive, with lush gardens filled with hibiscus and honeysuckle. She had a lemon tree that grew in the far corner and small patches of jasmine growing wild as chickens would come in and out. And on some days the sun would shine through the windows and illuminate the halls and the living room as though my grandmother's home were some grand cathedral, or a sanctuary filled with promises of immeasurable joy and laughter.

I wish I could say the same for my father's home.

While beautiful to some on the surface, everything held a much darker meaning in my eyes. There was no promise of joy or laughter. Just beautiful things in glass cases for the world to see. Perhaps, on some occasions I would find an old painting mounted on the wall. Other times I would see frightening masks and artifacts that had been stolen from their homeland. The only real semblance of color that I remember of his house was a Turkish dagger that he had found during a tour in the middle east. He never told me where he had found it. Only that the man who had sold it to him said that it had belonged to a group of nomads who had lost to him in a gambling match. The sheath was the color of vintage paper, patinaed by time into a shade neither grey nor white. But suspended somewhere in between. The hilt glinted sterling silver and could easily catch the eye of guests when they saw it. Unfortunately, such a thing was not enough for me to find a sense of joy, nor laughter in my fathers' home. It served more of a reminder as to what my expectations were. How to act, how to not embarrass the head of the household and how to stay silent, yet still manage to be interesting. It made me feel like a bird in a cage. And when my grandmother died, that's all I felt I was. And as time progressed and the houses changed, they always somehow stayed the same. Eventually they began to reflect how I began to see myself.

Now, as an adult, I find myself in a predicament. I know that there is conflict and challenges, but my will to overcome both is almost non-existent. The years of expectations have run me ragged and I have no accomplishments to show for it. I am weary of others. My ability to trust is faulty and I would be lucky if I could find some semblance of joy for only a moment. But now is not the time. As I hear screaming from up and down the hall of this crumbling house, I feel helpless. There are no words to comfort me as of this moment and I am not sure if any ever will.

It's difficult, focusing on the good things in your life when there has already been so much bad.

I could have everything I possibly want. I try to keep telling myself so, even though I have nothing. I come from nothing and I have no legacy. And as I sit and stare upon these walls of a crumbling house, with no sewage or running water, I wallow in my own potential grave. I have no way to get out. I don't have the money or connections I need to get out.

I am damned.

I am damned if I stay.

I am damned if I leave.

And I am unsure if escape is viable at this point.

THE UNIVERSAL ALGORITHM
BY SHEILA MENGERT

Amidst the flood of raw data that like a tsunami floods our collective consciousness on a daily basis there once existed tiny archipelagos of meaning that were referred to as stories. The best of them manifested various aesthetic qualities, among which was integrity. In other words they manifested certain integral and particular characteristics just as light may manifest as either a particle or a wave. The election of one or the other manifestation appears to be final and irreversible. A wave will remain a wave and a particle will continue to act as a particle after it passes through what has been called the double-slit experiment. The relevance of this reflection when viewed from the peculiar vantage point of our contemporary world is that data remains for the most part as a cacophony of unrelated momentary observations unrelated to any final arbiter of truth or utility until it is politicized and claimed by the residual groups and persons who are able to act as those who count, the privileged context makers of the day. Theirs is the power and the glory of interpretation. They are the merchants of constructed discourse that by appropriating mere facts bestow the aura of meaning upon them that can determine the fates of lesser mortals. Without an aura of presumed meaning facts are a mere chaos of waves lapping at the shores of our attention and beckoning for our loyalty as adherents and consumers. The net result of this phenomenon is a fragmented populace devoid of character. The utility of the masses is relevant only by virtue of the sign value of who they have chosen as the guru of the instant to reduce all this surplus of information to simplicity once again. We live in the age of trademarks and of identity politics. Who needs a well-argued discourse when a mere phraseology will be sufficient for most purposes?

In the days before such favored agents of articulation we looked to institutions and to the learned disciplines in order to form our views. The idea of a dominant and commonly shared mode of discourse may have reached its apotheosis in the law. Anyone who ever strolls through a well-appointed law library would be startled at the sheer volume of existing law. How can such a colossus of reading matter be brought to bear to reach a definitive solution to any single legal problem? How does one quarry into the unyielding strata of such multitudinous layers of meaning? Is this the justification for the high prices charged by law firms?

Horizon Law was one of Seattle's most respected law firms specializing in international trade, IPO's, and intellectual property. As befitted its wealth and stature it was located in one of the higher buildings gracing the Emerald City of Seattle. Its stature and elevation guaranteed an uninterrupted view of Puget Sound and the Olympic Mountains beyond. The firm was a newcomer amidst the top-ten firms on the west coast. Its novel image and ethos had made it the firm to watch. The partners had discerned early on that the traditional image of bookshelves filled with dusty volumes bespeaking the wisdom of antiquity, thick carpets, and comfortable leather chairs surrounding heavy walnut desks did not impress the young clients from tech firms who were as apt to show up in chinos and wearing Nikes as they were to arrive in Brooks Brothers suits and Florsheim shoes. Legal services were increasingly measured by the same standards of bottom-line efficiency as any other endeavor.

The firm was located in the right place at the right time to take advantage of the tech boom. The west coast, the silicon empire, was already viewing the great eastern cities, New York, Boston, and even the tri-state suburbia surrounding the nation's capitol as backwaters dwelling in the same twilight that was settling down over the European Union that had once promised to be the means of ending all wars in that fractured peninsula. Economic growth and historical significance was shifting to Asia as the arbiter of the new epoch of world history; Seattle was only an ocean away from what were to be the main players in the new century: China, Japan, Indonesia, South Korea, and India. As for the middle of the country, the soybean and corn prairie states, and the rust belts of Michigan and Ohio, hungering to return to an imaginary time gilded with soapy nostalgia and universal virtues the clock of progress had stopped ticking long ago never to be rewound.

Every Monday the firm began the work week with an overview, how the firm was positioning itself on the big board of strategic jurisprudence. The task was to enhance perception, to read the signs in the swiftly turning whirligig of international finance. The philosophy of the firm was that nothing was to be accepted as a given fact but only as an obstacle to be overcome or be circumvented by creative posturing. Law was a field like the space-time continuum, growing, stretching, altering according to the mass of objects existing within it. Each partner and associate was required to take a course in modern physics in order to provide them with apt metaphors to describe the character of the times. It would never do to speak in a Newtonian script even in legal matters when they are encased in the quantum realities of today. Communication within the firm was enhanced by creative use of space. Gone were the corner offices, comfortable citadels to flatter costly egos and to impress associates with the august power of the men who were sucking up their youth with billable hours requirements. The usual partner/associate divide was replaced by bonuses allocated by anonymous voting of the entire firm on an excellence grid kept for each attorney and partner and filled in quarterly. Contradiction was welcomed and bootlicking was anathema. The result was a motivation and *esprit de corps* that had left firms using older management practices to drift into dignified obsolescence. It wasn't that the Horizon Law firm was necessarily progressive in a political sense. Client morality and politics were still secondary to the calculus of power. The best that could be said for the firm was that it practiced the art of the skillful win; the machete was traded for the scalpel. Nothing pleased the collective ego there as much as to see an opponent look at every square on the board before tipping the king over as a sign of the recognition of defeat by a master hand. Style, that was it! The key was to win from another dimension so that even the loser was awestruck by the sheer beauty of the take-down.

Associates were screened to weed out precisely the types of greedy sycophants that were once considered the prime-cuts to be served upon silver plates to their paunchy elders just settling into reap the long-deferred benefits of their own period of indentured slavery in the grist-mill of briefs and citations. In the new digital world of e-law even established private practices were yielding to market pressures applied by astute in-house counsel. Efficiency was the watchword of the day. Established relationships might be severed by the swiftly altering composition of partners, lateral hires, and the attrition of burned-out attorneys who were not content to become mere fixtures as so-called permanent associates. Legal business was fluid, fleeting, transitory, and contingent to price and the fulfillment of expectations. Nothing could be assumed or assured and for that very reason the trend was towards the creation of a mobile and evanescent organizational design that could bring swift force to bear when needed and as swiftly to disperse back into a low-overhead celestial presence when business slackened. Seattle was only the center of an extensive web of cellular presences in external offices overseas. In this way the firm hoped to survive the carnage that was to come in the broad and expansive new world existing beyond traditional notions of applied jurisprudence.

The presentation this morning was to be longer than usual, one designed to locate the firm in the climate of shifting events that every day makes up the world anew from the detritus of yesterday. The question posed was how to face squarely the slow subsidence of entire edifices of market capitalism and the by-product of industrial human obsolescence. It was becoming clearer each day that industry after industry was submerging beneath the chill waters as the internet, foreign competition, and robotics replaced domestic human skills and expertise. The firm was committed to a course of strict acceptance of facts no matter how frightening or unpalatable they might be. Swift adaptation was the price of survival. Nostalgia and a mournful spirit of resistance were pointless; to look back was to risk being transformed into a pillar of salt.

This particular morning as the young attorneys filed into the conference room and took their places they saw a new face at the rostrum. There was nothing unusual in this. Insight was as likely to come from a lecture by an engineer or an anthropologist as from another attorney. As befitted the informality of the firm the presentation began even as the last associates were settling in to their places at the conference table.

"Good Morning Counselors. You have by now had time to

peruse my little biographical summary in the handout so we will not dwell upon my professional history or publications. I will also not waste your time or the firm's generosity by seeking to amuse you or to flatter your vanity individually or collectively. Our subject today is survival and the future. I will speak bluntly and trust that you will do the same.

As attorneys we preside over the social structure of the law, not because we are 'to the manor born' but rather because we have developed a habit of mind and a set of substantive knowledge that maintains order and peaceful transitions in social affairs. We are quite often resented for our expertise when the resentment should be directed instead at the system that we alone are trained to comprehend and to navigate across the stormy waters of events. The laws embody both stability and contingency. When the laws operate properly confusion is minimized and the prediction of consequences of various actions becomes possible. There is even an aura of majesty from time to time in the pronouncements of judges and the arguments of counselors. Yet for all of that law is not an aesthetic discipline but one ordained to achieve practical ends at the least possible expense. The residue of outcomes is due to the complexity of living rather than to any deliberate obscurity in the laws. Arcane speech is a function of tradition rather than delight in novelty in coded utterances. The result is the many-faceted crystal of logical legal discourse that melds thought and feeling, humanity and technology, form and function to serve the interests of our clients as advisors and advocates before tribunals.

Having said this though I may have given the impression that what we have been in prior ages may continue in its essence into the practice of law as it now presents itself, the same story repeated with only minor variations. If I have given that impression please allow me to correct it immediately. The burden of my presentation today is to alert you to a great cyclone while it still hovers black and menacing on the horizon. The cyclone is the loss of what might be called an anchor for hermeneutic expression in established and shared traditions. Each day witnesses an increase in factionalism waged between various absolutist positions. Meanwhile the roles of mathematics and algorithms have so far exceeded our ability to test various hypotheses that any relation to the ordinary experiential realm is marginal at best. We have outstripped our supply of readily available metaphors to describe reality in a human way.

This general trend in post-modern thought and in science is directly relevant to the contemporary practice of law. Illusions are costly to both your clients and to you so we will agree to dispense with them here today. I would like to begin our discussion with a rather startling assertion: law as a collection of stories is dead. Most of you were educated according to the empirical methods of case study and analysis as advocated by Christopher Columbus Langdell the originator of the case-study method. A few of you may have taken seminars that have focused on Judge Posner's emphasis on law and economics. Fewer still have approached law as part of the science of public policy formation and social engineering rather than traditional legal process analysis. I would venture though to say that each and all of these fail to put the emphasis where it truly belongs: procedural law. Why is this so? It is because human beings like stories; we are charmed by irrelevant facts that lend color to what should be as dry and uniform as a quadratic equation. Once having accepted that story is dead we can proceed to a new theory of post-humanistic jurisprudence; we can strip law of its 18th century accoutrements with all of the lace trimmings, powdered wigs, and professionalism humbug. Law is far more akin to engineering, to fluid dynamics and network circuitry than it is to the so-called social sciences.

The social sciences were what the humanities called

themselves when human beings decided to seek predictability in their own behavior. We have all heard of the equating of madness and creativity. What they share is a disproportionate response to initial stimuli in order to produce something new and unprecedented. Where will we find such great leaps forward in the 21st century if not in artificial intelligence? Where would we have sought such leaps in the past? Anyone? Too early on Monday to venture an opinion? Very well, we would have looked to the storytellers, the intuitive artists, the inventors, yes and perhaps even to the madmen and madwomen. Alas, no more; every mental aberration possible has already been reduced to the great encyclopedia of mental disorders in the DSM-5. Where are surprises to be found then but in story-telling? I would like you to take note that there is a difference between story and mere sequential incident recitation. I would define story as the disproportionate response of environment to events such that outcomes are unpredictable: if the results are disproportionately unforgiving we have tragedy; if the results exact only a token payment for folly or ill-will we have comedy. Perhaps best of all are those stories that provide a resolution to an ambiguous and indeterminate moral situation involving character as in the movie *Casablanca*. Only when the plane to Lisbon is about to take off do we know whether Rick is a hero or merely a disgruntled opportunist. I tell you these things in order to awaken you to the value of stories before the ability to appreciate them is lost forever. Lawyers in the past were storytellers. In rural America no greater form of entertainment existed than to observe a contentious legal proceeding at the county courthouse. Ah but that was when eloquence trumped a mere factual recital and the mechanical application of precedent, before arbitration and mediation, before the science of economics came to be the ultimate resort for policy determinations.

Perhaps an example will clarify my meaning. We would all

agree that various addictions have multiplied to the extent that they are now a collective human blight on the city of Seattle. Viewed individually of course each addict's story is an example of the great loss of human potential. Viewed collectively on the other hand these various encampments are the equivalent of the barbarian invasions of ancient Rome. I heard the other day that the Chinese have agreed to limit production and exportation of Fentanyl to help prevent drug overdoses. Ideally this will create a more reliable and safer drug-taking environment and decrease the number of overdoses. Lives will be saved.

But let us step aside for a moment and ask ourselves if such predictability is a good overall solution to the problem of addiction when seen as a predictably constant commercial transaction. In most commercial transactions the producer seeks uniform product control and purity in order to increase sales through reliable customer satisfaction. But what if one out of every one hundred vehicles inexplicably exploded over the product's span of existence? Would people keep buying cars? Would there not be consumer complaints or a switch to other modes of transportation? Then perhaps when seen in its more inclusive perspective it would be better in order to solve the epidemic problem of addiction to increase the risks of drug taking rather than to diminish them. No one can predict the exact ratio of danger to ecstasy of course but it does exist. Find that proportion and extinction of the behavior or at least diminishment must follow. The key is structural abatement over time. In an unpredictable world we must adapt by becoming accustomed to the breakdown of comforting generalizations, the folly of misplaced hopes that everything will magically as in stories just somehow work out in our favor as individuals. We must instead grow wedded to chaos while simultaneously attempting to manage and direct it. We must surrender the comforts of the storytelling world and become adamantine structuralists using every tool of systems theory to achieve productive ends."

There was a significant pause at this point. The speaker scanned his audience, one trained in legal analysis, selected from among the best and brightest of their law school classes to sit atop the majestic tower suite of Horizon Law.

"Are you troubled by my assertions any of you? Are any of you wedded to the prior paradigm or at least as the poet says tempted to indulge in "one last lingering glance behind" before consigning the storytelling phase to history so that deliberative social engineering can take its place? Or perhaps your agile minds have already zeroed in on the weak point of my presentation thus far, the question of what counts as 'productive.' Without metaphysical notions of some sort how is progress to be measured. Would anyone care to cross examine me on the point? I am not as formidable as I may appear. After all, I must leave here when my little juggling act is complete but you favored ones will remain here in this fortunate realm of reason and rationale towering over the great unwashed city that lies below you. Perhaps my age has already rendered my little testimony moot and you are willing to allow me to strut and fret my little hour upon the stage and then be heard no more. I may even be a cunning exemplar of precisely that bent towards storytelling that I pretend to decry and to despise. My habit of quoting from the enemy may give me away. What has a determined structuralist to do with literature? Ah but then as Walt Whitman said, 'Do I contradict myself? Very well, I contradict myself.'

I will answer your unspoken doubts by explaining that there is no absolute ground for what shall count as productivity. Zealous advocacy will allow you to vault over the question and simply serve those among the elect who can afford to pay you. Do not be persuaded that you must consider other voices in the great democratic vista of America. 'The people' is simply another poetic abstraction. Wipe from your minds that homespun image of the Norman Rockwell painting and its proud assertion that the individual voice matters unless it is mirrored by an extensive following in the social media. Do not expect sense to emerge from the great conglomerate of consumers. They are merely the clay to be molded to the designs that you must supply in answer to the desires of your select client-base. If you wish to save anyone from folly; save them. Structure has value because it surpasses personal motivation by dictating results at the highest and most general level. It is the difference between attending to the individual sheep and moving the herd. Storytelling is always damaged by its tendency to overvalue the particular; we shall manage by husbanding the most palatable generalizations in order to move multitudes at once. It is the secret of all leadership to weld the individual to the nearest coherent mass. A world of 7.7 billion people cannot afford the luxury of sustained debate about a problematic future. In the collisions of various cultures and mindsets only the most organized and determined mass propositions will prevail.

From this initial insight let us proceed to the next point. The philosopher George Santayana had it wrong when he said that those who fail to study the past are condemned to repeat it. He was wrong because it is precisely the past that law must repudiate if it is to keep up with the pace of expanding digital networks and artificial intelligence. It is not sufficient to ignore the rule of *stare decisis*; we must plunge a dagger into its heart. It is our expectations of the possible that constrain us in arriving at innovative solutions as lawyers; it is the presumption that substantive law is anything more than one option among many that defeats us on the threshold of new discoveries and social amalgams. We must see the past just as it is: as just so much detritus piled upon the refuse heap of history. We must cease looking for patterns or anticipating a return to past glories.

Where then shall we look to find the law, you are no doubt asking yourselves! Ah here you have anticipated my next point. Your metaphor is misplaced. The law is not to be found; it is to be created and it is creative procedure that tells us how this is to be accomplished. Lawyers are no longer to be merchants of the probable; they are to evolve into architects of the barely conceivable. Nothing is pre-packaged. There are no atoms only a swarm of sub-atomic particles zipping along through various fields of influence, attraction, and repulsion. There are only effects; causes are a waste of time because to determine them is to indulge in futile retrospection. We should abhor generalities as time-consuming exercises in self-indulgence. No two cases should be won in the same fashion. Where is the artistry in that?"

Another pause, the eyes of the speaker sought that same glint as of a jungle cat in the eyes of his listeners.

"I see that I have your attention at least but not yet your assent. Good! What conversion is worthwhile if it comes too easy? Let us move on. No doubt you realize that security is the illusion that must be most fiercely unmasked. The world is invented anew with each circling of the sun. Will Putin annex the Ukraine? Will he push the limits of our will to enforce the Monroe Doctrine in Venezuela? Will Kim Jong Un soon send a rocket on an arc that can re-enter the atmosphere without burning up? Will the Brits beg the Germans to let them come back within the fold of the European Union if a premature Brexit without an encompassing deal occurs? We are all part of one continuous newsfeed that makes the world up anew with each dawn.

A sense of story on the other hand demands continuity, ascertainable motivations, a context of stable meanings and values, and social recognition, what might be called resonance. Where are these treasures to be found in the digital age? The answer is nowhere;

we have extinguished them and our humanity with it. The human race has outlived its usefulness to the machines that we are meant to serve. Machines are our destiny. Machines are our soul. We are becoming machines!"

The room fell silent. There were a few troubled faces while the rest sat still, polite, and open to whatever was to come next.

"Does this all sound strange to you? If so you have not been keeping abreast of events. The world of carbon-based life-forms is dying. Silica is the new carbon. What will be required in the new age is a translation of the information content of our brains, the bits of jelly-fish goo in our skulls into endlessly replicable silicon micro-circuits. Someday that thing which is you will be backed up on the future equivalent of a thumb-drive. It does reincarnation one better: you will never have to repeat a grade. Your existence can be as fixed and absolute as the continents; you will be immortal even if no longer a willing agent. The human is something to be overcome just as the human left the animals behind with the invention of language. We finally located the problem. We made being human the status quo rather than what it is: a defunct appendage on the way to a new life-form.

Wasn't this what religion was really all about: to dream of immortality before we had the means to procure it by ourselves through our own efforts? Once realize the folly of humanity and the divine disappears as well. Who cares if God made the world; it's ours now. Nobody is coming back to save us. You're on your own baby; it's all up to you! That old song by Bob Dylan about a rolling stone had it right all along...

Of course most people will not be up to the transition. They will be un-reconciled to extinction just like the dinosaurs were. Our business, your business, the business of law is to serve those who would survive. Your firm is on its way to becoming the ultimate in boutique law practice: to help the rich survive what is coming. I think we all know the costs that nature is imposing each year in the form of storm and flood damage. What we have not faced is that this is the new normal. We are in a burning theater with no exit plan. Americans hate each other and still must live together in a world that would be all too pleased to see us finally go down. The prognosis is not good and democracy as our parents knew it will fail when our economy starts to slip and enter the long glide pattern of defunct empires.

Only a fraction of the human race will be so placed that lasting prosperity will be an option. The die-off will be like a bad winter season. If you have followed me so far you are no doubt waiting for the qualification that will make my assertions less grim and depressing. You are waiting for me to tell you that for you at least an exceptional fate may provide an escape. There is a way but it is not a matter of fate but of will. We must learn to survive without the comfort provided by any overriding loyalty to a mythos that directs our efforts beyond, towards any transcendent end; we must accept the death of meaning as meaning has always been understood. This is the great challenge of our times to face the utter loss of all illusions simultaneously: of progress, universal justice, the final triumph of equity, a remedy to restore lost innocence, everything promised by the various transcendent philosophies from the most august to the most self-serving and trivial.

Does my advocacy of what might be termed the universal algorithm sound excessive and beyond the demands of strict necessity, supererogation in the domain of nihilism? I assure you it is the price of survival in the transition of a dying planet! For the present all of the stories that have ever been elaborated since the dawn of consciousness are now coequally present along with their worshipful audiences and acolytes. But human beings have never learned to live together. Conflict and the will to appropriation are the only true universals. The great mingling and migration of races and languages has already begun. Look at Europe with its Syrian flood of refugees or America beset by wave from Central America bringing Catholicism to the land that gave the full flavor of the Protestant work ethic to the world as it armed to fight Germany and Japan in the last century. Weapons are everywhere! We will soon be tripping over missiles in the dark; all of them poised to blow this green and diversely populated earth into oblivion, the final testimony to our exalted species.

Such a pity that the great meditative whales abdicated the land to the conquest of the innovative monkeys with the overlarge brains and the opposable thumbs! Time itself has been foreshortened; we simply haven't time to evolve a new nature. We shout our stories to each other across the walls of our lack of sympathy and the barriers of our mutual comprehension. Once a story is fully integrated into the collective unconscious it becomes part of the operating system. There you have proper metaphors for the present hour."

The speaker paused and looked about the room as though challenging his listeners to object.

"Perhaps I leap too quickly to the holding of the case at hand without outlining first the relevant evidence and stating the applicable rules. Let us turn to the hodge-podge of events that in pre-digested format await us each day. Is any pattern to be discerned? Let us select a few. Ah, here is an item that the Sultan of Brunei plans on establishing death by stoning for anyone engaging in sexual relations between two members of the same sex. Here is a note that conservative Catholics are up in arms because the Pope is discouraging the ancient practice of allowing pilgrims to kiss the Papal ring on his hand. Here is a note that the Green New Deal has been voted down as idealistic and ill-conceived. Oh well, there are other planets available for colonization, a bit chilly on Mars but one must make sacrifices. Ah, here is an item! The President has decided to recognize the Golan Heights as the permanent possession of Israel and new conflict is already breaking out as a result. But then it will help gather strategic votes for the 2020 election, hmm.

What do we see daily but symbols and contention between opposed narratives. Where is the larger meaning that can align the fragmented pieces into a picture of general survival? Where are the grounds for mediation and arbitration between conflicting absolutist visions?

Look anywhere and you will see that as in nuclear fission highly active principles cannot survive close proximity without explosive consequences. Nowhere is this more evident than between opposing factions in America today. Each is a threat to each. The fence and the lock, the private security system, the walled perimeter, access codes, the veiled innuendo, the offensive phrase, the impermissible allusion, the unsolicited familiarity, the insult that demands retribution ... even the age of the vendetta seems mild in comparison to the dangers inherent in any form of discourse that may trespass upon forbidden topics or memes in a world of charged particles all zooming about in our great informational cyclotron.

Fortunately we are attorneys and opposition and conflict-ridden discourse is our bread and butter. But even we desire resolution at the end of the day and some measure of accord and satisfaction so that the social structure that is the fruit of the laws holds together. We bow our heads before the Constitution and give thanks that the spirit of independence and anarchy was so swiftly reduced to institutional regimentation. Let us pause now and allow this sense of temporary security to lead us to our noon repast. We can take a break now for I see that luncheon is ready and a little indulgence may pave the way for the next section of my presentation.”

Elegant and internationally mingled dishes to suit every palate from vegan to flesh-eater is one of the great advantages that accrue to meetings of this sort. The subject of the presentation soon yielded to chipper discussion and laughter all circling around whatever and whence each participant had managed to assemble in the hours of freedom and privacy not already bought and paid for by the firm's collective commitments. Individuality even among attorneys takes seed like grass after a flood has washed all else before it. Of course it is precisely these incremental seeds of private stories that it was the purpose and theme of the present seminar to eradicate. No great anxiety had been instilled yet that morning by the proffered thesis in the young minds and hearts sitting about the table. After all apocalyptic rhetoric was the order of the day whether it concerned the horror of the Green New Deal and the Democratic slide towards socialism or the prospect that Donald Trump might be elected to serve a second term of office as the nation's Blowhard in Chief. So as the presentation resumed that afternoon the bright and highly educated faces of the young and the more jaded faces of the old turned attentively towards the afternoon's source of illumination as he stood before them.

"Ahem, shall we continue then? Yes? Very well, you will recall that our pre-luncheon discourse ended with the proposition that change, even exponential change is not a doom as long as the will to assimilate and to respond appropriately exists. The quality of that response must be strategic and based upon a determination to face facts as they reveal themselves. I suggested that a precondition of that revelation is to abandon any notion of a return to the normal course of events as traditionally conceived. No amount of effort can put Humpty Dumpty back together again. There is a huge volume of content accepted as dogma that must be jettisoned because it is honeycombed with inertia, gangrenous with dead tissue, committed to out-of-date technology and antiquated managerial practices. Each of these has in common what might be called tenure, a right to collect present remuneration for residual value. The concept of property as a right to exclusive ownership is based upon landed estates, patrimonies, fiefdoms. These concepts make no sense in a shortened time perspective where statements fall prey to obsolescence or at least qualification soon after being enunciated. The echoes die and with their cessation all is created anew by some new concept that has displaced it. We must climb aboard the process or be left hopelessly behind. This is where cognition of process and of method must take precedence over substance, definition, and even over axioms. Physics sets the model of new metaphors before us. Even the principle of non-contradiction fails when we consider quantum measurements. The nature of law will be no exception; jurisprudence will be denied immunity. We as lawyers must accept this no matter how contrary to our habits and instincts this new reality of things as they are now constituted and as they increasingly will be constituted, may go."

The speaker paused for a moment to gage the effect that his words were producing before continuing.

"It occurs to me though that each case of abandonment must entail a period of mourning for what has been lost never to return. I mentioned that we must abandon the ancient concept of storytelling and the cause and effect sense that it nurtures. Before proceeding I wonder which of you has ever read Northrop Frye's, *Anatomy of Criticism* or Eric Auerbach's, *Mimesis: the Representation of Reality.* No one, ah, I thought not. What about Joseph Campbell's, *The Hero with a Thousand Faces?* Perhaps *The Romantic Agony,* by Mario Praz anyone? Ah, that is disappointing; whatever were you doing as undergraduates?

Suffice it to say that these works ground rhetoric in various ways of storytelling. We perceive according to various pre-existing templates that govern our perceptive processes. To not know these templates is to be subject to absurd generalizations and to be a ready victim for spurious propaganda ersatz, shopworn, and trivial. A day of reading various entrees in Mr. Trump's twitter account is a case in point. It has not been tested but it is not unlikely that a constant diet of such diatribes might be shown to lower I.Q. scores.

If we are to adjust to methodologies that are no longer story based we must learn to think in algorithms. We must see information content from a trans-humanist perspective and say farewell forever to the likes of Frye, Auerbach, Praz, and Campbell. I merely thought that you might look at them briefly as their burning ship sails out of the fiord towards the setting sun.

But we are all post-modernist pragmatists are we not, hard as diamonds and awash in terabytes? Besides, our time together is short, so we must press on. Let us turn then to a simple assessment of data and see where it leads us. I stated earlier that we are living in the age of the algorithm. Think of your daily task as attorneys like an extremely complex video game. The targets are moveable and constantly emerging and disappearing in random order; by the time that you prepare a client's case events will already have made many causes of action moot in the traditional way of proceeding. The world that we inhabit is ever-changing. Delay is often fatal yet we continue to believe in tools thought up by jurists in other centuries.

Of what use is discovery when the actions of yesterday are superseded by events happening in real time? What proposed injunction does not constitute irreparable injury? What standard of morality is sufficiently secular to encompass all personal rights in a free society? We must devise new procedures that will be as different from the old as the nuclear-tipped missile is from the cannons and mortars of yesteryear? We must show our clients a way to successfully opt out of the old forums provided by the nation-states. The structures of domination have shifted to private industry. Legislatures are mere theaters for sophisticated bribery by various interest-groups. The role of the individual is that of a grain of wheat to be ground into the dust by larger entities. Everything must be seen as a force generated by the size of the network that it can influence.

What is celebrity but a snowball rolling downhill and growing larger with every added follower? What does the retail apocalypse tell you about markets and the fate of established venues for commercial activity? The keys are connectivity and replicable sales across vast spectra of the fragmented universe of isolated consumers who can be reached in an instant by images and graphics. Law must evolve or become merely museum pieces along with the Code of Hammurabi.

Fortunately your firm is on the cutting edge of the possible because it understands when loyalty to past forms is not merely antiquated, it is suicidal, a one-way path to extinction. Look at the speed of attrition of many institutions that were once viewed as permanent and unchangeable. One needs only to look at the example provided by poor Pope Francis who is attempting to steer his unwieldy church into the post-modern age. The conservative Catholic media are out for his blood because he is attempting to look facts in the face rather than preserving formulations and ceremonials that are being shorn of all socially relevant theological meaning so that only the forms remain intact when they are no longer persuasive to the vast mass of Catholics. His pontificate is the dumping ground of every failure since the Second Vatican Council. All of the dust and neglect of prior pontificates is laid at his door. He has attempted to embody the Beatitudes in a visceral way by his simple life-style and compassion and all that various cardinals can see is the potential de-leveraging effect of the more horrific consequences of code violations and the power that it once gave them to command rather than to inspire, to enlighten, and to lead.

Or let us take the whole question of Constitutional interpretation: our most unifying document has become the very ground on which factions engage in demonstrating fixed positions and endless discord. Our highest values are reduced to the right of bakers to refuse to bake cakes for selected members of the body politic who do not share their religious views. Each commercial transaction is a potential moral moratorium. Show me an institution or established business model that is not menaced by the power of unrestricted connectivity or an area of private commerce that is not in danger of invasion and appropriation by computer hacking. This is the world to which our laws claim to privilege certain discourses as reliable, authoritative, and sanctioned by the common consent of the governed in our democracy.

Where is the evidence of silent consent amidst the factions that constitute the commonwealth of equal citizens, secure in their rights and privileges? The Ninth and Tenth Amendments are content-less admonitions, mere precatory language.

When substance fails to achieve its aims all that remains is mere technique and in the realm of technique the algorithm reigns supreme in its power to amalgamate and assemble data towards a given end. In other words power has finally found the perfect tool to achieve its ends by making everything mere disassembled pieces to be re-formed according to the dictates of those who can use the tools to attain results that are not tied to any merits or virtues as they have been traditionally defined and affirmed by story-telling cultures. This is the salient fact of the present hour.

The results are everywhere about us. Monoliths of established meanings and traditional loyalties are falling all about us like dead Sequoias. The vast mass of people is being rendered commercially irrelevant except as consumers of robotically produced goods. This is the trend that law as an institution must face and your firm is well-placed to address a reality that few are willing to acknowledge even while its effects are everyday more evident to the attuned observer. There is your challenge! As for the larger world ... well, I suggest that if we cannot jettison outmoded nationalisms and the residuum of various religious dogmas and arrive at a condition of massive toleration and synthesis of opposing positions in some sort of universal colloquium or willingness to pass each other unmolested and immune than we shall see a conflict soon that will dwarf the absurdity of the general conflagration triggered in 1914 by a shot at Sarajevo.

Having framed the issues thus I would be happy to entertain any questions or comments that you may have. Thank you for your attention."

Silence filled the room.

"Come now, we are no longer in law school; there is no room for back-benchers here. Do you agree with the thesis I have proposed?"

An associate spoke up. "If I understand you correctly, Sir, your thesis is that the age of storytelling is over and that advanced methodologies will determine content in the law and perhaps in everyday life as well rather than serving various determinations of public policy arrived at through democratic political processes in the unified nation-state."

"An admirable summation. (I trust that the partners are taking note.) You speak of democratic processes; let me ask you if you think that public policy is arrived at by a rational process or is rather the outcome of chaotic bargain and exchange, as I believe. Do not be afraid to disagree with me. Remember that my primary assertion is that procedure trumps substance; to argue well is to prevail in an indeterminate world."

"Very well, if you will allow me a question in return: 'Isn't your thesis merely a resurgence of the ancient arguments between the Platonists and the Sophists as to the nature of absolute truth?'"

"You make a good point, but my thesis is not based upon rhetoric alone but upon the deterministic character of technology. Even rhetoric is dependent upon a humanistic base whereas for technology, well, we have yet to sound its limits. There will be a time when rhetoric like stories before it trails off and all that will be left is non-linear dynamics and algorithms."

"Let me come back to your thought that bargains and exchange are chaotic; why do you say that; what becomes of the invisible hand of Adam Smith?"

"You are referring of course to *The Wealth of Nations.* Part, indeed a substantial part of my presentation today, was designed to hint that the world economy is moving beyond the utility of the nation. The bankruptcy of the striving of nations was revealed between 1914 and 1918 a hundred years ago. We are even a longer way from the Peace of Westphalia in 1648 that created nations from kingdoms. Immigration and multiculturalism has doomed the idea of a unified national ethos. How many Americans even know the history of their country or care to know it for that matter. Our radical groups are so ill-informed and lazy that they are willing to lump into their favored group all white people regardless of origin or history of prior animosity. How ridiculous they would have appeared in the 1990's when Croatians, Bosnians, and Serbs, former countrymen all, were at war with each other. America today manifests the same factions and fissures. It is anyone's guess when the riots and reprisals will begin. As lawyers we represent the idea of principled order. It is imposed upon us to accept the duty of shedding any *naiveté* that the mystique of our profession reaches any great depth of comprehension among those who are subject to the laws. Our citizens understand very little of the complex machinery of democracy beyond mere demagoguery. If we needed any demonstration of this we need only look at the peculiar exaltation of a pompous and empty-headed braggart to the highest office of the land. What do you suppose is behind his triumph?"

Another associate spoke up.

"I take exception to that. President Trump is addressing the very real concerns of the great forgotten middle-class in America. He is a master of the very rhetoric that you are exalting. How can you quarrel with his success?"

"You see him then as a revolutionary?"

"He is conservative. He wants to make America great again."

"But surely that implies some sort of fall. When did we cease being great?"

"Well Obama was undermining American freedom. We should each have the right to choose our own medical care."

"So you assume that as consumers Americans had equal bargaining power against the HMO's and insurance companies, the drug manufacturers, and the giant hospitals? What freedom is that but to be victimized; but you have raised a key point. Americans value their freedom do they not? But we as attorneys know that freedom is conditioned by the laws. We know that freedom of contract does not mean that each party has equal bargaining power. The law desires equity, but to impose it is beyond our power. We trust the political process to balance interests in pursuit of the common good. Look about you and ask yourself what process allows such vast accumulations of wealth and political influence that the richest eight individuals in the world possess the same wealth, or capital if you prefer that term, as the bottom half of the human race, that is to say half of 7.7 billion people. The laws of the world as presently constituted allow this unimaginable and iniquitous inequity, even enables this disparity through arcane laws and processes. Does that make any kind of sense to you?"

"So we should surrender our advantages."

"On the contrary, I expect the present conditions to get worse. To date we still see human beings as one species. How long will this quaint concept of a common humanity be allowed to exist? How long before the logic of mechanization divorced from the legacy of human values reaches the ultimate conclusion that the bottom half, or maybe even a little more than the bottom half, are already living lives that are nasty, brutish, and short and are therefore expendable? It is the only merciful thing to do, is it not?"

"I mean relative advantage here in America, social welfare, all that Alexandria Ocasio-Cortez, Green New Deal stuff."

"You raise an interesting point by your qualification. How much privilege is ethically tolerable in our democracy; are there any takers for that one?"

A partner spoke up. "Well here at least within the firm we have adopted a productivity calculus."

"But you are a community of sorts. What about outside these walls."

"Well, all in all Americans are doing well. We are still as a nation the world's largest economy."

"You are saying that we are great."

"Yes."

"Then what is understood by the phrase, 'making America great again' from whence comes this national inferiority complex?"

"Our national savings per capita is down and many just squeeze by," someone volunteered.

"So what we want is more of the good life, a mint julep on the porch and a swimming pool in the back yard?"

"Survival with grace," another volunteered.

"All that used to take was a chicken in every pot. Look where state socialism has brought us. Or perhaps a little Calcutta-style bodies of dead beggars in the street will motivate us again, hmm? Nothing is as finally persuasive to initiative as tripping over dead bodies on the way to the factory."

"Well I doubt it will ever come to that. We are Americans after all."

"But our logic is that the existence of vast accumulations of technologically induced wealth agglomeration is perfectly permissible, indeed it must be safeguarded as the guarantee of sovereign individual freedom. Isn't that why Republicans keep harping on the iniquity of the death tax and reap standing ovations for its abolition? Do you doubt the power of rhetoric as long as it triggers absurd presumptions that militate against the commonweal?"

Another partner spoke up. "But then we are hardly in the business of surrendering privilege. Our rent in these very offices determines our client base. We are international because from this hub we have outshoots, runners from the vine to virtual law offices in Beijing, Singapore, and Mumbai and further offshoots from them."

"You are undoubtedly cutting edge, but there are still externalities and encumbrances to be considered and ultimately that is why I am here today: to alert you to a great shifting of the world axis from nationhood to international corporate rule. Nations are mere bidders for business to world capital. Concessions in taxes and promised subsidies are the order of the day. Laws and taxation are for those who cannot afford the price of resisting the intrusive new form of colonization. If you can't contract yourself out of the system you will be subject to it.

Courts of general jurisdiction are the public swimming pools for the great unwashed masses. Prisons are the vanguard of what to do with superfluous persons. It won't be long until we outsource them to third-world nations. After we do so we won't want too much information about how well they are being kept. After all, every criminal is a domestic terrorist of sorts. The problem with Guantanamo is it is too small; try Afghanistan. They owe us something. Have I shocked you yet?"

One of the partners smiled. "We should have recognized the Socratic method."

The unnamed lecturer smiled in turn.

"Let us go back to this question of the rhetorical success of the Trump campaign. He definitely caught something in the American mythos. What do you think it was?"

"Freedom," one shouted out.

"The work ethic," another volunteered.

"Racial anxiety," a third suggested.

"Threatened entitlement," mumbled a forth.

"These are all good suggestions, but why Donald Trump of all people. Surely we could do better than that."

"Let me try," said a fifth. "His virtue is his sheer vulgarity; it betokens the common touch and makes him a faux populist."

"But I thought we were a nation of sophisticated argumentation with think tanks, universities, an institutional cordon of enlightened public intellectuals; what became of these?"

"Fake news!" shouted an associate laughing.

"Two words? Surely it must take more than that to convince skeptical Americans to underwrite all those golfing vacations to Florida on Airforce One. Whatever happened to Camp David? They used to reach accords there. Shall we take some time to reflect? Shall we take a brief break here before winding it up?"

The room dissolved into a chaos of activity and dispersal

before reassembling fifteen minutes later.

"I see that most of us are here; shall we press on? Good. I am afraid that we may have been distracted from our larger purpose by our little sortie into contemporary politics. However, some points of interest have emerged. We are at least able to see that the safety net of social institutional immunity in our supposedly advanced and multi-layered democracy is not as reliable as we once supposed since so many Americans have been willing to flirt with the 'hamburger and a cola version' of the Fuehrer Principle.

Trumpism is a symptom of the disease rather than the disease itself. What is evident is that Americans have little real awareness of the forces that govern their lives and no real idea of how to survive what is coming upon them with the inevitability of a melting glacier. We attorneys, grafted as we are to a dying institution, are little better. The tides of anarchy are rising about us and we continue as we always have assuming that somewhere in that vast arsenal of carefully reasoned decisions and statutes there is an answer to social dissolution when the barbarians are not yet at the gate but even more threateningly are the members of the commonwealth itself.

I came here today like Nietzsche's madman in one of his more aphoristic books, *The Joyful Wisdom.* You will recall that there the madman runs into the village carrying a lantern and proclaims that God is dead and that the collective will of the masses has killed Him. He realizes that he has come too early and hence will not be believed so he throws his lantern down where it is extinguished. He says that his mission is futile and will be ignored because of its very immensity and universal consequences. God was everything, the center of a civilization, and now there is only darkness and a plunging into endless night.

These were not the words of a complacent atheist but the *cri de Coeur* of a man who anticipated the full measure of damages that would soon be exacted by such a great dethronement in European culture The most troubling pronouncement is his ironic observation that the true wonder was that the people he had come to address had been the causative agent of God's demise. I often think of this when I reflect how many religious leaders, overlooking all else, have embraced Donald Trump as their new messiah. I suppose it is the logical result of the prosperity gospel and the anticipated coming of the millennium of Christian rule, but even then...

Oh, well, I am only an attorney after all and should be above being disillusioned by mere events; but there it is."

The room fell silent. A bank of clouds had imperceptibly moved inland from the sea. The Olympic Mountains that had been illumined for most of the day by an unexpected surfeit of spring sunshine now wore a ghostly aspect as mist poured over the peaks and valleys. Puget Sound had assumed a leaden aspect as the ferry traffic moved east and west across Elliot Bay. The supply of questions had trailed off giving way to the sense of waning time. Nerves that had found a few hours of refuge from the demands of billable hours began to quiver again with urgency. Tasks that can be deferred can never be escaped in a law firm. Perspective is all very fine, but its relevance must be proven by future events not in the molecular circuitry of a single reaction sequence. The quest for the universal algorithm must await some larger entity than the legal arena to find its definition and resolution. Besides, sufficient for the day are the troubles to be found therein. After a short applause, the Monday meeting was adjourned.

THE EMBODIMENT OF ART
BY CARRIE AVERY MORIARTY

Here we see the final submission to the collection," Hannah said. "Alexander was known for not only his artistic beauty with paint and clay, but he wrote beautifully as well. He titled this piece, 'My Beloved' in honor of his late wife, Beatrice, who preceded him in death shortly before he penned this piece. At twenty-nine, she was young, even for that time period. His son later collected all of his writings and transcribed them for publication, but kept each piece in its original format as well. You can find this collection, as well as prints of his paintings and copies of his sculptures in the gift shop on your way out of the museum."

Hannah had worked at the museum for a few years, and had always loved the collections they brought in. This one was extremely special to her, since she had studied Alexander Thornton in college, and fell in love with his work, particularly his writings. Her studies delved into his background and she found a lot of inconsistencies in what was readily available.

"We conclude our tour with this piece," she continued. "If any of you have any questions, please feel free to ask. Any of the museum staff can answer your questions. I want to thank you for visiting the Edison City Museum of Fine Arts today."

"Excuse me," a man said after the rest of her group disbursed.

"Yes," Hannah replied. "How can I help you?"

"You seem to know quite a bit about this artist," he said.

"I do," she replied. "While all of the staff are given extensive information about each exhibit we offer, this one is close to my heart."

"I could tell," the man said. "I had some questions that may sound odd. Would you mind answering them?"

"Not at all," she said. "I'm happy to help." Hannah led the man away from the crowd, asking, "What did you want to know?"

"First," the man began, "I'd like to apologize for the bizarre nature of my questions."

"I'm sure I've heard them all," she laughed. It was true, too. There had been questions she'd had to answer with a straight face when all she wanted to do was look at the person and ask if they were out of their mind.

"My studies have led me to believe that Mr. Thornton may have killed his wife," he said. "I know that you may not have this information, but I wanted to see what you might know about it."

"Well," Hannah said. She had to be careful when she answered questions that were not part of the training she received from the Museum, especially when it went to the more off the wall things people wanted to know. This definitely fell into that category. After gathering her thoughts, Hannah said, "We do not have any information regarding the cause of death of Beatrice Thornton. There were many who speculated the same as you, that he had a hand in her death. No report or other evidence has ever been made available regarding it."

What Hannah didn't tell the man, what she couldn't tell any visitor, is that she had heard the same rumor, and that she had investigated it, even going so far as to visit his home, which was now a national landmark, to see what she could dig up there.

"I know there's nothing official," the man said. "But I also know that you probably know more than what you are allowed to share here."

"I'm not sure what you mean," she said.

"Just that you gave much more information than any of your colleagues during the tour," he said. "Some of the things you shared were well beyond the simple information given to tour guides. My guess is that you did some studies on this artist on your own."

Hannah looked at the man, unsure how to respond. Every employee at the museum was required to study the art they showed, given a week, sometimes more, to learn as much as they could about the artist and each piece they would have on display. While most of the other guides did a cursory review of the information given, she was of the mindset that the more you knew, the better you could inform.

"I'll admit that I do tend to dig pretty deep when we get a new artist," Hannah said. "It's just part of my nature. I like to learn, and this job gives me the opportunity to get to know some of the most amazing artist that ever lived."

"This exhibit has been up for two weeks," the man said. "My guess is you got the information it would be coming a month or two before. Even if I give you the benefit of the doubt, that is still only a maximum of three months you could have studied his work. With the number of pieces in this collection, there is no way you could be as knowledgeable about them as you are without a foreknowledge as to his art. So, I'll ask my question again. Did Alexander Thornton kill his wife, Beatrice?"

"I'm afraid I can't answer that," Hannah said. "My capacity of information on this artist is limited to what we were given when the exhibit became available for our museum. That is all the information I am allowed to share with our patrons."

She was giving him a hint, that she couldn't talk about it at the museum. Now, she just had to hope that he was curious enough to ask her to give him the information outside the scope of her duties.

"It's been very nice speaking with you," he said. "Perhaps we will bump into each other in the future. In the meantime," he continued. "If you are ever interested in a career outside this one, please contact me."

He handed her his business card, black with white lettering on it. Simple and classic.

"Thank you," she said. "I look forward to possibly meeting you in the future."

With that, the man walked away. Hannah flipped the card over and saw his name and number. She would definitely be giving Mr. Bradley Graham a call. Not only was she intrigued by what his interest in the Thornton exhibit was, but also in the man himself.

Bradley walked away from the Edison City Museum of Fine Arts with a lightness to his heart he hadn't felt in years. His research into Alexander Thornton had been thrust upon him by his father, and his grandfather before that. Four generations of Grahams had been investigating the man, trying to discover what truly killed his wife.

When Beatrice had first married Alexander, the family was thrilled. Thornton was well known, having been the curator of the museum in their home town of Charlotte, and a philanthropist in the community back in the mid nineteenth century. Shortly after their son was born, though, she had withdrawn from her family, and from the community at large. Her father and brothers had discussed their concerns with Alexander, who simply put them off, saying she was taking time to be a mother and would return to her societal duties in the near future.

She returned nearly a year after Edmund was born, but was not the same. Frail and demure, she did not resemble the woman who had been wed to Alexander just three years before. Shortly after that, she took ill and was bedridden. Refusing to allow her family to see her in such a condition, it took her father, Reuben, months to convince Alexander to go against her wishes. He brought their family doctor in to examine her and ensure that she was being treated well and not being held against her will.

The doctor confirmed that she was ill, but could not determine the cause. Beatrice had been outraged with her father's intrusion and withdrew even further, cutting the family off completely. Alexander had been kind, continuing to allow Edmund's grandparents to visit him. They watched him grow while their daughter stubbornly refused to see them.

Shortly before Edmund's second birthday, Alexander called Beatrice's family to the house, telling them the doctor did not expect her to survive the night, and they should come to pay their last respects. When they arrived, the doctor told them what to expect: a shell of the woman they knew. Reuben went into a rage, demanding that the doctor find out what had killed his beloved child. The doctor said he could not explain it, simply that she failed to thrive once her son was born, and died from the heartache that she could not have another child. This was the first the family heard of her inability to have more children, and they demanded Alexander tell them why they were not told before. He'd informed them it was their daughter's wishes to keep it a secret.

That was the basis of Reuben's quest to find the truth. He scoured Alexander's artwork looking for clues as to what had truly happened to his daughter. The only clues he could find were the fact that the artwork all seemed to revolve around her. Everything Alexander created was in some way associated with Beatrice. From the paintings to the sculptures to the written word, everything was about her. Slowly, Alexander drew away from the Graham family, finding them too difficult a reminder of his loss. His son, Edmond, was the only connection they had, and that tapered off as well.

By the time the boy was of age, he wanted nothing to do with his mother's family. He blamed them for his mother's death, felt they had accelerated her demise and refused to even see them. This broke Reuben's heart. Year after year he tried to get in touch with Edmund, only to have his correspondence returned, unopened, with a note attached saying it was refused. Finally, Reuben gave up trying to connect, simply living with the information that was shared in the newspapers.

Passing the duties of finding the cause of Beatrice's death to her brother, Joseph, Reuben died a sorrow filled man, never truly knowing the reason behind his loss of not only his daughter, but a grandson as well. The task of finding the reason for Alexander's wife's death was passed down from generation to generation, always the eldest son taking the mantel of finding out the truth.

Now that it was his turn, Bradley had taken it upon himself to find every piece of art that Alexander Thornton created from the time he met his wife until his death thirty-seven years after her. While he'd been unable to acquire any of the pieces, he did take the time to visit each museum that held his work. Edison was the most recent, and he'd decided it would be the place he would find the answers his family had been searching for all this time.

"May I speak to Bradley Graham?" Hannah asked.

"Can I tell him who is calling, please?" the receptionist asked.

"My name is Hannah Collins," she said. "I met him yesterday at the Edison City Museum of Fine Arts."

"One moment, please," the other woman said.

Hannah twisted her hair with her finger while she listened to the music from the other end of the phone. She wasn't sure whether the man would remember her, or if he even meant that she should call him.

"Ms. Collins," a man's voice came over the phone.

Hannah was startled for a moment, but recovered quickly.

"Mr. Graham," she said. "I just wanted to see if you wanted to discuss the exhibit. I mean," she stuttered. "Well, you said you had some questions, and you thought that I might have some answers, but that I couldn't answer while I was at the museum and so I thought I'd just call you and see if you wanted to talk about it."

The words rushed out of her non-stop and she couldn't help but feel foolish for just blurting out so much.

"I'm sorry," she apologized. "I shouldn't have called. You probably were just being nice and didn't mean for me to call so I shouldn't have called at all. I'll let you get back to your work now and quit bothering you."

"Hannah," Bradley said.

"Um, yeah?" Hannah asked.

"I would love to meet with you," he said.

"Oh," she said.

"Are you available to meet for dinner this evening?" he asked. "Say around seven?"

"Um," she stammered. "Yeah, I think that's fine. I mean, yeah, that's fine."

"Great," he said. "I'll have a car pick you up."

"No," she said.

"Excuse me?"

"I mean," she stumbled. "Just that you don't have to send anyone. I can get to where ever we're going. Where are we going?"

"I'll have a car there at seven tonight," he said. "We'll have dinner at The Bayshore Club."

"I don't know if I have anything fancy enough for there," she said.

"I'll send something to you this afternoon," he said.

"I can't accept that," she said. "That just wouldn't be right."

"Consider it an early birthday present," he said.

"How do you know when my birthday is?"

"Ms. Collins," Bradley said. "It is my business to know things about my staff."

"Wait, what?" she asked.

"I am in the process of purchasing the museum where you work," he said.

"You are?" she asked. "I mean, I didn't know it was for sale."

"Everything is for sale, Hannah," he said. "I will see you this evening."

Before Hannah could answer, the call was disconnected. She realized that she didn't tell him what size dress she would need, nor where she lived. All of this was beginning to feel like she was stuck inside a book or movie.

Looking at the clock, she realized how late it was and decided she better get into the shower and get some things done, especially if she was going out to the Bayshore Club for dinner. She definitely needed to do some research on her date, too.

Bradley replaced the handset into its cradle and sighed. He hadn't intended to be so forward with Hannah, but there were two things he wanted from her. The first was any information she had on Alexander Thornton. That was the most important thing he needed. Selfishly, though, he wanted to get to know her. She had been impressive on the tour, pointing out things that he wasn't aware of, despite his extensive research on the man. While this had been a catalyst in asking her to dinner, he was well aware of his attraction to her. What he didn't know was how she would respond to his advances.

He pressed a button on his phone and said, "Stacey."

"Yes, sir," she responded through the intercom.

"I need you," he said.

"Coming," she replied and the door opened shortly after.

"I need you to get a dress appropriate for the Club and get it sent to a Ms. Hannah Collins," he said.

"Do you have a size?"

"She's about your size," he said. "Perhaps a little taller."

"Color?"

"Emerald green," he said. "I'll need a matching tie as well."

"Reservation time?" she asked.

"Seven thirty," he replied.

"Yes, sir," she said then turned on her heels and walked out.

Stacey was perfect at her job: discreet, polite, and a bull dog when it came to giving out information. She was also extremely loyal to him. He paid her well above what the position should garner, but she was worth it, and then some.

Sighing, he returned to the task at hand, completing the merger documents for the acquisition of his newest property. While it wasn't a big money maker, the museum turned enough of a profit that it was worth the investment. Bradley had gained enough properties to afford him the luxury of owning things which made him happy, and this museum was one of those things.

His computer pinged and he looked up. It was a message from Stacey saying everything was taken care of for the evening. How she did things so quickly was beyond him, but he wouldn't look a gift horse in the mouth. No, he would accept what he'd been blessed with and use it to his advantage.

"The Bayshore Club?" Jenna asked.

"That's what he said," Hannah replied.

"Is he cute?"

Hannah had been sharing an apartment with Jenna for the three years she'd lived in Edison. Neither of them made enough to afford a place on their own, unless they were willing to live in the sketchy part of the city. They were as different as two people could be. Jenna preferred the night life and party atmosphere, while Hannah liked the solitude of the museums and cultural centers the city boasted.

"Is that seriously all you are interested in?" Hannah asked.

"I'm just saying," Jenna said. "He's got to be rich to be able to take you to the Club. I just hope he's not one of those super rich guys who is uglier than a troll and hopes his money will buy him some action."

"Jenna!"

"What?"

"I can't believe you," Hannah said.

"Have you met me?"

It was their go-to question when one or the other did something so in-character that they couldn't believe the other was surprised. Hannah just rolled her eyes.

"Let's Google him," Jenna said. "I mean, you know what he looks like but I don't. Maybe he's not who he says he is and he's some crazy psycho who's just looking for a pretty girl to kidnap."

"Really?" Hannah asked. "That's what you come up with?"

"Happens all the time," Jenna replied. "Now, what's his name?"

Hannah gave Jenna the business card she received, then said, "I'm gonna take a shower. You figure out if he's a serial killer on your own."

Jenna grabbed the card and giggled. "I got you," she said, then pulled out her smart phone and went on the hunt for information. It was what she did best.

Hannah just rolled her eyes again and walked into her bathroom.

"I'm here to pick up Ms. Hannah Collins," the man said when Jenna opened the apartment door.

"Hannah," she shouted over her shoulder.

Hannah stepped out of her room, picking up her clutch from the kitchen table.

"You need me," Jenna said quietly as she passed her. "You just let me know."

"I'll be fine," Hannah said. "Good evening," she said to the man at the door.

"Good evening, Ms. Collins," he replied. "If you'll follow me."

He turned and walked back down the hall to the staircase at the end. Hannah followed, taking the stairs carefully in her heeled boots. While Jenna could probably run in her heels, Hannah preferred flats or tennis shoes to anything with a heel.

They stepped out of the building and she followed him to the awaiting town car. He opened the back door and she slid in. Once she was shut inside, he stepped around to the driver's side and climbed in. Starting the car, they were off for the short ride to the Club where he reversed his motions, coming around to let her out.

"Thank you," she said automatically.

"My pleasure," the man said.

She walked up to the door of the club where a doorman

opened the portal. The inside was just as she had imagined, polished wood and marble accentuated the foyer.

"Your name?" the woman at the podium asked.

"Hannah," she replied. "Hannah Collins. I'm supposed to be meeting..."

"This way," the woman interrupted.

Hannah followed her through the dining room to the back where she saw her date sitting at a table sipping amber liquid from a glass. He stood when she arrived and pulled out her chair.

"Thank you," she said as she sat.

"I'm happy to see you again," he said. "Thank you for agreeing to have dinner with me."

"You're welcome," she replied.

"I took the liberty of ordering for us," he said. "I hope you don't mind."

"Um, OK," she said. She'd never had someone order her food for her and wasn't sure what to think of it.

"Would you like something to drink?" he asked her.

"Just water will be fine," she replied.

She fiddled with her hands in her lap, unsure whether she should begin the conversation or wait for him. Since she didn't really know what he wanted, she decided to wait. It didn't take long for a waiter to come by with salads for both of them.

"Thank you," she said.

The waiter nodded and left. She again waited for a signal from the man across from her, unsure whether she should begin eating or wait. This was so outside her comfort zone she didn't know what to do.

Bradley picked up his fork, gave her a nod, and said, "Enjoy."

Following suit, she also picked up her fork. The salad was full of spring greens and had a nice raspberry vinaigrette dressing. The flavors burst in her mouth with the first bite, and she audibly moaned her appreciation.

"Glad you like it," he said and she blushed to the roots of her hair. "Don't be embarrassed," he continued. "Nothing wrong with enjoying your meal."

This only made her blush more.

"Let's talk about Alexander Thornton," he said once the salads were nearly gone.

"What do you want to know?" she asked.

"First," he said. "I'd like to know how you know so much about him."

"I was an art history major in college," she replied. "I did my thesis work on him. It was a really fascinating study into the history of his work, and the life he lived. There were so many things I couldn't get answers to, though, and that was really frustrating."

"How much do you know about his family?" Bradley asked.

"Besides his wife," she answered. "He had a son, Edmund. That's who gathered his collection and began the process of displaying it in museums. First it was displayed in the museum Alexander curated. Once that museum closed, the art was returned to his son for storage or to use as he saw fit. After that, though, it was taken out of circulation and thought to have been lost."

"Then how did it find its way to your museum?"

"That should be obvious," she replied. "It was found again. But we aren't the only one who displayed it after it was rediscovered. It spent time in several larger museums around the country, sort of a touring exhibit. When we were given the chance to acquire it, I pushed hard to make it happen."

"Because of your studies?"

"And because of its significance in the region," she replied. "Alexander Thornton was the most well-known artist to come out of the Carolinas, and it would be unfathomable to not have his work shown in his home state.”

“What happens to it once the exhibit is over?” he asked.

“For someone who is buying a museum,” she said. “You certainly don’t know much about how they work.”

“This is going to be my first museum,” he replied. “Most of what I own are clubs, hotels, and restaurants.”

“Then let me enlighten you,” she said. “We do not own the pieces we display, for the most part. Primarily, we are an exhibition place where work is shown to the public. Most artists don’t have enough space to show their own work, so we do host local artists as well. For the bigger shows, like the Thornton exhibit, we lease them from the owner, showing them within the guidelines they give us. I believe this is the way most museums work as well, though there are always exceptions.”

“Seems like you know quite a bit about the industry,” he replied. “Perhaps I should hire you to take over the museum once the sale is final.”

“And put Mrs. Lansing out of a job?” she asked. “I couldn’t do that to her.”

“I wasn’t quite serious,” he said. “I mean, you could do the job, no doubt, but I am not going to be making any staffing changes, at least for the time being. But I may want to have you work for me in some capacity. Would you be interested?”

“You don’t even know me,” she replied. “We just met a couple of days ago, and that was at my job where I was doing what I do.”

“Which is why I think you would do well working for me,” he replied. “Let’s get back to the Thornton exhibit, though.”

“Great,” Hannah said, relieved that the conversation was going to move away from her. She hated being the center of attention, especially when it was in a conversation with an extremely handsome man.

"You said the pieces were lost, then found," he said. "Do you know where the art was between when it was 'lost' and when it was 'found' again?"

"There are actually several theories about that," she began. "The obvious first one is that the pieces were put into someone's attic at some point and forgotten."

"How long were they missing?" he asked.

"It is clear that they were displayed in the museum he curated for about a decade after his death," she said. "After that point, though, is where we move into suspicion as to what happened."

"What do you know as fact?" he asked.

"Well," she said. "The museum remained open for just over ten years after Alexander died. Without him to manage it, though, it became a money pit and they had to sell it. At that time, the pieces still in possession of the museum were given back to his son, Edmund. He kept the collection out of circulation from any museum for the remainder of his life. His will deemed that they be offered for auction upon his death, since he had no family to pass them on to."

"That's where I lost track of the collection," Bradley said. "Who purchased them?"

"It was an anonymous bid that purchased them," she said. "They were shipped to New York where they disappeared. About twenty years ago, one of the pieces, the one titled 'My Starlight' showed up as a piece at the Met."

"What do you mean, showed up?"

"Just that," she said. "It arrived in an unmarked box with an index card indicating the artist and name of the piece, along with it's place of origin. The curator was stunned and tried desperately to find out where it came from."

"Obviously they did," he surmised.

"Actually, they didn't," she corrected. "The courier who brought the piece in said it was dropped off at their location with instructions to deliver it to the museum."

"Who dropped it off?"

"A taxi," she said. "When the company was asked about it, they were told it came from a hotel, which had no further information. They said that it was found in a storage closet on the premises with the note to deliver it to the museum, and the manner in which it was to be sent. There was also cash to pay for the delivery."

"Then where did they get the rest of the collection?" he asked.

"The same way," she replied. "Every month or so, another piece would be dropped off. Same information as to how it got there, from a different hotel each time. No one could piece together where the pieces were coming from."

"All of it going to the Met?"

"Each piece went to a different museum in the tri-state area," she explained. "It was a real mystery for the curators to figure out. Of course they talk, we're all in the same business. We share pieces regularly, and work together to make sure that each of our collections compliment without competing. After a year or so, the collection became rather large, with no one owning more than a couple of pieces. It was decided that the museums would work together to share this collection, gathering it all in one place to show the full scale of his work. It started at the Met, then moved around the tri-state area, followed by a tour of the country. When we were notified that it might be coming to the area, we pushed hard to be the ones to display it."

"Why is that?" he asked.

"Because this is where he was born," she said. "Alexander

Thornton grew up in Edison, married here, raised his son here, and died here. He's buried in the cemetery on Water Street, next to his wife and child."

"I thought he was from Charlotte," Bradley said.

"His museum was in Charlotte," Hannah explained. "But he lived just outside of Edison. His house is a national landmark. I'm surprised you didn't know that."

"But he was originally from Charlotte," he said.

"Technically," she replied. "But he always said that Edison was his home."

"So," Bradley said. "What do you make of the rumors of his having something to do with his wife's death? I know you can't comment officially as a member of the staff of the museum, but my sense was you knew more than what you said the other day."

"Some of them are so ridiculous they're laughable," she said.

"Like the fact that he used parts of her in his art," Bradley agreed.

"Or that she was the true artist and he was jealous of her work," she continued.

"That's the one that baffles me the most," he said. "It is obvious that he was the artist since many of the pieces from the collection came after her death."

"Unless you take the rumor that she didn't die when they say she did," Hannah said.

"That's a new one," he said.

"Really?" she asked.

"From what I know," he began, "she was buried and her family saw the body. They even had her examined."

"The research I read said her family didn't see her body," she replied. "What I learned was that he had his own doctor examine her and give the report to her family, but that he refused to let them see her after she passed away."

"I think we'll have to agree to disagree on this," he said.

"How do you know so much about it?" she asked.

"Let's just say I have more than a passing interest in his artwork," he said.

"Is that why you're buying the museum?" she asked. "Because, we don't own the artwork."

"I'm buying the museum because it is a good investment," he said. "My interest in the collection is personal, though."

"You're the one who is in negotiations to purchase it," she said. "I should have known."

"Why?" he asked.

"Your last name is Graham," she explained. "That was Beatrice's last name before she married Alexander. You're family, aren't you?"

"That I am," he confirmed. "Our family has been trying to gain access to the artwork in order to do some testing on it. We also believe that since Alexander had no other family, and his son never had children, it rightfully belongs to us."

"Why did your family not claim it upon Edmund's death?"

"Unfortunately," he said. "It was sold prior to our becoming aware of his death. Her brother, my great, great grandfather, was unaware that Edmund had died. He didn't find out until well after the collection and everything else in the house was sold. Nothing was left to her family."

"Who brokered the auction?" she asked. "I mean, did they even try to find family?"

"You know we're talking about the late 1800's, right?" he asked. "At that time, if there was a will, that was what happened to the property of the person who died. Since he had no children, there was no one to protest the will, and the artwork and everything else in the estate was auctioned off. My family wasn't even notified that it was taking place."

"Why not?" she asked. "I mean, it seems that in this small of a town, they would have known he died and could have asked about what was going to happen to everything."

"His will was very specific," he said. "His father's was as well."

"What do you mean?" she asked.

"It was specified in Alexander's will that everything was left to his son, Edmund," he said.

"That makes sense," she replied.

"There was also a stipulation that once Edmund passed away," he continued. "If he had no heir, then the property was to be sold at auction, and the Graham family was banned from purchasing any of it. It would be passed down generation to generation until no heir was alive, then it was to be sold."

"Banned?" she asked.

"Yep," he replied. "That's why no one knew it was for sale."

"Then how could an anonymous bidder purchase the collection?" she asked.

"My guess is that the person who purchased it was not anonymous," he replied. "They simply didn't want her family to know who it was."

"How did it get split up and sent to the museums, then?"

"It's been over a hundred years since the original sale," he said. "There was no provision in the will that stipulated it not be sold or sent elsewhere once the final heir let it go. Because of this, whoever purchased it originally was able to parcel it out and send it to the museums."

"Wait," she began. "It was originally sold in 1897 as a whole collection. After that, it disappeared for over a hundred years. It began showing up in 2000 or so. That's a long time for it to just be sitting in someone's garage or storage unit. Where did it go?"

"I don't know that that particular mystery will ever be solved," he said.

"If your family had known about the auction," she began. "Do you think they would have asked someone to bid for them? I mean, that would be a way for them to get the pieces without it faulting the will."

"The person who purchased it had to sign a guarantee that they would not be giving it to our family," he said. "Which means that whoever purchased it couldn't have been hired by my family because they would have had to lie on the paperwork in order to gain possession of the pieces."

"And you know they were purchased as a set," she said.

"By one entity," he confirmed. "From there, they simply vanished."

"If the will says that the person can't sell them to your family, how are you going to purchase them now?" she asked.

"They are not owned by the original purchaser," he replied. "The owners are the museums. By the time I am ready to purchase the collection, I will own your museum and will be able to properly show my ability to display and protect them."

"You've thought this through thoroughly, haven't you?"

"Very much so," he replied.

"So," she said. "How can I help?"

"I thought you'd never ask," he replied.

"Did you go back to school when I wasn't paying attention?" Jenna asked Hannah.

"No," Hannah replied. "It's for Bradley."

"It's Bradley now?" she asked. "Didn't know you were on a first name basis, yet."

"We've been working on this for five weeks," Hannah said. "We went to first names within the first week."

"Interesting," Jenna said.

"What's that supposed to mean?"

"Just that you've never given any guy a second glance before now," Jenna said. "Suddenly, some guy shows an interest in your favorite artist and you're all swoony."

"I'm not swoony," Hannah protested.

"You are," Jenna said. "You keep looking at your phone, wondering if you'll get a text or call or email from him. You're doing so much work after work that it's like you're studying for a doctorate. When I suggest we watch something or go out or do anything other than your research you snap at me and act like I'm trying to steal your favorite toy."

"That's not swoony," Hannah said. "That's moody, and it's because you're disrupting my flow."

"The only flow you've had is information overload from research," Jenna said. "You seriously need to take a break. There is more to life than art, you know."

"I am taking a break," Hannah said. "Tonight, Bradley and I are going out to dinner."

"But you'll be discussing Alexander Thornton," she retorted. "That does not constitute a break."

"We'll talk about other things," Hannah said.

"Will you be talking about going on a real date?"

"This is a real date," Hannah said.

"No," Jenna said. "A real date is where you go to a movie or to dinner or something. Not where you talk about work. That's not a date at all."

"But it's something we both love," Hannah protested.

"Even so," Jenna said. "You need to do something besides

talk about that artist."

"The purchase is supposed to go through next week," Hannah said. "Once that's done, Bradley will be moving forward to purchase the collection from the various museums."

"Which will take another month of you doing nothing but research," Jenna said. "I need a girls night."

"Next week," Hannah said. "I promise. We'll go get manicures and pedicures and watch stupid movies."

"But I get to choose," she replied. "None of those foreign films you like so much. I want something with a sexy guy in it, preferably one who has his shirt off most of the time."

"You're ridiculous," Hannah laughed.

"Hey," Jenna replied. "You used to love those movies."

"I still do," she said. "I just think I'd rather have the real thing."

"Are you trying to tell me something about you and Bradley?"

"There are moments when I think he's interested," Hannah said. "But then things happen and it's just like I'm a business associate or something. It's sometimes like he doesn't see me as a woman."

"Maybe he doesn't see you as someone who is befitting his stature," Jenna said.

"Because I'm not rich?"

"Or because you are about to become an employee," Jenna replied.

"He doesn't act like that," Hannah said. "I mean, OK, maybe he does a little. But honestly, I think he sees me more as someone he works with instead of someone he could spend more time with."

"Then maybe it's time you made him take notice," Jenna said. "When do you guys meet next?"

"After tonight, we're supposed to meet on Tuesday," Hannah said. "Dinner to discuss the final pieces of the purchase."

"Then we need to make sure that he sees more than just a cog in his wheel of fortune," Jenna said. "I've got a plan."

"Why does that make me nervous?"

"Because my plans are awesome," Jenna said.

"Or because your plans sometimes fail miserably," Hannah replied.

"Not always," Jenna said with a blush.

"Just when they involve guys," Hannah said. "Do I need to remind you of Wilson?"

"Please don't say that name," Jenna cringed.

"Then don't set me up like you did that time," Hannah replied. "I don't think I could take another episode like that."

"No one wants that to happen," Jenna said. "Never again."

"We're signing early," Bradley said.

"Really?" Hannah asked. "When?"

"Tuesday," he replied.

"So, we're not going out, then," Hannah said dejectedly.

"We're going out," he replied. "It'll be a celebration, though."

"Wasn't it already going to be a celebration?" she asked.

"This just means it'll be official," he replied.

"Where are we going?"

"Have you ever been to Lincoln Center?"

"I don't exactly make the kind of money for that place," she replied.

"Then you're in for a treat," he said. "They have the best blackened Cajun catfish."

"Sounds delicious," she replied.

"I'll pick you up at seven," he said. "Will you have enough time to get home and changed?"

"Tuesday is my day off, so it won't be a problem," she replied.

"Great," he said. "Wish I didn't have to cancel tonight, though. I was looking forward to seeing you."

"Work calls," she said. "I understand. I'll see you Tuesday."

"See you then," he replied.

The call disconnected and Hannah pulled it from her ear.

"Canceled?" Jenna asked.

"Until Tuesday," Hannah replied. "He's finalizing the sale early, though, so we're going to the Lincoln Center for dinner."

"What are you going to wear?"

Hannah's phone buzzed and she looked down, seeing a text from Bradley.

I'll send something over on Monday for you to wear.

"That's apparently been taken care of," Hannah said, turning her phone to her roommate.

"He certainly likes to dress you," she said. "Isn't that kind of creepy?"

"I like it," Hannah replied. "Makes me feel like he pays attention to me."

"Or pays attention to how you make him look," Jenna said.

Hannah looked at her friend and said, "He doesn't treat me that way."

"Has he made you feel like anything more than an employee, though?"

"That's what I am," Hannah protested.

"But you want more," Jenna said.

"Of course I do," she replied. "That doesn't mean that I have to push it, though."

"Once this purchase goes through," Jenna began, "what's to keep him interested? I mean, you'll have done all the hard work. Where's the incentive to keep you around as more than just an employee?"

"That's not what this has ever been about," Hannah said.

"Be honest with me," Jenna said. "You want more than just a working relationship with him and you know it."

"It would be nice," she replied.

"Then we need to do something to make sure that once he's got the museum, he'll want to keep you around."

The determination in her friend's voice was a surprise to Hannah. She knew that her friend loved her like a sister, and would do anything for her. What she didn't get was why she was so set on Bradley being the one for her. She'd never been that interested in who she dated before.

"Love the red," Jenna said. "Did you know he was sending something in this color?"

"I wasn't sure what he was going to send," Hannah said honestly.

"But you got new heels," Jenna said.

"Black, patent leather," Hannah replied. "They'll go with anything."

"Fine," Jenna said. "But we've got to do something spectacular with your makeup."

"I like a classic, clean, fresh look," Hannah said.

"Not with that dress," Jenna replied. "That dress calls for dramatic, and that's just what we're going to give him. He sent the dress, you'll supply the pop."

"Just don't make me look like a French whore," Hannah protested.

"Have I ever?"

"Wilson," Hannah said, and Jenna cringed, saying, "Fine."

The next hour was spent with Jenna flitting and brushing and pressing and glossing and all other means of primping Hannah. By the time they were done, Hannah felt like she was wearing a pound and a half of cake on her face. When Jenna turned her to the mirror, though, she looked like a movie star.

"Now for the hair," Jenna said, pulling out a brush, comb, and all sorts of other paraphernalia. Hannah wasn't sure what her friend had in mind, so simply sat and let her play.

Another hour went by with pulling and combing and spraying and finally Jenna seemed satisfied.

"Perfect," she said and turned Hannah back to the mirror.

Hannah's jaw dropped open at what she saw. Staring back at her was a vision from the silver screen of yesteryear, as if she'd been dropped from a movie from the '50's.

"Wow," she said.

"I know, right?" Jenna replied.

"How?"

"Magic, my friend," she said. "Pure magic."

Jenna pulled the towel she'd draped across her friend's shoulders, uncovering the satin that hung off her shoulders.

"Shoes," she said and Hannah dutifully went in search of the new pieces, sliding her feet into them.

"Well?" she said hesitantly, doing a slow turn in front of her friend.

"You are a vision of beauty," Jenna said. "He's not gonna know what to do with himself."

"I don't care about that," Hannah replied. "I care whether he knows what to do with me."

"If he doesn't," Jenna said. "Then he doesn't deserve you."

Just then they heard a knock at the door.

"Showtime," Jenna said as she went to open it.

"Ms. Sanders," Bradley said.

"Mr. Graham," Jenna replied.

"Bradley," Hannah said as she came to the door, her black clutch in her hands.

"You look stunning," he said with a smile.

"You two have fun," Jenna said, nearly pushing Hannah out the door.

"Night," Hannah said just as her roommate gave her a wink and shut the door.

"May I?" Bradley asked, holding his arm out.

"Thank you," Hannah replied, taking it in her hand.

They made their way down the stairs to the lobby of her apartment building, stepping outside into the cool spring air. When he walked up to a silver Porsche she faltered. It wasn't that she didn't appreciate the beauty of his car. Oh no, she loved it. The problem was it was too much of a reminder of her brother. He was the black sheep of the family, always in trouble. One night he stole a car very similar to this one, went for a joy ride with friends, and found himself wound around a telephone pole. In an instant, she went from a big sister to an only child, and her parents were never the same.

"Is everything all right?" he asked.

"Just bad memories," she said.

Bradley opened the car door and ushered her inside. Hannah closed her eyes and took a deep breath. She hadn't realized how tense she was until the smell of the man she was heading to dinner with filled her senses. Somehow it had a calming effect on her, giving her a sense of peace.

"You sure you're all right?" he asked when he got in.

"Yeah," she said, smiling. "Let's go celebrate."

"Let's," he replied.

"Have I told you how beautiful you are?" Bradley asked.

"I think seven or eight times, now," Hannah replied.

"I'm sorry," he said.

"I don't mind at all," she replied. "It never gets old having someone tell you that."

"Then I'll say it again," he said. "You are absolutely stunning."

"Thank you," she replied.

"Did you enjoy your dinner?" he asked.

"It was delicious," she replied.

"Good," he said. "I thought you might want to take a drive by the waterfront."

"That would be nice," she said.

"If you're too tired, though," he began.

"No," she said. "I'd like that."

Bradley handed his valet ticket to the kid at the podium and they waited for him to bring around the car.

"What is your ultimate goal as far as your career?" he asked while they waited.

"I'd love to be the curator at a museum," she replied. "I know I can do it, I just have to find the right fit for myself. I don't want to leave Edison, but I'm afraid I won't be able to go much further until I venture into a larger city."

"Have you thought about my offer to work for me?"

"You haven't really given me a job description," she replied. "I don't even know what the job is. And you don't know whether I'm capable of handling the job."

"After watching the way you dove head first into the project I gave you," he began. "On top of what you already do, I think you have the right work ethic for my company. And I know how smart you are, simply by the information you've given me from the studies I needed."

"What is the job, exactly?" she asked.

"I'd like you to work for me as an assessor," he said. "I'm

going to need someone to review and authenticate any pieces I might want to add to the Thornton collection. I don't know of anyone more qualified than you to take that on."

"Except you," she replied.

Just then the young man drove up in Bradley's car. Opening the passenger door, Bradley helped Hannah into the vehicle, closing the door behind her. He walked around the car, pressing a large bill into the kid's hand as he passed, then climbed into the driver's seat. They drove out of the parking area and made their way to the waterfront, neither talking on the short trip.

"I'm serious," he finally said. "I want you to come work for me."

"That isn't what I studied," she said quietly.

"But it is what you are good at," he countered.

They'd found a place to park in a lot that looked out over the bay. Bradley turned the car off and shifted in his seat to look at Hannah.

"When I took your tour in the museum," he began, "I knew you were the one I needed to help me with acquiring the Thornton pieces. It was my third tour at Edison, and my seventeenth overall."

"You've been following the exhibits?" she asked.

"Does that surprise you?" he countered.

"I guess not," she said.

"No museum held enough of the exhibit for me to see its extent," he continued. "I wanted to see which pieces were out and what was and was not being displayed from the collection I knew existed. My goal has always been to be able to collect the entirety of the collection in one place. While there are many pieces you have in your museum, there are so many more that haven't been displayed. That's why I wanted you to do the research. If I'm going to have the whole collection, I'm going to need to know what has been rediscovered.

"The number of tours I've taken have told me that he isn't as known as he should be," he continued. "It also showed me that you are one of the only people besides me who is aware of the scope of his work. I think if we work together, we should not only be able to procure the remaining pieces of his work, but also figure out exactly what happened to Beatrice. That is my ultimate goal."

"Wow," she said.

"I know it's a lot to take in," he replied. "Honestly, though, you are probably the smartest person I've met who has as much of a passion for this project as I do."

"What do you think we'll find once we have the full collection?" she asked.

"The truth," he said simply.

"Do you need an answer today?" she asked, unsure whether she really wanted to delve into this with him or not.

"I'd really like an answer within the next week," he said. "But I want you, so take as much time as you need to find a way to say yes to me."

Hannah blinked at him, unsure if he'd just said what she thought he did.

"I just realized what I said," he said, almost reading her thoughts. "I mean, I want you for the project."

"So you're not interested in me," she said. "Other than my mind."

"That's not what I meant," he said. "I'm very interested in you as the beautiful woman you are. There is no question about that. I just don't know whether we should be involved in a relationship if we're going to be working together."

"I understand," she said dejectedly.

"Oh, no," he said, suddenly embarrassed by what he's said.

"Let me start again. Hannah, I'd love for you to come work for me. I would pay you a good salary and give you quite a bit of leeway within which to work. Additionally, I'd love to see you on a social level. I know it would be awkward with you working for me, so if I have to choose…"

He paused and she looked at him.

"Please don't make me choose," he whispered.

The vulnerability on his face was more than she could bare. The longing she saw in his eyes was something she'd always wished to see. Because he had asked her to work for him, she felt it would never happen. But here he was, asking for both.

"I really like the idea of working for you," she said and held up a hand to stave off his interruption. "I also really like the idea of dating you."

"Then you'll do both?" he asked.

Taking a deep breath, she nodded. The smile that broke on his face was the most beautiful thing she'd seen in ages.

"Don't ever feel like you can't tell me anything," he said. "I mean it. If something is bothering you, if you want to stop the dating, if you want to stop working for me, anything. Just tell me."

"I will," she replied.

Two Years Later

You're sure?" Hannah asked into the receiver. "In each sample?" she asked again "Thank you."

"Well?" Bradley asked.

They'd finally gotten almost all of the pieces they were aware of from the collection. Each had been tested for anything out of the ordinary, and the results had just come back.

"Traces of human DNA," she said.

"I knew it!" he shouted, then scooped her up in a hug. "You're a genius."

"That's only half the battle," she said as he set her down.

"I know," he replied. "But it's the biggest piece we've found to date."

"Mr. Graham," came the call from Stacey over the intercom.

Bradley moved around the desk and picked up the receiver. "Yes?" he asked.

"I have a package for you," she replied.

"Bring it in," he said, then hung up the phone.

The door opened and Stacey stepped in holding a small box. Bradley took it from her and thanked her, then brought the box to the desk. He picked up the letter opener and sliced through the tape holding the box closed. Folding the flaps back, he reached into the packing peanuts and pulled out a smaller package.

"What is it?" Hannah asked.

"I'm not sure," he replied.

Pulling the tape from the smaller box he pressed the flaps back. Inside was a small bottle and a card. He handed the bottle to Hannah and opened the envelope, pulling the card out.

You have completed the collection. This final piece is what is left of Alexander and Beatrice Thornton. Please ensure that this is kept separate from the other pieces. Lock it in a safe, keep it in a bank, move it to another city. Whatever you do, do not take it near the rest of the collection. The risk is too high. You are now trusted with this secret, one which can never be told. They can never come back.

"Is this real?" Hannah asked.

"Are you willing to risk finding out?" Bradley countered.

Hannah looked at the bottle in her hand, twisting it in the light. The dark liquid shimmered where it caught the glow and she shuddered, handing the bottle back to Bradley.

"I'll lock it up," he said, walking behind his desk.

He pushed a plant to the side and pressed on a panel in the wall which opened revealing a safe. Bradley pressed the buttons on the front and it popped open. He put the bottle back in the smaller box and placed it inside, closing the door and putting the wall back in place.

"Are you sure it's safe there?" she asked.

"It has to be," he replied.

"Maybe we should send some of the collection to another museum," she suggested.

"You're saying you believe the note," he said.

"My guess is you do, too," she replied. "Otherwise you wouldn't have put that bottle in the safe."

"I'll leave it there until I can get it tested," he said.

"The rest of the pieces are together at the lab," she said. "If you don't believe that card, why don't you take it to the lab now?"

"Why run the risk," he said.

"Then you do believe," she replied.

"What I know is that there are trace amounts of human DNA in the pieces at the lab," he began. "If this also has DNA, and it is my guess it does, then we do run the risk that the note is correct. We will have the rest of the results from the testing in the next week. By then, we'll know whether it is strictly Beatrice in the art, or whether Alexander put some of himself in it as well."

"If it's both of them," she began, "what will you do?"

"Either way, I need to reveal the truth," he said. "When I do, though, it will be a shock to the art world."

"I think that's an understatement," she said.

"Yeah," he replied. "Perhaps the understatement of the century."

"It's here," Bradley said.

"I'll be right there," Hannah replied.

The door to Bradley's office opened nearly immediately after he replaced the receiver on his phone.

"Let's see it," Hannah said.

Bradley sliced the envelope with his letter opener and slid the sheaf of paper out.

"They couldn't condense it?" she asked.

"I wanted the full report," he replied.

"Please tell me they have a summary sheet," she said.

"Right here," he said pulling the top page off the stack.

Sequencing conclusion 1: Singular, male, not related to Graham sample.

Bradley looked at Hannah who read the sheet over and over again.

"It's not her," she said.

"Definitely not her," Bradley replied.

"Then are we at square one?" she asked, looking at him.

"Let me look," he said, going back to the desk. He flipped through the pages to one that was marked with a flag. "Here's another results sheet."

"Why are there two?" she asked.

"Second sample," he replied walking over to her with the second page.

Sequencing conclusion 2: Singular, male, related to Thornton.

"It's him?" she asked.

"Apparently," he replied, rereading the second page.

"Where did you get a Thornton sample?" she asked.

"From the last piece," he said.

"You had that tested?" she asked.

"I did," he replied. "It came back as blood from their son, Edmund."

"Then how is it related to Alexander only and not to your family?"

"I asked the same question," Bradley said.

"Well?" she asked when he didn't offer anything further.

"It seems that Beatrice never was able to bear a child," he said.

"But…"

"That's why she declined so rapidly," he said. "Edmund was the son of one of their servants."

"I thought…"

"Let me finish," he said. She waved him on, so he continued. "Beatrice found out right after their marriage that she was unable to bear children. She wanted a child, and wanted Alexander to have a child. They decided to have one of their servants, someone who looked enough like Beatrice that the family would be fooled, bear him a child. Since women were not seen as much during their pregnancy in that time it worked. When Edmund was born, they presented him as their own.

"Beatrice soon became insistent on having more," he continued. "When Alexander refused to have another with the servant, she went into a rage, attacking him. He defended himself, but she was injured in the process. The reason she died was because of that injury. Alexander threw himself into his art, focusing on it rather than his son. By the time Edmund was old enough to understand what had happened, he cut all ties with the Graham family. He blamed them for his father's state."

Hannah sat with her hand over her mouth, unsure what to make of the story she'd just heard. "How did you find all of this out?" she finally asked.

Bradley went to his desk and pulled out another stack of paper, this one very old looking. He handed it to her and she pulled the front page back and began to read. The more she read, the more she realized that Bradley was right.

"Where did you get this?" she asked.

"It came the day after the bottle," he said.

"Why didn't you tell me?" she asked.

"I wanted to authenticate it," he replied. "I didn't want to muddy the waters until I had all of the facts."

"This is so sad," she said. "It changes everything about his work."

"You are the one who knows his work best," he said. "I want you to write a book on it."

"What do you mean?" she asked.

"I have a vested interest in the story coming out," he said. "But the story is the important part. It needs to be written by an outside party."

"I'm hardly that anymore," she replied.

"But you are," he countered. "You and I may have a relationship, but you are not family. Everything you've told me has helped to find the truth. I know you can do this, and you deserve the credit."

"I didn't do anything," she said.

"Your desire to know everything helped push me to get to the bottom of it," he said. "Without you, this never would have seen the light."

"Where did this book come from?" she asked.

"I don't know who sent it," he said.

"Do we know it's authentic?" she asked.

"What is your gut telling you?" he countered.

She looked back at the book in her lap, the pages so old she feared they would rip if she weren't careful. Finally, she nodded and said, "It's real."

"And?" he coaxed.

"It needs to be shared," she finally conceded.

"Then you'll do it," he said.

"I'll need help," she said.

"My resources are at your disposal," he said.

She looked at him again, unsure whether to ask, but decided she needed to know. "Where does that leave us?"

"I'm not going anywhere," he said.

CANTATA
BY DAVID MECKLENBURG

The brief afternoon is almost over and I am finishing my piece of *Himbeerkuchen*. I pay Nicholas after he drops off the second *Kannichen* of black coffee.

"Where will you be wandering today?" He smiles and asks me. His hair is fashionably long, and he isn't very good at obscuring flirtatious glances with it. But he is trying, and I think that far more adorable than a practiced seducer. I was won over by his dark brown eyes and his prominent Adam's apple, the sort that looks remarkably fragile under his pale skin.

"*Heute? Wie ein Kind wandere ich durch die Weinachtsmarkt.*" I answer. I have told him that I will help him practice English if he helps me with my German. He pauses a bit longer by the table, looking at his hands, the bill. "*Fragst du mir etwas?*" I ask.

"Frau Ludenow… would you like to hear a cello recital?"

"*Du?*" I ask. I am not about to keep to formal pronouns. "*Studierst du an die Universität?*"

"*Ja,*" he answers without thinking.

"*Was spielst du?*" I ask him.

"The Cello Suite Number Five in C-minor," he says this somewhat proudly in re-composure and English. "I am not very good, but it would be nice for you in your visit here." He tells me where and when. It is an early practice recital. I know the composer, because this is Leipzig after all and one does not even need to name him—only which piece.

"Did Nicholas just ask me out?" I ask myself as I leave Kaffeehaus Riquet, and I do not know if I am flattering myself or he was. But in a minute or two I am free of such thoughts, because I can wander the *Weinachtsmarkt* by myself, "like a child." Ironic, not because I am far from being a child, but things were a bit more restricted when I was one. I had the limitations of parochial Arden in Sacramento, living in an apartment complex with above average vacancy and few friends nearby.

Oh, but those were the days and yet I didn't really know it, having grown up in them. In Felizia,—a city I had imagined and where I knew I truly belonged—Cathness Kleppers glided in, filled from the keel to the sails with spices, rare dried fruits, silks and kurz fabrics, the textiles of dreams and billions of now dead korty bugs, who, like their silkworm cousins made a good snack once boiled and deep fried.

But Felizia is somewhere I visited only in my mind. So I have Leipzig.

Why Leipzig? *What is Leipzig? I never heard of it.* Leipzig is roughly the same size as Seattle, and the urban area around has roughly the same population as King County, so it feels familiar. Leipzig has always been a trading city and is still famous for its trade fairs. I am not here for one of them. I don't have to come to terms with Leipzig, because I have never been here.

It is late in the year and the Leipzig Christmas Market ramps up for the darkness. It has been luxuriating all day. There is *Glühwein*, fat loaves of *Stollen* dusted in sugar, tiles of *Lebkuchen*, furs from

Finland, knives, ornaments for *die Tannenbäume*, many of which have been cut and make the place look like a forest. Maybe it's the *Glühwein*, perhaps the largesse of the Market, but my head, while not spinning, finds itself swimming in the sunny city that Girl once inhabited.

That Girl waited for an Ursean Hauler, decked out with 23 masts and carrying 8 million bags of the highest quality rags and an equally formidable cargo of livestock: bleating, mooing , oinking and shitting across the seven seas for seven years. No one in the port ever really knew why the sailors burdened themselves with such a cargo since some of them were so terrified of labor that they stood stark raving mad, the victims of a terrible catatonia.

Her Daddy would be out there, trying to help unload the *Rover*, and what she wanted wasn't a pig or a rag. No, the *Rover* carried, deep within its massive bulk, the One Thing she wanted: the last installment of *The Bishop's Dream*. The city had been gripped, well, some of them, by this serialized tale. The Girl had begun, like the rest of the literate populace, at the end, for narrative runs backwards in Felizia.

In the first (or last) chapter, the Player slid off the bench as the last notes of the Mass lingered in the stonework. Everything had been meticulously researched and printed according to the principia of the era, which meant that the Audience had patiently assembled the performance space over centuries, just as it would have been done traditionally. Time was now something to be savored and not waded through.

The Player looked at the beautiful ceiling arching far above, as the Corrin's Disease, an unfortunate side effect of the Mannoid Process, rendered flesh into a chocolate marble shot through with veins of what looked like alabaster and carnelian. The first arm, the one used on the upper manuals went stiff and tight. Then the second arm. Finally, the third and fourth limbs froze as well. For so long had they been lithe in manipulation of the stops.

"Now I understand," the Audience said.

"And I have been used?"

"You are assigning teleology. Fascinating. I have not tasted that word since we first brought back the unicorns."

"Möchten Sie das Einhorn kaufen?" The woman asks me, and I am back in Leipzig. My gaze lingers in the reflected fire kindled like a real flame in the depths of the crystal unicorn. The unicorn hangs like imperishable ice on a bare branch in her menagerie of Christmas tree decorations.

"Nein, es ist sehr schön. Es erinnerte mich nur an etwas…" and fortunately another customer, much younger than I, holds up a grinning gnome. Her father is already getting out his wallet full of Euros. I do not have to explain what I am remembering, and the saleswoman does not seem to mind.

There is a lack of pretense here: the Germans are aloof and wrapped deeply in the warmth of their own *Privatsphären:* the private spheres of their own lives, unlike Seattle where fuss is made over appearing open, friendly, but ultimately the ice wears thin on those frozen ponds and you will fall through. I think again about how much I prefer this Christmas market than the pay-on-entry drinking scenes in Berlin. My ex is a Berliner, and I got to know that beautiful City quite well through loving her. So that is one reason I am in Leipzig. Astrid is and always was far away from here. I have Leipzig to myself.

The Girl was not so lucky, I think as I walk back to my hotel. I can almost feel the breeze as her mother threw a tin can at the Girl's head.

The Girl, who'd long been the target of tin cans, peach pits, cigar butts, and a *Collection of the Lesser Odes by Burbank Anusol* had learned to shift her head with just enough effort to avoid the missile at hand.

"Git me some of thar beer you brat shit oh GAWDZ why did I ever scrape you off that stump after the crow shat you out and the sun hatched you and there you were with eyes that couldn't even peep and ever thinking of yourself and your dreamy worlds. Do you git me?!"

The *Rover* was hauling 7 million barrels of porter, it was famously said. Her mother knew, the Girl knew it. Everyone knew it. But it gave the Girl a reason to go! She jumped off the old pyutl crate the family kept as a chair on their houseboat and ran out on deck. But how to get there? Her father, whom she seldom saw and suspected was not her blood father, was already a jumble of smokestacks and masts and wheelhouses crowded by the *Rover*. She looked down at the harbor punt tied up alongside their houseboat and jumped in.

Out upon the water was where she belonged. She was tall, unlike her mother and supposed father, which is why her pedigree remained unconvincing. She was strong and sculled the punt across the choppy waves with expert strokes from lean but iron-hard muscles. She often thought of getting a sailboat or something and just sailing out of the harbor. But then, of course, she would never have gotten to the beginning of *The Bishop's Dream*, with which she had fallen in love. As she delved deeper into the story of the poor Player, she had seen a bit of herself.

"Why are you complaining?" The Audience had asked the Player in the second installment.

"Because this performance is the most important, that's

why," the Player said. "I am beginning to feel stiffer and the willow bark extracts you have brought in from the domes no longer succor me. If I am so precious, why did you make me to age? Did you think I wished to be born?"

"Ingratitude. A learned response? From where?"

"Are you so sure that I cannot have a single thought on my own?" the Player asked.

"A sense of pride, perhaps. This is most delicious. I haven't seen it in centuries. Oh, to think that in the architecture of these pillars, God Himself was made in the image of a Man, with beard, feet, arms, nipples. It was all they could do. Is that pride? Or the worst kind of idolatry?" The Audience was speaking to themselves again, as they often did.

"Hey! I am here you know!"

"We appreciate your patience for that which you do not understand. Are you prepared?"

"It is what I was born to do. Even though I never asked to be born."

"Came into this world is a better phrase."

The German side of my family came into this world in Lübeck, so that is not why I am here.

He is here, though. He's been dead over 268 years, but I could just as easily expect to meet him on any street. Without the wig of course. I was never a huge fan, to tell you the truth, although in my family he lives in the same Olympic Mountains as do Schiller, Goethe, and Beethoven: these were the Germans I was taught to offer up to the world when I was called a Nazi at school because of my name and half my heritage. How they could really call a black-haired girl with my complexion a Nazi is beyond me, but the logic of bullies is selectively effective.

Know that his music played in the houses of my family. My Uncle was an engineer for Aerojet and like many engineers he's crazy about the guy—the music has a mathematical certainty to it. Perhaps it's this place, but I feel kinder to him now that I see where he lived. I lay in my hotel bed with the curiously inept pillows I find all over Germany and remember the light in Sacramento, the music coming from the stereo which was a large cabinet in the living room of my Grandparents' house. I would play with toy boats on that floor I think... arguments and maneuverings on carpet like a harbor.

"You can't come aboard, we have enough of your kind on board, scuttling around and distracting the crew."

"I don't want one of your sailors, I want a book."

The mate looked down on her and scowled. "Oh, you're one of them readers. Shove off and buy it through a proper bookseller like Jezzos Bros.

"No, thank you. Fine. If you continue like this, I am afraid I shall have to inform my father."

"And who might that be?"

"The Captain of this Ship," she was going out on a yard-arm, she knew, but she also suspected that her father *was* the captain of one of these ships.

"Ha! I have no doubt of your bastardy, because I really don't have any alternative facts at hand and by the look of you, you somewhat resemble Captain Dooley, but he prefers boys not women, so you had best shove off and get in line at Jezzos Bros." She looked about and noticed there were quite a few anchor chains for the vast ship, so she made her plan. For *The Bishop's Dream* she was willing to try anything because it taught her something about persistence, even in the leering face of the inevitable. She remembered the Player's struggles.

"No, it isn't working,' the Player said to no one in particular, although the Audience was always around. In all the years the Player had been perfect; knew only this music; practically *was* this music. The Player knew the notes as objects, as something four dimensional in their shape and plasticity through time, how syncopation would leave the notes stretched, or chipped and yet they were always the same in the score.

The Player learned Lutheran theology and the Species counterpoint theories of Mazzola: anything to avoid the conclusion that stole up the aisles, floated over the empty seats, evaded the light of the Sun and came to rest its ghostly hand on the shoulder of the Player.

Sometimes the mornings in Germany enhance my irritability. I blame this on the darkness, although by now I have thoroughly reset my clock and while it's dark compared to Seattle, it's not that dark. But I know what it is. It's been 5 months since my last period and that one lurched forward, stalled, lurched and stalled like a teenager learning to drive a stick shift. It gave up in the end and sat in the wide parking lot and cried.

I am getting old. My skin feels different. I notice it especially in the pale light of the hotel bathroom because it is a different light to be naked in. I am trying to make myself appear attractive for Nicholas. I won't lie. But the real reason is I hope I look young enough to be his girlfriend is that I know people will otherwise think I'm his mother. I sit on the strange square toilet of this hotel and count out the years. It's within the realm of cruel mathematical possibility. Perhaps Nicholas was being nice. How swift I am in discounting agreeable manners and optimism with Machiavellian charity. But I remember his gaze... those brown eyes and think it's nice to be seen. Many women my age are no longer seen.

But the Girl could have used some of my invisibility.

The anchor chain was heavy and unrelenting, but she was strong. In the general hubbub of the *Rover's* arrival she could inch up the chain easily enough, but upon foisting herself up the side, she saw another mate, leaning against the capstan. She immediately ducked and nearly lost her handhold. When she peeped again at him, she saw that he hadn't noticed her. Whether this was because of his strabismus or the captivating final chapter of *The Bishop's Dream* which he relished, she couldn't tell, blinded as she was by her own desire and now rampant jealousy.

A seagull, who could not read and did not need to, was more interested in her tensile fingers and waddled over to peck at her. Peck peck. One, two fingers slipped. Peck peck peck. Three more.

The young Player fell into the perfection of the Variations. It was not the climbing victory of perseverance and final mastery, but realizing instead that this had all been made easy. The 20th Variation had not been a problem. With four arms, it was easy to avoid crossing hands over the manuals. But the Player, at the height of power, failed on the 25th. The chromaticisms sounded forced, and the enharmonic tapestry of the music tore apart in lame swatches, like fine fabric cut with golden, yet dull shears.

"I do not understand."

"That is precisely the problem, we think. That is not mere logical tautology. But you will understand that like leaves, birds, you will fall through time into death."

"Is that the Meister's meaning in the 25th?"

I think of the poor Player, like this student (the one before Nicholas in these recitals); there is a lifetime still, hopefully to learn the 25th Variation. The student manages the Aria de Capo well enough I think, but it sounds a bit clunky. Rather than elegant footfalls toward a sleep, there is the hollow clunking of boots falling to the floor by the bed.

The recital hall is plain. The lights seem too bright, but I have to remember this is a place for practicing music. Maybe the light makes the music brighter, easier to learn? Or maybe it is a better light in which the proctors and auditors can probe the weaknesses of the students. My German is not good enough to know precisely what they are telling the pianist. She shows grand German resolve, even though she has a very Chinese name on the program. But I like to think China and Germany share a few things: both of their languages are good to yell in. The cuisines are based on pork, cabbage and salt. She listens to their criticism and nods sharply. She stands and bows to the audience and like the only American I am there, I smile at her. She frowns, glances over to the door and I see she is looking at Nicholas as if to say: "is this the dumb American you brought here?"

I look down at the program and realize my Girl has been in worse places. And she was hardly stupid.

Felizia's harbor is often oily from the ships and their various oils, both in the form of petroleum, converted vegetals and spilled renderings of animal fats and so when the Girl surfaced in the water, her long hair (of which she was secretly vain) was coated in a fine lipid film. She cursed the seagull and gravity (which had it especially in for her) and swam toward another barge.

"What are you doing here?" a stevedore asked as she scrambled on the deck.

"I was trying to get on the *Rover*. I..." She fell silent and held her hands before her private area because she felt wet and oily and all of her clothes stuck to her with perfect adhesion, revealing every curve-to-be-perhaps after puberty, every muscle, every bony projection and other embarrassingly salient appurtenance. The stevedore eyed her silently. Then approached her with a lustful glint in his eye.

"I know what you want, girl. I want it too."

"I'll bet you do…" she said.

"It looks like a Woman," the Player said. "Like from the paintings you have showed me."

"Regardless of its historic shape, it is the shape and that is important for the acoustics," the Audience said.

The Player held up the Viol de Gamba gently, cradling the base which had been crafted of maple that had once again grown free and clear upon the reclaimed slopes of the Apennines. The viol had seven strings according to Monsieur St. Coloumbe.

And there is a first time for everything, even if they are nothing more than vestigial memories. The Audience did not worry about desire, but perhaps it should have before it programmed the gonads out of the Player. Originally the entire aspect of sex seemed to be a ridiculous component of the old Form. Like many clumsy heuristics, it had outgrown its usefulness as a reproductive method and had become an emotional liability. The Player was better off without all of that nonsense. The Player wasn't meant to perform Led Zeppelin, after all.

"We can start with the Sonatas for cembol and viol."

"I do not understand. Why don't you just imagine this, Mother. Why do I have to play it?"

"That will take some explaining. And I wonder if you know what you're saying when you say 'Mother.'"

"I have read the instructional water, I know what a placenta is, how you fashioned it for me."

"You fashioned it, but you know that I am neither female nor male. You know that I am as much stainless steel and nanocarbon as unlimited regenerative flesh.

"Did I not grow inside of you?"

"What do you mean by that question?"

"I mean the direct answer of 'yes' or 'no.'"

"Specify, do you wish for a literal answer, or a figurative one?

"What can I understand?

"Besides the Cantatas and the Partitas?"

"Yes."

"I am not sure. Perhaps in a way you did grow inside of me. Oh, this is what they must have experienced when their children came for to ask the impossible questions."

'What questions?"

"Of meaning, direction, purpose. The Categoricals grasped and let go, like ape babies in the zoo looking at a blade of grass or discarded Coke bottle."

Nicholas has large hands. He would have been a very good piano player. But they give him a strength and reach on the cello that seems to suit him as he plays through music that sounds like introspection at the end of a life: not of good times, nor bad, but missed chances. A stairway not climbed. A beach on a beautiful morning driven by. A lover unloved. A life not lived. I suspect that C minor and the register of the cello are perfect for the expression of grief.

I like music, that much must be obvious, but I have neither formal training nor theory. Most of what I know comes from listening, reading and some occasional commentary from my uncle. At my elementary school a music teacher had come and set us all on fire for band. I wanted to play the clarinet because Jenny was going to play the clarinet. (And what school in California in the 70's did not have a Jenny who played the clarinet? Jenny, if you are reading this, I admired you. I think you knew that).

There was an open house at the school for band. All of us went, even my mother. She looked at all the instruments, considered them in some way and then sat down to listen to the presentation about how important music was for the development of our brains. Afterward, she went up to the band teacher and asked. "What instrument makes the least noise? I don't want to hear her practicing."

Afterward, during band hour, I had a note to go to the library: "She'll like it there better anyway. She's always reading," my mother's handwriting said. During those afternoons I would read, but sometimes I would sit and imagine how much better life was for the free and strong Girl.

Like her, the stevedore was one of those people cursed with chronic inflammatory literacy, and nothing but the new episode of *The Bishop's Dream* would quench his desires. Within moments on the deck, their mutual recognition and respect became apparent and enabled a session of strategy-&-tactics immediately after her extraction from Felizia's harbor, although they did waste some time in a needless yet indulgent sidebar discussion of who was better: Crimrose *pere* or *fils*. But then they got to business.

"Just make sure you don't drop it in the water or get caught."

"I won't. Give me a bag or something I may sling over my shoulder."

"And how about a knife to carry between your teeth in Buccaneer style?" The stevedore said.

"Don't be ridiculous."

"Look, every minute we stand here talking those bastards

from Jezzos Brothers are off-loading another crate and we'll never get to read it without paying their exorbitant markup."

The stevedore moved her aloft with his crane usually used for loading barrels of anchovies, so it smelled of oily fish but the Girl was oily anyway, so it really didn't matter. Now she was going to get two copies of the text. The stevedore of the barge expertly nudge-flung her into the *Rover's* rigging and she caught, swung, dipped, spun and brachiated through it like a gibbon until by the 3rd mizzenmast she espied what she was looking for: boxes of books.

The Player was the equivalent of five human years. Old enough to start with the linear octaves on the piano. It still had to learn how to arrange its augmented limbs to play the music originally designed for only two hands. But even then, the Player could not understand how the Meister, who presumably only had two hands, could write such music.

Because the music lessons had begun early, before the alphabetic and pictographic systems were introduced, the Player knew the staves, bars and clefs. Yet this method was not solely relied upon. Music filled the child's life. Books, which were an antiquarian curiosity and thoroughly archaic, were not present. Perhaps one day the Audience would create a poet: someone who would wander through the vast deserts of the empty libraries. But not just yet.

"Nein, noch nicht heute abend, aber montags gehe ich nach Dresden." I explain to Nicholas I was leaving Leipzig soon.

"But you have said you haven't even been to the museum yet? You went to that tourist trap of Feuerbach's Keller…"

"Das war für Goethe."

"Yes, but Weimar and Frankfurt are Goethe's cities. This is the Meister's city. Come, we have a few hours. I will take you there."

We drink our *Glühwein* quickly, leave the *Weinachtsmarkt* and walk towards the St. Thomaskirche, through the rush of the crowd. We pass by the old booksellers in the Old Town Hall and I turn briefly like Orpheus, but my Eurydice tugs on my arm, enfolded in his.

"*Komm, wir haben nicht viel Zeit.*" he says. Time is too short for English. I laugh and remember how the Girl avoided the booksellers and publishers.

Because it wasn't theft per se, if she could have paid the publisher: Bendix, Bendix and Chandra, if she could have. At least this was the rationalization she made as she swooped down and landed as gingerly and delicately as a bird behind the boxes. As nonchalantly as she could, she opened her jack-knife and sliced open a box. The men around were occupied in the task of casks, rolling the heavy beer barrels up the ramps, hauling them out with cranes and so no one really noticed the thin girl opening up a crate of books, neatly laying the excelsior aside and stowing two copies of *The Bishop's Dream* into her swag sack but then:

"You, what are you doin' there!" a voice screamed at her.

Fleeing as swiftly as she could, the crew members pursued her, but they were encumbered by *everyone else*. The entire dockyard population had gang-rushed the *Rover* as bales of billy goat tails also swung through masts, and seagulls cried and porters waited with barrows, yelling and popping their pimples while waiting for the clamor to die down. A bosun grabbed at her ankle.

"You'll pay for that, you little thief!" he yelled, and she felt her body slipping.

It was at that precise point that her expert, yet distant partner intervened. He quickly counterswung his articulated crane and knocked the bosun safely into a waiting mainsail with a barrel of porter. The Girl then clung to the barrel and its hitches and harness for dear life as it hurtled through the air, cleared the deck of the *Rover* and descended with aplomb to the barge.

"*Shut up and hide,*" he whispered, and she rolled right up to and burrowed into a pile of rags. Gods, she was so close! She had read all the way up to the womb and remembered how it was wheeled into its position.

The first beam of sun from the Vernal Equinox shone upon the Player's face as it emerged. The elastic glass swelled slightly with each pump of blood and nutrients into the Player's umbilical cord, (the first of many chords) and it bathed in an amniotic fluid composed of rigidly programmed salinity, yet, as the Audience understood, a certain degree of variance, of aleatory heuristic influences, would result in a subtle and therefore profound existence. A touch of lavender, onions, ambergris, anthracite, and gluten all made themselves seats in the orchestra of the Player's gestation.

Was this not a selfish thing to do? The world, being understandably vast, far vaster than the Audience's progenitors could have imagined was a difficult place to make categorically imperative decisions. But there was a certain element of morality involved and a perhaps it was the investment in a living being, a being that would experience joy, sorrow and absurdity, that gave the Audience pause. By endowing the Player with musical precociousness, the Audience knew that the crossing bridge between bars, the required silence of music and the interstitial ontologies of notes would result in emotion. The limbic brain was always there, and even the Audience understood its deep algorithms in its own being.

"I want to hear someone play his music." That declaration continued in repetition, sometimes gaining in harmonic strength with the often-forgotten encoding of adenine, thymine, guanine and cytosine; no matter what the scrambling, the genes maintained

Schopenhauer's relentlessly amoral will to live and reproduce. But wasn't there a selfishness in the desire for music? Especially the music for which the Player had been bred?

I understand why someone would be selfish enough to want to hear it. Nicholas and I pay the fee and leave our coats in the lockers. The museum is directly across the Thomaskirchof where the Meister was the Thomaskantor for many years. His statue presides over the square and a couple were having their wedding pictures taken with him in the background, like a bronze photo-bomber.

We walked through the exhibits, most of them were the playful, interactive kind where you can push a button and hear music. I loved the case full of period instruments and I was fortunate to have such a skilled guide with me.

"At some point, maybe I will switch to Viol de Gamba. Study with Jordi Savall. It is a little dream of mine," Nicholas said, and I looked at him and smiled. He was very sweet, and very young. For a moment I remembered what it was like to have my life in front of me like that. I can still dream, my own change in life is proof of that, and the arguments make a sort of sense now. Nicholas is climbing out of adolescence and I am climbing out of fertility. Upward upward scales, like a well-tempered clavier.

It is late and we seem to be alone in the museum.

"Come, the manuscript room is this way," he says.

"Are they gone?" The Girl asked, popping her head above the rags like a marmot.

"Aye, they're gone, although they didn't make much of a fuss," the stevedore said. His craft, as full of beer as it allowed, was calmly, albeit slowly puttering back across the bay.

"Aye," she said. "Well you have your book and I have mine.

The sun and weather are fine, are they not?"

"They are."

And she sat back in the pile of rags and opened the book. It was a slight volume, candy striped on the cover beneath the plain brown paper wrapper. She looked over the volume for oil stains and saw none. "How long do we have before we make land?" she asked.

"What?" The Stevedore was reading as well and not paying close attention to the Girl nor the course.

"How much time do we have, and where are we going?"

"I didn't get volume 5. What's this business with the centaur?

"Oh, a manufactured animal, just like the Player."

"For what?" It was then she noticed how much the stevedore's nose was like hers. How long and strong his hands were, and the particular grain and wave of his black hair was like hers.

"You're Maria Hardanger's Girl?" He asked. There was a strange, wistful look in his eye, then a feline, knowing grin.

"Aye."

"What is your name?"

"Ada."

"A pretty name. We have as much time today as we need to finish this book, Ada," and he winked at her.

The Player had been bathed in the music since parthenogenic conception. Synthesized and perfect forms, of course, but the Audience made sure that historic recordings were also present during gestation. The tone color and excitement of Horowitz. The mechanical, uncanny force of Gould. Perahia's fluid craftsmanship. Fliter's attack.

A cursory review of Buddhist philosophy, both before and after the conception, yielded the same results for the Audience: the attachment to the world remained a flicker of noise in the great silence of the void. Earlier experiments with the unicorns and centaurs were essays in the craft, and while they were alive in the world, the Audience did not take these actions as godlike. Yet, the Audience wondered if the notations in staves and clefs revealed some hitherto-dreamed consciousness of the Universe. Even some of the Audience's ancestors had pondered that. The Audience manifested that vision in the gently pulsing, embryonic flesh of the Player as it turned in its artificial and therefore perfect uterus.

That music could careen across the harbor in a myriad of purples and oranges as the sun set, and The Girl felt her toes itching on the coarse rags, which reminded her for a moment that her ungainly mother was waiting for beer and no account of smoke stacks, or flying through rigging like a gibbon would assuage. She learned that her probably-father was finally nearby, reading the same book, as the seagulls conducted their parliaments above the waves and the eels feasted on offal below, and all of the perpendiculars of buildings in perspective, the rounded forms of ships and fractal miracles of ever-changing clouds also sprang from this music when the little Girl in Sacramento, under a different yet similar sun, would listen to the music.

So that when she was older, she finally went to Leipzig: the place where the music, like the Player, first emerged into life, death, love, and time.

I can see it there, almost pulsing under the glass: Johann Sebastian Bach's fine manuscript in oak gall ink that eats up the parchment in microscopic mutability. I know that the *Goldberg Variations* score is only notation, yet it suggests a reality Bach had heard, perhaps dancing through the harmonics of truth at the horizon that marks the beginning and the end of the Universe.

MAY

THE PROMPT

Forgotten in one corner, cloaked in cobwebs and decades of dust, it was a survivor merely by default, by being over-looked, silent and unobtrusive, not big enough to be an imposition and so allowed to remain—a receptacle of memories, an eye witness to everything that came before.

FIREWORKS
BY JENNIFER DiMARCO

When I was in my early twenties, I read a story in a magazine while sitting in a clinic waiting to hear I would never carry a child. It was cold—inside the clinic, outside the clinic, in my chest, in the eyes of the doctor who knew I had no husband, had never been with a man, had no right to really want a child in the first place. New England was beautiful in the fall, brutal in the winter, and might as well have been both heaven and hell the way my time there turned my life upside down and inside out.

It was winter that day. It seemed like it had been winter for years.

But in the calm before the storm, ignorance is bliss and I sat there in the waiting room on a cheap chair and read that story about childhood abuse and not being believed. A story about retreating into your own head. About your only allies being the teddy bear, the hobby horse, the stuffed hippo with the big black button eyes that saw everything, that were my witnesses to everything... except they weren't *my* witnesses. It was just a story.

I felt exposed.

I also felt seen for the first time.

It was two sides of the same coin.

"Geraldine? The doctor will see you now."

I looked up at the thirty-something nurse with the thick glasses and up-turned nose and I stood. I intended to look back at the author's name. I intended to tuck the magazine under my arm and take it with me when I left the clinic. I intended a lot of things. But my existential trajectory changed over the next twenty-two minutes and by the time I emerged from the back office out a door at the end of the hall that led me to the elevators that took me to the lobby that opened out on the parking lot and my car and my rented home on the lake, I had forgotten the magazine, the story, and any revelation about being exposed, about being seen, about being anything other than what I was: Infertile. Barren.

Lacking.

That last one wasn't new to me.

Twenty Years Later

It stood forgotten in one corner, cloaked in cobwebs and decades of dust. A survivor merely by default, by being over-looked, silent and unobtrusive, not big enough to be an imposition and so allowed to remain—an unlikely receptacle of memories and an unexpected eye witness to everything that came before.

I'd been here a month and I didn't remember it. I didn't remember the story in the magazine. It had been two long decades and, understandably, that day at the clinic wasn't one I tried to revisit or recount on the regular. Right now, with the burden of stress on my shoulders like Rand's Atlas (far more bitter than the Grecian titan) I barely remembered what I had for breakfast. Or if I'd even eaten.

"How could you possibly keep all this crap." It wasn't a question but neither was it an accusation. I'd learned a long time ago that's just how Lydia spoke. Like fireworks, bright and a little too loud, taking up your entire field of vision whether you wanted her too or not.

I turned toward her and away from the forgotten thing. I liked turning to Lydia. I had come to rely on her blunt, tactless honesty and I relied on no one.

"How could I not?" I joke with her, picking up a soccer trophy I 'earned' when I was nine. That was the year I got confused and kicked the ball into the wrong goal resulting in my furious little teammates tackling me on the field. One fractured scaphoid carpal later, no one bothered to ask, *Why didn't the parents intervene?* "You love a jock, right?"

Lydia laughs and I feel the timbre of her voice like sparks jumping up my spine. I'd kiss her—soft and sweet, waiting for her permission to proceed—but she's already putting on her dust mask. "This is the danger of inheriting your childhood home."

I can't disagree but there are lots of things I can't do right now because I'm staring as Lydia walks to the only window in the attic and opens the warped wooden shutters. She has a great ass.

She turns back and I look up quickly. Her hands on her wide hips, sunlight falls past her, framing her no-nonsense posture, her take-no-prisoners, modern-and-empowered, all-American housewife-by-choice vibe. "Let's make this attic our bitch," she proclaims and it's my turn to laugh; I love it when she swears.

And yeah, I'd much rather she make *me* her bitch but I'm not on the schedule and Lydia is all about the schedule. Already, she's sorting boxes from bins, *tsking* in that wordless way she shows displeasure whenever she uncovers an errant squirrel or mouse nest.

I pointedly turn away, facing the other side of the room so I don't wind up staring at her all day and getting nothing done; I can't imagine anything that annoys Lydia more than getting nothing done.

I kneel down and the first box I open is falling apart before I even touch it. The cardboard flaps are placid, ready to give up the last of their structural integrity and unburden their contents onto the dusty floor. The stacks of paperwork inside are from an era long gone, an era when carbon paper and typewriters were at the top of the administrative food chain. I recognize my father's small, precise handwriting in all capital letters. Columns of numbers from his mind-numbing, meticulous assessments as an insurance adjuster. He spent his life deciding what property, objects, and even people were worth. His was a life not arguably well-spent but certainly spent, nonetheless.

I'd inherited the house from him. Not by favor or preference, certainly, but because my mother had given him one child and only one. I was Inheritor by Default (not a title I ever wanted but here I am).

I don't need to touch the papers to know they've fused into a single mass. I don't want to either. It took me a month to remove signs of my father from the house itself; Lydia even helped me patch the walls where his fist or my head had left their impressions of false entropy.

I'd moved out at sixteen, never returned for holiday or event, and yet the holes had remained. Were they his trophies? Like animal heads mounted in smoky studies. Did he drink whiskey with his fellows and when their eyes drifted to the holes in the plaster did he tell them with a smirk that was where he beat the 'faggot' out of his daughter? (He was never very good at lexicon.)

I take a deep breath and cough on mildew. I imagine I'm inhaling his handwriting, swallowing his orderly, uniform letters that perfectly symbolize how the rest of the world saw him. It's like being choked on grains of sand.

"You have a problem."

You're telling me. My thought isn't a question. Maybe Lydia is contagious.

Lydia puts a hand on the back of my neck and I look up at her. She's standing beside me motioning up with her other hand. I peer where she's pointing even though all I want to do is lean into her, enjoy the touch of her skin on mine. Enjoy the feeling of resting my head on her thigh.

For one hot flash it's last weekend again. And that's exactly where I am: My head resting on her thigh. There's a wine bottle empty on the bedside table. A dessert wine, expensive and sweet. There's a beveled pocket mirror on the bed, a new razor, an empty amber vial.

"Is it my birthday?" I'd asked when I'd opened the door four hours earlier.

"No." She'd closed my door behind her, locked it, tossed me the vial and lifted the wine out of her *Only Good Vibes* handle bag. "It's mine."

That's the other way she reminds me of fireworks.

"You have a leak."

And I'm back in the attic, in the present, in this new moment with Lydia. A new moment not quite as fun as the old moment.

Well, fuck. She's right. A sliver of daylight shows through the failing lathe and cedar shingles. Dad's box of paperwork had apparently been a rainwater sponge for years.

"Jesus...." I say no more because she moves forward and leans over me to peer into the soggy box of water-logged history. Her skin smells like lavender body wash I'd never be able to afford to buy her and her belly isn't flat; she's no slave to StairMaster or Pilates. I'm so enamored with her it's easy to pretend she's not my escape.

There is no reality where I wind up with Lydia in more than my bed. Our lives run parallel but never the twain shall meet. I mean... I suppose we 'meet' occasionally when she shows up at my door unexpected and unannounced with wine and cocaine and black satin panties under her Givenchy gabardine trench coat.

"Is this your mom?" Lydia plucks a damp, warped photo out of the otherwise unsalvageable box. This time she's absolutely asking a question. She crouches beside me and I take the photo reluctantly. "She looks just like you."

Let the Freudian field day begin.

My mother. I have two memories of her. In one she's alive and in the other she's dead. Very black and white. My brain works like that—in absolutes—and absolutely opposite from the real world.

I was told (many, many times) that I also watched her die

at the bottom of the stairs as she seized with a massive stroke and my four-year-old self sat on the landing with my wooden bumblebee and didn't call for help or run for the phone but just watched like the idiot I was and maybe still am.

Lydia carefully corrects herself, "You look just like her."

In the photo, my mother stands in a garden somewhere, a rose garden, with the cultivated and manicured plants arching and weaving between ornate, black wrought iron trellises. Is it Sicily? Victoria? The image is black and white with a thin white border and almost square so I know it was taken by my father with his ever-present Kodak used to document dry rot and birthdays alike. My mother is looking into the middle distance, her thoughts private and entirely somewhere else, her Amelia Earhart scarf and trousers quite avant-garde for a woman of her station and time. She was, after all, ten years my father's junior.

Every picture I've ever seen of her, she's like this: Distant. Candid. Already halfway gone.

In the photo, in the rose garden, I stand at her side—thin and non-remarkable—looking up at her with such obvious yearning. It's almost painful except that I lived through that pain and the wound has healed. Now I look at the scrawny girl child and instead of hurting *with* her, I hurt *for* her... but I also know she survived. It did, as all the hashtags promise nowadays, get better.

Also, it's true. My heart-shaped face and mop of dark hair? I do look like her.

"What are you holding there?" Lydia taps my clutched hands in the photo. Lydia's nails have just been done. I know the salon she likes and the deep reds she prefers. Her nails are neat ovals, just enough to tap an impatient rhythm on a countertop or leave trails down my back.

I swallow. My throat is dry. "A toy."

I look away from the photo. This was not my memory of my mother alive so I'm not sure where the garden was and I'm not sure anyone bought me the toy I clung to. I may very likely have walked out of the garden gift shop with it tucked against my narrow chest. Maybe the shopkeep took pity on me as I tagged along, all but forgotten, trailing a few steps behind my parents where they preferred me.

I glance back at the photograph, almost sidelong, and even in fading shades of gray, the garden is gorgeous in riotous bloom. A description which could easily be used for my mother.

I'm trying so hard to stay here, in the attic—this final dungeon of memories, the last place where relics of his life remain. I'm trying not to be torn in two between the past and present. If I don't stay focused, somehow he wins. Even dead, he wins. Then these dusty beams and stairs and walls will remain his forever—or at least until the paperwork reservoir overflows under the leaky roof and the whole attic crashes into the dining room that no one ever used for anything other than my mother's wake.

I am, instantaneously, a child clinging to her wooden toy with its black and yellow stripes loaded with lead, and a grown woman, trying to excise her demons by obsessing over the unobtainable. And I know those two things are interconnected or point/counterpoint like Freud is to Jung so maybe I'm not quite an idiot after all.

"Geri...."

I look up. Lydia has removed her dust mask. You'd think the world had come to an end and the Blessed Virgin had appeared before her with a command; Lydia does *not* remove her mask when detritus is a threat. Then she tugs off her gloves and I know for sure the world has ended and only Lydia knows it. Which, you know, is probably exactly how it would go.

"You'll get filthy," I protest because her behavior is unsettling me. My voice is huskier than normal. Probably the dust.

"Shut up."

There is such incredibly tenderness in her tone. I tell myself not to feel it. To let it drift past me like a cool breeze in summer but my world is tilting and I'm not entirely in control. Damn it. This was supposed to be two friends (with undefined benefits) cleaning an attic—nothing more, nothing less.

She sinks all the way down beside me in one fluid movement like she's in a Hollywood movie where everyone and everything is graceful—men, women, cats, lamps. I can't *not* look at her. I am compelled. I am no longer entirely here.

She reaches up carefully and cups my cheek in her palm. She strokes her thumb under my eye and I feel my own tears for the first time; their existence seems convenient and contrived. I've always hated crying I feel a rush of cold embarrassment that's hardly alien to me.

She's looking at me like she can read my mind, like she knows me, which, I suppose, she does and doesn't in equal measure. She's my closest friend and has been for a decade but I'm also a cagey bitch and can't remember the last time I had a heart to heart with anyone.

No. That's a lie. I do remember.

Is it here somewhere? Somewhere in these wet and dry boxes, among the mildew and dust? Genderless (read: safe), timeless, and waiting. Maybe in the back corner, away from the window...?

I almost get up to look but I catch Lydia's expression. She is looking at me like I'm a precious thing she wants to save, or own, or become. I'm not sure which. I suppose we're both cagey bitches.

I grow a pair (of ovaries—get the irony?) and ask her suddenly, "What are you thinking?"

I have so rarely asked her anything. Our relationship exists of her actions and my reactions. She could put a gun on the table and I would pick it up. She could point to the moon and I'd shoot it from the sky.

"I'll deal with this box." Again she makes a statement—not a question or request. The decision is made. She has forgiven my impropriety but she will not answer me. She takes the photo then: "Only a monster would hit that child."

I should turn and kiss her palm against my face. I should ask her to move in. I should tell her she's my lifeline, my soulmate, my first thought every morning and my last thought every night when I touch myself and imagine another life with another past, present and future.

I miss my chance. Her hand falls from my face and she's pulling on her gloves and tugging down her dust mask again. She's shaking out a black, heavy duty garbage bag—a contractor bag, they call them, even though they remind me of mobster movies and disposing of bodies.

It isn't a revaluation for me to hear someone call my father a monster. My memory of my mother alive? She called him that. And after her? Countless therapists. To be honest, I think I always knew. I knew at three and four and ten and sixteen that other people's fathers didn't slam their faces into walls, didn't threaten and demean them, or fuck them on the regular because they were too small to resist (effectively) and so accessible in the convenience of his own home.

I'm shaking. We're bagging up my past and dropping it through the trap door in the floor to the hallway below. I'll haul it all to the curb and pay for an extra pick up. The realities, the mundane follow through, crowds my brain but my emotions are messy as fuck and it's a good fifteen minutes before I can move again.

In that time, Lydia billows a garbage bag over the fused stack of my father's handwriting and, stealing glances at me, she consumes him in black plastic, tying the bag, tying it again, then dropping the body through the trap so that it misses the drop downstairs and lands with a muffled, moist thump in the hall below.

I stand up.

Lydia is across the attic. She's holding a Waterford Crystal candy bowl. It's blue like her eyes. She says nothing. Stops completely and watches me walk to the corner of the attic. Pretense is gone. She is worried I will... what? The window doesn't open and it's at the opposite end of the attic. When I was fourteen, I fantasized about hanging myself up here. About pulling the stairs up behind me so no one would know where I'd gone until the smell of my corpse alerted the world. I read somewhere that the scent of decomposition is impossible to truly get rid of so part of me would have haunted the house forever.

I think that's why I never did it. Not fear. Not the will to live. I just didn't want to be stuck here.

There was a lidded plastic bin, not as old as the boxes but untouched for far longer, shoved into the far corner under the sloping trusses of the roofline. On the side in small block letters: Geraldine. This was everything I didn't take with me. My entire childhood in one twenty-five gallon Rubbermaid. In the shadows it appeared black and dark gray but when I dragged the tote out into the light of the window and the single bulb that dangled from the rafters—cobwebs snap, crackle and popping as they gave way—it was actually a murky blue like a darkling sky before a night of rainstorms. I broke the seal on the lid and smelled roses.

"Do you know why I married Greg?"

Lydia is standing beside me and we're both staring down into the contents of the bin. There are two completely different conversations going on—one verbal and one not. She gently lifts out a teal hoodie with silver stars.

"You love him."

I take the teal hoodie from her and put it in the nearest garbage bag, adding a few more clothing items and a couple posters rolled, crumpled and actively aging.

Lydia lifts a few stuffed animals—a teddy bear, a hippo—and considers them, trying to ascertain how much dust and decay each furry creature contains. Neither of us look at one another.

"It's because he doesn't ask before he kisses me."

I see it then. So much smaller than any memory or photo could make it out to be because I've grown up and wooden bees don't. I lift it from the bin and it fits in one hand like a worry stone. The antennae springs have a fine coat of rust and the bright yellow paint is more ochre now. But the round black eyes are the same, speckled with white like starry nights and glossy with lacquer.

Lydia takes my free hand and squeezes just enough to tell me she's there. That I'm there. She whispers, "You don't have to be so tame."

"Actually..." Our two conversations collide and I look at her. "I do."

For just a moment she seems startled. The pressure of her hand lessens. I will her to not look away. I will her to see me. Not as she wants me to be but as I am.

She says, very quietly, laced with sadness that I can hear, "That's a shame."

"I agree."

We stand together and she searches my face as if for the first time. My gaze is steady and sure. I wanted that connection so badly. Not a connection with Lydia. Not a connection with a lover but the connection between a parent and a child. Life (and death) had robbed that from me. Then my own body had done it again. I suppose I should have adopted. I suppose I should have dated a woman with children and become the best stepmom the world has ever seen. But instead I was standing in his attic—my attic now—forty-six years old, basically single, basically alone, because the only person in my life wanted me to be someone I could never be.

Wouldn't a child love me unconditionally? Wouldn't I love a child the same way?

I let go of Lydia's hand and held Bee with both of mine.

Three hours later we're done. With the attic. Not with each other. I know that day would have been the right day to end whatever it was we had but I felt... happy? That's not the right word. I felt content. Content to have Bee in my pocket, to be back together, to have something that survived, like me.

We carried bag after bag out to the curb together and then I stood in the open doorway and Lydia stood on the porch steps. The sun was setting and beyond her, across the quiet street, out over the bluff and the meadows and trees and mountains, the sky was pale orange and almost translucent pink.

The hippo had fallen out of a garbage bag and she picked it up. "We'll never get the mildew out of the stuffed animals."

I put my hand in my pocket. Good thing Bee is made of wood.

She says, "Let's buy paint tomorrow."

Bee saw everything.

She says, "I'll come get you after Greg leaves for work."

Bee remembers.

She says, "New paint does wonders."

Bee understands me. And really? That's all I need.

That night I burned the house down. I drove away as the flames reached the attic windows and the sirens and lights were already adding to the fireworks display. Bee sat in the passenger seat.

I guess I was done with Lydia after all.

It felt like Independence Day.

ECHOES
BY LAUREN PATZER

Gallus and Dyntrie entered the small cabin cautiously. Gallus always entered first as his darker hair and complexion gave him a little more stealth than his fair-haired and fair-skinned partner. Though they had been summoned and had every right to enter the building, they'd both been stung enough times by Carlyle's whips and darts to remember caution could save their life one day.

As Gallus' eyes adjusted quickly to the interior, he noted the fire burning in the small cook stove in the corner as well as three lamps burning into the night. Carlyle, a haggard man who always looked a stone's throw from death but surprised the unwary with his strength and flexibility—proved wiry and deadly to opponents who underestimated him. He raised a gnarled finger and beckoned them all the way to the small table he sat behind.

Carlyle eyed the two young men as he sharpened a short diamond-tipped blade on a stone. They nervously looked at each other, wondering if the blade was meant for them.

"I have a mission for you two, both profitable and dangerous," his voice cracked as he spoke. The young men were never sure if this was his real voice or just an act. He set the blade down on the table and pointed at the chairs next to them. "Sit."

Gallus and Dyntrie sat as nonchalantly as they could manage. After six years of training under Carlyle's tutelage, they'd learned to be both alert and cautious. They'd also had it drilled into them to always carry more than one blade and always diamond-tipped. The jeweled requirement was never explained, but they'd chalked it up to Carlyle's eccentricity among his other interesting traits.

"Relax," Carlyle said, his gruff voice sounding lighter than they'd ever heard before. "This is a serious mission. You've completed your training. You'll face death enough when you're in the field."

"If that was supposed to relax us..." Gallus said in his light voice.

"Mission accomplished!" Dyntrie finished, a gleeful smile painted his face.

Carlyle sighed. "That levity may be the only thing that helps you keep your sanity," he said. He pointed at a piece of parchment on the desk.

The thieving duo leaned forward to look at the dark ink marks on the page that created a crude map of a square room. A circle in one corner opposite the door was etched in red.

"The current Baron of Givenchy is rumored to have dispatched a nobleman without the proper authorization. He denies said impropriety, but the rumors persist that he did the deed in his dungeon, well away from prying eyes... or so he believed," Carlyle said as he pointed to the red circle. "This ornamental gem appears identical to the others, but it has a magical property in effect since it's installation during the prior Baron of Givenchy's reign. Alone in the dark, it captures a visual record of all that transpires. Forgotten in the dark corner of what is now a fully functional dungeon."

Gallus and Dyntrie looked at each other and frowned.

"Is this rumored to be in this corner? Who vouches for this tale?" Gallus asked.

"Surely the current Baron is aware of this feature, learned from the last Baron either voluntarily or through other means," Dyntrie finished.

"The previous Baron was unaware as I was the one who installed it without his knowledge," Carlyle said as he thrust the freshly sharpened knife into a cube of cheese and raised it to his mouth.

"You?" Gallus frowned. "Surely you weren't a stonemason in a past life."

"I had a patron of my own who wished for information of an ill nature he could use to overthrow the Baron. Sadly, my patron passed before the gem could be retrieved and so it remained." Carlyle took a draught of wine and smiled. "I was still paid handsomely before my patron passed. I gave it not a thought before I overheard this bit of palace intrigue."

"Who else knows of this? What dangers of discovery will we face?" Dyntrie stood and paced as he spoke. Carlyle grunted as Dyntrie paced, knowing this was his way upon considering a task before him.

"I'm your only liability," Carlyle said. "No one else knows

and I'm covering the reward myself. I'll be gaining other riches beyond justice with the recovery of the gem."

"What is the reward?" Gallus asked from his seat. His style was more relaxed. "More importantly, what danger does the Baron pose to us playing in his domain?"

"One hundred gold each," Carlyle said.

Dyntrie stopped pacing. Gallus sat up. They both looked at each other.

"That's Insane," they said in unison.

"The requisite danger is death at the hands of a sadistic Baron who will no doubt torture you for information before skinning you alive… or so the rumor has it for his preferred method of execution." Carlyle stabbed a piece of meat and popped it in his mouth. "From what I understand, he rules by fear. Asking the local populace anything about the Baron would likely lead to your immediate deaths. I obtained that last tidbit from the sole survivor of a band of merchants that chose unwisely to visit the barony four years ago."

"Guards? Defensive structures? Contacts?" Dyntrie asked.

Carlyle chuckled and pointed at the crude map.

"On the east wall, there is a waterfall. The pond at the bottom hides a passage under the water that leads directly to the dungeon. Given your stealth capabilities, I trust you'll be able to slip in and out unnoticed." Carlyle sat back and sighed. "The rest is up to you. Any contacts I had in that barony have long since perished. I haven't been there myself in decades. In truth, I'm not entirely sure the hidden passage is still there, unguarded or otherwise safe to traverse. It is the only information I have on the building other than the gem's location—hence, the rather substantial fee for acquiring the item."

"Why not retrieve it yourself?" Gallus asked.

Carlyle looked down and was silent for a few minutes.

"Hard though it is to admit, I'm not as young as I used to be. I'm certainly spry enough to keep two students on their toes, but I've lost a bit of pep in my step. Combine that with my face being known to several mercenary factions that may be operating in the area and you can see how I'd be in considerable danger before getting anywhere near the Baron's fortress," Carlyle said as he stood up and stretched. "Besides, a wise man acknowledges his own limitations and plans around them - which I have, by your considerable tutelage in the thieving arts."

"Fair enough," Gallus said and turned to Dyntrie. "Satisfied?"

Dyntrie nodded.

"You have your blades?" Carlyle asked as he always did.

"Of course, Master," they replied. Carlyle tossed a small bag to Dyntrie. It clinked when he caught it.

"Good. If the Baron catches you, use them on him or perish. Prisoners don't live long at the barony. That's sixty silver to see to your transportation and lodging costs," Carlyle smiled. "An advance against your reward upon completion of the task."

Gallus shook his head. "Still teaching us the business end of things, I see."

"Would you prefer a lesson in dagger catching?" Carlyle asked.

"No!" Dyntrie said. "We're on our way."

Dyntrie grabbed Gallus by the arm, pulling him up from the chair he lounged in. They left the building quickly.

Three cart trips and several miles hiked on foot later, the duo entered Givenchy. They found the nearest tavern for a drink while they checked out the local populace for any danger signs they might be watched. No one had even inquired as to their business in town, so their carefully concocted stories of a traveling cobbler and stonemason looking for work were never tested. People seemed content to keep to themselves for the most part. The hushed tones everyone spoke in didn't seem to be in reaction to the visitors; it was more like no one wanted to draw attention to themselves. Even the women seemed subdued, dressing plainly to appear less appealing.

"The sooner we leave here, the better," Gallus said. "None of these people really seem alive."

"It would seem the Baron's sadistic tastes weren't exaggerated," Dyntrie said. "We'd do well to follow their lead - keep our heads down and we might survive the next couple of days."

Several ales were consumed before they made their way back out onto the dusty streets and into a fairly modest-looking inn. They shared a room to keep costs down; Carlyle had literally beaten frugality into their heads many times over the last five years. Still, the promise of hot water to soak their aching feet drew them to this particular inn more than anything and the extra cost was worth it. Fortunately, while sore, they didn't sport any blisters from their days on the road.

The innkeeper smiled briefly at them as they paid ahead of time. He looked around the small common room of the inn and then whispered quietly.

"Go out not at night, kind visitors. All who do are left to the

Baron's pleasure." He nodded to them both and then took them to their room.

After a small meal at their bedside, they quickly fell into a deep slumber.

The next day found them both refreshed and ready to do some exploring. Givenchy was a medium-sized town with large tracts of well-maintained farmlands surrounding it. High above the town, the towers of a keep could be seen nestled deep in the forest on the mountainside.

"Our quarry, I presume," Gallus said.

"Most likely," Dyntrie replied. "There doesn't appear to be much else that could qualify. Woods seems kind of thick. Hope they didn't divert the water from our anticipated point of entry."

Gallus opened the small backpack he carried. It contained two chisels, small hammers and some rope as well as a bundled set of torches, flint and steel wrapped tight in waxed linen for waterproofing.

"You've got your blades?" Gallus asked. Dyntrie looked at him incredulously.

"Of course! When have I ever not?" Dyntrie shook his head. "You're beginning to sound like Carlyle."

"Good," Gallus replied. "Then we might come out of this alive."

Dyntrie grunted but didn't disagree. He walked into the forest taking his steps carefully to remain as quiet as possible.

After two hours of careful movement, they reached the outer walls of the fortress. Watching from cover, they observed the buttresses for over an hour, but saw no one.

"I don't like it," Dyntrie whispered. "No guards in town and none on the walls. Who protects the Baron? Who enforces the laws?"

"We need to get in and out quickly, before it gets dark," Gallus said. "There's evil afoot. I can feel it in my bones."

They made their way silently to the rear of the fortress where a spring-fed waterfall still flowed from the middle of the keep wall. The pool at the bottom was clear. They watched briefly for guards, but still none appeared.

Stripping off their outer clothing and boots, they strapped the blades back on and secured the backpack. They both dipped under the water and found the opening a few feet below the surface. It couldn't be seen from above; had Carlyle not told them it was there, they never would've known.

They emerged into a small chamber leading to a single passageway, not tall enough to traverse without crouching down. The room was sparsely illuminated by sunlight coming in through cracks in the wall hidden by the waterfall outside. It was just enough to allow them to get out of the water and get their torches out and lit.

Cobwebs lined the single path leading from the chamber; not surprising after decades of abandonment. The ground was slick from dew and moss growing in the dark confines, so they made their way down the descending path carefully. Handholds were naturally present in the walls of the roughly hewn tunnel. Near the end of the passage, the smell of death began to filter in from somewhere in the darkness. Dyntrie held up his hand and Gallus stopped moving.

Dyntrie handed his torch back to his partner and moved to the end of the passage which ended below an old rusted grate overhead. A small hole underneath led to the sewer system far below.

Dyntrie held his head cocked slightly so he could listen to anything happening in the room above. A small drip of liquid splattered on his neck as he held himself perfectly still, confirming there was no movement or sound in the room. He beckoned Gallus forward with a wave of his hand. Gallus scrambled quietly to him holding both torches.

Gallus gasped. Dyntrie turned to frown at him. Gallus pointed at his own neck. Dyntrie raised his hand to where the liquid had dripped on him. It was a deep crimson. Dyntrie locked eyes with Gallus and took a deep breath. He sniffed in annoyance and pointed to the grate above. Gallus moved one of the torches so it better illuminated the obstacle. Even though heavily rusted, there was nothing but gravity holding the grate in place. Dyntrie pushed it up and stood slowly, holding the metal above his head.

In the dim light coming from below, Dyntrie could see the floor around him was clear enough to set the grate down silently and out of the way. He climbed out of the hole and held a hand down. Gallus passed the two torches up to him. Gallus then joined him in the large dungeon chamber above.

As their eyes adjusted to the light, the room came slowly into focus revealing numerous torture apparatus in the roughly forty by forty-foot room. In addition to large red gems lining the walls about waist high, there were three relatively fresh corpses entangled in the apparatus. It was clear they'd died horrible deaths and fairly recently as the blood still trickled from two of the corpses. Dyntrie stared at the nearest body, a woman of perhaps twenty years of age hideously impaled on spikes. Her arms and legs were strapped to cylinders that had been slowly lowered so the spikes entered her bloodied form at a slow, anguished pace.

Dyntrie jumped as Gallus set his hand on his arm. The room flickered briefly with light from the jostled torches Dyntrie held. Gallus pointed at the door at the far side of the room and then behind them where the gem they sought would be embedded in the wall. Dyntrie nodded and they quickly removed the tools from the backpack and got to work.

The mortar was decades old and fell away easily so they had little trouble removing the gem quietly. So it was with no small surprise that they jumped when they heard a deep voice say "Only a matter of time before he revealed the life stone and sent fresh meat for me to carve."

From beside the closed door, a dark figure seemed to erupt from the shadows and fly toward them, blood red eyes glowing and fingers ending in claws. It was upon Dyntrie before he could move.

Gallus stabbed at the creature with the chisel in his hand, embedding it deep in its throat. It turned its head and laughed at him, spitting blood all over Gallus' chest.

"I'm not a mere mortal, boy!" it shouted. Then it jumped back, screamed and clutched its chest revealing Dyntrie holding his diamond-tipped short sword, black ichor dripping from the blade. Without pause, the duo whipped their throwing daggers into the fleeing monstrosity's back. It exploded in a shower of flesh and fire, rocking the foundation of the fortress and knocking them off their feet.

"Get the gem," Dyntrie said, grabbing at the scratches left by the creature as it tore through his shirt. The echoes of falling masonry peppered the air above them. "If that wasn't the Baron, you can be sure he knows we're here."

Gallus picked the gem up from where it had fallen and looked at it briefly. It glimmered with an otherworldly light. He tucked it in the backpack without another word and jumped down into the hole. Dyntrie dropped the torches into the passage and followed Gallus, replacing the grate quickly. They scrambled up the passageway bringing the torches with them and extinguished them in the pool at the top of the tunnel.

They slipped quietly into the water and dove down until they reached the opening. They rose to the surface of the pool outside quietly, taking in a breath as hushed as possible. Proving their stealthy credentials, they quickly slipped into the forest and never looked back, only stopping to dress when they'd made it halfway back to the road. Gallus paused as Dyntrie tried to walk by him toward the road. Gallus grabbed his arm. Dyntrie looked back and saw his partner shaking his head. Dyntrie nodded and they resumed their way to the town passing through the forest and avoiding the only road that connected the populace to the fortress.

As they got closer to the town, a large crashing sound shook the forest and an orange light erupted from the direction of the fortress. A loud crack followed by an explosion dropped them onto the forest floor as flames and debris rocketed past them. They quickly got up and ran from Givenchy as fast as their legs could carry them, never looking back.

Days and nights passed wandering the wilderness until they managed to find a trail leading to a small village in the neighboring county. Their training came in handy as they lived off the small game, plants and insects they could find during their trip. Even so, they were parched beyond reason when they got to the town and gratefully accepted their fill of water from the village's well.

Nearly a week passed before they reached Carlyle's cabin. By then, the scratches on Dyntrie's neck had become inflamed and he was feeling weak and feverish. Dyntrie leaned on his partner as Gallus reached to knock on the door. It opened before his knuckles reached the surface. Carlyle appeared in the doorway, reaching out to help Dyntrie into the room. As the stricken thief fell in a heap onto a soft chair, Carlyle looked at Gallus expectantly.

"The Baron or whatever that was scratched him before we killed it," Gallus said.

"The gem," Carlyle said, holding out his hand. After a brief look of shock, Gallus' face became grim. He pulled the gem out of his pack and handed it to Carlyle. Gallus glanced at Dyntrie; the grim look remained on his face.

"I hope it was worth it. I'm not sure Dyntrie will make it," Gallus said. The tone was somewhat accusatory, but he couldn't be too upset. They knew what they'd signed up for—a life or death mission.

"It was," Carlyle said smugly. Dyntrie and Gallus both frowned at him. Carlyle chuckled.

"He'll be fine," Carlyle said as he walked to the hearth.

"It recorded us killing the Baron," Dyntrie said weakly.

"No," Carlyle said as he opened a small jar on the hearth and tossed the contents into the flames. The fire turned blue. "I'm afraid I told you both a bit of a story there."

"Yeah," Gallus said. "We guessed that much when he

called it a life stone before he tried to kill us.”

“Ahh, it’s a bit more than that. It’s a sophisticated trap, actually,” Carlyle said. “I’m going to have to ask you to trust me again even though I lied a bit about the stone.”

Carlyle pointed at the table behind the duo.

“Your reward and the deed to this small parcel of land are on the table there. It should be enough to set you on to be whatever you want to be after today.”

Gallus looked at the table and then back at Carlyle. “You won’t need it?”

Carlyle shook his head and tossed the gem in the fire. He walked to the men.

“I won’t be here much longer, but I’ll remove the venom and infection from Dyntrie before I go. The least I can do for you boys releasing me from my prison,” Carlyle said. The fireplace popped as the fire cracked the gem and Carlyle slowly morphed into a beautiful angel before their eyes.

The angel reached out to touch Dyntrie’s neck. Blue and green light flowed from the injured man and he sighed. The color returned to his face.

“Fifty years I’ve been trapped here,” the angel said in a lilting golden voice. “Magicks hard to fathom were brought into play. It took decades to unravel the puzzle. Now I can return to reclaim my home after this long exile. Thank you both.”

“But how…” Gallus began.

“Darkness and light are always in eternal conflict, even within each of us. Today you struck a blow for the light. Tomorrow, who knows? That path is yours to decide. Farewell.” The angel rose up through the ceiling leaving the two shocked men staring at the thatched roof above.

"Of all the ways I expected Carlyle to go out," Gallus said as he looked at Dyntrie. "That was not one of them."

Dyntrie grunted and got up. He grabbed the side of the chair to steady himself. "Well, no reason we shouldn't raid his wine stash now, is there?" Dyntrie said and wobbled toward a cabinet in the far corner.

"I suppose there isn't," Gallus said.

BE FAE DO CRIMES
BY HIROMI COTA

Humans say things like, "Be gay! Do crimes!" Which is just terrible.

I mean, which crimes am I supposed to do? There are so many! I've probably done crimes just by being me, but that doesn't count, I'm sure. And how many crimes ought I do? There has to be a specific number. Does it fulfill the request if I just do two? After all, that makes it crimeS. But what if I do the same crime twice? That probably doesn't count. That's not crimes; that's just one crime multiple times. I find this lack of specificity vexing. But I'll document my crimes anyways. After all, if I don't write it down, then it never happened. At least that's what Da said. He'd know. He's been ignoring lots of things that I did without recording.

So, the crime! I picked graffiti. It was loads of fun.

It wasn't easy, though. First, I needed to get paint. The human male at the hardware store did *not* want to sell me any. First, he told me that I needed an adult to buy them for me; said I was too little to be buying spray paint. I assured him that I was big enough to not fly back when I pushed the button. He didn't look like he believed me. Then, he told me that I didn't need 17 cans. I told him that I did if I wanted to do a good job. AND THEN! He said that he didn't take gold coins. Can you believe it?!

He changed his tune when I told him I had lots of them. I made three piles of gold on the counter and his eyes went ... well- You know how when your uncle's been drinking for 17 days and then sleeps for 17 days and you wake him up? How he makes a face like "Auch. What did Aw do?" and you have to tell him that he thought that he'd found the goddess Aine and wanted to be her husband more than he wanted his left ear. But your uncle wanted to be better than King Aulom, so he visited Aine every day, giving her offerings and poems and asking her out dancing. But she said "nay" every time. Until the last of the 17 days, when she finally agreed, and he got the parson out of bed to wed them that very evening. Long story short, my uncle's now married to the red mare in the stables. Yeah, the shopkeeper at the hardware store made that face. My uncle too.

Anyways, the human at the hardware store saw the three piles of gold and said, "That better not be fairy gold!" and took a taste of a coin.

"Oh! Rumbled! You found me out!" I replied, making finger guns at him like I saw on the telly once.

But he scooped up the coins and waved me off. For a second, I thought it might count as a crime when coins turned back into leaves, but I don't think it does. I told him that he'd rumbled me, and he still took the coins. A deal's a deal.

So, I got the spray paint cans and took them to the local constabulary. I also heard humans say "fuck the police" but I'm too young to be doing any o' that. But, the f-word comes with a lot of meanings, so I'm sure that one of them ought to fit what happened next.

I started building a base layer for my graffiti with a great many of the white paint cans. Well, I say "white", but they had daft names like "off-white," "mountain peaks," "dove feather," and other nonsense. After a few minutes, a gent in blue came over and asked me what the hell I thought I was doing. I told him, but he was still mad and tried to take the can out of my hand.

He grabbed the can and jerked this way and that, but it didn't spoil my aim any. I had to stop spraying a few times when he got between the can and my canvas, though. He grabbed my wrist with both hands and held on, but it didn't do him any good. It was a good long while before he got annoyed and reached for a pair of handcuffs. They looked like they might be iron, which was a bit of a fright for me, so I tried to keep my hands safe from his. But he was a tricky one and eventually got a cuff on. Not iron. Whew. He tried attaching the other cuff to my left wrist, but I certainly wasn't going to help him do that.

After a minute of avoiding the other cuff, his face was red, and he was grunting and growling. He was apparently upset at the noises he was making because he secured the other end of the cuff to his own wrist. He said he did it for crying out loud. I guess that's a crime worthy of cuffing. The silly thing was that now that he was attached to me, I just dragged him around the painting as I worked. I'm not sure if that's a crime, but he wasn't happy about it, so I'm pretty sure that I "fucked the police." Mission accomplished. Well, that mission anyways. I still had crimes to do.

I started on with the blues and blue-greens and greens and

grays. Strange that two colors ought to have so many words. My painting was really coming together now. I could almost feel the unicorn's restlessness on the surface of the wall. The flare of her nostrils. Hooves yearning to break through the ground.

The blue boy was weeping, crying out for me to let him go. That didn't make any sense to me. After all, he was the one with the keys, wasn't he? If he didn't want to be attached to me anymore, he could just unlatch the cuffs. It wasn't that far to the ground. I floated twenty feet lower and gave him a "well?" look. He didn't see it because he was crying. Can't say I didn't try, though. I gave the unicorn a tousled mane with a few hundred quick flicks of the can.

An annoying man gargled through a speaker that someone was under arrest. Whoever that was had five seconds to release their hostage. Four seconds. Three. Two. "Do it now!" he said. He was very serious for someone who forgot how to get to one.

"You forgot one!" I helped.

"Come down to the ground and let the hostage go!" he shouted back. I hadn't seen anyone else flying, so it dawned on me that he might be addressing the blue boy. I yelled over my shoulder.

"Oh, I'm not a hostage. I'm OK. I don't know why he attached himself to me, but it doesn't really bother me. He can stay if he wants to."

"No! You! With the pink hair! Drop the hostage!" Apparently, they thought the blue boy was the hostage, which didn't make any sense. I decided to help them for free.

"You're in error. He put these cuffs on us. No one here is a hostage."

"You're under arrest!" he yelled.

"That can't be right," I replied and dug through my hip pouch for the last color I needed.

The man with the speaker yelled something about a fire, but I didn't smell smoke, so I assumed I was upwind of it. Presumably, Speaker Man had many alarming things to yell about today. I wondered if that was his job.

Lightning flew from the ground and struck my blue friend. He did not appreciate it. Nor did I, since it gave me a mild zap through the cuffs. It happened again. And again. Speaker man said nothing about this strange lightning, so I assumed he was too busy paying attention to the fire to notice. Blue Boy sobbed.

"Aren't you going to get in trouble for crying out loud so much?"

He replied in a language I wasn't familiar with. Whatever tongue it was involved a lot of sniffing.

"You gave me this cuff, so I'm going to keep it, but you clearly own the other half. How about I just split it in the middle?" His head twitched. I'm pretty sure it was because of the lightning striking again. Still counts, though, so I broke the chain between the cuffs. He dropped to the ground faster than he ought to have and landed like a horse plop. I guess the lightning interfered with his flying ability. "Sorry!" I shouted down at him.

I finally found the right color to finish the unicorn and gave my painting a long, bold stroke. Speaker Man's speaker crackled like he was going to be angrily wrong about something again as the 30-foot-tall unicorn whinnied and tore itself free of the police station wall, raining bricks and dust on those below. The speaker stopped crackling, and screams came from below me. The unicorn leapt off of the wall, exposing several floors of the police station. The people inside started screaming, too. I joined them just in case it was fun.

It turned out that screaming *was* fun. Unfortunately, it involved a lot of closing my eyes and raising my head upwards, so I wasn't paying attention when the unicorn ran me over. That hurt. I'm not certain how many ribs I'm supposed to have, but I don't think I have that number anymore. In hindsight, I should not haven painted iron horseshoes on a unicorn. On the plus side, I had definitely performed a crime.

A crime. Just one. So far.

I danced over towards speaker man, who was huddling against a police car. I squeezed his hand and the device inside it. The speaker crackled and I started to sob and wail into Speaker Man's contraption. Crying out loud. Nailed it.

Been gay.

Done crimes.

What else ya got, World?

THE CURE
BY AMBER RAINEY

Johann stood by the window, peering down at the darkness below. His spine stiffened when he noticed a black sedan turn on the street. As expected, the sedan stopped in front of his house and idled, a black menace distinguished from the dark of night only by the headlights.

"What if this doesn't work?" he sighed, turning away from the window.

"It must."

Johann nodded to Eleonore. She was right and she looked at him with such earnest hope mixed with desperate pleading, he was loathed to argue. He took a moment to really look at his wife. He wished he could erase the dark circles under her eyes - put there by long days working in the lab. It was the only feature he did not like on her otherwise beautiful face. He missed the days of her easy laughter—the laugh lines he knew hid just under the surface. Her green eyes could sparkle with such mischief. Now, they contained worry as she looked down at the crying bundle in her arms. He was at a loss for how to comfort them both. She'd known what would happen long before he'd accepted it.

His musings were interrupted by a car door slamming on the street below. He looked out the window again, watching as two men in suits entered the light of the building's doorway. Johann closed his eyes, sending up a prayer for his family and turned back to Eleonore.

"They're here."

Eleonore nodded and handed him the now sleeping baby. She smoothed her hair and straightened her skirt. She leaned over the baby and kissed Johann briefly. He looked down at her, wanting very much to wipe away the tear threatening to fall down her cheek but knowing Eleonore needed his strength, not his empathy. They both jumped at the knock on the door and Johann gave her a wink and shrug, trying to lighten the moment. She smiled and he locked the memory of her face in that exact moment away for later.

"Doctor Strasburg, open the door," a stern voice called.

Eleonore kissed the top of her baby's head and walked calmly to the door. Johann watched as she straightened to her full height and calmly opened the door. Immediately, the two men from the street walked in and handed her a piece of paper. They gave her a moment as she read it, standing silently but imposingly over her. She nodded and looked back over her shoulder at Johann. He saw the desperation in her eyes only a moment before she clamped it down and then mouthed, *I love you both*. She turned back to the men.

"I'm ready."

"Doctor Strasburg, you are being charged with high

treason and are under arrest. Please follow me."

Johann watched as Eleonore walked out of the room. As if sensing the change in her mother's presence, the baby began crying again.

Years Later

Monika peered into her microscope, wondering if she had done the assignment incorrectly. Her final grade depended on the lab assignment and she desperately wanted to pass. It was the only way she would be accepted into a job at The Institute. Her entire life, she'd wanted to work there, just like her mother. Now, the tests she was running on her blood was not working correctly and she was not getting the expected values on the assignment. She looked around the room, noticing she was the only one left in the lab.

"You still working on that?"

Monika jumped at the sound of her friend's voice. She looked up and rolled her eyes. Abelard chuckled and sat down next to her. He picked up the test reports Monika had run and his brow furrowed.

"These don't look right."

"Really, it doesn't take an Einstein to know that!" Monika huffed.

"Very funny."

Abelard raised his eyebrow at her and looked back down at the reports. He double-checked Monika's equations and rubbed his chin. He lifted his eyes to her but not really seeing her as he did the mental calculations. Then, he dropped the reports back down on the table and gestured for her to move. Monika did so and

Abelard peered into the microscope.

"Hmmm."

Monika banged her head on the table. "I'm doomed."

Abelard put a steadying hand on her shoulder.

"Maybe the sample was contaminated, you should run it again. It can't be missing the marker. You've had the illness just like everyone else."

Monika lifted her head up, rubbing the spot she had hit a little too hard in her desperation.

"I have... I ran it four times."

Abelard whistled.

"I know. It doesn't make any sense. I've been super careful. I know the sample isn't contaminated. I followed every. Single. Step. *To the letter.*"

Abelard sat in stunned contemplation, opening and closing his mouth several times. Monika watched in agony. If anyone could figure out the issue, it was him. Finally, he shook his head sadly and Monika let out the breath she didn't know she was holding.

"You're doomed," he said jokingly.

Monika's face fell.

"Monika... I didn't mean..."

Monika jumped out of her chair, stuffing her report in her backpack, and fled from the room before Abelard had time to stop her. He peered into the microscope again. Then, looking around the room to make sure no one was watching, he took the slide and placed it in his pocket.

"Monika?"

Johann walked into the house, flipping on a light switch. It was very unusual for the house to be so dark when he arrived home from work. Normally, his daughter had music blaring and every light on in the house. He looked around, noticing her backpack tossed carelessly on the floor. *Ah,* he thought, *it is one of those days.*

Monika rarely got overemotional but Johann had learned the typical signs of his daughter's moods and he knew he would be in for a long night of consoling his only child. He went into the kitchen, making a plate of cookies and a glass of milk. Then, we went in search of his sulking daughter.

"What is it this time, my love?" Johann asked with a hint of humor in his voice.

The room was dark except for the lights of the streetlamp filtering through the window. A lump in the bed confirmed that his daughter was somewhere under the mass of covers and pillows. Monika peeked out from under her pillow and then sat up, glowering at her father.

"I'm not a little girl anymore, Papa." She scowled.

"True, true. Should I take them back to the kitchen?"

Monika shook her head. "One won't hurt."

Johann chuckled lightly and offered the plate. Monika took a cookie, then reached over to switch on the lamp by her bed.

"That is better. Light always wins over darkness," Johann offered with a smile.

Monika huffed. She ate her cookie and then gestured for the milk. Johann gave it to her, waiting for her to begin the conversation. He had found, through the years, it was best to let her gather her thoughts and speak on her own terms, rather pushing her into giving up her secrets. He could see so much of Eleonore in his daughter, a fact that often frightened him but more often than not gave him comfort. Monika, like Eleonore, was a fighter.

"Papa?"

Johann roused from his musings and met his daughter's eyes. Immediately, she began to sob and tears streamed down her face. Johann moved to the bed and gathered his daughter in his arms.

"What is it, sweetheart? Whatever it is, we can fix it," Johann said soothingly, all the while smoothing her hair.

"I... I wanted to work at The Institute and now I can't!" Monika wailed.

Johann stiffened slightly, "Monika, why would you not be able to get any job you wanted?"

Johann did not want to stir up their ongoing argument. He did not want his daughter anywhere near The Institute but, like her mother, she could be stubborn when she wanted something. He had hoped to persuade her to turn to other employment but had yet to be successful. Monika leaned away from her father and angrily swiped at her tears.

"Something is wrong with me, Papa. I won't be able to pass my final."

"I'm not understanding. Have you not studied?"

"I have."

Johann scratched his head, "Then you will pass with flying colors. What has you so worried?"

Monika shook her head, "Papa, you don't understand. The final is me. My blood. I must run a specific test on my blood and reach a specific outcome, then I will pass. However, my samples are not cooperating. Even Abelard can't..."

Johann's blood ran cold. Monika trailed off as he stood abruptly and rushed out of the room. She threw back the blankets and followed after her father. She found him, fists clenched and head resting against the wall in the hallway. She put a hand on his shoulder and felt him tense. He turned to her, grabbing her arms and staring into her eyes.

"You must abandon this idea of working at The Institute. Immediately," he said frantically.

"What? No..." Monika argued.

Johann shook her a little. Monika's eyes widened in fear at the crazed look her father gave her. She bit her lip and held back the fresh tears forming in her eyes. She searched his face for reason but found none.

"Papa... I don't understand."

Johann took a deep breath and pulled Monika into a tight hug. She hesitated a moment then returned the hug. She tried to ignore the tears dropping onto her cheeks from her father's. She had never seen him vulnerable, her Papa was always strong. Johann's knees crumpled and Monika helped him sit on the floor. She held his hand while he finished crying. They sat silently in the dark hallway, each afraid to broach the topic of her employment again.

After a long while, Johann wiped his cheeks and stood. He held out a hand for his daughter, then helped her up. Monika looked at him quizzically. She saw him make a decision and nod his head.

"It is time," he simply said.

Johann walked towards the living room and Monika followed. He crossed over to the window, peering down into the street. Satisfied by what he saw, he closed the curtains and turned back towards his daughter.

"Monika, I have to tell you about your mother."

"Papa, you've told me about her. She worked for The Institute. She created the medicine for the illness. She kept hundreds of people from dying but died trying to find the cure."

Johann shook his head. Monika watched as he went over to the curio cabinet in the corner of the room. He reached up to the top and pulled out a dusty key. He blew the dust off and inserted it into the cabinet. Monika walked over and joined him at the cabinet.

"Do you see that cube?" he asked.

Monika's brows furrowed and she looked into the cabinet. On the second shelf, there was an iridescent cube. She could tell it had once been bright and shiny but now it was dull from years of dust collection. It was not unique in that aspect, every item in the cabinet was covered in dust. Monica lifted the item out of the cabinet and sneezed. She handed the cube to Johann and watched curiously as he gingerly wiped it with the hem of his shirt. It was the size of his palm and the lights of the room caused it to cast rainbows in a prism effect as the dust gave way to the iridescence. Once it was cleaned, Johann handed it back to his daughter. He sat down on the couch, gesturing for her to do the same. She hesitated, then sat down, placing the cube on the table in front of her. As she did so, something triggered and suddenly an image of her mother appeared before her. Monika gasped at the lifelike image.

"Hello, my dear girl. It appears the time has come for you to know the truth," Eleonore's image said.

Monika sat in stunned silence, her eyes wide. She glanced over at her father, noting the weariness on his face. She wanted to console him but was also furious with him. Everything she'd known was a lie. She was at a loss with how to deal with the revelations from the cube. Johann reached over and grabbed her hand, giving it a squeeze. A knock sounded on the door and both their heads snapped towards it.

"Quick, hide the cube," her father hissed.

Monika grabbed the cube and thrust it back into the cabinet, locking it. She watched as her father rubbed his face and straightened his hair. She tossed the key on top of the cabinet and did her best to straighten her own face. Johann peered through the peephole and Monika let out the breath she was holding when the tension in his back eased. He put on an easy smile and opened the door.

"Ah, Abelard, so nice to see..." Johann trailed off as Abelard rushed into the room and slammed the door.

Abelard leaned back against the door, trying to catch his breath. He was as pale as a ghost and Monika rushed over to him. He looked into her eyes with terror.

"Is it your blood?" he demanded.

Monika jerked back in shock.

"What?"

"Is it your blood?" Abelard repeated.

"Why don't you sit down," Johann offered.

Abelard nodded and sat down on the couch. Monika sat

carefully next to him, waiting for him to catch his breath. Johann handed him a glass of water and he downed it in one gulp. Abelard ran a hand through his hair. He pinched the bridge of his nose and then looked between Johann and Monika, who shared a glance. Abelard closed his eyes.

"This is the cure... You are the cure," he said, pointing at Monika.

"Abelard, that's absurd," Monika tried to lie.

Abelard shook his head. Johann sat heavily in a chair, watching his daughter and her best friend. He could only hope the boy was a true friend. Abelard pulled a notebook out of his backpack and shoved it into Monika's hands. When Monika didn't move, he opened the book and pointed to a page.

"I recognized a signature in your report and I took your slide."

Abelard shrugged at the glare Monika gave him. She looked back down at the pages, flipping through them.

"It's unmistakable, Monika, the blood on that slide is a cure for the illness. Is it your blood?"

"Abelard, my boy, perhaps..."

"It's okay, Papa. I trust him," Monika reassured her father.

Johann nodded and stood up. He peered into Abelard's eyes for a moment, searching for any hint of malice. When he was satisfied, he kissed the top of Monika's head and left the room.

"It's true?" he asked.

Monika nodded.

"Why didn't you tell me?"

Monika sighed, "I just found out. Papa never told me."

"How?"

"It is better if I show you," Monika explained.

Abelard, once again lost for words, watched as Monika retrieved the cube from the cabinet and triggered the playback of her mother's hologram.

Two Years Later

Monika paced the antechamber, nervously checking her watch every few seconds. Johann sat in a chair with his eyes closed. She knew her father was as nervous as she was but he had a knack for looking calm, even in the worst storm. She began worrying they were making a bad call and it made her more nervous.

"Everything is as it should be, my love," Johann soothed.

"What if—" Monika started to argue.

Johann held up a hand. "*What if* is a game. This will work."

Monika smiled at her father. If he had confidence in their plan, she knew they would succeed. She looked up when Abelard entered the room. He nodded at her and she nodded back.

"It's time, Papa."

Monika stood before the microphones in front of the massive crowd. She tried to ignore the cameras and the people and focus on her mother's face staring back at her from the large banners hung around the square.

"Twenty-five years ago, the illness struck our land without regard to wealth, age, status, or gender. My mother worked tirelessly to find a cure for the illness. It was believed by everyone, including myself, that she had only succeeded in finding a medicine to treat the illness."

Monika watched her father tense and noticed two men in dark suits near the edge of the dais. One spoke into a microphone at his wrist. Johann squeezed her hand and she squeezed back. She took a deep breath and continued.

"Today, I am pleased to announce the creation of the Eleonore Strasburg Foundation. Its sole mission will be to disburse a cure for the illness, free of charge. The government and The Institute will no longer hold you hostage to a costly medication. We have taken measures to ensure that the governments of every country affected by the illness will also have access to the cure. Today, we are liberated from the ravages of the illness."

Monika smiled as the reporters began barraging her with questions and the two men and suits slinked away from the crowd.

UXB
BY MARSHALL MILLER

Robert Dodge once again mouthed the silent refrain of *"Why Me"* as he looked at the state of the art interplanetary shipping container with the one hundred kilos of personal property. Robert knew the basic answer to why his Great Uncle Johnathon "Doc" Dodge's property was shipped to him. The somewhat famous man had gone to his final resting place in Outer Space and left Robert with the task of dealing with his remains.

Of course, Robert had been Great Uncle Doc's favorite grand nephew, as Robert actually was interested in some of his tall tales. Doc Dodge had been one of the original 'Rock Hounds,' those intrepid early explorers of the Asteroid Belt located between Mars and Jupiter. More famously, the great uncle was one of the Rock Hounds who helped to corral six large asteroids, join them into one planetoid, and propel them to an orbit just outside of the Earth's Moon.

Thus was created Earth II, the planetary body in which

Robert Dodge and his family resided. In the year 2100, Earth Time, the interior of Earth II was a significant way station in the expansion of humanity into the solar system.

As a direct result of the Dodge Family's involvement in the creation of Earth II, Doc's brother Richard and his family, including the then young father of Robert, Richard Junior, had been one of the first 'settler' families of the manmade planetary body. Great Uncle Doc never married, never had any official offspring (though famously randy) so by default, his brother's family took on the mantle of the repository of his heritage.

Richard Junior had taken a wife from another of the original families, Mary Watson, and produced a son, Robert, and a daughter, Rhoda. Robert had followed in his father's footsteps and found a career in space travel, stayed on Earth II and now had his own wife and family. Currently the Vice President for Operations of Earth II Industries, he was a mover and shaker in the expansion of humanity in the Sol System and beyond. And now he had to deal with these one hundred kilos of memories and junk.

Robert sighed. He had liked his Great Uncle Doc, if for no other reason than he was the antithesis of Robert's staid father, Richard. Doc had regaled him in all the tales of life on the edge in the Belt, searching the asteroids for valuable minerals in the early days. Private enterprise transportation advancements in the first half of the Twenty-First Century enabled people like Doc to push the envelope and tell world governments to go screw when it came time to push out past the Earth's Moon.

Robert had to smile when he remembered Doc telling him about porking a Chinese mission commander in Zero-G who had been sent to 'reign in' Doc and his crew of ne'er to wells. Doc had an animal magnetism Robert's father had never inherited. Robert had to drag himself back to the job at hand. The important man needed to return to his VP duties before some rising a-hole tried to stick a knife in his back to climb the corporate ladder.

Robert checked the tagging, which stated the container and its contents had been decontaminated before sealing and shipping. Everything was vacuum packed as any type of air was precious in Outer Space. Robert pumped some stale atmosphere into the container before popping it open. The spin put on Earth II provided a form of artificial gravity due to the Coriolus effect. Thus he did not have to worry about chasing odd pieces of whatever junk Uncle Doc had chosen to save as it floated by in Zero G. The production of artificial gravity was one of the lead projects of Earth II Industries Robert needed to pay close attention to, rather than sorting his great uncle's stuff.

"Well," he said to himself," the sooner I sort this crap, the sooner I can get back to real work."

At least everything was secured in stackable polymer boxes, each with its own description tag. That was, all but one noticeable item.

Forgotten in one corner, still cloaked in cobwebs and decades of dust, was a survivor merely by default, by being over-looked, silent and unobtrusive, not big enough to be an imposition and so allowed to remain—a receptacle of memories, an eye witness to everything that came before. It looked like an old military-style duffle bag, jammed in among all the neat boxes as an afterthought.

Robert's slender and gangly body, a by-product of life at less than an Earth Gravity, enabled him to slide into the shipping container and retrieve the odd bag. Robert had been to Earth only once and had no desire to re-visit the seven billion controlled populace and more massive gravity. The powers to be wanted more people on Luna, Mars, and Earth II, with no intrusive government trying to control what happened in the bedroom. Thus, Robert and his wife Jane had two healthy children.

Robert moved the duffle bag onto a small work table. There was a clear plastic envelope attached to the oversized zipper handle. Robert opened the envelope and unfolded a piece of paper with 'Robert' scribbled on the outside. He frowned as he read his Uncle Doc's writing.

"A mystery inside a conundrum, grand nephew," it read. "But it may make you famous like me. Keep it from Space Command."

"What did you get yourself into, Doc?" Robert mumbled. The unzipped military duffle bag revealed a bunch of what some would call space junk. A very used and rolled up jumpsuit with every organizational patch imaginable. The senior manager thought it might get be worth money to some collector. Old photos of Doc and many of the early pioneers (plus some nude women), manuals, books, and some currency from what seemed to be from ninety percent of the countries on Earth. Again, maybe all the bills combined may be worth something.

Then Robert found It.

The company vice president gingerly lifted the softball-sized jet black object. It was so smooth it spoke of being machined, but the texture seemed to be more rocklike than metal. Plus, it was heavy for its size. Then Roberts saw the writing and froze. For he had seen the symbols before.

Just a year prior, Earth II intercepted what first seemed to be outer space noise from some far off star. Then, a week later, a similar signal but with some nuanced differences. The second burst of radio waves may have been put in some file to be examined later, but then another transmission came the next day. Then the next day. Then the next.

Space Command latched onto the transmissions and tried to classify the lot of them, but it was too late. Earth II was governed by a private company, as were most of the tiny colonies on Mars and the Moon. World governments in the 20th Century had created a problem for themselves when they said no one country or government could claim a planet or moon. However, if that was the case, how could they prevent a private party from landing on it and homesteading? No one foresaw all the private space exploration companies. Thus, 'free people' staked out plots of real estate on the Moon, Mars, and created Earth II. The alien transmissions were found by Earth II personnel, so short of invading them, Earth One and the United Nations just had to pound sand.

However, Robert and the Board of Directors agreed to limit the amount of specific information supplied to the news media. Thus, people knew 'Contact' like in a favorite movie of the 20th Century was made with actual Outer Space Aliens. What the great unwashed did not realize was the extent of successful translations of the transmissions.

Robert saw the symbols on the object were like those used by the Arrivals in some of the video transmissions. They looked similar to language believed to mean "Careful" like a warning label on some commercial products. In first attempts at translation, some officials thought the apparent efforts to talk about danger and possible warnings meant the Arrivals were trying to frighten humankind with threats of violence.

Then as the piecing together of the communique became more accurate, the powers-that-be realized the aliens were trying to warn them of some ancient danger. At this time all the governments and private parties realized the Arrivals had been to the Sol System in some ancient past. The translations of the messages shared with the public became scrambled as there was now a real fear that every nut case UFO Conspiracist and religious fanatic would resurrect all the stories of government coverup. The private expansion into the Solar System already shook up countries used to controlling their population. No one needed or desired any more threats to World Order.

"Shit," Robert cursed out loud. "I need this like I need a hole in my head." Then he stopped. He looked at the written note again. A grin formed on his face. Great Uncle Doc was right. Robert could be famous, especially if he had a chance to examine this object before he turned it over to the Board who were bound to give it to Space Command. Too many of those in charge were, in Robert's estimation, old biddies with visions of Alien Invasions dancing through their heads. Hell, new sensors and telescopes had pinpointed the messages and the Arrivals to a cluster of objects (probably hollowed-out asteroids) some twenty-five light-years away. Even if the aliens had 'light hugging' technologies, could travel close to the speed of light, it would take over twenty-five Earth years to arrive. If Robert could be the originator of some new-found knowledge from examining the softball-sized shape, he and his family would be set for life.

"Might even be some new material or mineral," Robert mumbled as he turned the object over in his hands. Then his communicator tab buzzed. He cursed and placed the object back into the duffel bag before he activated his communicator

"Robert, here."

"Sir, Susan, here. The Board called an emergency meeting. Something about our…friends."

Robert refrained from cursing over the open line. Susan was an efficient and attractive assistant all the Board members wanted for their own. Robert did not want to risk offending her or give someone an excuse to transfer her. Not when he had just consummated a tet de tet during a late night office meeting. Some of Uncle Doc's randiness had rubbed off.

"Be right there, Susan." She knew Robert was with his Great Uncle's remains and would cover for him until he arrived. Robert shut the door to the container but did not lock it. This small loading bay belonged to the Vice President for Operations. No one dared screw with it.

As Robert left for the meeting, he had failed to account for two possible flies in the ointment who did not care about his position as Vice President. As Robert hurried down the passageways across Earth II, his Fraternal Twins, Jack and Jill poked their heads around the corner of the loading bay entrance. Brown-haired and lean, they both took after their father.

"See, Jill. I told you Dad had Great Uncle Doc's stuff here."
"Why is this important?" his sister asked Jack. "We never knew him."

"He was one of the original Rock Hounds. Remember that from history class?" Jack confidently went up to the unlocked container door and opened it. He spied the unzipped old duffel bag and glommed on to it. Jill quickly assisted him in divesting the bag of its contents.

"Look at this cool jumpsuit," said Jill. "I bet you no one at school has one of these."

Jack picked up the black and round object. "This is heavy. Maybe lead. Or gold under this black color." Jack turned it around in his hands. "Come on. I'm taking this to school. Bet you, I can use it for a science project."

"I can use this jumpsuit for History," Jill chimed in. In moments, the two maturing ten-year-old thieves made off with their booty down hidden passageways only kids seemed ever to find.

The Board members were in a tizzy. Robert sat and drummed his fingers in frustration as he watched the eleven other meeting attendees dither and squawk like a bunch of old chickens. On a broad vision screen was displayed the signs and squiggles of what served as the written language of the Arrivals. The Board Members all gestured at the display and tried to talk at the same time. Finally, Robert pulled out a mechanical metal pencil, older than anyone on Earth II, and tapped a crystal water glass. The loud ringing noise grabbed everyone's attention.

"So Ladies and Gentlemen. We have another message saying 'Danger' and 'Careful' in a long sequence of messages. That makes, let me see, fifty such communique out of some seventy we have received."

"But this one, Robert," stated the Board President, Charlene Quest, "uses what was newly translated as words for fighting and conflict."

"You mean, War, Madam President."

Charlene frowned, then looked at the displayed message. "That does fit the tone and form of the message, Robert." "So?? They had a War in this neck of the woods. Shall we say, a hundred thousand years ago at least? They do not even mention we humans, using the word which seems to denote us." Robert leaned forward.

"They are warning us about a conflict which did not involve our ancestors. A situation that did not seem to include Earth. Why and how could that harm us now? "

Back in his room, out of sight of his mother, Jane Dodge, Jack probed and prodded his stolen treasure with his inquisitive fingers. As he did, a small surface section suddenly recessed into the black globe.

"Hey! Something m…"

Jack never finished his comment.

Investigation by Earth authorities as to what exploded and split Earth II back into the asteroid parts of its creation was still ongoing two years later. What was evident was the effects of the explosion. The Lunar settlements were decimated as chunks of space rock and destroyed humanmade structures rained down. Two oversized pieces made it to Earth's orbit, where they split up like shotgun buckshot when entering the planet's atmosphere. Downtown Oakland, California took a direct hit from a piece that did not burn up on re-entry. Another mass-casualty strike happened in Vladivostok, Siberia. An airburst from an exploding rock bent the main supports of the Eifel Tower in Paris, France.

There was one survivor from the near 3,000 souls in Earth II. A maintenance technician had been on the airless surface in a protective suit and was blown out towards an approaching Space Command craft. After dodging the Earth II debris, the crew of EXPLORER FIVE recovered Technician Huang Tsu. He and the Space Command personnel became famous on the talk show circuit.

A recreation of the recent message from the Arrivals was studied. Finally, the best human linguists stated with ninety-nine percent certainty what the communication said.

DANGER! EXPLOSIVES!

ADDENDUM.

UXB. Abbreviation used in World War II for Unexploded Bombs which resulted from Hitler's air attacks on England. UXB disposal units disarmed them. Unexploded munitions are still found on all the battlefields of Earth.

THE UPHILL BATTLE
BY ELIZA LOEB

It's funny when others say that standing, walking, and breathing is easy. They've obviously never had to claw their way through the mud while trying to make it to the top of the hill. And during the climb, have their hands bitten by poisonous insects that plague one's thoughts and bring them to a mental state of unrest or have heavy boots stepping all over them both intentional and not. And the heavier the footfall, the more inclined its owner is to hurt, to cause harm, to stop the climber from reaching what it is that they want to achieve. No one will know what the motivation is that will cause that amount of pain. Few will forgive it and will let it roll off their back.

For me, personally, it is a matter of timing. It is a matter of whether dwelling will solve anything or bring importance to an issue or a topic. And I like to think of ways to approach things that have happened in the past, so I can use it in the future. But I still acknowledge that no matter what I do, I am still on that uphill slope. My face is still buried in the mud and I am no better than anyone else. I can't deny that I've hurt others unintentionally. I cannot say how deep the trenches go with others, because I am not them. What I can say, however, is that no one realizes how easy it is to fall until they must start climbing their way back up on their own. And frankly, I envy those who have yet to do so. I envy those who have others to lift them out of the mud and pull them back to the top of the hill, but I also find them to be irritating. Because those people are the people who have taken too many things for granted in my eyes.

You can tell who they are.

They're all over the place and in their mind, everything is easy.

The most belligerent are the people who say "Your disability is in your head. Stop being so lazy." Or "Medication is a gateway to codependence, you don't need medication to keep your seizures in check." These people have had many advantages in life that, to me, deprives them of compassion. They have never lost the ability to walk or to do the things that they want without worrying about how it affects them. They've never had to figure out ways to manage their stress in a way that wouldn't cause a cumulative shutdown. And that's only the medical part of it all.

You don't, you can't, and you are, are all double-edged swords that can bring both the giver and receiver to their knees and push their faces back into the mud if used improperly. The giver can destroy their reputation and harm the receiver. But the giver can be one of the few who can help convince the receiver of the positives.

You don't have to give a toxic person your time.

You can go home and take care of that novel or painting

that you've been working so hard on.

You are a talented and good-hearted human being who deserves so much in this life.

These things being said can do a lot of good for a person who has been clawing their way through the mud all week. These things can do a lot of good.

I remember life with my grandmother and how she would constantly encourage me to continue drawing or reading something out loud. I remember how she would describe my feet as being firmly planted on the ground and how she would come along with a hairdryer and an umbrella if it dared to turn into mud. And one day when I asked her what would happen if it became too much, she looked me in the eye and said, "Well, if it becomes too much, I will hand you the blow dryer and the umbrella." Upon hearing this, I began to feel a part of myself sink. My five-year-old brain began to feel as though I had to be perfect for her to love me.

"But..." she would begin again. "I will still be here with an extra umbrella and hairdryer, if you begin to get tired."

I don't know if she realized at the time. But those words always seemed to make my day when they came from her.

It wasn't until I was seven when the rain started to pour harder in my life. And by age eight I was already struggling to stay on top of the hill and by twenty-six, I'm still struggling to make the halfway point. I guess it comes from feeling as though I had been forgotten in one corner, cloaked in cobwebs and decades of dust, having been treated as a survivor merely by default, by being over-looked, silent and unobtrusive, not big enough to be an imposition and so allowed to remain—a receptacle of memories, an eye witness to everything that came before... as dramatic as it sounds.

The thing that many don't seem to realize is how easy it is to fall. It's one thing when someone is constantly there to lift you up or be able to manage your own solid grounding. It's another to lose it all and struggle to keep yourself up. It's another not to have anyone there or someone there who lacks empathy or compassion. Especially if those people are your own parents or family members. And you become closed off. Which makes the mud deeper and more difficult to manage, and it gets to a point where you just want it all to go away. And when you try to push and power through it, the trying stops being enough and it eventually fades into disappointment. You start to doubt yourself and whatever expectations you may have had of beating that damn hill are never met.

And it gets to a point where you want to take your own life.

Looking in the mirror, I recollect the times I have. I wouldn't wish anything that goes on in my brain onto anybody. I see the struggles that many have on a daily basis and my heart goes out for them. And I almost want to ask what they went through. Sure, depression and many cases of mental illness are genetic; however, in many other instances, there are triggers. There are root causes and those who are neurotypical are none the wiser.

For those of you, who like me, are struggling with that same damn hill. I see you.

I see your pain.

I see your struggle.

And I am proud that you have managed for this long.

People have died on this hill and have been buried by the mud. Many are beneath our fingers or have been delivered by what flowers grow near the top.

That could be you.

That could be me.

But it isn't.

We are here.

And we are fighting to stay alive.

SHOREWRACK
BY SHEILA MENGERT

The psychologist's office was quiet, comfortable without being too suggestive of fluffy comfort and maternal nurture. The psychologist was male, middle-aged, and sufficiently weathered that he was beyond awakening competition and Oedipal feelings in his male clients or quickening Electra complexes in his female clients.

His chosen methodology was client-centered without being vapid and directionless, but he did believe in allowing his clients to solve their own problems and at their own pace. He avoided any semblance of secret knowledge so that dependency quagmires could be avoided. He never took a client for over a year not believing in what he called "chronic therapy." He considered therapy to be an intervention rather than supportive in nature. His advice to narcissistic patients who were always confined to a single session was, "You aren't the center of the universe." His prescription for people with Borderline Personality tendencies was equally short, "Stop using drugs, things, and people for your own advantage."

He had a framed statement on the wall of his office that said, "Life is short so don't waste my time or yours."

The psychologist had many clients, but this was his first client who was a writer. There is an assumption that writers possess the secret of happy and successful living until their actual biographies are read. Perhaps their genius is rooted in the sheer sensitivity that they possess or in the compulsive desire to express the common human condition that drives them on. The best authors extend our grasp of form by finding new ways to express what we already intuitively know. It is the recognition that dispels our uncertainty by reducing supposition to conviction. Maybe Plato was right and everything is really a recollection. Our lives already existed somewhere before we were even born, not pre-determined but already in some fashion part of the eternity that we must perish in order to re-enter again when the cycle completes itself. The psychologist couldn't answer questions like these not being a philosopher and philosophers do not maintain consultation practices. It was not the business of a psychologist to give us reasons for living but rather to kick us out the door with enough force that we will take up our lives again wherever they happen to have ended up. Their job is to get us look at our lives fully and to see them whole to the degree that we are able to do so, to realize that for us the clock is still ticking and that we possess the miraculous ability to go on.

The session for today with the writer began.

"Well, what would you like to talk about today?"

"The Maltese Falcon."

"Book or movie?"

"The idea."

"A huh, would you like to elaborate on that?"

"Well, I was thinking about the way that at the end of the story the quest for the Black Bird goes on. Its value in purely monetary terms has become irrelevant to the seekers. The characters have been so long involved in the quest that they can't give it up even though it is destroying them. The Black Bird is like the carrier of some latent virus of human greed, a whirlpool that draws anyone that comes into contact with it to his doom. Even the innocent bystanders like Miles and Floyd Thursby are not spared. Its history is one long line of casualties."

The client took a sip from his glass of mineral water.

"So do you have a Black Bird in your life?"

The client smiled, "There have been several."

The psychologist nodded before suggesting, "And you would like to…"

"Give them up."

"Why now in particular?"

The client reflected before answering, "Maybe because I can finally see things clearly, apart from the dream, that aura of golden mist that once surrounded it, that… hope."

There was an electricity-driven pump in the office that caused a little waterfall to cascade over a pool of quartz and ebony rocks. It prevented that awkward silence in a room that can stifle insight when the therapeutic clock is ticking over like a taxi meter.

"I went back down to the Oregon coast recently. I visited some property we once owned that for so long was a cincture of my dreams of the future, my own private Maltese Falcon."

"Was there something different about it this time?"

"There always is. The land on which it rests is in a fault area. There are many areas of the Oregon coast that are gradually sliding down and into the sea. There are visible geologic traces. It is sort of like watching a great ocean-liner fill with water, lean-over, and slowly founder beneath the waves. The place about which I am speaking manifests this sinking and erosion year by year but in recent years I have noticed it more than I once did. Trees that I have known and sat under in years gone by to gaze out to sea now litter the beach down below. Sandstone cliffs crumble; beach growths of salt-grass and evergreens that once hugged the banks become dead due to salt-spray and die. The whole solidity and integrity of the land breaks up and what have you? I can close my eyes and still see it as it once was, extensive, majestic with its winding access path, its hiding places back in the trees, and the artists that once gathered that first year, painting and sketching at the northern point beneath the low cliffs. I thought I had found a little corner of paradise."

"And how is it now for you?"

"Oh it is still beautiful but I see it with eyes stripped of the possibilities that were the greater part of its value for me. For one thing we don't own it anymore... The funny thing is that in many ways the coast as a whole is more open to me than ever before. We got a good price for it when it sold. Now I just pay for the visit to hotels and someone else pays the taxes. There are no headaches in just renting. But ownership, that sense of permanent investiture and the right to exclude the entire world from one's possession is gone. I see now how impermanent things are and how illusory is our sense of possession."

The psychologist nodded.

"You see the land was a part of me. It made me feel somehow invincible, bigger than my mere self. I could bring people down or show them pictures of it and know that it would be there long after I died but altered in some way by what I had done to improve it and what I had built there… Did I mention that it is well within the Cascadia earthquake's probable inundation zone? No? Well it is. The tsunami that will probably arrive sometime in the next fifty years will reduce anything there to rubble and debris, so I guess even the earth is never still or secure."

The client paused, "I hate that. I would like at least some proximate version of immortality."

"Yes?"

"Last year I met an ornithologist who was banding and studying wildfowl. The sea is heating up you know and the fish are diving too deep for some species of birds to reach them. They have to fly out to sea farther to areas where the colder waters percolate up from the ocean floor in order to get their food. Their numbers are decreasing. It seems so unfair. They were so accustomed to their local environments and now… Well, like them I want to find a place in the sea cliffs to nest."

The psychologist spoke up. "Give up your migratory habits?"

"I suppose it's a sign that I am getting older, this nesting urge. It sounds so…"

"So…"

"Well, this urge to root oneself in the life process is something that women do. For men it's always that search for change and adventure, to not be tied down that keeps us alive.

Commitment is always rather the beginning of the end."

"Is that what you think?"

"Isn't that what most men think? Isn't that why women are always attracted to precisely the men who want little to do with them after the novelty of conquest wears off? What good is catching a mate who doesn't struggle to escape the traces? And afterwards, men wilt in captivity."

"Is a normal desire for security the equivalent of captivity?"

"No. But to give up the search for something better in one's life implies the prospect of fortuitous change, of surprises in life. Migration may be the bird equivalent of the two-home syndrome, the English country house or the aerie on the cliffs at Capri before returning to one's London townhouse."

"True, but even for such fortunate people there are patterns of migration, habits of return to the familiar. What has yours been?"

"One of mine was simply coming down every summer to our ocean property just hoping that this was the year that we would finally build a family getaway and we never did."

There was a pause. "Can you let that go now?"

"I have to don't I? But I feel like such a fool for entertaining the dream for so long. I could have done other things, found other people to center my life around."

"I thought we were talking about a place not a person."

"Well we need to people the stage of our dreams with a cast don't we?"

A pause ensued and the sound of the waterfall became salient in the room.

"A woman?"

"Yes. Her name doesn't matter. Maybe she could have been anybody who came into my life at just that particular time, when she was needed. She embodied then for me … oh I don't know, the sheer possibility of regaining lost time, of doing it right this time, redemption. I thought I could spare her at least the price exacted by my own delay in discovering what is of value in life."

"Like that huh," the psychologist suggested noncommittally.

"Isn't it always like that?" asked the client.

"Not always but more often than you may think; it's an old story but not a universal one."

"I saw her against the wonderful background that the ocean provided. I guess that I thought that between the two of us we could stand against the leeching force of time itself, make death stand still in sheer awe of what we could be to each other and for each other. Isn't that what immortality means, at least in a Pagan sense?"

Pause.

"As I said an old story."

"But unfortunately a very long story, too long; I couldn't realize that just like the land that I loved so much that was sliding irrevocably into the sea she was sliding deeper into the abysses of addiction year by year. I couldn't bring her into my world. Instead, each year took me deeper into whatever new cycle of incessant misery was on order for that year. The turning that I kept hoping for never came. Would it sound strange if I said that she possessed a genius for degradation? After awhile I forgot what freshness and joy could mean. There was only relief when she would cycle to the surface to catch a few breaths before diving again into the dark waters. Still, I couldn't manage the obvious and simply walk away. You might say it was all misplaced loyalty or an unwillingness to read signs and take them at face value, but I think the real problem for me in regard to her was that I had a template for happiness that simply had no basis in her version of reality ... or unreality."

"Well addressing recovery is what I am in business for."

The client smiled, "Yes, I guess that's true. But why do we hang on so hard to precisely what we should have known early on was hopeless?"

"It must have seemed worth it at the time or you wouldn't have done it."

"But I could have done differently isn't that it?"

"But you didn't. So what are you going to do now?"

"I don't know. I lost myself somewhere in those years or at least the momentum of living. It's like venturing out on a cliff-face handhold by handhold and suddenly finding that you can't go higher and retreat is impossible. In relationships like that an interchange of genes or DNA takes place so that the damage done to both of us may be irretrievable. Neither could give the other enough of the other's survival traits to create a whole life."

"Why do you call it irretrievable?"

"Because it's too late for another shot at making it right for whomever I was then."

"You talk about yourself in the third person. So you want to go back in time; pull the relational equivalent of the land back out of the sea?"

"I guess I do."

"And what would that accomplish."

"I wouldn't have made such a big mistake and such a stupid one at that."

"Who's keeping the record?"

The client paused to consider.

"I wanted a life you know with no sidetracks, no wasted days, no…"

"Learning and regrets? Who ever told you that life could ever be like that… or history either for that matter? With every added level of complexity the possibilities of catastrophic breakdown increase exponentially. Or maybe you just wanted a dull life after all, one that could pass any test that an outside observer might impose."

"Hardly that! I wanted to sample every level of existence; even to walk on the wild side as long as I could avoid consequences and maintain my innocence."

"It sounds a little like Oscar Wilde's novel, *Portrait of Dorian Grey*. Maybe you got off cheaply after all. She lived the dysfunction and you got to watch her downward spiral and be the redeemer. It plays right into everyone's hope for bargain-basement omnipotence. I see it manifested here all the time in my practice."

"But what did she want?"

"She isn't my client so does it matter? We're working on you."

"But this whole thing just throws me back into the street waiting for someone new to walk by."

"I can see that you haven't let go of the old set of presuppositions that set you up for precisely that type of relationship. You don't think that your experiences can be real until they are filtered through the medium of somebody else. It is like one of those plants that cannot create its own chlorophyll so it must depend upon another plant to feed it. The whole process is derivative – each trying to engineer the other person to a version of the perfect host organism. Until you alter your agenda; you will only repeat it by finding someone just like her."

"So I am doomed?"

"Only if you go back to an inadequate template for your life…"

"I don't know any other way to be!"

"I thought that you were the one with a God-like plan for everything and everybody."

"Only after I get my teeth into something; before that there is only this great emptiness."

"Maybe that's what the two of you shared: the inability to simply be without any need for an outside reflector to tell you that you existed. It takes responsibility to take up life and to accept consequences even if they are beyond the zone of our predictability and control."

"That's depressing."

"You always want to read life's menu before ordering? It isn't depressing; it's only a little scary and at times unpleasant. It's up to you if you want to get depressed about it."

The client considered this.

"So what would life be like without a template? How can you know whether you are on course to achieving appropriate goals?"

"Isn't that what learning means—to resolve uncertainty by encountering new data? It sounds to me like you think of life as a play where you as the playwright can sit in the wings while others and a projected version of your ideal self act out the lines of an already written script—or worse life as an endless series of rehearsals that never comes to the opening night. There is no risk in that.”

“But if I only get one life then it has to be perfect the first and only time around.”

“Do you have any examples of such a life?”

The client smiled. “How did you know that I like biographies?”

“Why do you like them?”

“They are mines for raw material.”

“So you can step somehow into their shoes rather than your own?”

“Well, I don’t want to miss anything.”

The psychologist shook his head. “It sounds very tiring keeping to someone else’s itinerary. Would it be so hard to simply make a choice no matter how trivial and then just take what comes?”

“No if it was only a matter of a single choice but it is the pattern of successive events that I am seeking and that pattern must have a beginning somewhere so the first choice suddenly becomes simply part of an irrevocable change, a chain of infinite linkages, and I am paralyzed.”

“Do you approach your writing in the same manner?”

“No.”

“How is it different?”

“Well, since the advent of computers revision is an easy process—I just write.”

The psychologist looked at the writer with unusual emphasis as he asked, "How is living different then from writing?"

The client considered, "Costs."

"What costs?"

"Well in life there is engagement, the world around us changes according to our choices and is not immediately subject to being put back into its original order."

"Have you ever heard of forgiveness?"

"Of course but there is always the residuum isn't there; God forgives but the damage remains. Our imperfect world even leaks its way into eternity and demands that somehow we make it right – the doctrine of purgatory."

"Do you understand Purgatory?"

"Yes, it's like hell only temporary."

"Sounds like bad theology to me."

"Well how do you see it, presuming that you believe in Purgatory?"

"Well to begin with as I see it Purgatory is more like heaven than hell because you know that paradise awaits you. Also, the correction of damages may be more beyond the control of the agent than you suppose; after all he or she is dead."

"Then who fixes things?"

"Maybe no one does. Maybe Purgatory is the final acceptance that we cannot be like God knowing good and evil. Our grasp of things is always partial, tentative, subject to correction. We are not able to freeze even salvation into a permanent form, some *quid pro quo* where God owes us salvation. Isn't that the ultimate presumption and impiety to think that we can control God, to somehow hold Him bound to a contract?"

"I never thought of it like that."

"Few people do. It would mean that religion above all else should remind us of our humanity and not of our efforts at self-deification."

"So you are telling me that I'm trying to be God."

"You are, at least insofar as your own life is concerned. When you realize that you can't have everything your own way without the chance of making mistakes you freeze or worse you try and adjust life to some ridiculous pre-existing idea of how everything should turn out."

"Isn't that what Nietzsche meant when he reduced everything to the will to power?"

The psychologist smiled, "And it drove him mad. He ended up frozen into the awareness that the instinct of compassion was still alive in him. He would never be a superman ... and neither can you."

The room was silent and the sound of the waterfall continued patiently and without ceasing.

The client spoke up at last. "Alright, so what do you recommend?"

"You mean take two aspirin and call me in the morning?"

The client smiled. "Yeah."

"Why don't you write a story about your experiences down there on the coast and how it relates to some of the other of your discontents that we have been discussing during your sessions with me and we'll take a look at your composition together next time?"

"Alright; any length requirements...?"

"It isn't an assignment; it's a suggestion. The rest is up to you. I won't be grading it. Next week then…"

"Right."

The client turned again before leaving.

"Oh one more thing though…"

The psychologist looked up.

"Yes?"

"I'm still not that happy about all of this, this whole therapy process."

"Well, take two aspirins and…"

The client interrupted smiling, "Call me in the morning."

"No, just show up next week and give yourself a break once in awhile. Just live."

Coastal Credo

I discovered the Oregon coastal towns early in my life. I would have discovered them earlier still had prudence not opposed my will, when I proposed to my father a plan to follow Highway One to California on my little burgundy-red one-cylinder Honda 90 Scrambler. The fact that it could reach a speed of sixty miles per hour on level ground and with a tail wind did not augur well for any sort of highway travel. My proposed adventure was met with an immediate veto as manifesting the same optimistic frame of mind and impulsive desire as when I proposed to raise a pet alligator in the shower stall that no one ever used of our home's auxiliary bathroom.

For me the impressive idea always came first and thereafter one naturally used the means at hand. I managed to preserve well into adulthood a sense that fantasy could not only infuse reality it might actually be found there just waiting to be discovered. I had little conception of the dull struggle for existence that pervades most coastal communities as logging and fishing waned leaving only tourism and retirement as bases to support the economy. For me there was only the majestic presence of the sea and a dim apprehension that a pirate galleon under full sail might at any moment round the rocky headlands to seek shelter in one of the bays that provide illusory shelter due to the presence of treacherous reefs.

I was raised in a benign and complacent era when good and evil seemed equally matched in a bi-polar, Cold War obsessed world. It was a world in which men like Simon Templar, also known as The Saint, could work their magic of detection and justified violence against villains without the more realistic limitations that beset the hard-drinking detectives of the 1930's like Sam Spade or Philip Marlowe whose exploits were honored with little more than effort, neglect, and at most an uncrowned moral victory. In those early days before the tide of fantasy had waned I wanted to write mystery stories.

In the golden age of Agatha Christie, Mary Roberts Rinehart, and Mignon Eberhart, all women writers, and of Ian Fleming, Earl Stanley Gardner, Rex Stout, and Mickey Spillane the male writers, the world was peopled by spies, smugglers, and an illustrious international set of seductresses. All of this was bound to keep the hearts of readers beating as they served to bridge the gap between childhood and the pubescent dreams of adolescent romance. But perhaps the writer I most admired was Daphne Du Maurier whose masterpiece *Rebecca* revolved around Max De Winter and his hereditary manor house, Manderley. Coincident with this was the television series called *Dark Shadows* with the great estate of Collinwood, haunted by ghosts and the remnants of ancient loves. It was these that set the parameters of my quest for the perfect coastline where I could set up shop and quietly become rich and legendary. I saw myself walking the sea cliffs in a heavy fog drawing inspiration from mysterious vessels hovering just beyond the moaning channel markers manned by a crew of indeterminate but desperate nationalities and determined to deliver a cargo of raw opium or enriched uranium to various criminal masterminded societies whose cunning operatives were waiting to arrange a rendezvous. Even into my late twenties I had not surrendered these visionary versions of my life that supplanted sensible career planning; so when I drove up from California one November day to begin graduate school in Washington and spied Whale Cove just south of Depoe Bay I thought I had found at last the site of my retreat from the boring world and the base for my future literary eminence.

As a gesture to realism and a possible academic career (just in case) I set aside my immediate impulses to embrace years of study allowing texts to speak for themselves stripped of any semblance of authorial intent or idiosyncratic readings tracing the impact of various personal signifiers when filtered through a post-Marxist sensibility. I had already seen industrial America up-close and personally and vowed that this experience was to be my only concession to necessity in a life of sustained rebelliousness. At best it might provide a resource to add a seamy texture to some future narrative that would touch in passing the squalor of rust-belt America, the legacy of the cost of our collective involvement in the endless struggles between the various European empires for relative dominance, and a warning to America to return to a comfortable isolationism.

It is hard to say when life ceases to be an adventure like the one that painted my early dreams with romance, when magic finally resolves itself into a sober and severe appreciation of the nature of life and its struggles, but my attendance in law school might have had something to do with it. The legal mind is gradually attuned to the vast amount of human preconceptions and ideas that are simply legally irrelevant. This breeds a certain cold-blooded attitude if it is not counteracted by a stern prior grounding in the humanities. It is these literary studies that explore the tension between human aspirations and the workings of what the Greeks called fate or fatality.

The world of the 21st century is an engineered age. We have come to believe that technology can answer most problems and that information and the flood of data will fill in the insuperable gap between our limits as human beings and the worlds of quantum physics and fields that provide the stage for all human actions. What cannot be coded and reduced to software is held to be immediately suspect in such a world. It is a world where the old conflict between story and fate has been superseded by mere narratives that may be further subdivided into atomistic signifiers assembled into chains.

All of the above is a mere prelude to the real subject of this … well call it a reflection on the position of the author as he approaches his senior years. (I will not say retirement years because few authors ever retire. The flow of ink becomes a habit). My early experience of the Oregon Coast was an interwoven one: a blend of July sunlight, salt and sand, and my body still bursting with that nuclear life-force that we imagine will endure unaltered as the years progress. I felt its power when body-surfing in the chill waves, that the great Pacific and I were equally matched. Yet for all of that there was a sense that the sheer multiplicity of possibilities before me entailed their own sorrow.

Already you see I was facing the peculiar way that a thread of fatality becomes gradually interwoven with our lives until the garment it weaves takes definite shape and acquires the stiffness of form that finally leaves us with a sense that we have lived the majority of our days and nights without reaching any of the definitive resolutions that we once imagined that we alone could provide to the eternal dilemmas of existence. Of course I may be presuming too much when I say, "we." No doubt many people assume a place in life that is defined by a context of limited economic and cultural options but as a child of the sixties who believed that I was part of a generation with a new explanation, anything seemed possible to me then.

Americans have always been arrogant and optimistic while at the same time haunted by a sense that in the last analysis we are intruders bearing a burden of guilt for the atrocities committed by the previous generation of dreamers. I suppose that the real burden carried by the recent rhetoric of "Make America Great Again" is a desire to restore the lost virginity of the land so that we can rape it all over again, the search for clean coal as a modern day version of the search for the Holy Grail. My own sympathies have always been with the writers of what might be called the American Gothic sensibility, writers like Nathaniel Hawthorne, William Faulkner, and Edgar Allen Poe. Writers like Edmund White and Andrew Holleran have explored our national epic of paradise lost after the brief effulgence of 70's gay America. Perhaps that was when the tipping point occurred, before the election of Ronald Reagan condemned America to making the rich richer and to exalting a new Puritanism as the remedy for the excesses of that age of reform and revolution that still has my personal allegiance.

It was an allegiance refined by early disillusion and rebellion. In my youth I had a tendency to only grow indignant after the fact, when my first instinct towards escapism had failed me. I expected things to be easier than they were turning out to be. I was spared the trauma of personal involvement in the fighting in Viet Nam but fell into the same national trough of disillusionment post-Watergate. My early forays into a definitive career were met with disappointment. I took as a remedy that traditional anodyne of becoming an expatriate on a bargain budget. I left a job in rust-belt America and fled to Paris and beyond anticipating garrets, café culture, and discussions about the future of a post-colonial world. The decision to travel abroad seemed quite heroic even if not as unique as I supposed it to be.

When I returned from studying in Europe I was determined to become a writer so I proceeded to steep myself in our American prophetic authors, men like Walt Whitman and Henry David Thoreau, while imbibing yellow Chartreuse while I read, a decadent recipe for instant advancement into the ranks of the immortals. I hoped to make it easier for my future biographers by living my life in discrete periods each punctuated by a signature stylistic development and passionate commitment to inappropriate but promising attachments.

I discovered no unique vices, was sheltered by a

providential sense of caution, and managed to skim along the ridge of the various disasters that have weeded out so many creative spirits over the course of my life. The end result is that I am still here to reflect upon the interplay between story and fate that so perplexed the Emperor Marcus Aurelius in his meditations. Perhaps his primary insight was that fate is governed by the whole as opposed to the particular so that even an emperor could not expect to be held immune from the trials of fortune that often seem so disproportionate when viewed from the point of view of suffering individuals. He considered it the height of impiety to ask that the universe adapt itself to our needs and desires rather than the other way around. The task of the man of wisdom is to adjust his expectations to results in the vast web of cause and effect that surrounds us. To do this of course works a termination or at least a severe corrective to most human meta-narratives, to all of the vast projects and projected dreams on which we repose our hopes for a fortunate set of outcomes to our actions from the major to the trivial.

American idealism of course finds such a limiting proposal to be anathema to its national creed. What are we if we cannot dictate events? This is not held to be special-pleading; it is our richly deserved destiny. But so deeply rooted is this ethos and perception that it has become the underlying theme of the present hour in its most extreme form, determining national policy and domestic economics. Many people already sense that we are hovering at the fulcrum-point between two historical eras. The magnitude of the incipient changes has forever altered the balance between story and fate among us. Our ability to dictate the text is restricted by the fields that must be filled in before the document may be forwarded to whatever central processing unit is recording the perhaps inconsequential history of the human experiment. It is precisely at such a time that the past is to be consulted it seems to me.

So by this circuitous introductory route we return to the Oregon Coast where my spirit has of old found that sustenance that makes life possible. Nothing so reminds us of the brevity of our days than the all-witnessing, all-embracing tumult of these immense waters. Sameness and succession—can any two words better express the course of our lives as individuals? Uniqueness combined with mortality—therein is the source of all tragedy. It takes a mind like that of Marcus Aurelius to take the oceanic view of insentient futurity and to make it his own—to the rest of us it is precisely the local, the particular, the things that we love that must somehow survive the welter of events, the accidents, the deep currents of the irrevocable. So when I grow weary of the sea with its play of light and shadow, its winds, fogs, and squalls I seek out the wisdom of the ages in the many bookstores that act as a sponge to absorb coastal visitors when the insouciant and constant interplay of water and atmosphere bring rain, wind, or fog to the coastal environs.

The siren call of used bookstores is universal at least among that sector of humanity that is willing to court solitude as the price of deeper colloquy with the written word and those generous minds that are willing to sacrifice a portion of irreplaceable time to communicate across an abyss of anonymity with unspecified strangers. It is no small part of community to create these spaces where fortuitous meetings are made with antiquity. The best evidence of tangential immortality is provided by the written word. I for one feel the same sense of intimacy with many long-dead authors as for people whose time I share but whose minds are more elusive despite our propinquity.

It is said that every city contains a million stories, most of them unnoticed and hence untold. All of them share the interplay between desire and outcome, expectation and result. When the law of disproportion favors us it is called good luck or fortune; when the disproportion emerges like a great sea monster to devour us and to maim us forever it is called a tragedy. Between these two there is only the dull passage of linear time, the quiet meeting of presupposition and outcome that we call ordinary life. We depend upon routine and a blanket of supportive relationships to act as twin custodians; yet we sometimes contemplate trading boredom and obscurity for exposure and renown the two biggest enemies of the private life. Limited individuality is the progenitor of story as opposed to history which traces only the great abiding current of events. This foments the illusion that storytelling is trivial precisely because it is not general or immediately replicable as science-mindedness demands that it should be to qualify as data to feed the hungry gigabyte maw of the information superhighway.

Of what use is it to meander as I do down the country lanes of coastal villages or to look back upon eras that are already being washed away by sand and surf into yellow-paged oblivion? Yet still we write. We join the silent denizens who have left only this medium behind as witness to their passing perceptions and reflections, deficient in graphics, irreducible to design and governance, demanding of attention that would otherwise be drawn into countless multi-tasking inventories that keep feeding the great totality of the theoretically accessible but inconsequent sloshing-about of the tub of raw data devoid of organizing principle and final utility to us as human beings. So in its place we alter not our narratives but ourselves as constituent parts of whatever the abiding technology demands of us. This is the background, the setting, and even the thematic undertone that drones through our days and nights like a wailing foghorn; this is the thing that reduces us to cells and corpuscles, mere sea anemones clinging to rocks waving our fragile tentacles about for whatever might come our way to nourish our fragile selves.

As a writer I am absorbed and enmeshed in the ecosystem of fates and of personalities that surround me, the antidote to the fatal introspection of youth that because it fears that no one can ever really care fears to reveal itself fully, to transform confessional into tale. As a writer I feel a sense of story in the ebb and flow of the human tides about me, each as individual, each as hopeful as I am that it all has been worth it, that my life matters, and that wisdom differs in some essential way from the noise of the political hour. I hope for more for Americans even as the MAGA-Hat wearing throng cheers for embodied banality in the incarnation of the great hamburger-glutted attention glutton who migrates between his golf course in Florida and his television tuned to FOX News in Washington. The wreckage left behind gluts the American mind in an unprecedented way and makes books suddenly seem to be irrelevant counter-cultural artifacts. Why add to the supply of dinosaur bones of the already expressed when only such clinging store front repositories as are found scattered in abundance on the coast preserve what the publishing warehouses have already long since remaindered? Shouldn't all utterances be only momentary effusions, blogs and broadcasts, meetings over coffee and gossip?

The sea breaks and I know the answer. This impulse to select and to refine is as constant within me as these waves. Recognition will always lead the avid seeker to harbor in these labyrinths of authors describing and interfacing with other times and places finding there the still and solemn pulse-beat of the eternally human spirit that unites us all and bridges the gaps of age and sex and nation. I in turn will leave the sea of tranquility of the desiccated moonscape of this present hour of our tormented history hoping for something better, knowing that the value of ideas only emerges when thinking itself falls into shadow as in the innumerable dark ages of humanity that have come and gone before us.

Perhaps we took progress too much for granted in the days of my youth so that this present penitential era was foredoomed. Attentive observers might have remarked more on the general drift towards self-interest and materialism long before various algorithms doomed us to sordid repetitions of yesterday's atrocities: new tears for old stories, another shooting, another hate rally to stoke our fears, another evisceration of the fabric of our collective lives. Fate only becomes story when story ceases and response becomes pointless because the market has already discounted the response in all of its possible permutations before it happens. Out of this realization grows resistance opposing wind and wave by the transient but undeniable fact of our own existence. This is the remnant of the confidence that was once in my youthful arrogance presumed to be a permanent possession rather than lent to me for an indeterminate span of days and nights while all along the fabled coast of cape and estuary the great Pacific quietly whispered its name.

In precisely this way we come from the realm of past convictions and present concerns to the present minute of undigested life. A single kite flies over the beach. The morning clouds have fortuitously cleared away; an empty Tudor-Style and steep-roofed store front across the cobbled way still beckons for a tenant. A swift dust-devil just gathered its burden of dried soil in the unpaved parking lot. Couples are passing or coming in for a swift coffee or sandwich. An unclaimed guitar leans against the window. The afternoon ebbs and the light on the sea changes, grows more slate blue and silver as the emerald green of morning has waned away while I write. The swift haiku of impressions melts and improvises. Is it story or is it fate that I have endured so many times and places to write these words this day? Where is the floor of my being on which all impressions are grounded? Is my skull a shell where a little grey creature lives? What will become of me when it is ground to gravel and sand and washes away? Yet who can deny the prescience of the moment when I may decide to strike the next keystroke or indulge in the cup at my side with its coating of cream and mocha, long since a victim of my ardor and subject to my neglect?

What have become of my usual haunts and the people who once gave texture and substance to my life at home? Where is my home, this thing that I am always leaving behind and then perpetually trying to regain? The insight, the conclusion, the reduction to formula, they are as always elusive. Has my cranial balance sheet gone up or down in this particular trading session of inquiry with my own mind?

I look up to decide and suddenly I realize the full impact and color of the ocean as though I had never seen it before, realize its absolute beauty. I think of those who I did not know how to love. The crowd passes me, each retaining their secrets and the sea is as ever breaking along the coast. The lighthouse out on the end of Yaquina Point is blinking, warning the night-bound vessels to maintain their seaway and steerage room until the fog clears. The day dawns and they can then proceed safely onwards to harbor while I, guided by only a dim and flickering inner light, must seek again the open sea.

NEW BEGINNINGS
BY CARRIE AVERY MORIARTY

What kind of storage space does it have?" Karen asked as they finished their tour of the upstairs.

She and her husband, Cliff, were looking for their first home, knowing they couldn't stay on base much longer. They hadn't told their family yet, but they were expecting a baby right after the first of the year, and that had given Cliff enough of an incentive to retire from the military. They'd been fortunate that his most recent station was near where they both grew up, so they were looking to settle down and raise their family in their home state.

"Storage space in these older homes is sometimes hard to find," the realtor said. "But this one has an attic on the third floor, easily accessible up these stairs."

The woman showed them to a door at the end of the hall.

"Can we go up?" Cliff asked.

"Absolutely," the realtor said as she opened the door. "You go ahead and explore. I'll wait downstairs for you when you're finished."

Leading the way, Cliff climbed the narrow set of wooden stairs. The sun came in through the dormers, filling the small space with a soft light. Looking around, he noticed a handful of boxes lining one wall, but the space was otherwise empty.

"It's perfect," Karen said as she stepped up behind her husband.

"You should be able to paint in here with the light no problem," he replied, smiling at his wife.

"May take some work to get it cleared out, though," she said, noting the boxes.

"Doesn't look like much," he replied. "Who knows. They may have this all gone by the time we move in."

"Does this mean you're sold on it?" she asked.

"Right neighborhood, right price, perfect amount of space," he began. "No reason to look any further. I think we found our dream home."

Grinning up at her husband, Karen said, "I love you."

"You, too, Bunny," Cliff said, kissing her on the lips. "Let's go tell the realtor."

"This is nice," Gayle said to her daughter. "But are you sure you can afford it?"

"Mom," Karen said. "We've been over this. Cliff has a job offer for as soon as he is discharged. That means he won't spend any time without work, which means we won't miss a paycheck, and we've got some bonus money coming with the new job. It's the perfect time for us to buy."

"I just wish you'd have let your dad look it over before you signed the paperwork," Gayle replied.

"They did just fine," Charles said, brushing his wife's concerns away. "It's a great house, Bunny," he said to his daughter. "I'm really proud of you."

"Thanks, dad," Karen replied.

"Fine," Gayle succumbed. "What's the first plan of attack?"

"Cleaning," Karen said. "The realtor said that no one has lived in the house for about three years. It's just been sitting here collecting dust. I've got cleaning stuff in the kitchen already, so let's get started."

"I'm going to go mow the yard," Charles said, excusing himself and getting to the task.

"He's always quick to find something else to do when the word 'cleaning' comes up," Gayle laughed.

"Cliff's the same way," Karen replied.

"So," Gayle began. "Why the sudden desire to settle? I thought he was going to be reenlisting."

"We're ready," was all Karen would say.

"They never cleared out the attic," Karen said.

"Wonder why," Cliff mused.

"I guess whoever owned the house didn't want any of that stuff," she replied.

"Did you go through it?" he asked.

"You know how mom is," she began. "Everything in each room has to be spotless before we can move on to the next. I'm surprised we got more than the downstairs cleaned, honestly."

"Is she coming to help again tomorrow?"

"She's got some kind of committee meeting tomorrow,"

Karen said. "I'll get the attic cleared out and swept so I can bring my painting stuff up. Maybe I'll even be inspired."

"Are you sure you're up for it?" he asked. "I mean, are you worn out from today?"

"I'm not a fragile doll, babe," Karen said. "My body will tell me when to take breaks."

"When do we get to tell them?"

"Let's announce at the housewarming," Karen replied. "That way we can celebrate two big things."

"Perfect," Cliff responded.

"But for now," Karen said. "I think I'm ready for bed."

"Thought you weren't worn out," Cliff said playfully.

"Hush," Karen replied with a smile.

"You need to see this," Karen said as she came downstairs, carrying a small box.

"What did you find?" Cliff asked.

"Look," she said, holding the box open.

"What are they?" he asked.

"I'm kind of afraid to touch them," she said, setting the box on the counter.

Cliff reached into the box, pulling out one of the small stuffed animals. "They're kinda cute," he said.

"We are not keeping them," she replied. "I am not letting our baby touch those things."

"Maybe we can donate them somewhere," he suggested.

"Fine," Karen replied. "Just as long as I don't have to look at them anymore. They're kinda creepy looking."

"It's just the dust," he said. "Once they're clean, they'll all be really cute."

Karen just shook her head.

"What else is up there?"

"Don't know," she replied. "This was the first box I opened."

"Maybe you'll find some antique that's worth a million dollars and we'll be set."

"Wouldn't that be nice," she retorted.

"Need help?"

"Nah." Karen shook her head, then said. "You finish getting the wallpaper off this kitchen. I can't do the '70's look. It'll kill me."

"What will we do about the countertop?"

"I really don't care," she said. "Burn it to the ground?"

"I'll figure something out," he said.

"You always do," she smiled.

"Holler if you need me."

Karen kissed her husband and said, "I will always need you."

"Cliff!"

The shout startled him and he rushed up the stairs to the attic. Out of breath he panted, "You OK?"

Karen was staring into a box, hand over her mouth. When she turned to him, her face was streaked with tears.

"What is it, baby?"

She shook her head and clung to him, burying her face in his chest and sobbed.

"Hey," he cooed, rubbing her back. "What is it?"

She just kept hold of him tightly, shaking her head back and forth. Patting her back, he released her and walked over to the box she'd been peering into.

"Oh, baby," he said, seeing the small urn inside.

"It's just so sad," she hiccupped.

He pulled out a pamphlet that was laying beside the urn and turned it over. On the cover was the face of an infant with the words, 'In Loving Memory' below the picture. Flipping it open, he read the inscription about a child who was lost before their life ever got a chance to begin.

"Baby," he said, turning to his wife.

"I can't imagine losing our baby," she sobbed.

"We're going to be fine," he comforted. "This is from years ago. There is so much more that we know about caring for medical issues now."

"Why would they leave their baby here, though?" she asked.

"Let's see if we can find out who the parents are," he suggested. "Maybe we can return her to them."

Karen nodded, trying to dry the tears still staining her face.

"Are you sure it's her?" Karen asked.

"She's the only one I could find," Cliff responded.

It had been a week since she had discovered the small box with the pieces of a broken life. An urn with the ashes of an infant inside, the program from the funeral, and the wrist band from the hospital where the baby was born and died. Cliff had promised to try to find the family of the baby, and had finally come up with a name and address for the mother listed on the paper.

"What do I say to her?" Karen asked.

"That you know how much it would mean if someone cared enough to return your baby to you in the same circumstances," Cliff suggested.

Taking a deep breath, Karen finally said, "OK. I'm ready."

Holding his wife's hand, Cliff walked through the automatic door to the nursing home he'd found.

"Can I help you?" the receptionist asked.

"We're here to visit someone," he said.

"Great," the receptionist said. "Sign in here."

"We're not family," he said. "We've never met her, and we aren't sure where she is."

"What's her name?"

"Dorothy Sparks," Karen said.

A look of sadness came over the receptionist's face as she said, "Mrs. Sparks doesn't get any visitors."

"Well," Cliff began. "We'd like to see her, if it would be all right."

"I think she would like that," the receptionist said. "If you'll sign in here, she's in room 302. You can take the elevator there to the third floor."

Karen put their names down on the sign in sheet, then they pressed the button to call the elevator.

"You're sure you want to do this?" Cliff asked once they were inside.

"I have to," Karen responded.

They took the rest of the ride in silence until the bell chimed that they'd reached the third floor. Stepping out, they saw a caregiver waiting. "Can you tell us where we can find Mrs.

Sparks?" Cliff asked.

"Are you family?" the caregiver asked.

"No," Karen said. "But we have something that belongs to her. We purchased her old house and it was left behind. We think she'd want it back."

"She's just down this hall," the caregiver instructed. "First door on the right."

"Thank you," Cliff said.

"You're welcome."

They took the few steps down the hall and came to the door marked 302. The name plate next to it showed two spaces for names, but only one was filled. "Ready?" Cliff asked.

Karen took a deep breath, then nodded. They stepped into the room, walking past the empty bed near the door to the one closer to the window. "Mrs. Sparks?" Karen asked. The woman in the chair didn't respond. Stepping closer, she tried again. "Mrs. Sparks?"

She was small, fragile almost, with white hair done up in a bun on the top of her head and a light pink robe covering a floral night gown. When she turned, her eyes held no light, only a sadness that seemed to be soul deep.

"Are you Mrs. Dorothy Sparks?" Cliff asked. The woman nodded, but was clearly confused as to who they were.

"We bought your house," Karen explained. "The one on Fir Street." No real response came from the woman, she simply stared at the intruders.

"We found something that might be yours," Cliff explained.

Karen pulled the small box out of her bag and opened it.

She brought out the paper with the baby's picture on it and handed it to her husband.

"Is this your daughter?" he asked, showing the paper to the woman.

A single tear broke from her eye, trailing down her cheek. She blinked and more fell as she turned to Karen.

"We thought you might want her back," she said, pulling out the urn.

Reaching a frail hand out, the woman grasped the urn. Karen helped her bring it to her lap, not wanting any of the ashes to spill, nor the vessel to break. Once it was in the woman's lap, Karen let go. Tears rushed down the woman's face as she gently ran her hand across the urn. Unable to stop her own tears, Karen placed her hand on the older woman's shoulder. Looking up, eyes bright with tears, a smile crossed the woman's face.

"Thank you," she whispered, her voice barely audible.

"Welcome back," Charlotte said.

"Thanks," Karen replied. "Is she doing well today?"

"She has been getting better and better," the receptionist said. "I think your visits are really helping her. The staff has noticed as well."

"I'm just glad I can help," Karen replied.

"When are you due?"

"Three weeks," she replied. "I feel like a whale."

"But you're glowing like an angel," the receptionist said.

Smiling, Karen made her way to the elevator, riding it up to the third floor. Stepping out, she walked to the room she'd been visiting for months.

"Karen," Dorothy said. "You are absolutely beautiful."

"Thank you, Mrs. Sparks," Karen returned.

"So?"

"Here you go," Karen said as she handed over an envelope.

Flipping the top open, the older woman pulled out the card inside. Looking at the younger woman, she opened the card.

"Look at that," she exclaimed.

"Wonders of modern technology," Karen said as she sat in the chair next to the older woman.

"I can't believe this," the woman said, running her fingers across the image. "It's almost as if you can see her."

"Three-dimensional imagery at its finest," Karen laughed.

"Oh, what I wouldn't give to have had this back when I was young," the older woman said.

"I wanted you to be the first one to know," Karen said, growing serious.

"What's that, dear?"

"We've decided to name our baby Evelyn," she said.

The older woman looked at Karen. "Why?" she squeaked out.

"Because she brought us to you," Karen said, tears threatening to spill. "We're naming her Evelyn Dorothy."

The older woman brought her hand to her mouth, tears spilling down her own cheeks.

"Now don't you cry," Karen said, tears falling from her own eyes. "We'll both be a mess."

"I don't know what to say," Dorothy nearly sobbed.

"We'd like to know if we can have her call you grandma."

"Oh," the older woman said. "I'd like that so much. I really would."

She reached her hand out and Karen took it, holding it tightly in both of hers. "I'm just so glad that little house is going to actually hear the pitter patter of small feet."

"Maybe we can bring you over," Karen suggested. "Let you see what we've done?"

"I don't get around too well," Dorothy offered.

"Cliff is strong," Karen argued. "He can carry you if need be."

"Oh, stop," Dorothy chided.

"We really want you to be part of our lives," Karen admitted. "We feel like you've given us so much, it's the least we can do."

"Well, maybe," the other woman said.

"Then it's settled," Karen said.

"Here," Dorothy said, offering the card back to Karen.

"That's yours to keep," Karen said.

Dorothy pulled the card to her chest and smiled.

"I've got a doctor's appointment, otherwise I'd stay longer."

"No fuss," Dorothy said. "You just stop back by when you get the chance."

"I will," Karen said as she hugged the older woman.

"She's perfect," Cliff said, holding his daughter.

"She really is," Karen agreed.

"Knock, knock," Gayle said as she came into the room.

"Mom," Karen said, reaching out.

Gayle came into the room with a small bag, handing it to her daughter as she embraced her. "Dad and I thought we'd get something for the little one."

"You've done so much already," Karen said.

"We couldn't resist," she said.

Karen pulled the tissue from the bag and gasped. "You found her," she whispered as she pulled a battered stuffed rabbit from the bag.

"We've been saving her for the baby," Gayle replied.

"Ready for visitors?" Charles said as he stepped to the door.

"Daddy," Karen said.

"I've brought someone who wanted to see the baby," he said, stepping aside.

"I hope you don't mind," Dorothy said.

"Come in," Karen said through tears. "Come meet Evelyn."

The older woman made her way slowly to the bedside and sat in the chair Gayle offered her.

"Grandma Dorothy," Cliff said, placing his daughter into her arms. "Meet Evelyn Dorothy."

Taking the baby, Dorothy peered into her eyes. "Aren't you just perfect," she cooed.

Karen looked at her husband and smiled. 'Thank you' she mouthed. He nodded, confirming that bringing the previous owner of their house into their family was the right thing to do.

THE CAMERA DOES NOT LIE
BY DAVID MECKLENBURG

You come and go in my life. This question always comes up when I am moving because that is the time when I think of you the most. I suppose it does for many of the things we keep that remind us of someone, especially when they are stored away and not out in the community of our daily acquaintance.

Right now—in my middle age—there is a beautiful woman from Japan who, in the mayfly lifespan of fame, teaches Americans how to tidy up their homes with joy. On Netflix. That is how it's sold, but you remember I spent some time there. The Japanese can also tidy up with wistful nostalgia or sorrow—emotions that illustrate the mutable nature of the world. Kept objects may even provide the illusory counterpoint of obduracy, because that's the point: a rock, or a Nikon camera.

What a multiplicity of Second Persons. In animistic systems it must be the main form of address for the world: it's no wonder Japanese has so many pronouns for different levels of address, mood and formality. That's where part of you is from after all.

Am I afraid of you? Did you capture part of my soul? I think there is a default system somewhere in my being that believes this scenario, sitting resolutely alone in a world before magic, yet rife with noumenal threat. Another, equally sensitive but modern window of existence has a very different reason for leaving you where you are. Rolled up in the silver halide sheets is a thirty-six-year-old woman—at the height of her powers and beauty, perhaps.

My breasts were still firm and high. I exercised on a very regular basis. I ate well. I slept well. I fucked well. And I was in love with the most beautiful woman in the world. I often used to think of that time as my apex.

You know. You were there. You always corrected me. My teeth weren't straight. You got me into Pilates to tone up my ass and abs and I've never really stopped. My hair had grown back out since the Berlin bob, but you said you liked it better long, but not all of my hair—I was still waxing my pubic hair for you. You said you didn't like the hair in your mouth. I figured that if Paris was worth a Mass, then you were worth a waxing. I suspect it was really because of the artwork. "I can't see you with all that hair." Snap.

"Don't look at me." Snap. You said that often. With a fast shutter speed, you caught the disappointment in my face before I obeyed and looked away. That look is what you wanted.

"Don't you dare get your nose done, ever. Even if we break up I will find you and cut off whatever they've done. The shadows it casts are beautiful there on your cheek. Sit still."

Snap.

Would you think I am still as beautiful as that alluring woman standing in the surf, which the sun burned in crystal white stillness. Does my graying hair fly like her rich black mop in the wind? Inside the darkness, there is still a flash of a smile. The palm trees, the detritus on the beach. Driftwood, my limbs, my body reclining. Your photographs are unearthly; everyone always said it and I agree. Yet you left the quotidian world we shared alone.

It is up to me to remember the bed we shared, our little breakfast table where you ate the muesli I blended for you because you liked extra cardamom and rye berries. The curves of the archways in the hallway; the scuffed 1/4-inch round molding that circled our living room; the yellow shower curtain and antique clawfoot tub that was our refuge on late Sundays; the vanity with the shared combs full of thick hair, lipstick tubes laying down (mine), organized in their rack (yours).

You said it was simple: *"Unsere Zuhause ist nicht für die Fotografie."* I cherished that decision, that wall you built around us. You photographed when we traveled. Sketched and painted when we were at home. *"Ich brauche die Unmittelbarkeit von Macher zu Hause, meine Ada. Ich möchte mich an unserer Reisen erinnern, also war der Film.*

At home, you let yourself go with paint: the half-squeezed tubes of Phthalo green and Burnt Siena, palettes—old and crusted with paint—the canvases, framework, the hammer, staple gun on the floor. The easel. The fan brush, I remember it well and I remember me—somewhere in all of that mess with paint on my feet and naked for you on a stool. The immediacy of paint was slow. I posed for hours, but so did you. I remember the full-length mirror you used to document your divinity.

There is no fine detail in your paintings; they are unreal but in a different way. The world is divided up into great slabs of orange and blue, colors *die Brücke* could have used along with barely discernable figures. But when the enlarger casts your photographs, everything comes into a deep focus—so unreal from human perspective. But you said human perspective was never the point.

You liked digital for quick studies, but for art it had to be a

Real Camera. You wouldn't deign to use autofocus. "For amateurs *und Kindern.*" You preferred to control the focal depth and f-stop. I learned all of this on the other end of the lens from you: understood why I was often distorted by your optics because you liked wide angles and deep focal lengths.

But my memory enforces a kind of *bokeh* on your carefully composed spontaneous captures. I see the camera, and run my gaze over its lines, its solid blackness, notice the reflection points that slyly give it shape, but know that the rest of the trip, that last roll of film is blurred in my recollection.

I could say the camera takes pictures, but that is not entirely true. It is no longer in your hands and it was always your camera. I didn't know how to operate it anyway, aside from the obvious shooting button.

And the camera does not lie. Except it does lie. Right now, it lies in the old cabinet that I will have to move. Photographs were for travel. Perhaps it was the very simple logistics of the camera, but you were never in those pictures. I am omnipresent, but only because my form was your subject of omnividence.

I am leaving, not traveling. Travel is different. While one may move in space and time, from one place to another place, one does not need to remain one's self owing to the anxious reassurance that a trip does not last. At least if you are a nostalgic traveler who, even if she does not own a home and lives on jet planes and in hotels, always longs for home whether that is a city or a lover's embrace.

I loved traveling with you. We were a team, a pair of mountebanks, the daughters of Hermes with our own argot. Whether we were looking at the calm reflection of churches along the Trave river, or eating mangoes in Merida, I always had your arms and the sparkle in your eyes at sharing the novelty of the world with me.

The irrefutable, subterranean end was coming, a cenote hidden beneath the deep jungle in the form of a trip to Mexico for a commissioned photo shoot. That was what you called it. A rich couple, "some software people from Redmond," liked your work at the McKay Gallery. They wanted "more, 'more of the brunette woman' is what they said. That's you, love."

"Photographs? I thought you were showing paintings there."

"No, some photographs too. I didn't tell you? It doesn't matter. People thought they were studies at first, but Jules knew they weren't and so he put them up in a special room."

"Can you tell who I am?"

"Of course."

"And I'm naked."

"*Genau, ach Scheiße, bevor haben wir diese Konversation, Ada. Du wüßte daß ich sie Akte von dir hier anzeigt.*"

"*Ja aber nur Gemälde, nicht Fotos.*" You *had* said the only representations of me were the paintings, not the nude photographs from Berlin.

"Are you fucking kidden me, Ada?" Such was your power, that for a moment I wasn't sure if you *had* actually said you would never show photographs of me but only paintings. I feigned, I retreated to making fun of your English.

"Kidd*ing* you bitch. Jesus how many times have I told you?"

"Fuck you, Ada" and you threw the coffee cup on the floor, the paintbrush at me and stormed out of the studio.

I went in to the dark bedroom later. You had smoked outside. I could tell, but it didn't bother me because I still felt terrible whenever I disappointed you. I snuggled up behind you and brushed your hair away from your ear. I wonder if you remember: that was our ironic signal that I was ready to listen.

"This is my chance, Ada. My paintings are *Scheiße*, no shut up and let me speak. If there is a future in them it's for perhaps a split use. Something like collage bases for photographs to work with. You are so beautiful, more so in the photos. I don't know why you keep some bourgeoise shame of being seen naked. Like a well-to-do friend of yours will see you on Pine street and hold her gloved hand in front of her mouth saying "ooh." Those people don't exist. You are my beautiful girlfriend and I want to show you off to the world sometimes. I think that couple saw that love. That spark that wasn't in my paintings. That's why they wanted more pictures of you."

"I am sorry."

"It's a hacienda in Mexico. In the Yucatan. We can stay there for a month. Can you imagine?"

"I can. But I can stay here with you and be happy."

"Oh God, Ada. This is my chance. Our chance. You know? Do you care or do you just want to sit in this shitty apartment for the rest of your life reading your books and letting me paint and fuck you and occasionally you pretend to be some kind of domestic goddess? You are beautiful and smart, and I'm tired of seeing such a wonderful woman go to waste. We are so much more together if we are on the what... same page."

I knew that when you struggled for English idiom your practiced words were coming to an end. I could have asked some more questions to pry out of you what you were really getting at. But I didn't need to. I was too boring, and not enough of a muse for you.

"I guess I am just afraid, baby," I said. "Change is never easy you know."

"I don't, but I am glad you can see it that way. This will be fun."

Another reason I don't get rid of the camera: I know that somewhere inside of it is a woman who believed that the trip would be fun. That it would revive our love. Before you think of this as some ham-fisted foreshadowing, know that the woman on the film *did* enjoy the trip. She got to see Chichen-Itza, Tulum. She got to swim naked at midnight with her lover in the Caribbean. She could eat avocados to her heart's content and see her lover smile over coffee in the sprawling Mercado of Merida.

In the undeveloped film, I suspect I am nothing more than organic feminine archetypal form. My image is clear, but so is everything around me because of the deep focus and that 28 mm Zeiss lens: the sparkling water, the seaweed and flotsam on the coral sand, the shadows of the palm trees, the grackles, the ceibas, the bougainvillea, and the iguana that ate hibiscus flowers.

Within the jungle, within the darkness of the hacienda, there was no distance. We were close in those moments. In the shop with all the dark lustrous brown honey, gathered from every flower in the Yucatan, there was also silver and turquoise jewelry, candles, and the black forest of the owner's hair, like mine. You held my hand out of nowhere and squeezed and were happy.

Yet, amongst the old dark door panels and marble floors of the hotel in Merida, you pointed out that: "horizons are everywhere. We carry them with us wherever we go. See how the lines converge, *dort im Wanderschicht.*"

"*Sind wir über den Wanderschicht?*" You were lying close behind me and marked the vanishing point beyond the diaphanous curtains and hotel walls for me. Your arm was another line leading to the horizon—could you see us beyond it?

"*Wir wissen das nicht, Liebe,*" you said, and you rolled back into the distance of the bed. I saw horizons everywhere after that. There is probably some agglutinated word your language is so well known for that explains this phenomenon. But I did not seek it. I simply saw the horizon out beyond Cozumel, it lay beyond the mirror in the hacienda's bathroom, and it rested on the tarmac of the Cancun airport.

I am not sure when you loaded the last roll. But we were at Sian Ka'an, of that I'm sure. That was our last f-stop: out beneath the stars, backed up against the palm tree, beneath the netting that glowed like a ghost. The sand was everywhere but for one last episode of encounters I did not care because I knew that I was losing you and the sand would let me remember.

As far as the roll of film? I have forgotten precise poses, although I remember the ones you were fond of. I stood in the surf with one arm, usually my right, up and resting on my head. Or maybe I was standing with arms akimbo looking at the rising sun. Looking down to the right and smiling when you made a joke about my mother.

The film is over 13 years old now. My mind and heart went round and round after the trip, after us, but it took a long time for that pronoun to dissolve. My daily dialectic: why am I afraid of getting rid of you? Is there still some hope I can give you back? I put you away when I met Ralph, an intense distraction away from the questions of: why did you get rid of me? Is there still some hope I can get you back? But once he was gone you came back like ants in the spring, crawling around the kitchen counter, trying to find honey, sugar and what had been.

"*Du bist ein Dieb, you cunt,*" you had written.

You know that I was born in June under the power of Hermes. I can't help stealing. I get so turned around in the dark city at night, having fallen in love with my precociousness in tunnels, alleyways, all reverse routes to throw off the police, my supervisor, and my mother. I often wind up robbing my own house because I can never remember what the front of it looks like. That is because I never use the main entrance. I sneak out the back. Does it have pillars? I have no idea. You would know. Maybe it has Spanish archways.

I remember those because they were in the box of photos you threw on the back step along with your note. In the prints, I posed like some Maxfield Parrish muse. You didn't like the comparison, I remember. That was at the beginning of the trip. The archways were courtesy of our hosts, the rich couple who loved your work and sent us to their hacienda. But you kept all the negatives.

Well, not all of the negatives. You took the butterfly but couldn't hold onto it, could you?

I saw a write up for your show at the McKay Gallery in *the Stranger* and argued with myself about going. The opening night would be out of the question because you and your patrons would be there. I don't even have to ask if you remember them because from what little I know, you are still living with them. It must have been easy to leave me when you had a bed, breakfast and everything else in the San Juans, or Redmond, or Quintana Roo.

So on a Wednesday, I left work at lunch and went to the gallery to see me. And the pictures were beautiful. I was beautiful, clothed at most in the diaphanous curtains you let the wind caress me with. There were the early pictures of the playa where I was stark nude, and the Mercado where I wasn't, yet I was barely there. Your deep focus was set on shoes, other sides of meat, fresh fish, armies of fruit and chiles, the old men, the children.

The centerpiece was the agave triptych. A large one grew within the courtyard of the hacienda and you liked the prehistoric shapes of the turgid leaves. And the thorns, like the one I cut my leg on. Because I would do anything for you, especially then when you had explained how your horizons were different than mine. So I tried to climb into your horizon there on that plant and I was cut, pierced.

In the photograph my blood was black, touched with flares of reflection so that it looked like onyx on my skin, and the agave had the cool translucent grey of marble. It was the closest your Protestant genealogy could get to Catholicism. But you did it well.

The handsome young man at the front desk made the customary rounds an associate does, perhaps more out of boredom than hope for a sale. I didn't notice him until he made some deliberate sound, a sniff, or ahem.

The man looked at the central agave portrait. "These are really beautiful and my favorite in the show, don't you…" and I could tell there was more in his script. He had turned and looked at me, then fell silent. Then he glanced back at the other me as I looked at him from the agave leaves, again with the contrast of my hair framing some impossible dream. He then turned to this me, and gaze ran up the length of my nose. I blushed.

"Oh! I'm sorry…"

I left immediately and didn't let him finish. I went to a bar in a dim-sum restaurant in Chinatown and got drunk overthinking what he meant. How much did he know?

I hold you in my hands for a moment, glad that is all past. Glad that I was too drunk at 7:00 to even think about opening you up and exposing the last of me that loved you before the end. I tried to dial your number I think, but I couldn't even manage a drunk call or text, so I threw up the shrimp dumplings and Crown Royal and went to sleep.

I will lay you back into the box I bought for you at the swap meet in Burien. The woman who sold it to me said her brother made them in Michoacán and he crafted them to hold precious things. I knew you would rest there as soon as I saw it on the table: because the box was not made on the Yucatan, and because he had lovingly inlaid the deep cause of your rage when that cold German exterior was rolled back and the angry *Walküre* emerged.

"Where is my camera?"

"I don't know. You probably left it there."

"*Du lügst, ich weiß, ich weiß. Gib es zurück.*"

"I'm not going to give it back, you bitch, because I don't have it. You probably left it there. Why don't you go back with your patrons and fetch it? Take some pictures of them with it."

I slammed the door on you. It had been our door. You pounded on it for a while until the manager called up the stairs threatening to bring the SPD into our little drama. I thanked Mr. Sung later, and apologized. What I really wanted to tell him was my gratitude for his intervention because I would have opened the door and let you trample me.

I know what the rage was for. It is the morpho butterfly on this undeveloped film. You had me posing, nude of course, out in the jungle leaning against a ceiba tree when a morpho butterfly in brilliant blue came and landed on my breast. By the time you had the camera ready it poised on my nipple, fanned its wings and then disappeared. You had framed us perfectly. I was looking straight into the lens as you had trained me. But what are we there? Besides your masterpiece, for I saw that accomplishment in your gaze.

"Too bad that's not color film" I said. But you waved it off.

"That's not the point, *Liebe. Die Farbe macht nicht. Es wahr Perfekt. Ich habe dich und den Schmetterling.*"

What a terrible word for such a beautiful creature, I thought.

I put you back in the butterfly box from Michoacán. Now I can ask: why would I want you back? Would you even know me? Would you even care? I am still that boring, unambitious woman with the same haircut. But now I'm older. Aren't I better off without you?

But you know me. In the synesthesia of my memories, there is also the lyre of sunlight and lemon that kisses the orange flame of mango, the labial red of the hibiscus flowers that grow along the lazy Paila I can never step into again. And you were with that younger woman. You captured her on film, and so she shall remain with me— she is not trapped in the darkness of the camera in its case. She and I remain free in the interplay of brightness, contrast and exposure. Black, white. Gray.

ABOUT THE AUTHORS

JENNIFER DiMARCO

A PNWC and Bumbershoot award-winning poet and Seattle Times bestselling novelist, Jennifer DiMarco first toured nationally as an author when she was nineteen years old. Her resume of publications includes contemporary drama, science fiction, high fantasy, and mystery novels as well as poetry collections and stage plays. For the last ten years, DiMarco has worked as a filmmaker writing and directing more than a dozen feature films, half a dozen mini series, and more than a hundred short films. She lives in the Pacific Northwest with her wife, author and actor Brianne, and their children, author and illustrator Maxwell, and producer and actor Faith. Find out more about DiMarco at www.jenniferdimarco.com.

LAUREN PATZER

Hailing from Tacoma, WA, Lauren has been an information technology guru, actor, writer and film producer among other pursuits. From the earliest days when he could sit up in a chair, he typed happily away at his grandparents IBM Selectric typewriter, writing somewhat less coherent stories than he does now. He feels the best part of writing short stories is the ability to briefly immerse yourself in a brand new world (even if it's modern day America) and tell the reader a complete, entertaining and /or thought-provoking story in just a few short pages. When he's not spending time with his wife, three daughters and grandson, Lauren is pouring over the details of his next pursuit.

HIROMI COTA

Hiromi Cota has been a special operations heavy weapons expert, an adjunct professor, a rave journalist, and the flaming-sword-swinging lead in a heavy metal opera. They (singular) have lived in nations around the world, but have settled down in Seattle with their spouse Randi and their (plural) dog Nasus. Outside of crafting queer science fiction/fantasy, Hiromi writes roleplaying games, produces the inclusive and comedic D&D radio drama podcast "Dear High Elves," programs video games, and gets into sword fights as a member of the Seattle Knights actor-combatant troupe. A reasonably complete list of their work can be found at: HiromiCota.com

AMBER RAINEY

A mom first in all things she does, Amber just happens to also be an author, actor, and award-winning filmmaker. She lives in Texas with her engineer husband, precocious son, and two cats, who vie for her lap while she writes. Amber has yet to find a medium she doesn't enjoy so she writes novels, short stories, and screenplays. Her first novel, *Eternal Willow*, can be found online at Amazon. You can visit www.amberrainey.com and www.tiny.cc/amberrainey for more about Amber and her work.

MARSHALL MILLER

After retiring as a Senior Special Agent/Federal Criminal Investigator, Marshall found a second career in writing and has a published four book series called THE TSCHAAA INFESTATION. These in-depth science fiction/speculative fiction works examine the human condition, and what people would do to survive when threatened with being eaten by an invading intelligent alien species. His thirty years of law enforcement experience and world travel provides him with the basis for the many varied characters which populate his literary works, demonstrating the good, the bad, and the ugly.

ELIZA LOEB

A United States actor, Eliza stepped in to the writing field in 2018, beginning with *Prompt Generation 1*. Originally born on Guam, they had spent their life reading, writing and creating with many artistic influences. Today, Eliza channels their creativity and experiences through their writing and does their best to reach out to their readers with a subtle portrayal of empathy or compassion. Sometimes, by allowing the reader to get close to them through the pages, other times by a means of fiction. Most times with wine that rarely touches the glass. A recently published piece of Eliza Loeb's work can be found on Amazon in the horror anthology *Unnerving*. But for those of you who would like to see the human behind the writer with occasional writing tidbits, feel free to follow Eliza on Tumbler at imelizaloeb.tumblr.com.

SHEILA MENGERT

A transgender novelist, dramatist, and poet, Sheila is also a political commentator. She has a Masters Degree in English Literature from the University of Washington with an emphasis on the works of James Joyce and Virginia Woolf. Her stories in *Prompt Generation 1* are a debut effort for her in a new genre. Her previous books include a non-fiction book on Borderline Personality Disorder and a seven volume epic re-telling of the Sherlock Holmes Saga published under another name. The story of her transition is told in her book *Transsexualism and its Discontents: A Political Profile* available from KitsapPublishing.com under the separate editorial imprint of Trannie-Goddess Press. Sheila is currently at work on an eighth volume sequel to her Sherlock Holmes Saga dealing with The Great European War of 1914-1918 and its critical aftermath in the Peace Conference of 1919 in Paris.

CARRIE AVERY MORIARTY

Born and raised in the Pacific Northwest, Carrie still lives there with the love of her life. She raised two wonderful, if not slightly warped, children who both live close to home. When she's not yelling at her hometown sports teams on the television, she's cheering them on from the stands. She loves nature and spending time enjoying it with her family. And you don't want to attempt to beat her in any board game. They are meant to be played to the death. Find more from Carrie at www.facebook.com/AuthorCarrieAveryMoriarty/ and on Twitter or Instagram @camoriarty13

DAVID MECKLENBURG

Much like his unseen Gemini half/fictional narrator Ada Ludenow, writer & illustrator David Mecklenburg was born in Sacramento, and moved home to Washington to attend the University of Washington. He has worked as a chef, tech support specialist, and capital project manager. You can often find him on the Washington State ferries commuting to and from Bremerton where he now lives. His stories were written "on the water." For more information about David (& Ada) please visit www.hagengard.com.

ABOUT THE EDITOR

BRIANNE DIMARCO

A published short story author, poet, and writer of more than a dozen short films, Brianne has been captivated by the written word from an early age and doesn't even remember when she learned to read. She currently works as a full-time volunteer for Blue Forge Group and is the Senior Editor of their publishing division, Blue Forge Press. Brianne lives with her wife, Jennifer, and their children on the Olympic Peninsula in the Pacific Northwest.

www.ingramcontent.com/pod-product-compliance
Lightning Source LLC
Chambersburg PA
CBHW070157310726
48976CB00001B/125